TEPHLON FUNK!®
テフロン ファンク

TEPHLON FUNK!
テフロン ファンク

Created and written by
STEPHANE METAYER

Illustrated by
DAVID TAKO
NICOLAS SAFE

Dark Horse Books

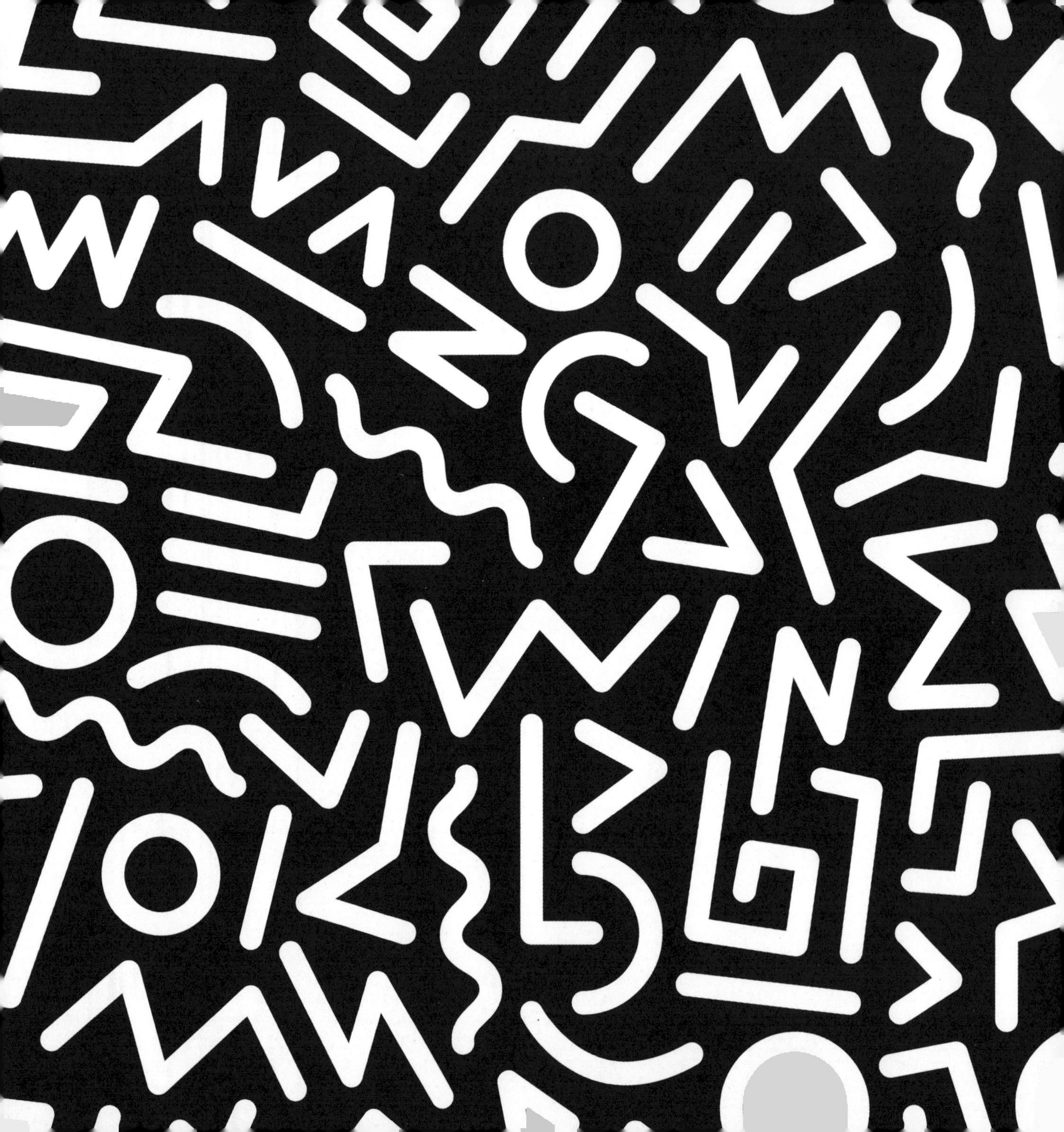

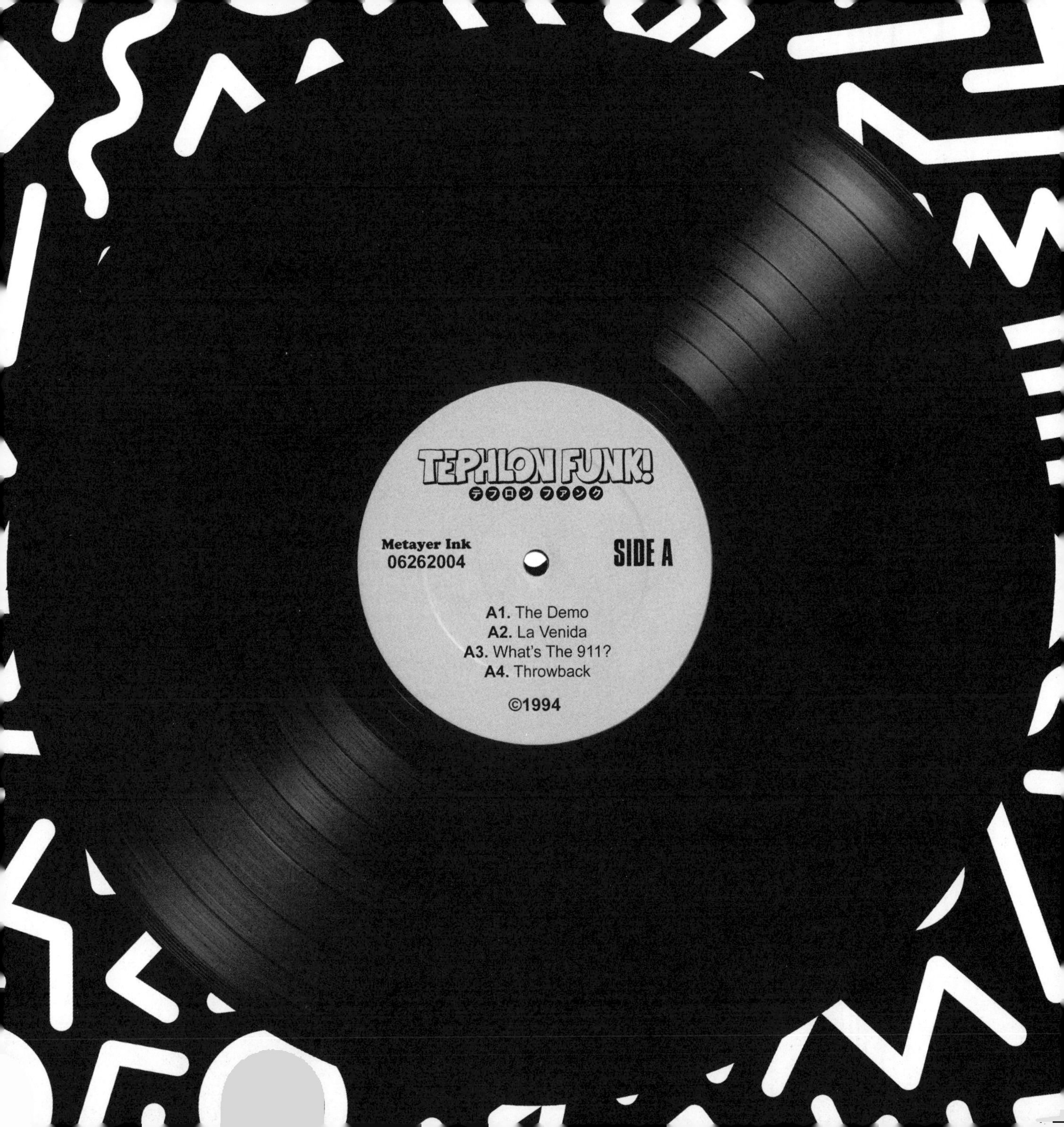
TEPHLON FUNK!
テフロン ファンク
Metayer Ink
06262004
SIDE A
A1. The Demo
A2. La Venida
A3. What's The 911?
A4. Throwback
©1994

Inez Jozlyn

AGE: 14
HEIGHT: 5'4"
WEIGHT: 122 LBS
DOB: MAY 5
QUEENS, NY

A SENSIBLE BUT TROUBLED
YOUTH WHO'S LOST ALL
HOPE. INEZ CAN NEVER SEEM
TO CATCH A BREAK FROM HER
HARSH UPBRINGING. HOWEVER,
WITH HER DILIGENCE SHE'S
DETERMINED TO CHANGE THAT,
NO MATTER WHAT THE
CONSEQUENCES ARE...

Gabriel Ainsley

AGE: 17
HEIGHT: 6'2"
WEIGHT: 214 LBS
DOB: FEBRUARY 27
BROOKLYN, NY

EXTREMELY CHARISMATIC AND
FEARLESS, GABRIEL IS
NOTORIOUSLY KNOWN FOR HIS
AMAZING ATHLETIC PROWESS.
THE BIGGEST PROBLEM IS THAT
HE'S NOT WHAT OTHERS BELIEVE
HIM TO BE. HE'S DESPERATELY
SEARCHING FOR SOMETHING,
BUT WHAT EXACTLY IS IT?

Cameron Phoenix

AGE: 24
HEIGHT: 5'9"
WEIGHT: 153 LBS
DOB: JUNE 29
BRONX, NY

A YOUNG AND AMBITIOUS COP WITH A STRONG SENSE OF JUSTICE, SHE'S AS SHARP AS A RAZOR. CAMERON CAN BE HARDHEADED AT TIMES, BUT HER DETECTIVE SKILLS ARE UNLIKE ANY OTHER. SHE WALKS HER OWN PATH AND ANYONE THAT GETS IN HER WAY BETTER WATCH OUT...

Giselle Rodriguez

AGE: 25
HEIGHT: 5'8"
WEIGHT: 148 LBS
DOB: AUGUST 11
NEW YORK, NY

MYSTERIOUS, COOL, AND VERY LAID BACK, GISELLE IS CONSTANTLY PURSUED BY ALL TYPES OF MEN. IF ONLY THEY KNEW THIS BARTENDER HAPPENS TO ALSO BE A SWORD-WIELDING BOUNCER! UNFORTUNATELY, HER CHECKERED PAST COMES BACK TO HAUNT HER ALL OVER AGAIN...WILL SHE ENDURE?

TEPHLON FUNK!

テフロン・ファンク

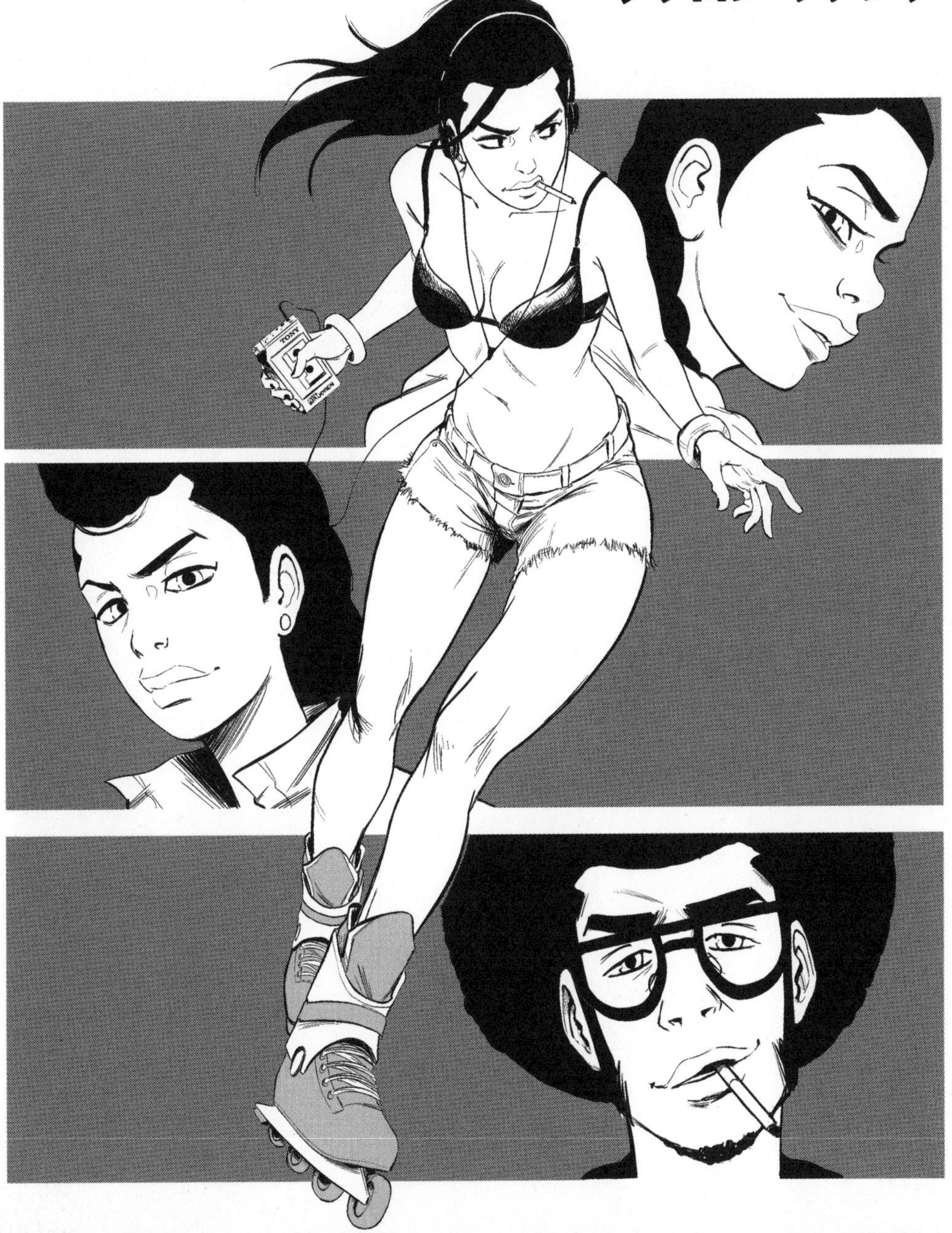

SIDE A

1994

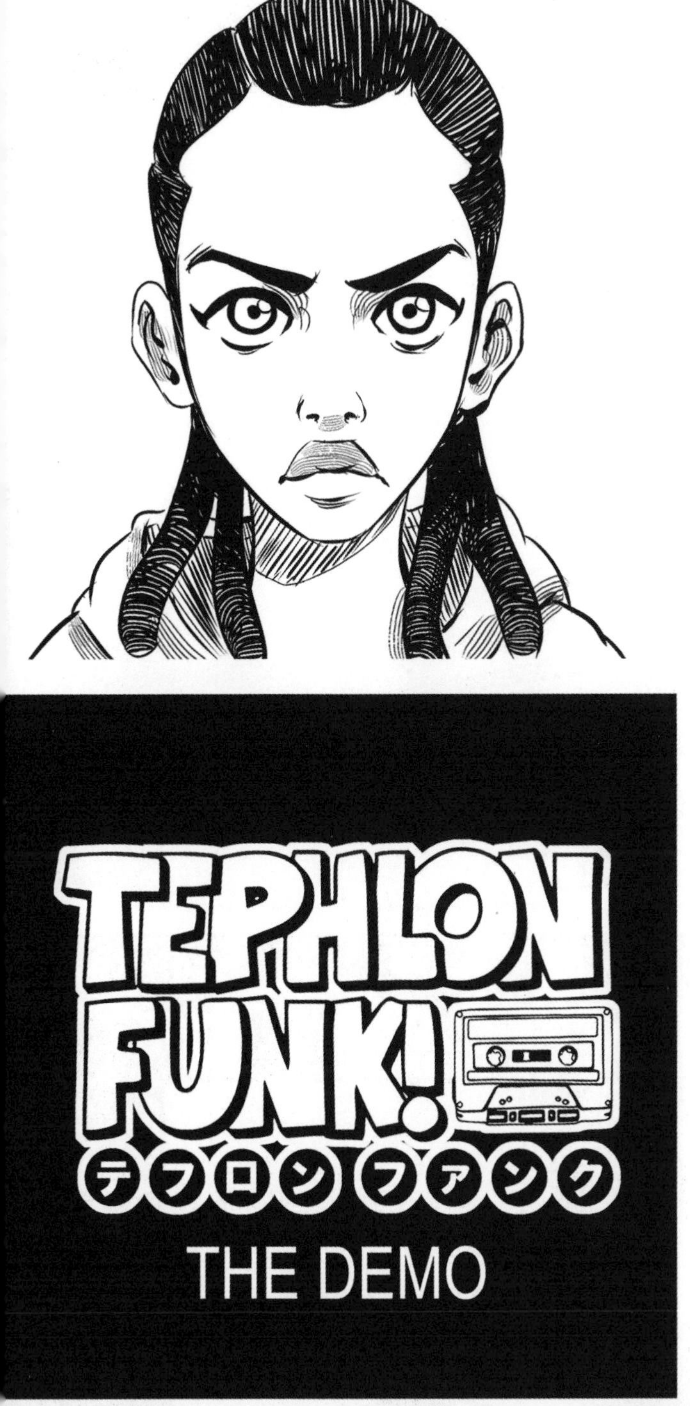

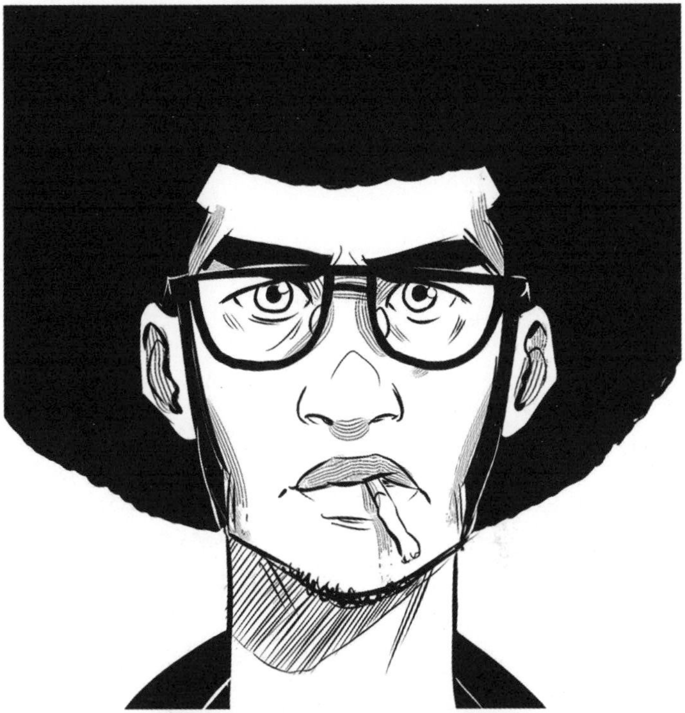

TEPHLON FUNK!

テフロン ファンク

THE DEMO

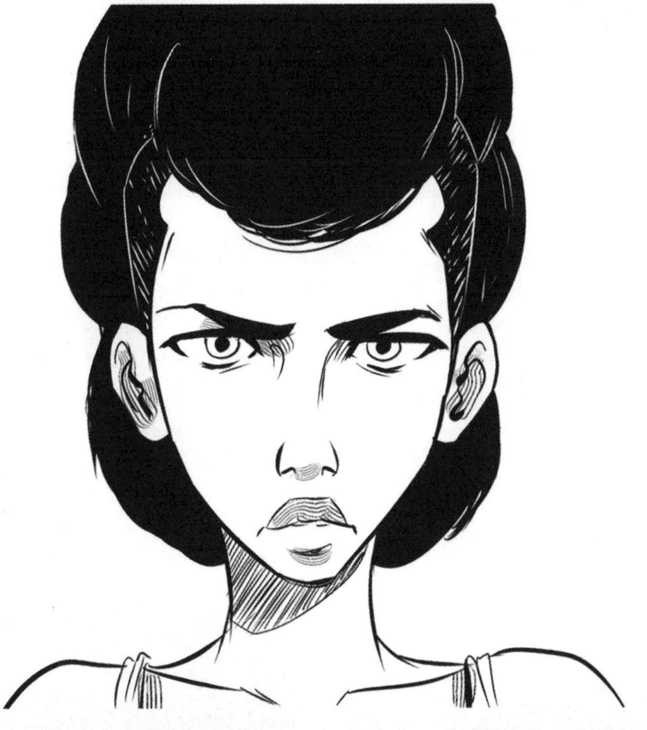

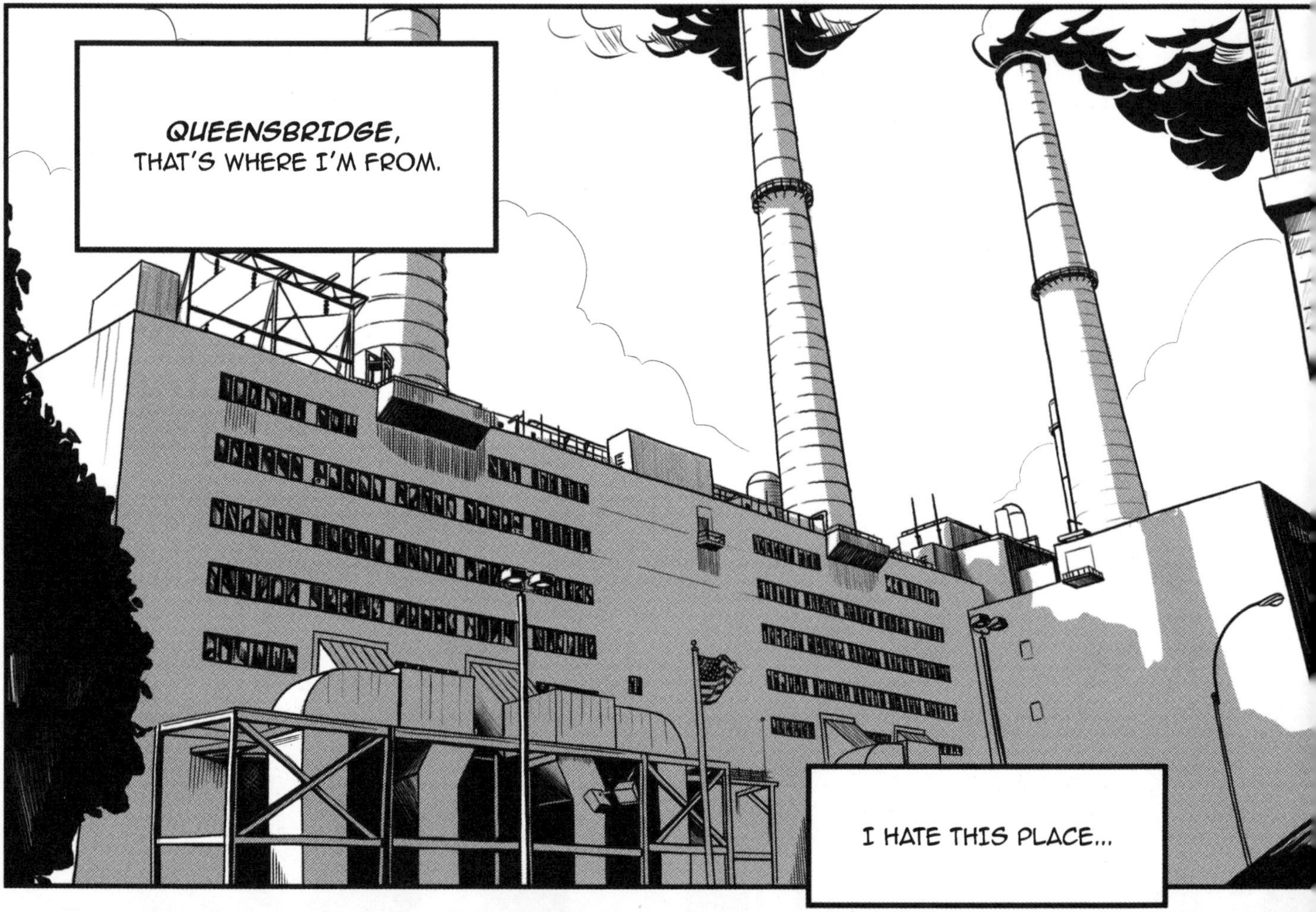
QUEENSBRIDGE, THAT'S WHERE I'M FROM.
I HATE THIS PLACE...

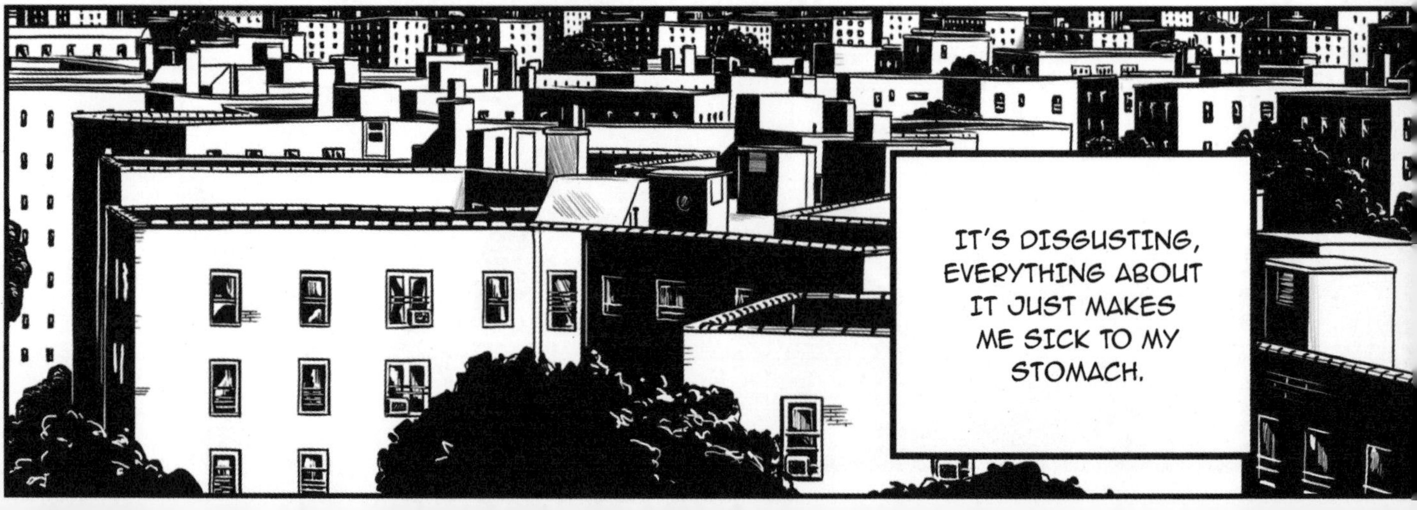
IT'S DISGUSTING, EVERYTHING ABOUT IT JUST MAKES ME SICK TO MY STOMACH.

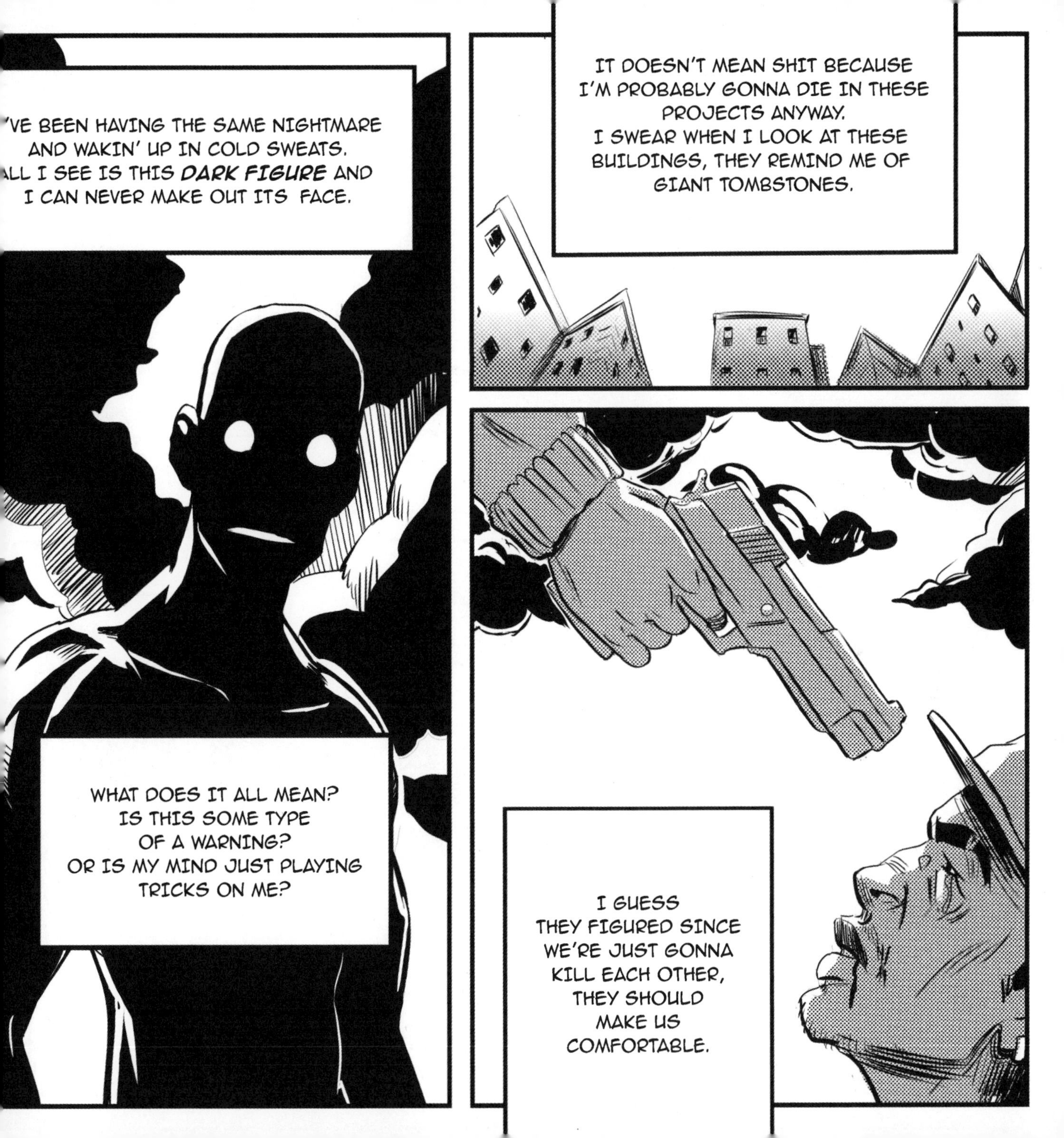
'VE BEEN HAVING THE SAME NIGHTMARE
AND WAKIN' UP IN COLD SWEATS.
LL I SEE IS THIS *DARK FIGURE* AND
I CAN NEVER MAKE OUT ITS FACE.
WHAT DOES IT ALL MEAN?
IS THIS SOME TYPE
OF A WARNING?
OR IS MY MIND JUST PLAYING
TRICKS ON ME?
IT DOESN'T MEAN SHIT BECAUSE
I'M PROBABLY GONNA DIE IN THESE
PROJECTS ANYWAY.
I SWEAR WHEN I LOOK AT THESE
BUILDINGS, THEY REMIND ME OF
GIANT TOMBSTONES.
I GUESS
THEY FIGURED SINCE
WE'RE JUST GONNA
KILL EACH OTHER,
THEY SHOULD
MAKE US
COMFORTABLE.

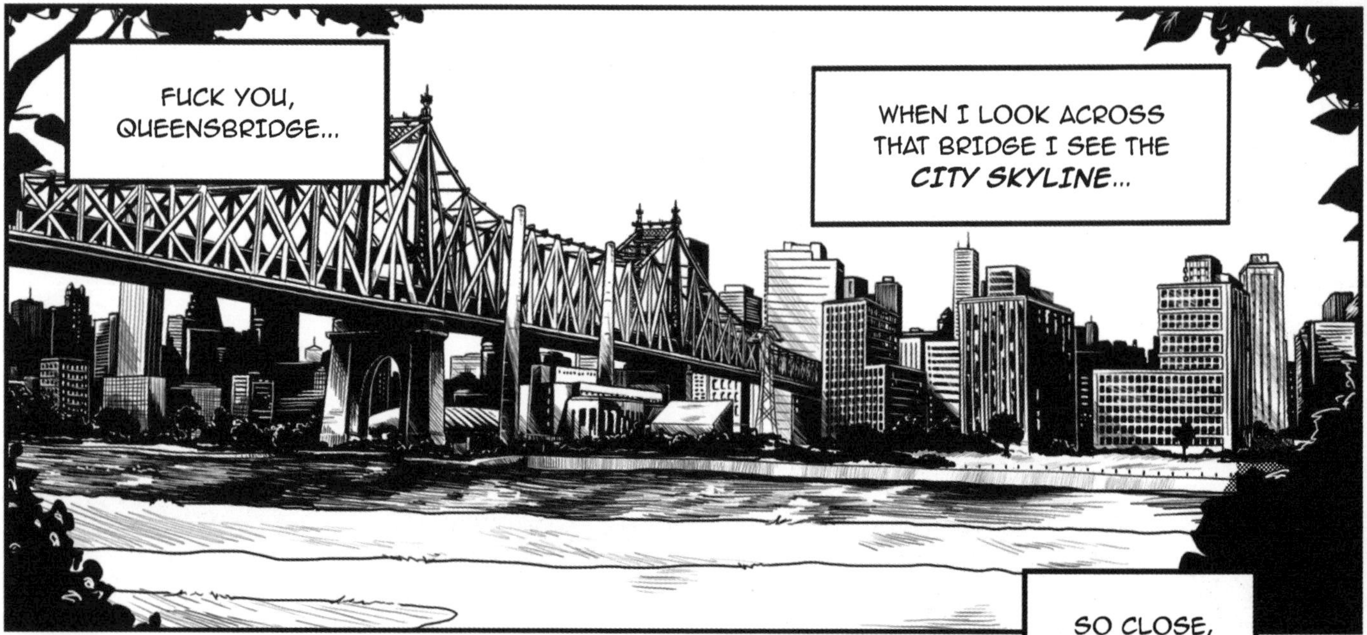
FUCK YOU, QUEENSBRIDGE...
WHEN I LOOK ACROSS THAT BRIDGE I SEE THE *CITY SKYLINE*...

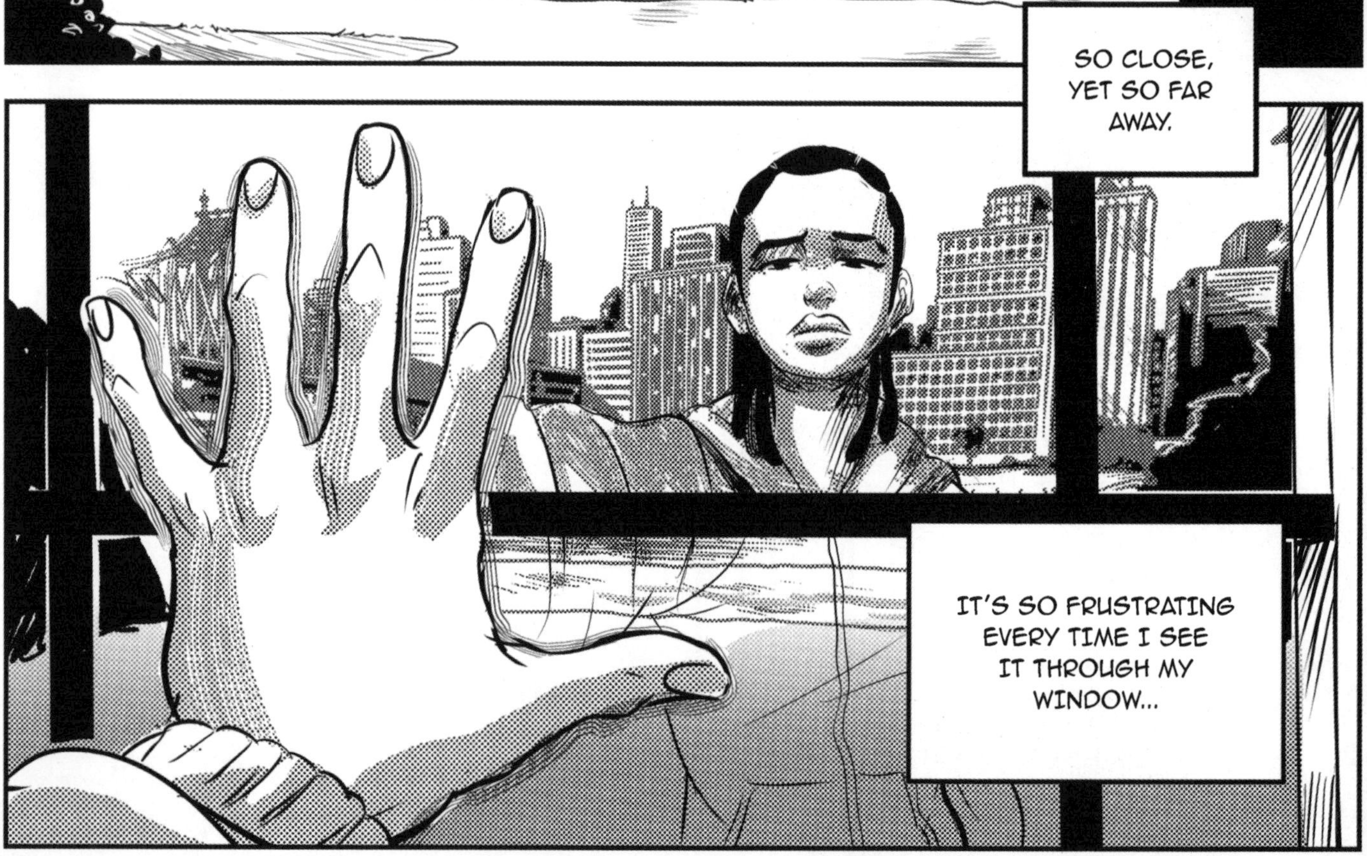
SO CLOSE, YET SO FAR AWAY.
IT'S SO FRUSTRATING EVERY TIME I SEE IT THROUGH MY WINDOW...

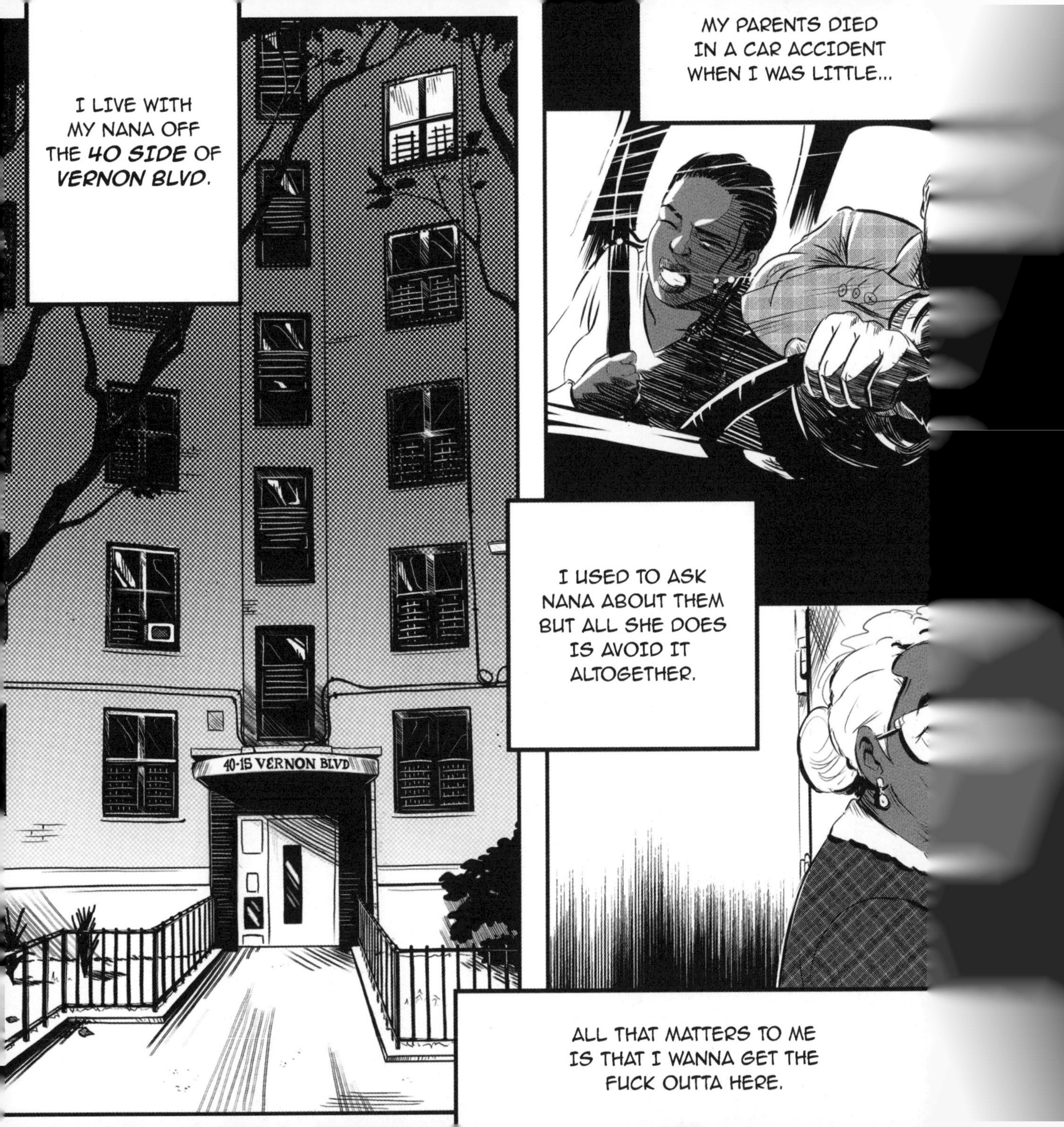

I LIVE WITH MY NANA OFF THE *40 SIDE* OF *VERNON BLVD*.
40-15 VERNON BLVD
MY PARENTS DIED IN A CAR ACCIDENT WHEN I WAS LITTLE...
I USED TO ASK NANA ABOUT THEM BUT ALL SHE DOES IS AVOID IT ALTOGETHER.
ALL THAT MATTERS TO ME IS THAT I WANNA GET THE FUCK OUTTA HERE.

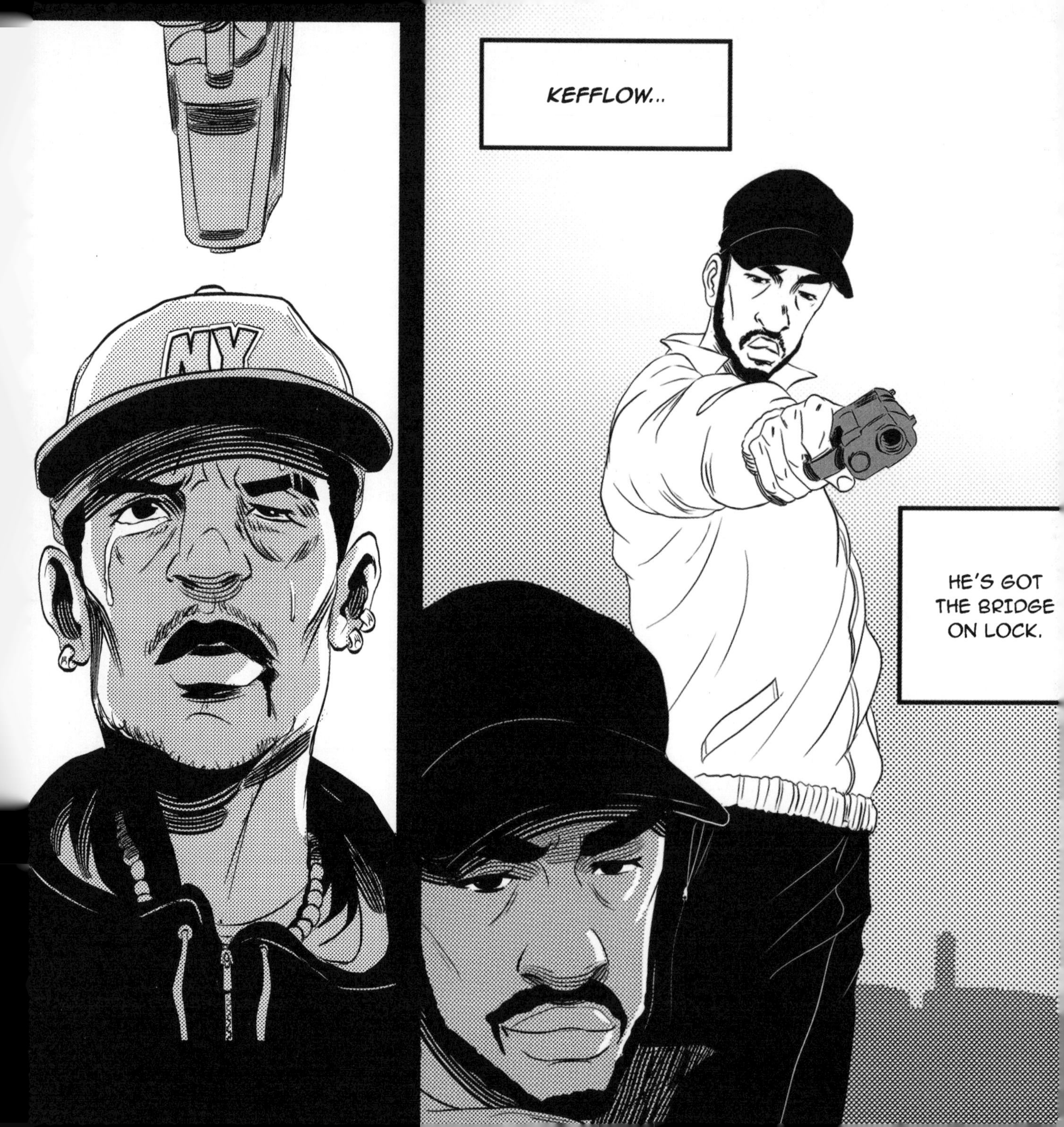
KEFFLOW...
HE'S GOT THE BRIDGE ON LOCK.

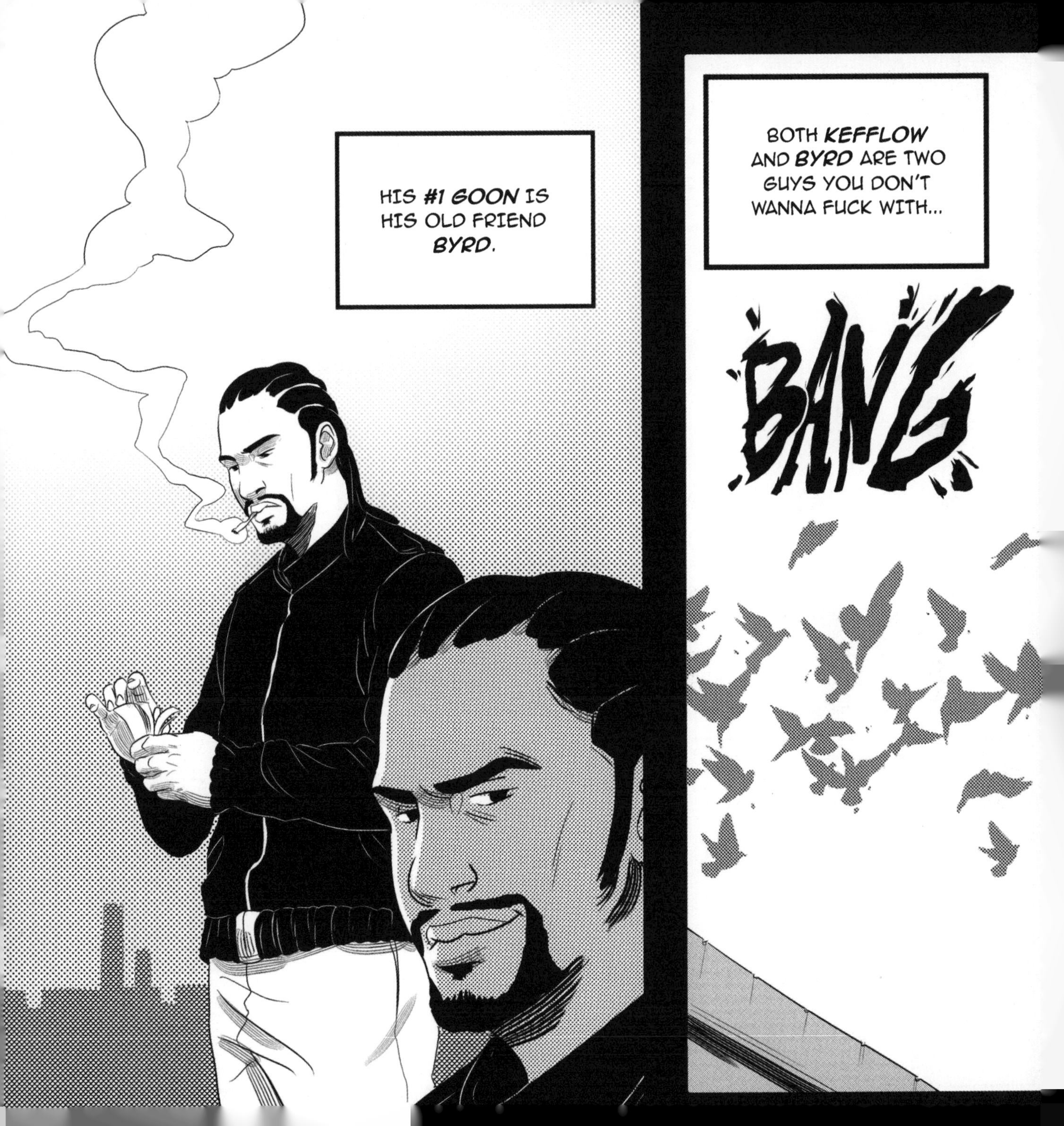
HIS #1 GOON IS HIS OLD FRIEND BYRD.
BOTH KEFFLOW AND BYRD ARE TWO GUYS YOU DON'T WANNA FUCK WITH...
BANG

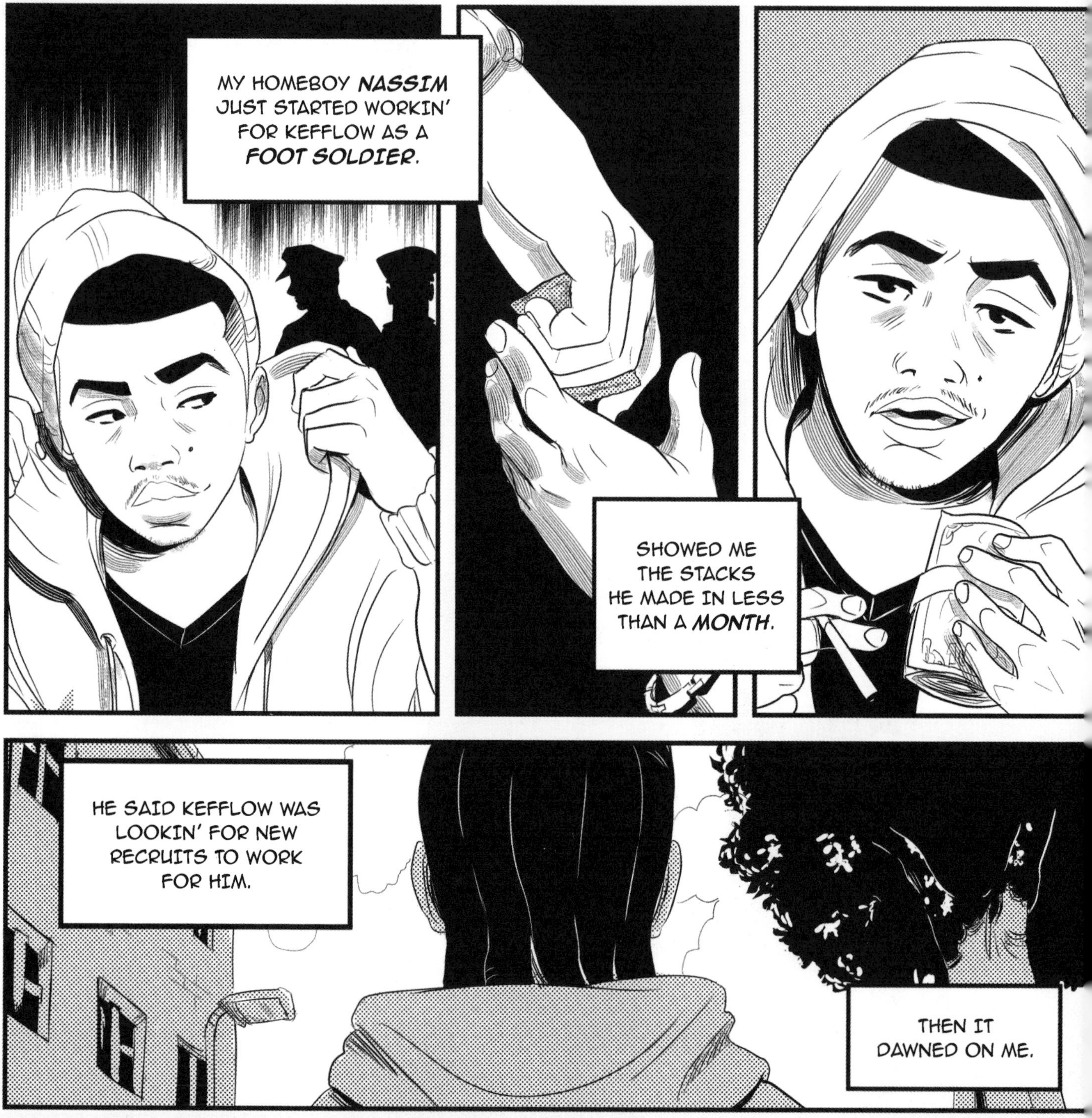

MY HOMEBOY NASSIM JUST STARTED WORKIN' FOR KEFFLOW AS A FOOT SOLDIER.
SHOWED ME THE STACKS HE MADE IN LESS THAN A MONTH.
HE SAID KEFFLOW WAS LOOKIN' FOR NEW RECRUITS TO WORK FOR HIM.
THEN IT DAWNED ON ME.

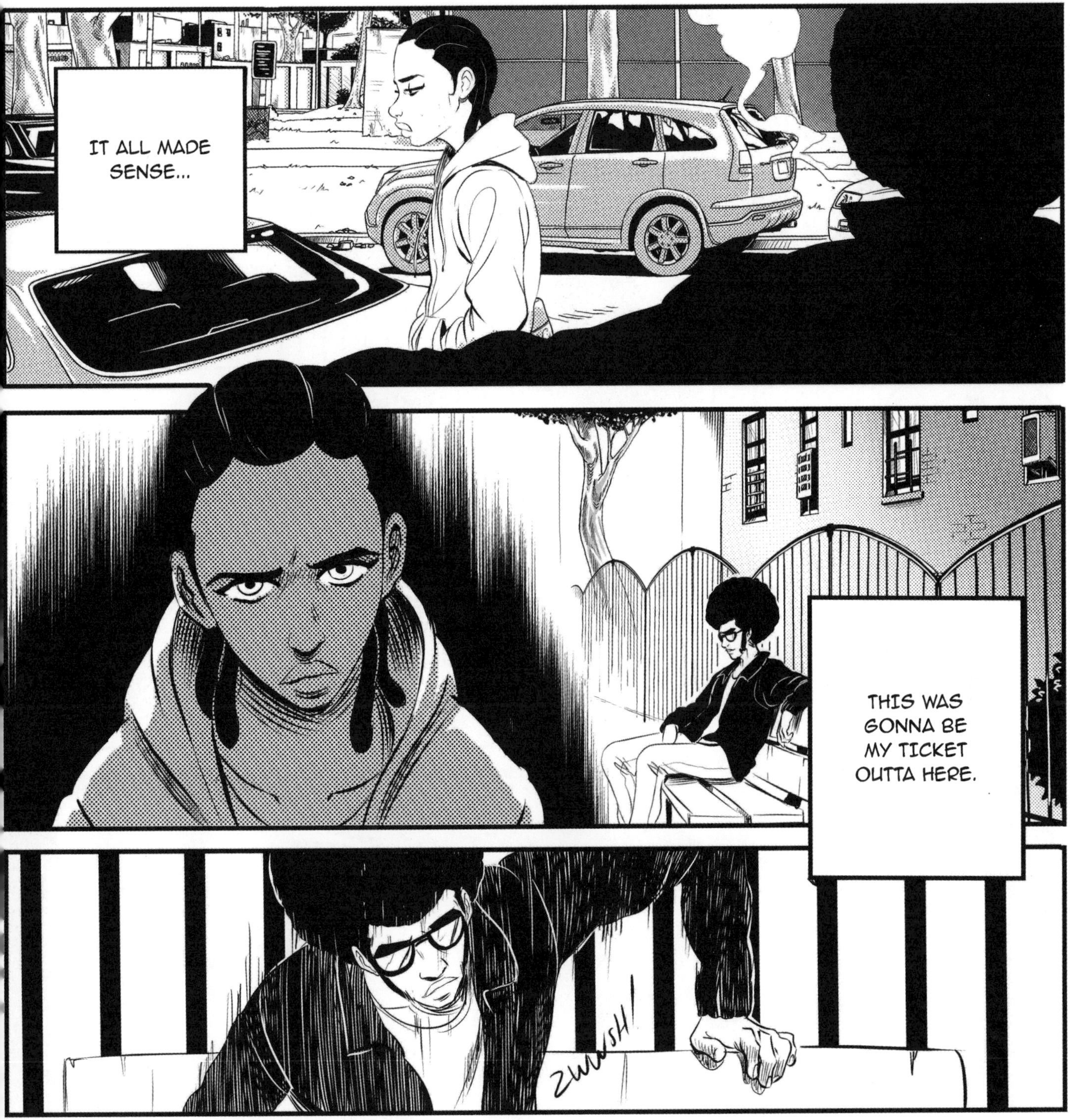
IT ALL MADE SENSE...
THIS WAS GONNA BE MY TICKET OUTTA HERE.
ZWWSH!

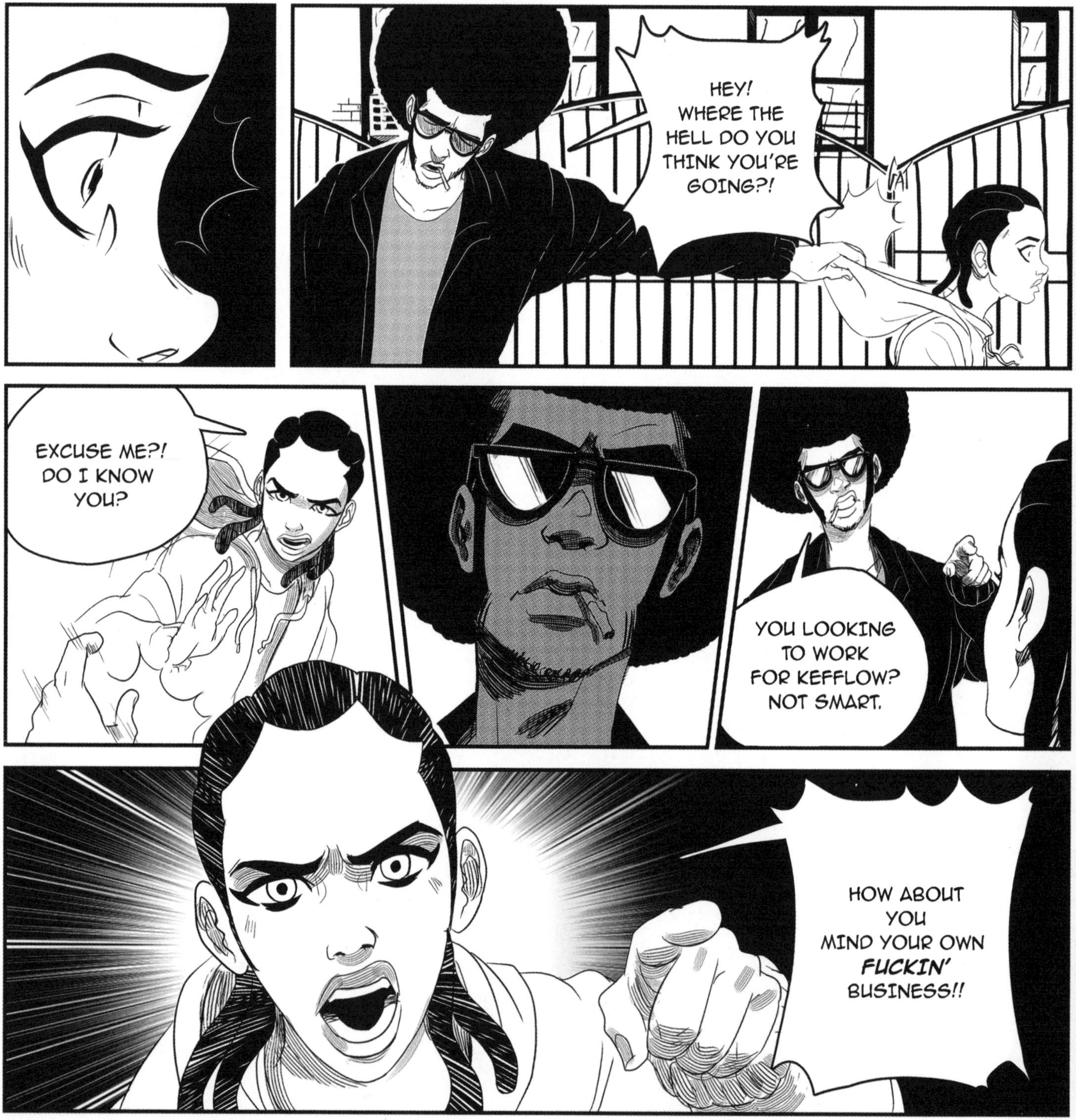
HEY! WHERE THE HELL DO YOU THINK YOU'RE GOING?!
EXCUSE ME?! DO I KNOW YOU?
YOU LOOKING TO WORK FOR KEFFLOW? NOT SMART.
HOW ABOUT YOU MIND YOUR OWN *FUCKIN'* BUSINESS!!

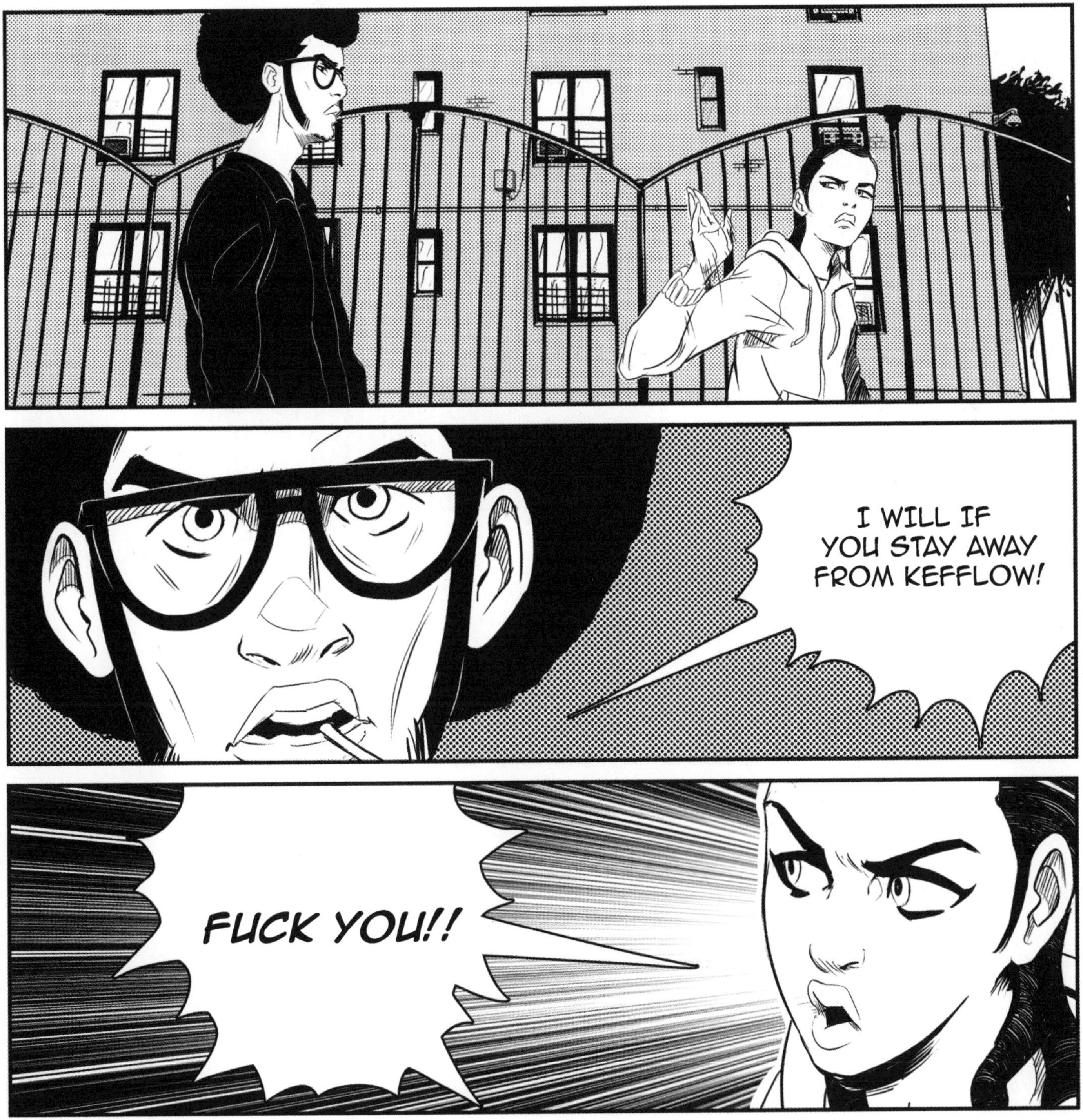
I WILL IF YOU STAY AWAY FROM KEFFLOW!
FUCK YOU!!

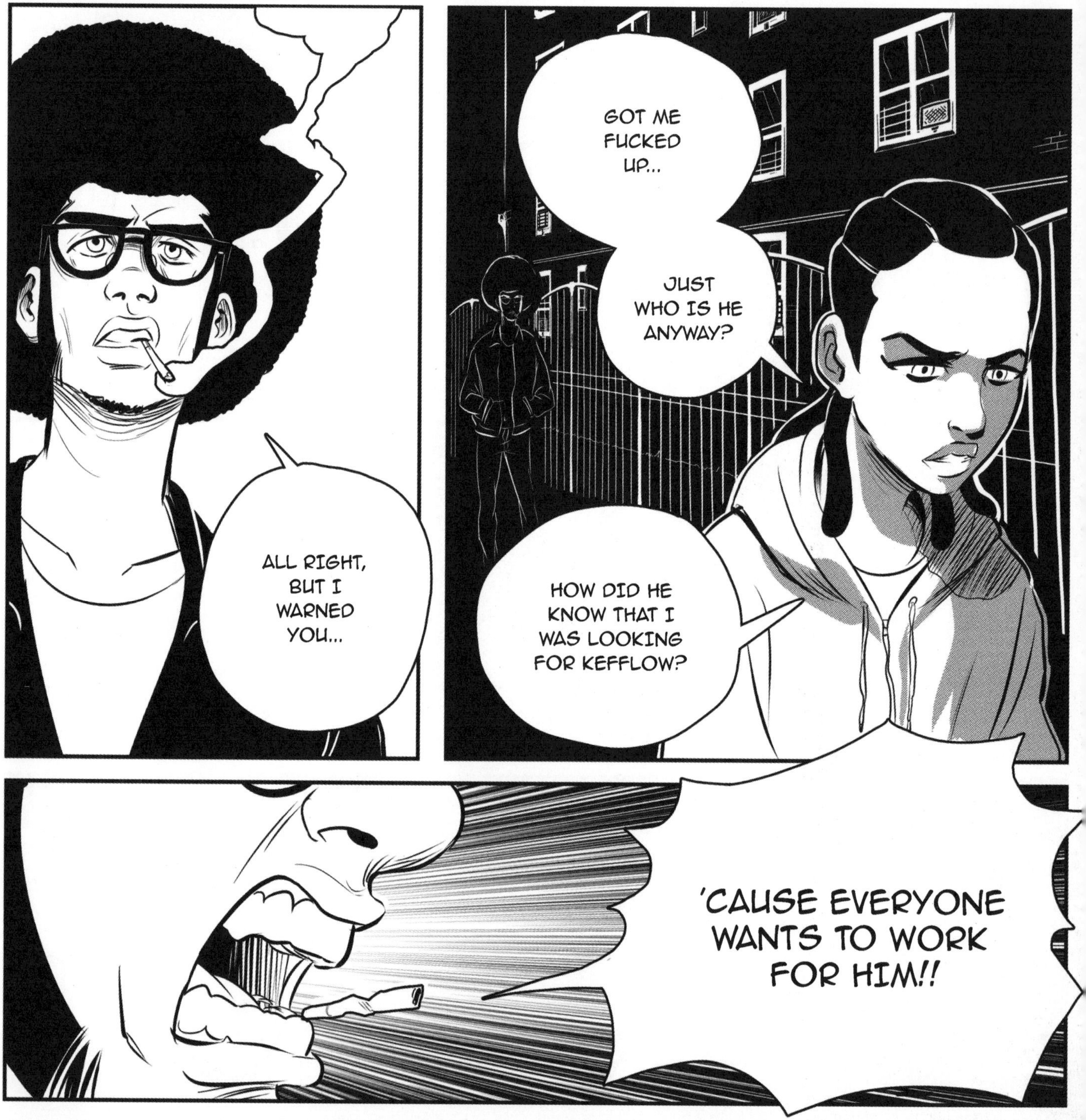
ALL RIGHT, BUT I WARNED YOU...
GOT ME FUCKED UP...
JUST WHO IS HE ANYWAY?
HOW DID HE KNOW THAT I WAS LOOKING FOR KEFFLOW?
'CAUSE EVERYONE WANTS TO WORK FOR HIM!!

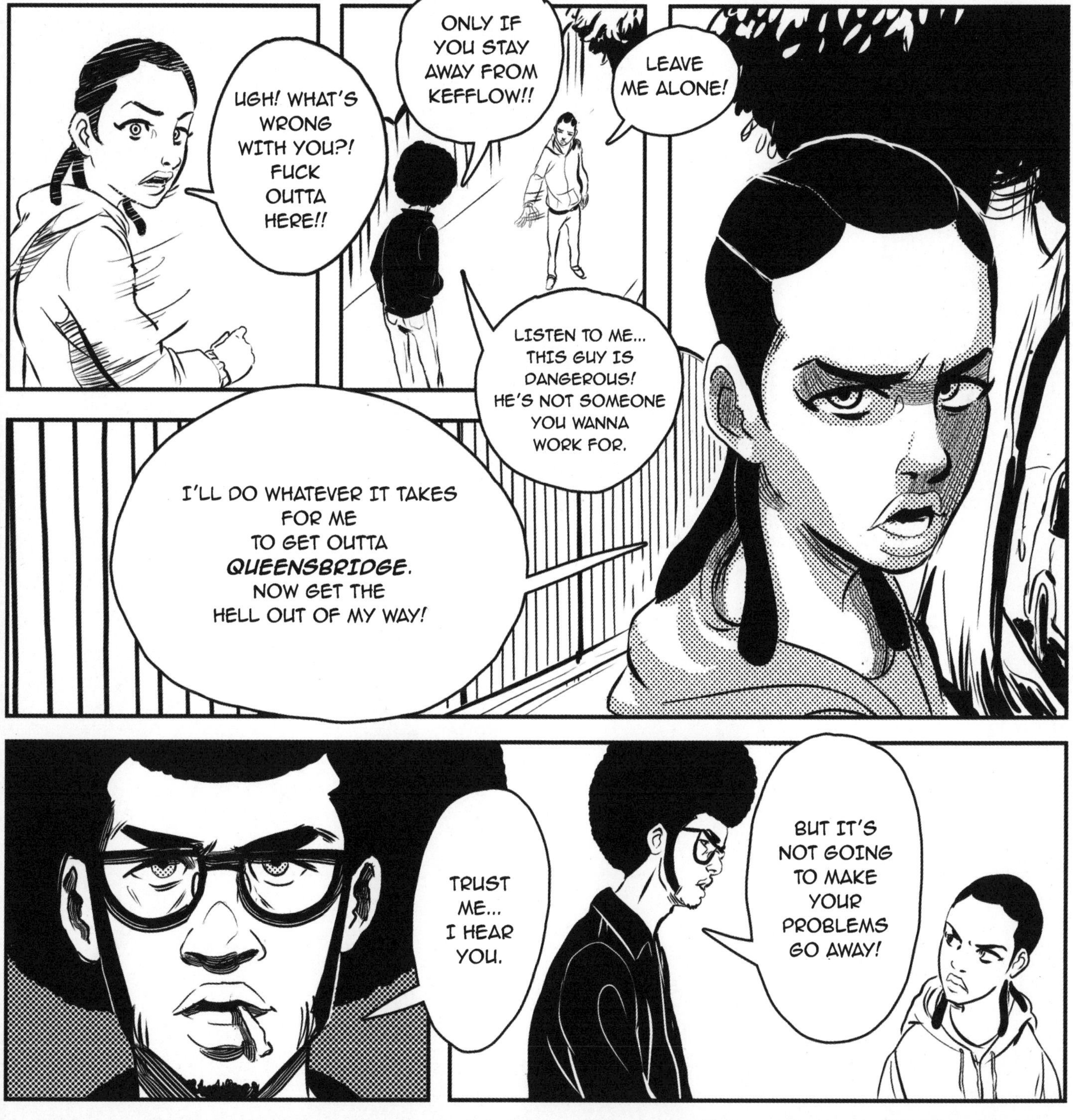
UGH! WHAT'S WRONG WITH YOU?! FUCK OUTTA HERE!!
ONLY IF YOU STAY AWAY FROM KEFFLOW!!
LEAVE ME ALONE!
LISTEN TO ME... THIS GUY IS DANGEROUS! HE'S NOT SOMEONE YOU WANNA WORK FOR.
I'LL DO WHATEVER IT TAKES FOR ME TO GET OUTTA QUEENSBRIDGE. NOW GET THE HELL OUT OF MY WAY!
TRUST ME... I HEAR YOU.
BUT IT'S NOT GOING TO MAKE YOUR PROBLEMS GO AWAY!

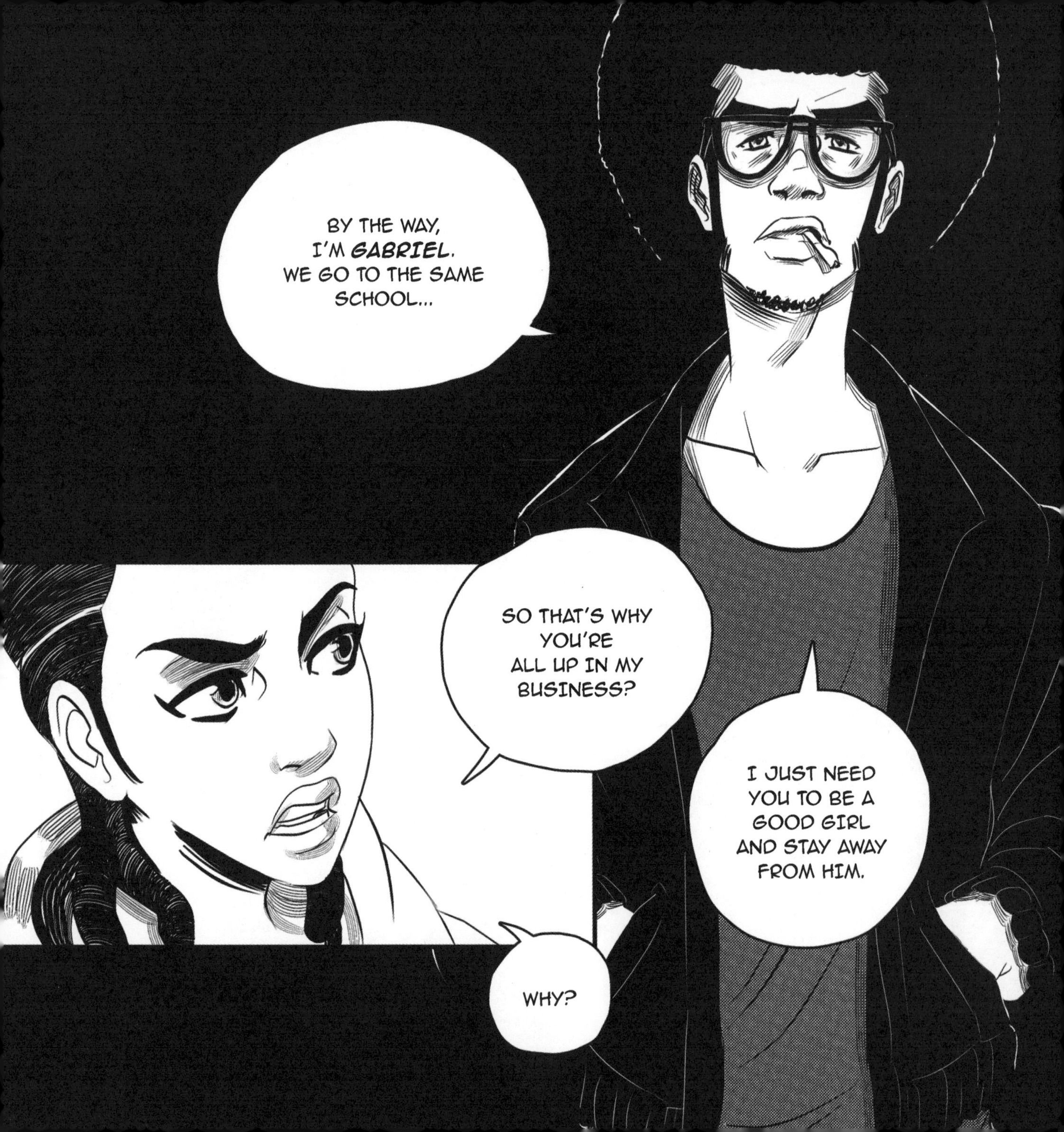
BY THE WAY, I'M **GABRIEL**. WE GO TO THE SAME SCHOOL...
SO THAT'S WHY YOU'RE ALL UP IN MY BUSINESS?
I JUST NEED YOU TO BE A GOOD GIRL AND STAY AWAY FROM HIM.
WHY?

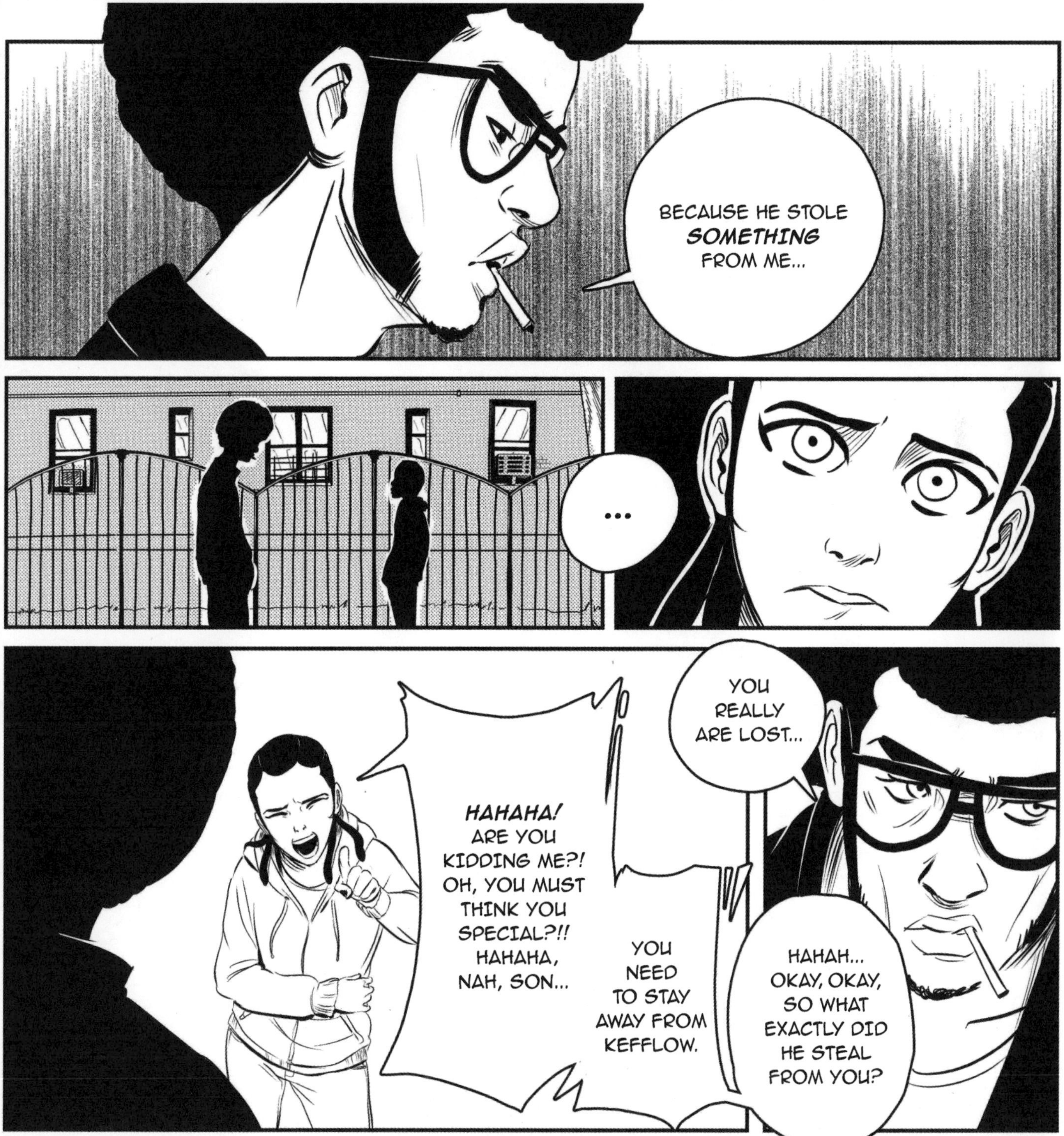
BECAUSE HE STOLE *SOMETHING* FROM ME...
...
HAHAHA! ARE YOU KIDDING ME?! OH, YOU MUST THINK YOU SPECIAL?!! HAHAHA, NAH, SON...
YOU NEED TO STAY AWAY FROM KEFFLOW.
YOU REALLY ARE LOST...
HAHAH... OKAY, OKAY, SO WHAT EXACTLY DID HE STEAL FROM YOU?

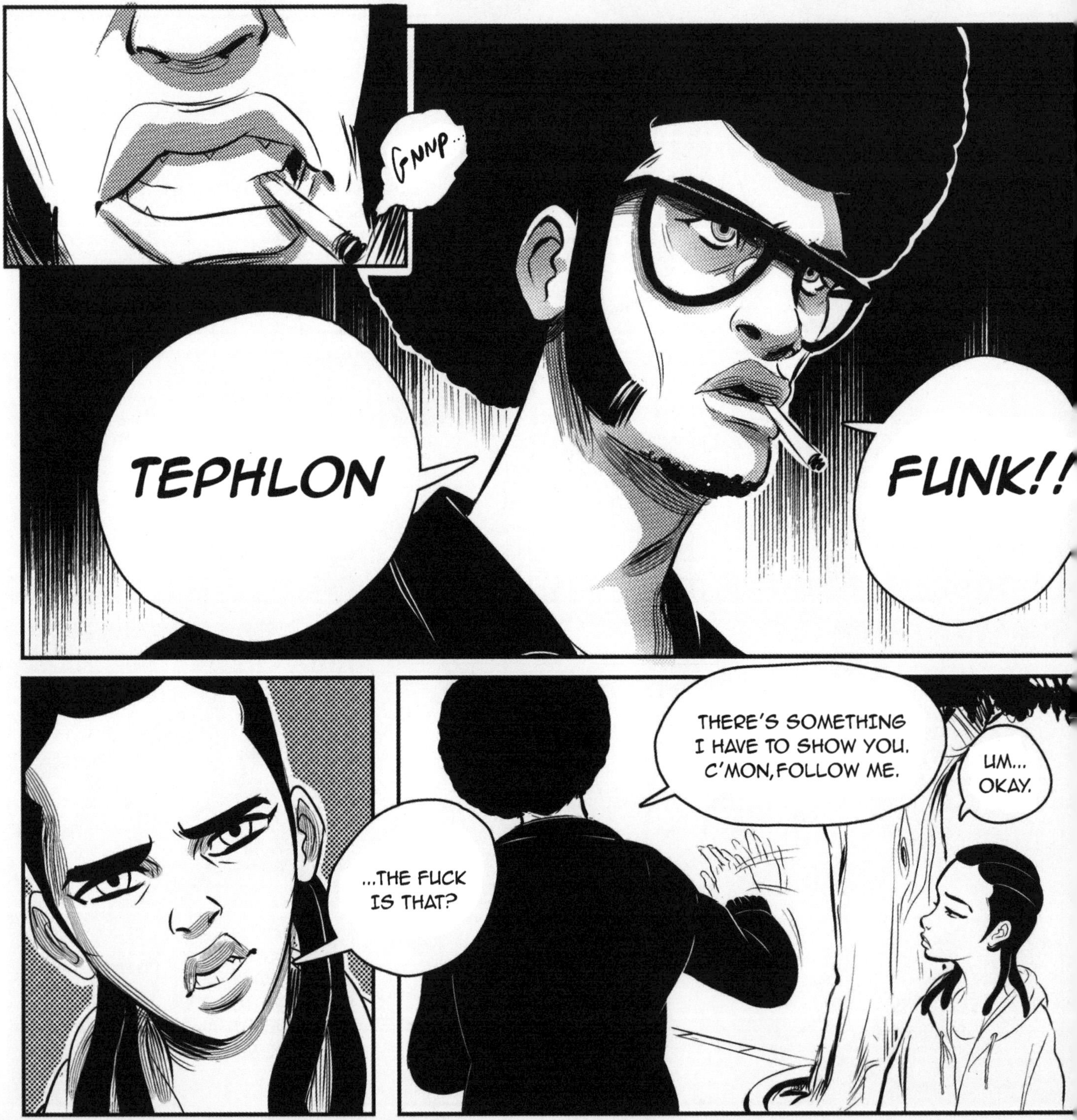
GNNP...
TEPHLON
FUNK!!
...THE FUCK IS THAT?
THERE'S SOMETHING I HAVE TO SHOW YOU. C'MON, FOLLOW ME.
UM... OKAY.

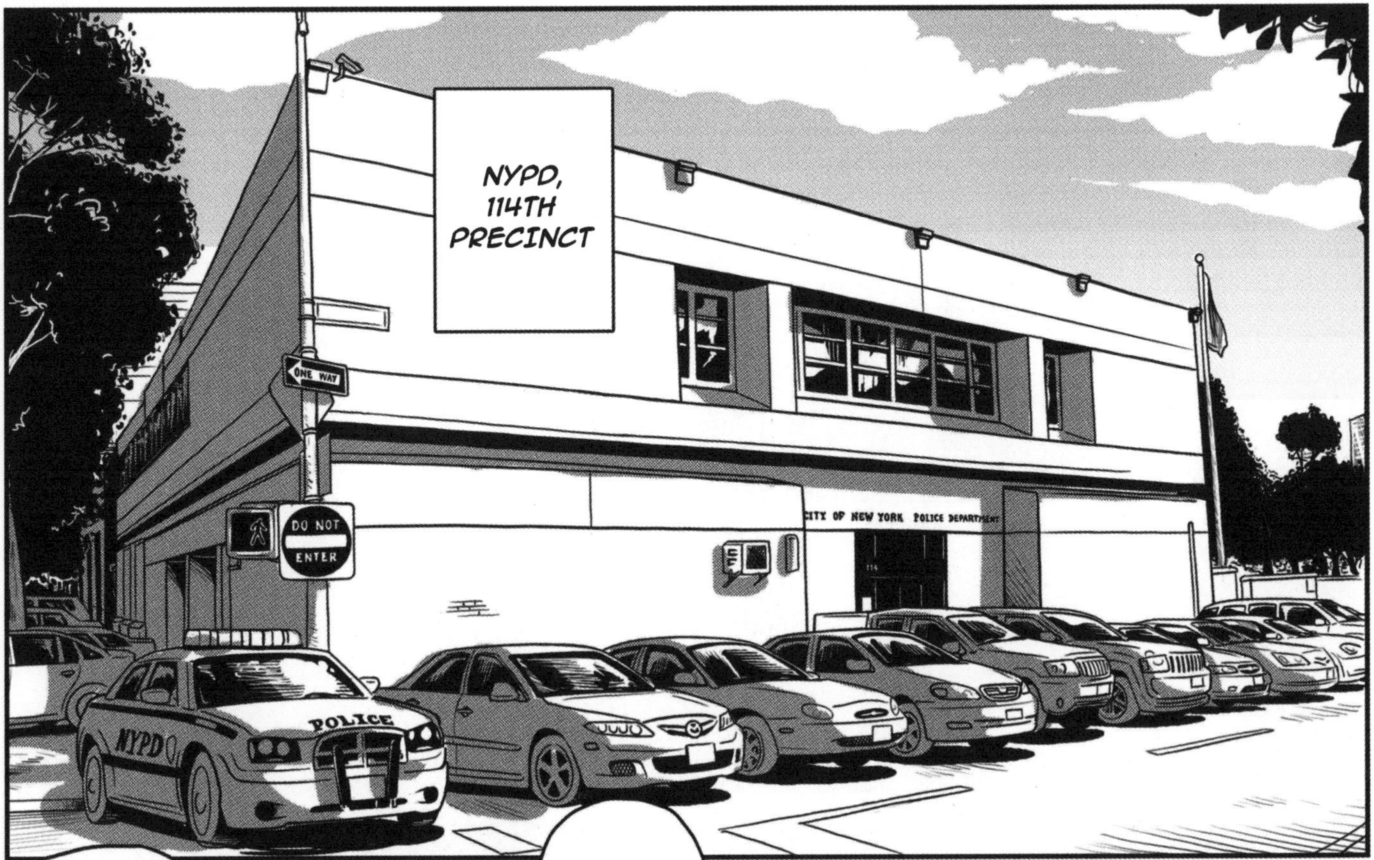
NYPD,
114TH
PRECINCT
ONE WAY
DO NOT ENTER
CITY OF NEW YORK POLICE DEPARTMENT
POLICE
NYPD

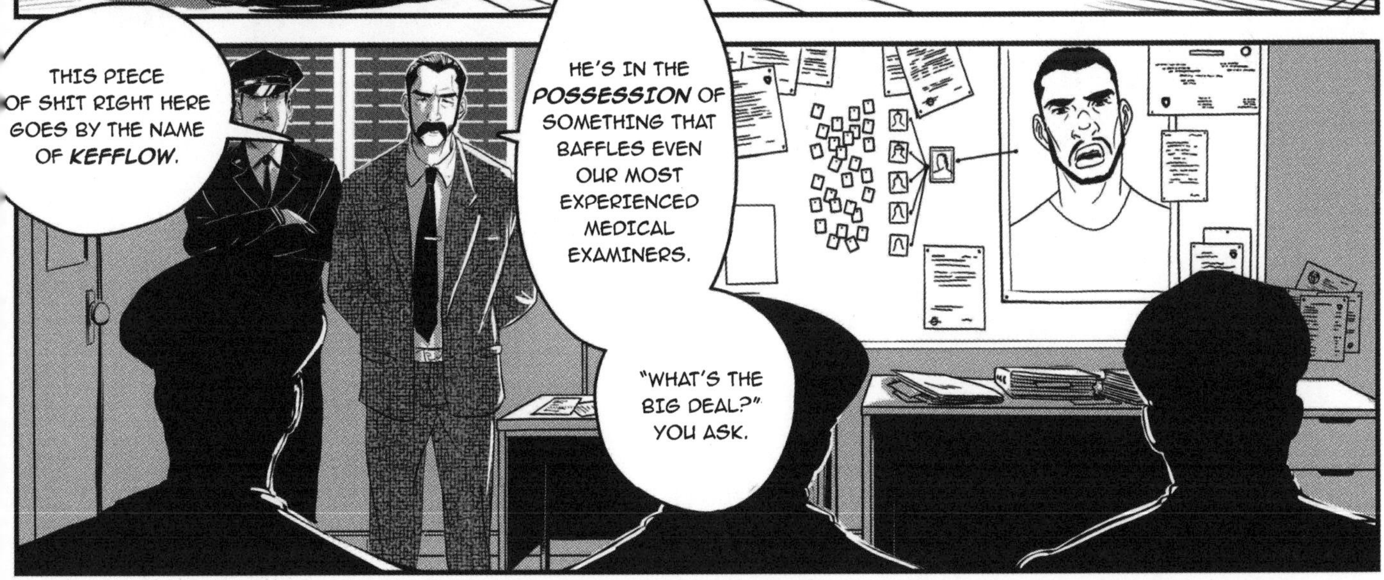
THIS PIECE OF SHIT RIGHT HERE GOES BY THE NAME OF KEFFLOW.
HE'S IN THE POSSESSION OF SOMETHING THAT BAFFLES EVEN OUR MOST EXPERIENCED MEDICAL EXAMINERS.
"WHAT'S THE BIG DEAL?" YOU ASK.

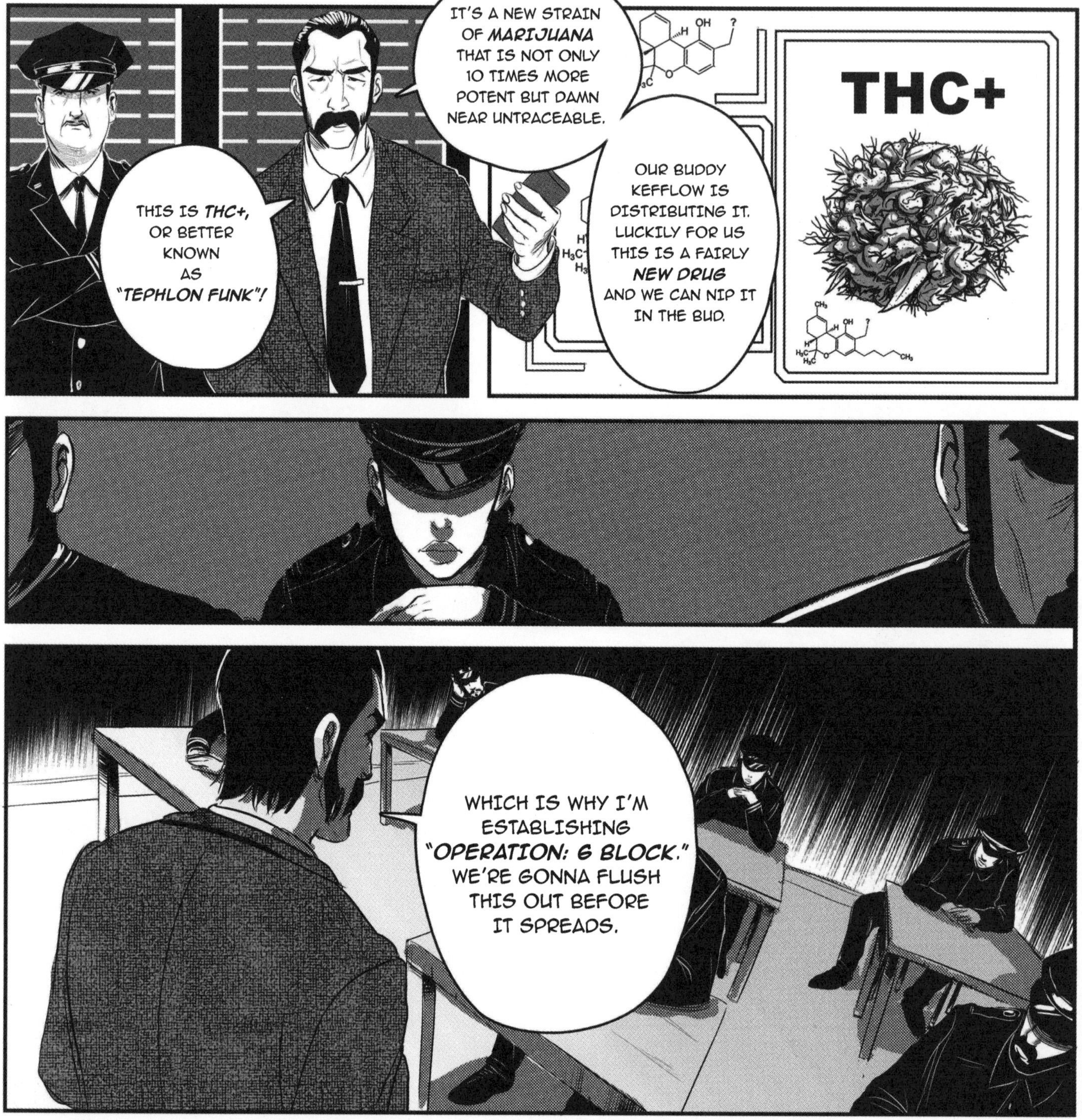
THIS IS *THC+*, OR BETTER KNOWN AS "*TEPHLON FUNK*"!
IT'S A NEW STRAIN OF ***MARIJUANA*** THAT IS NOT ONLY 10 TIMES MORE POTENT BUT DAMN NEAR UNTRACEABLE.
THC+
OUR BUDDY KEFFLOW IS DISTRIBUTING IT. LUCKILY FOR US THIS IS A FAIRLY ***NEW DRUG*** AND WE CAN NIP IT IN THE BUD.
WHICH IS WHY I'M ESTABLISHING "***OPERATION: 6 BLOCK.***" WE'RE GONNA FLUSH THIS OUT BEFORE IT SPREADS.

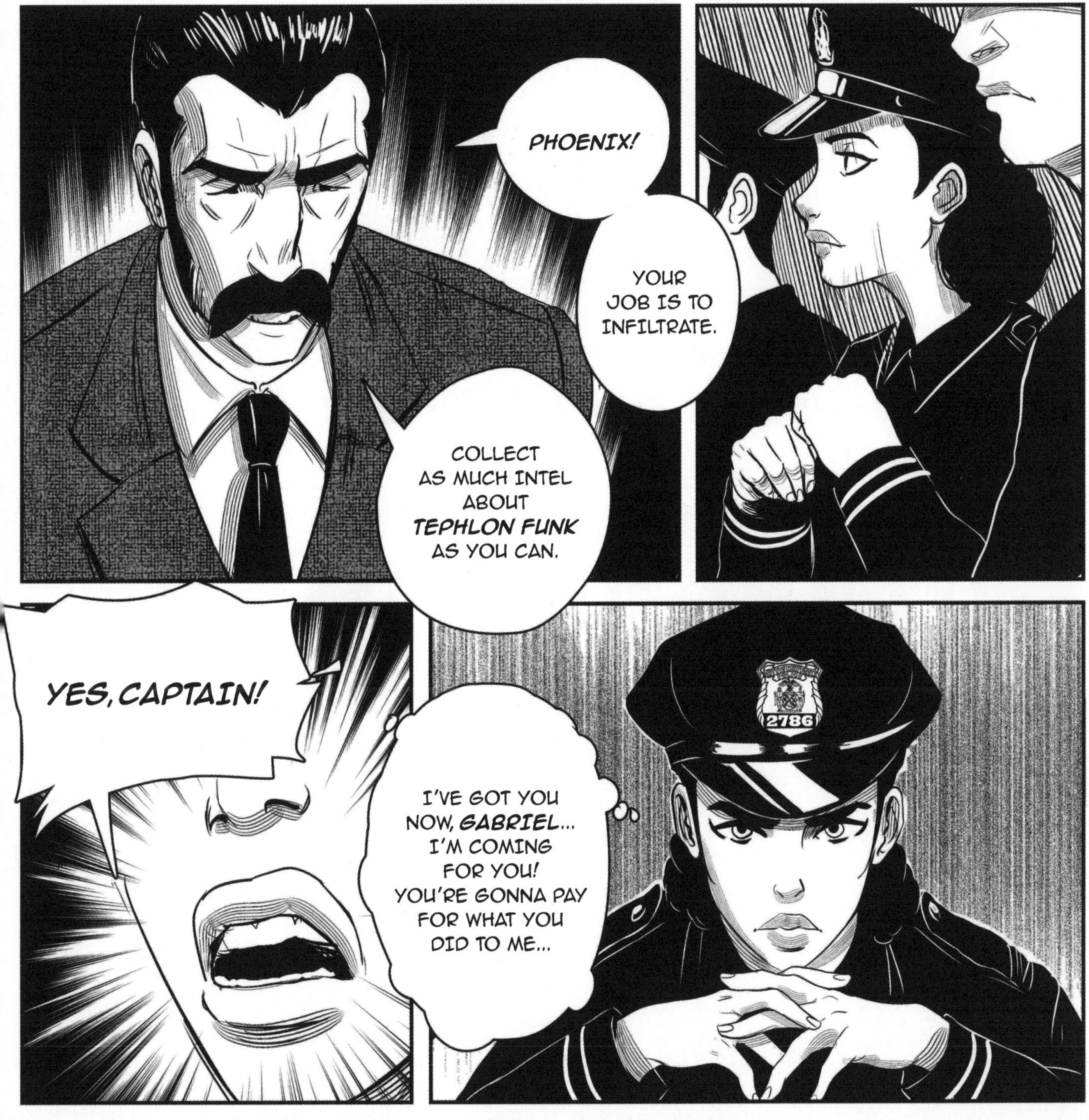
PHOENIX!
YOUR JOB IS TO INFILTRATE.
COLLECT AS MUCH INTEL ABOUT *TEPHLON FUNK* AS YOU CAN.
YES, CAPTAIN!
I'VE GOT YOU NOW, *GABRIEL*... I'M COMING FOR YOU! YOU'RE GONNA PAY FOR WHAT YOU DID TO ME...

Welcome to...

QUEENSBRIDGE
HOUSES

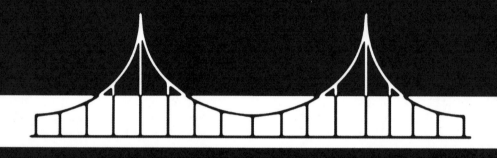

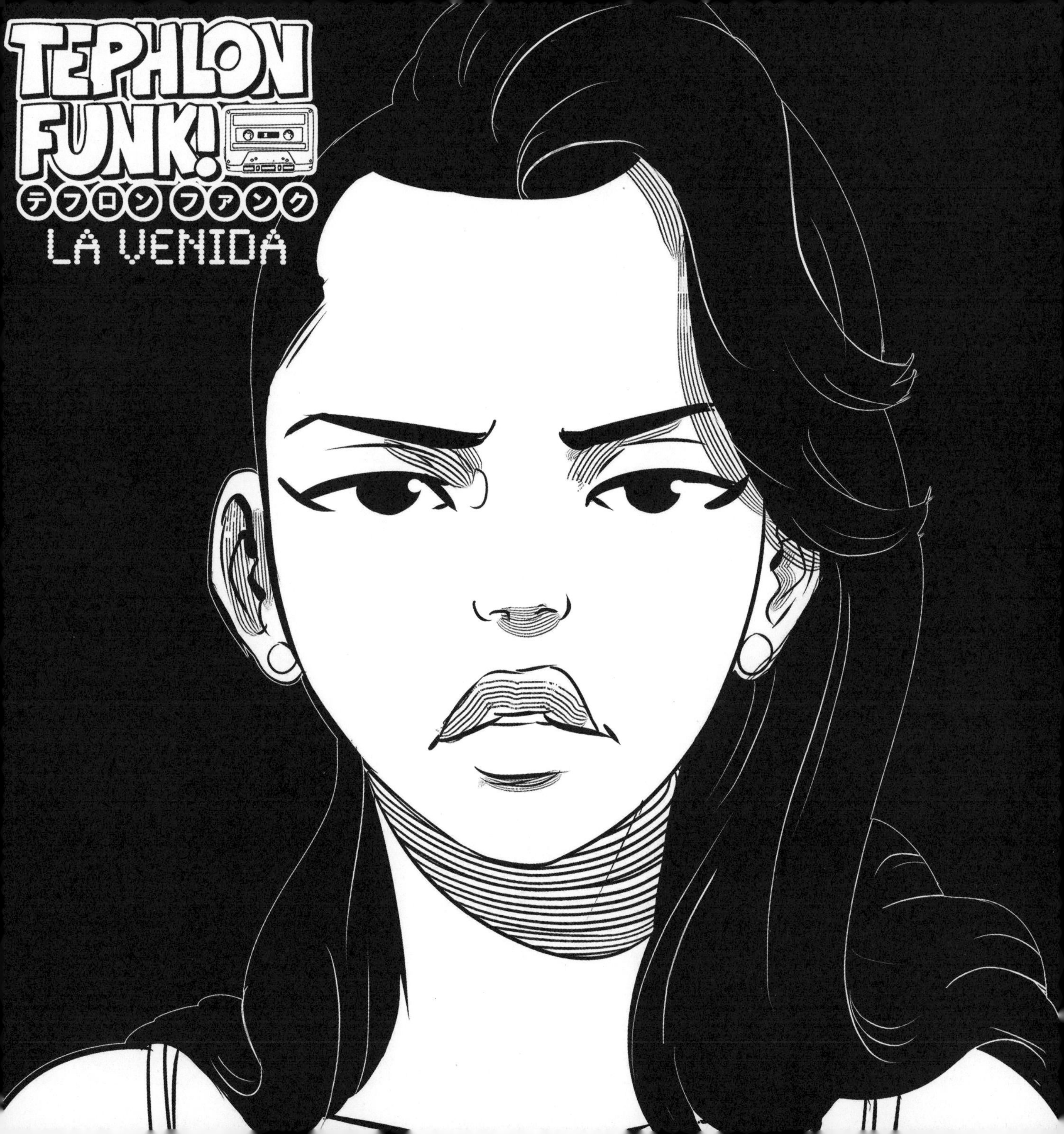
TEPHLON FUNK!
テフロン ファンク
LA VENIDA

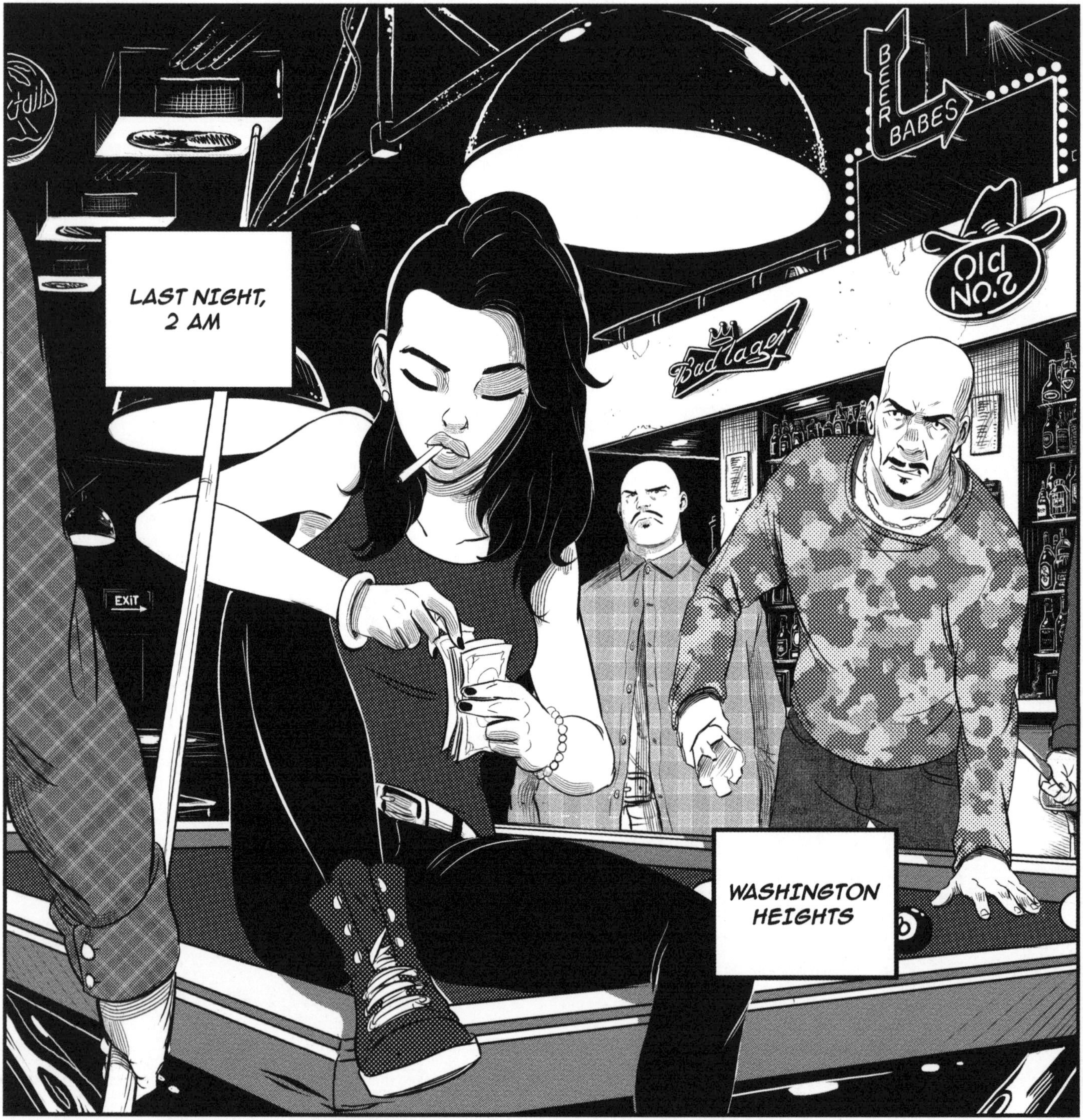
LAST NIGHT, 2 AM
WASHINGTON HEIGHTS
BEER
BABES
Bud Lager
Old No.2
EXIT

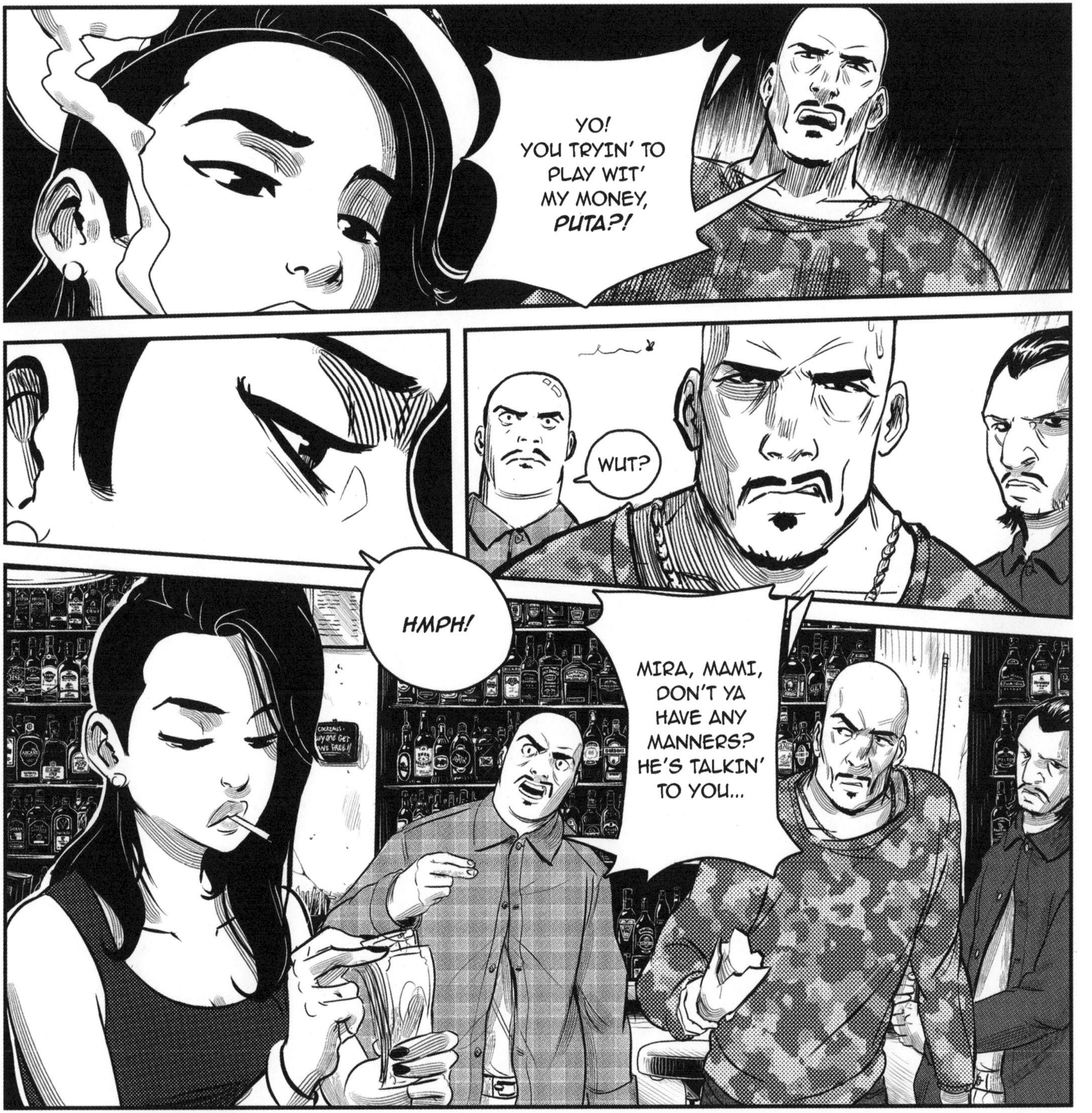
YO! YOU TRYIN' TO PLAY WIT' MY MONEY, *PUTA?!*
WUT?
HMPH!
MIRA, MAMI, DON'T YA HAVE ANY MANNERS? HE'S TALKIN' TO YOU...

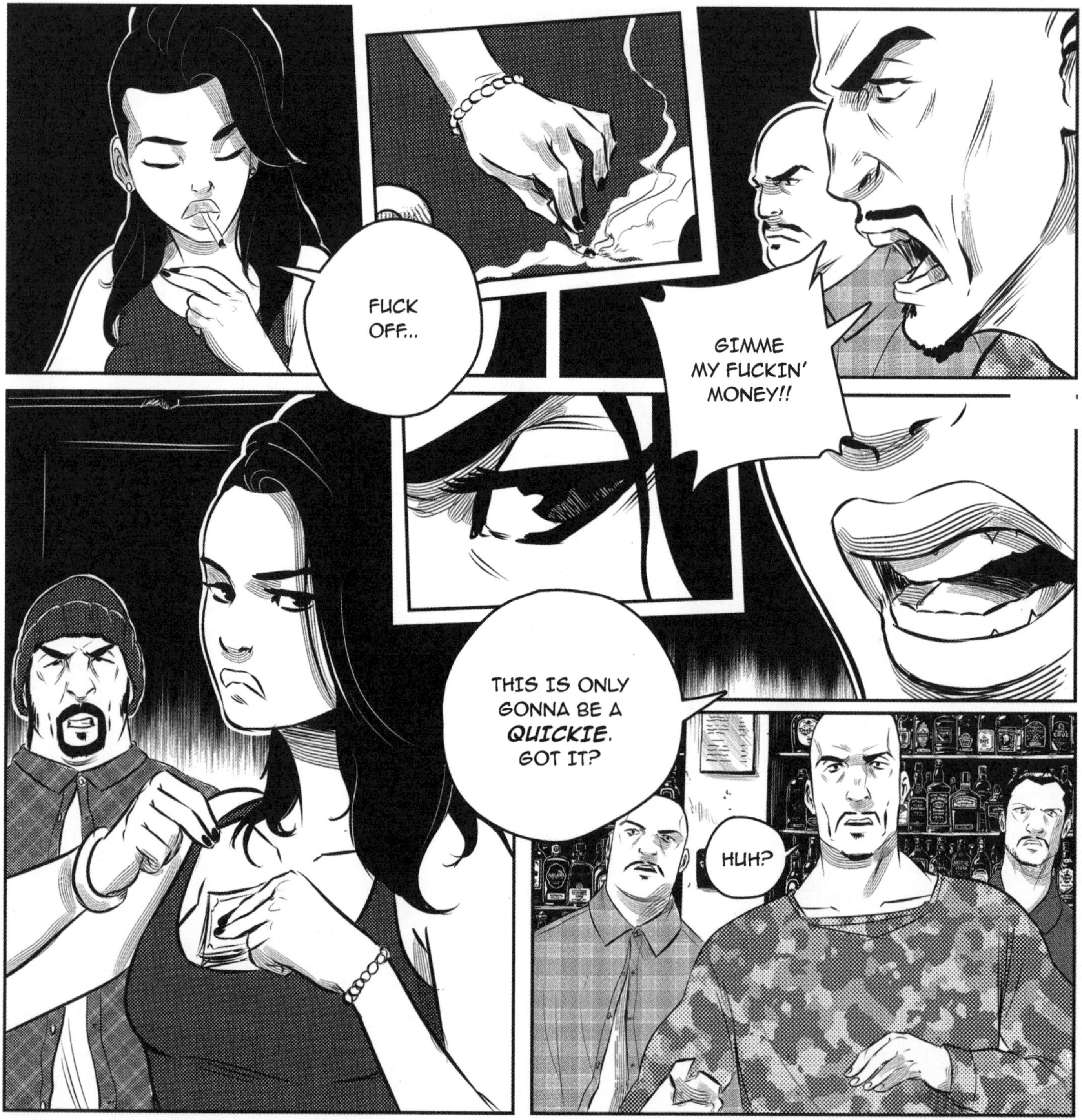
FUCK OFF...
GIMME MY FUCKIN' MONEY!!
THIS IS ONLY GONNA BE A *QUICKIE*. GOT IT?
HUH?

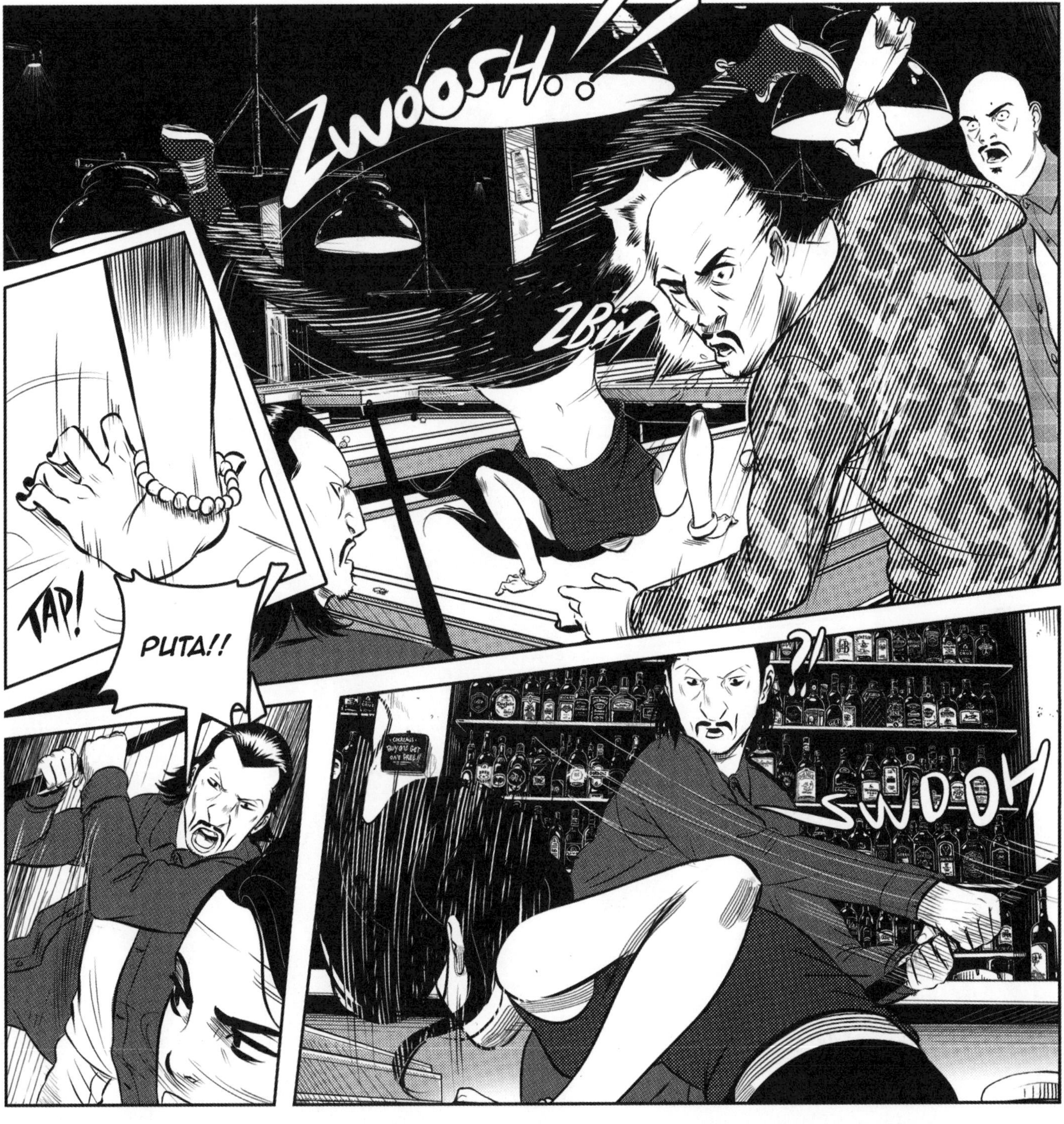
ZWOOSH!!
ZBIM
TAP!
PUTA!!
?!
SWOOH

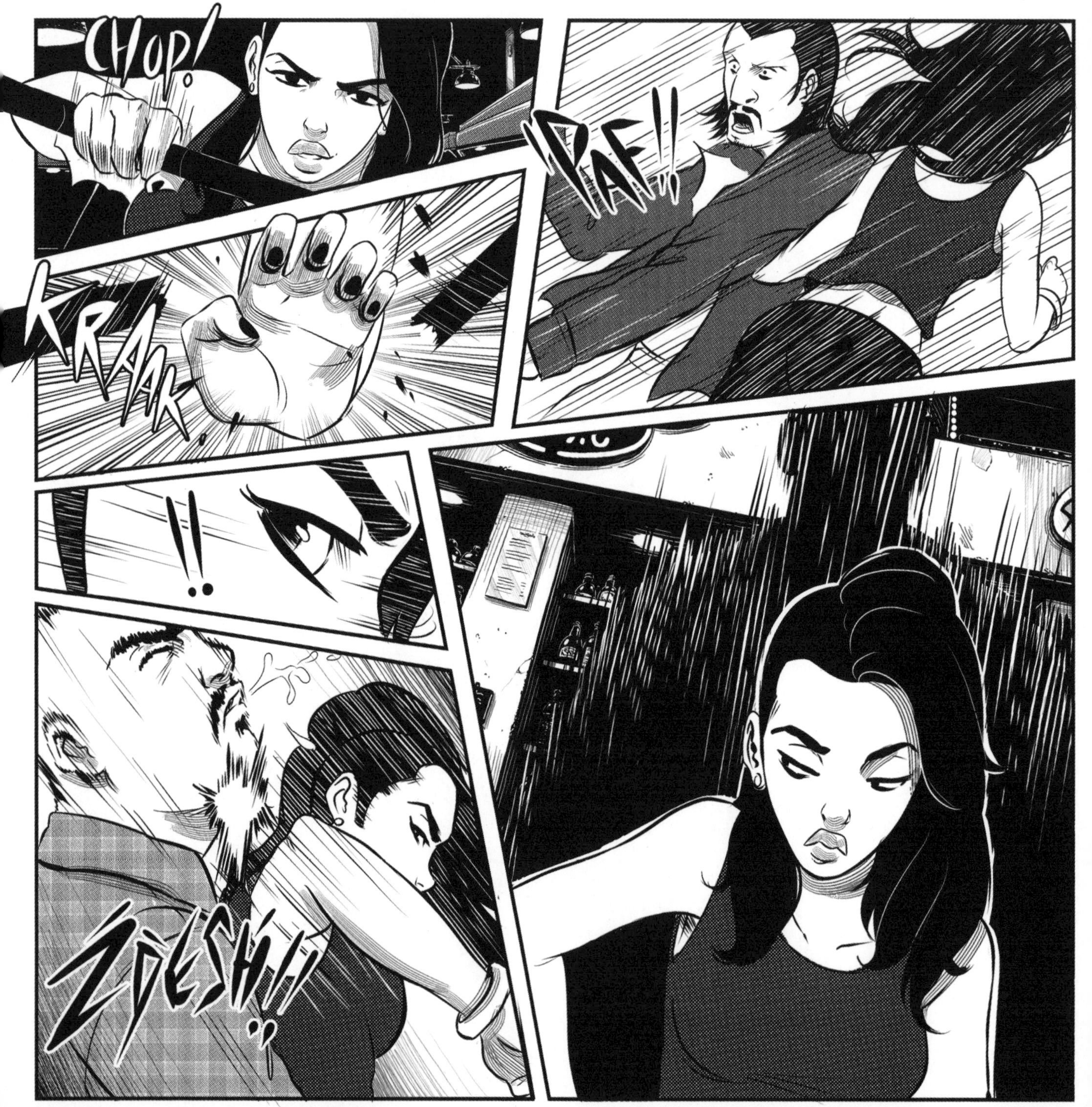
CHOP!
PAF!!
KRAAAK
!!
ZDESH!!

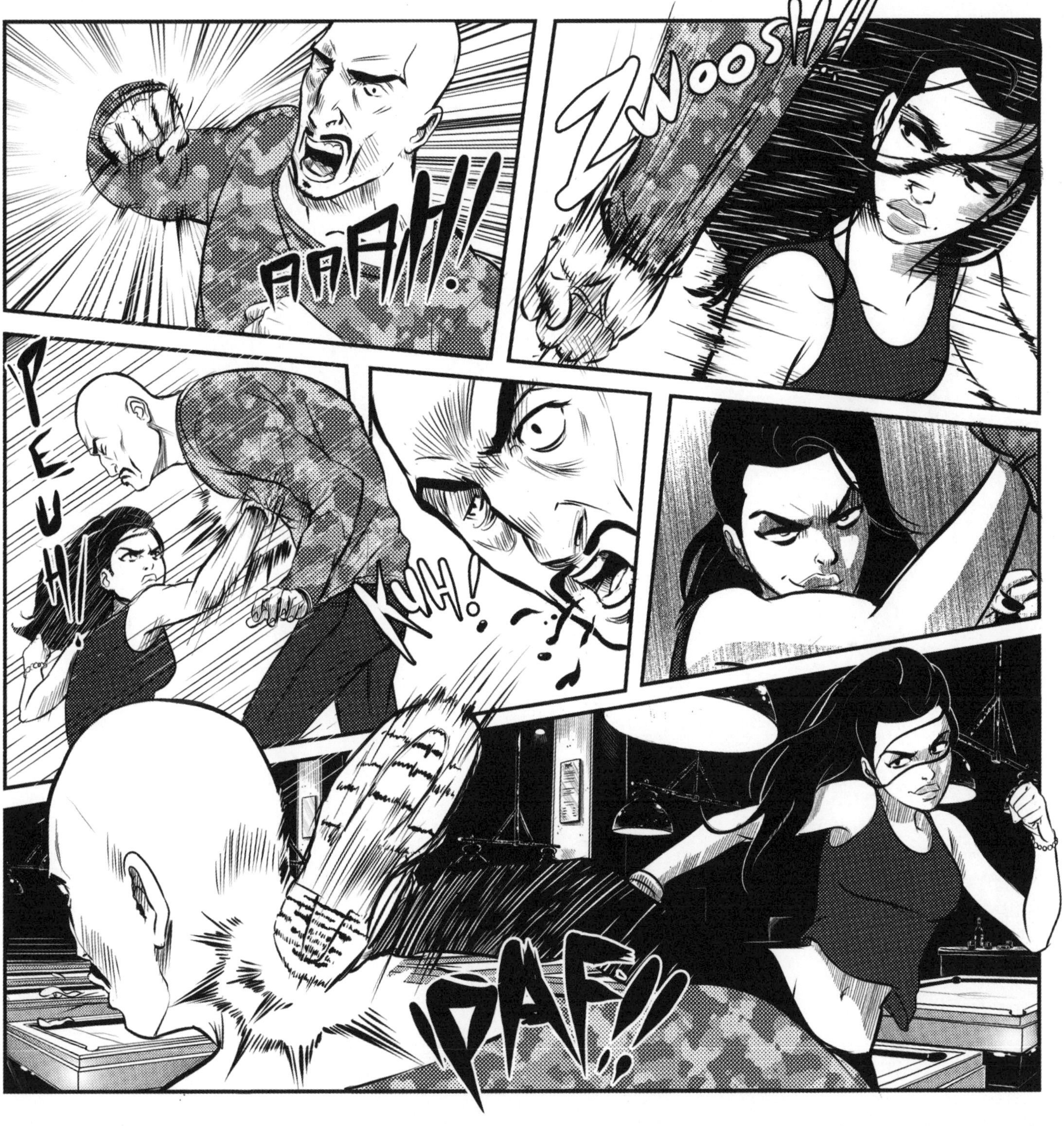
AAAH!!
ZWOOSH!!
PEUH!!
KUH!
PAF!!

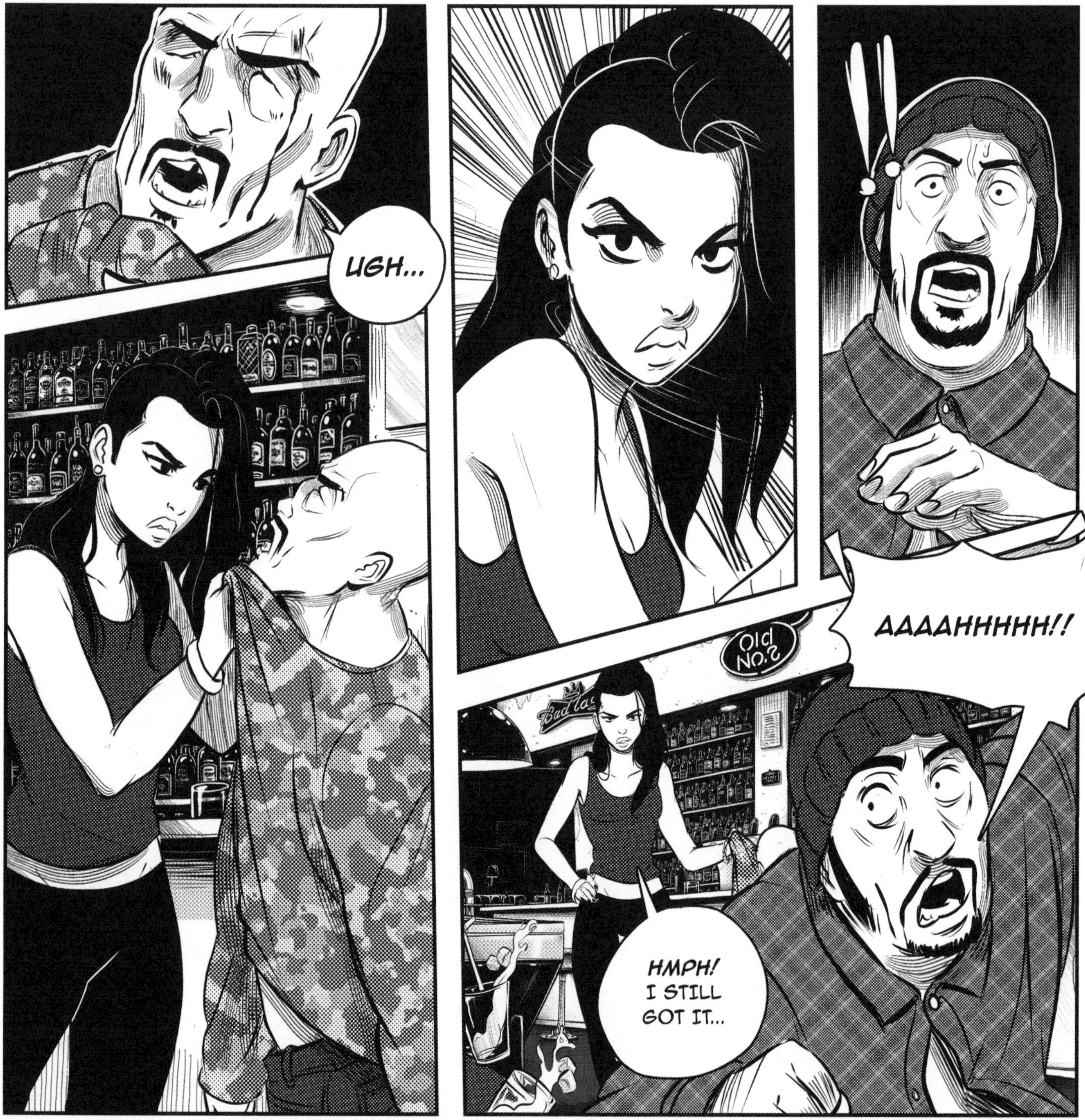
UGH...
AAAAHHHHH!!
Old No.7
HMPH! I STILL GOT IT...

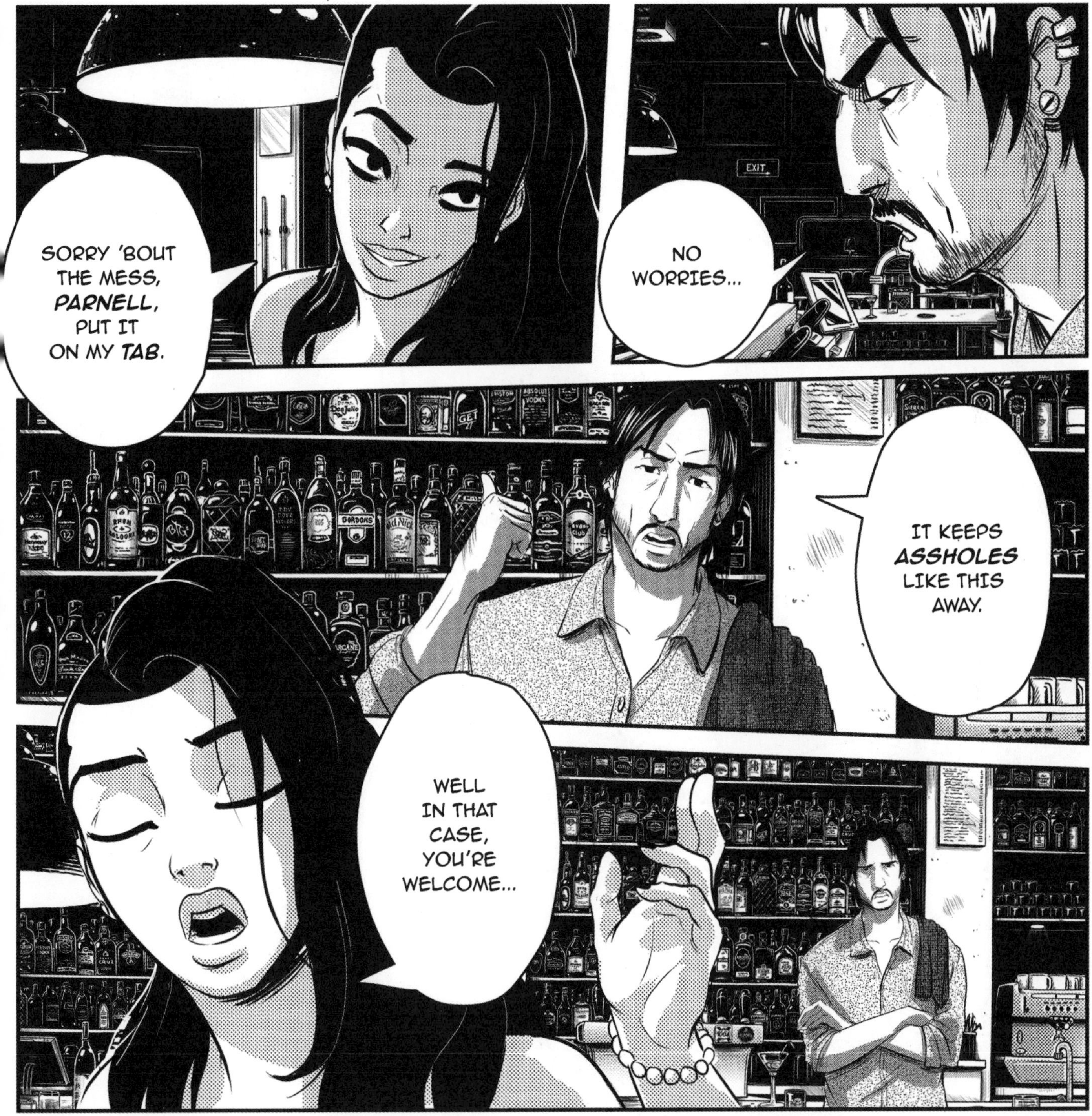
SORRY 'BOUT THE MESS, ***PARNELL***, PUT IT ON MY ***TAB***.
NO WORRIES...
EXIT
IT KEEPS ***ASSHOLES*** LIKE THIS AWAY.
WELL IN THAT CASE, YOU'RE WELCOME...

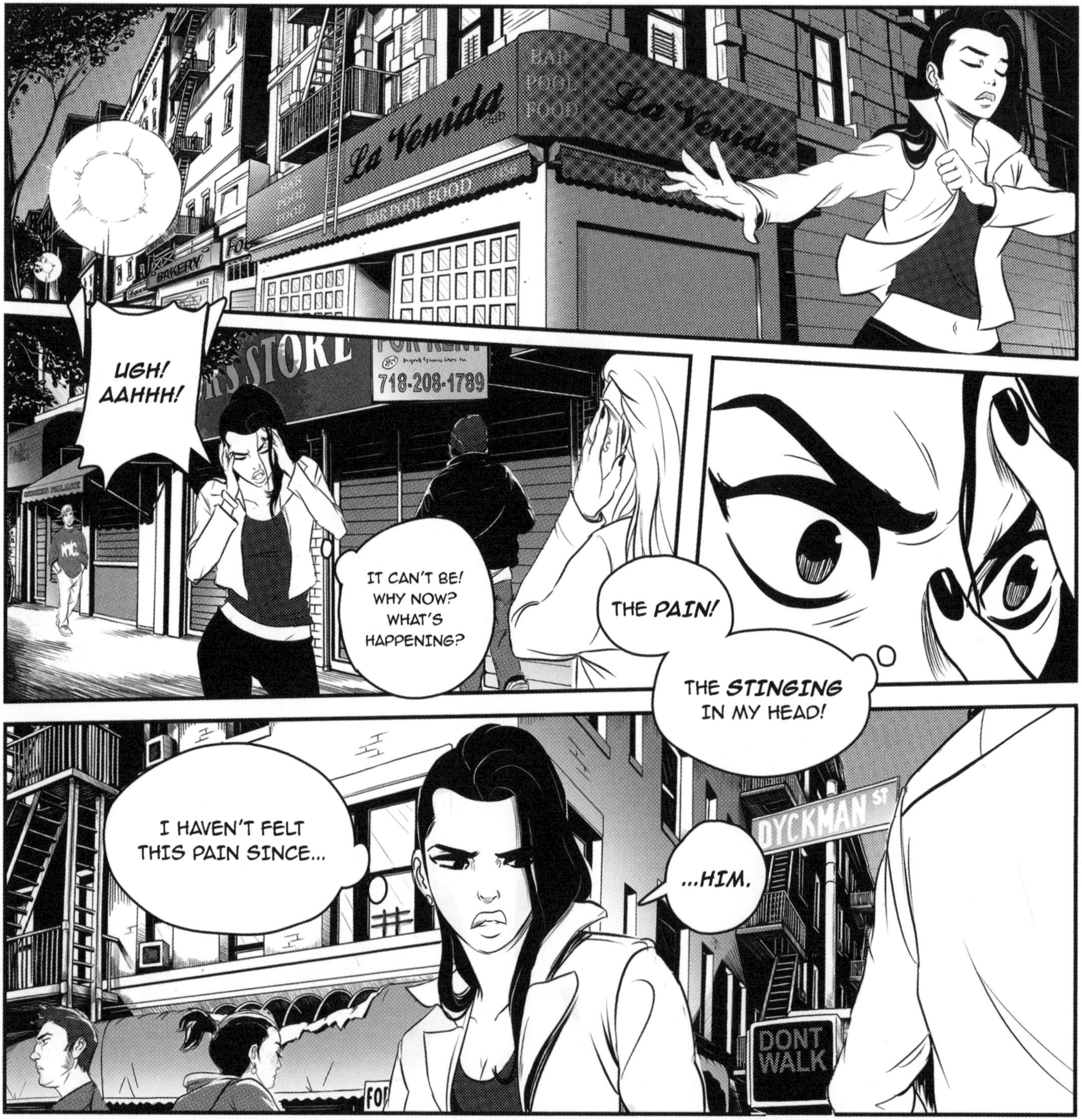
La Venida
BAR POOL FOOD
UGH! AAHHH!
718-208-1789
IT CAN'T BE! WHY NOW? WHAT'S HAPPENING?
THE PAIN!
THE STINGING IN MY HEAD!
I HAVEN'T FELT THIS PAIN SINCE...
...HIM.
DYCKMAN ST
DONT WALK

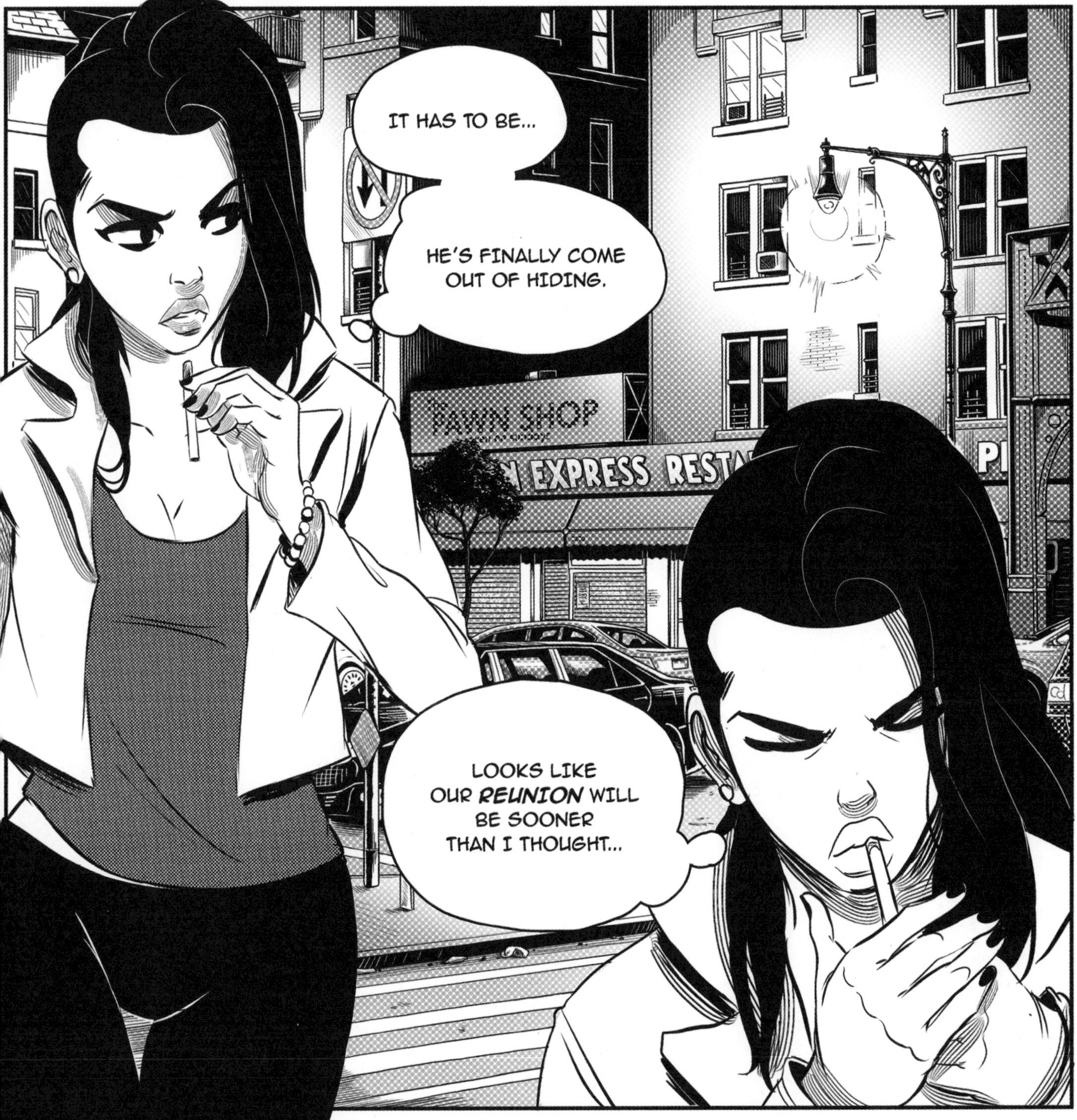
IT HAS TO BE...
HE'S FINALLY COME OUT OF HIDING.
PAWN SHOP
EXPRESS RESTA
LOOKS LIKE OUR *REUNION* WILL BE SOONER THAN I THOUGHT...

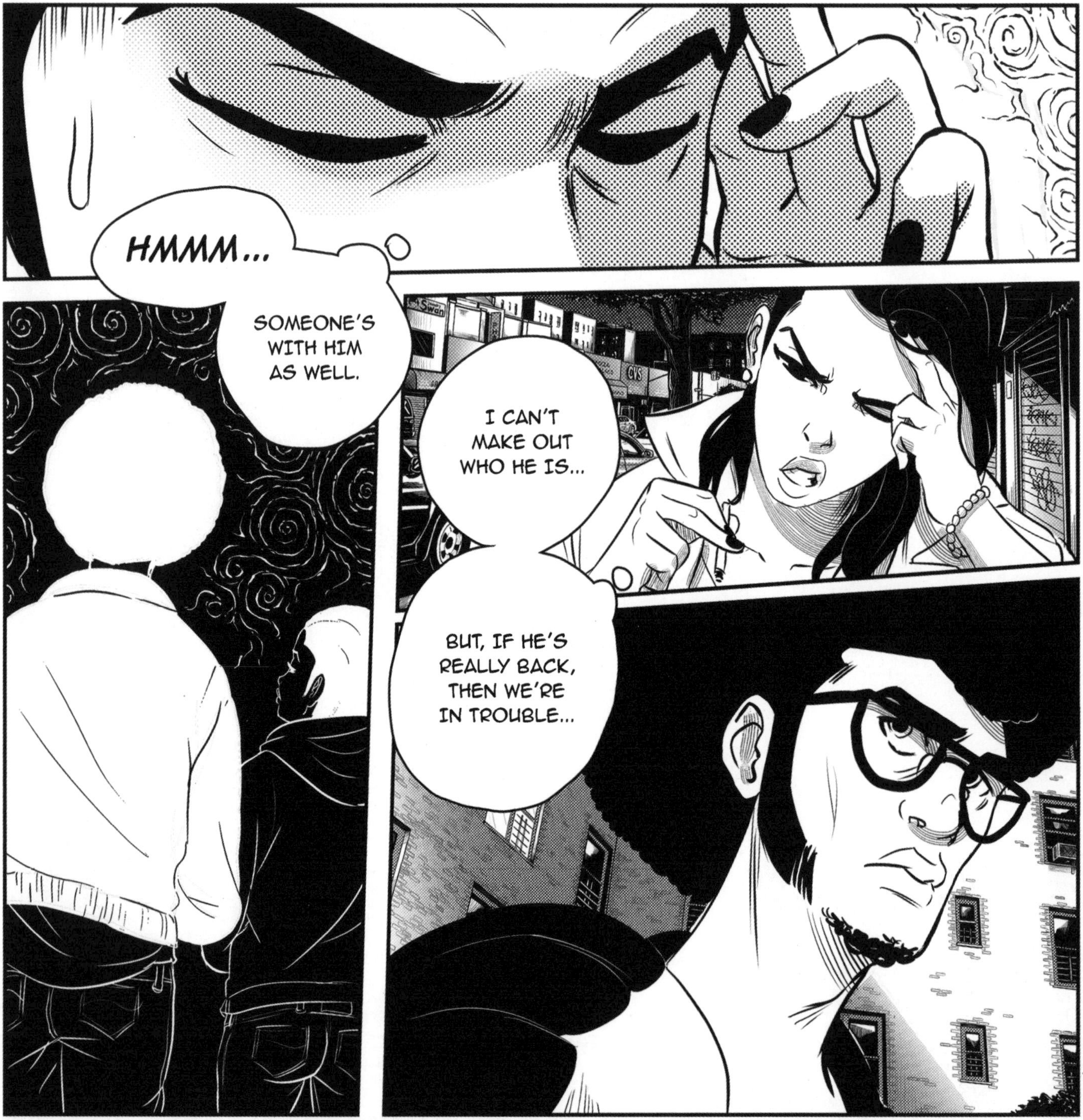
HMMM...
SOMEONE'S WITH HIM AS WELL.
I CAN'T MAKE OUT WHO HE IS...
BUT, IF HE'S REALLY BACK, THEN WE'RE IN TROUBLE...

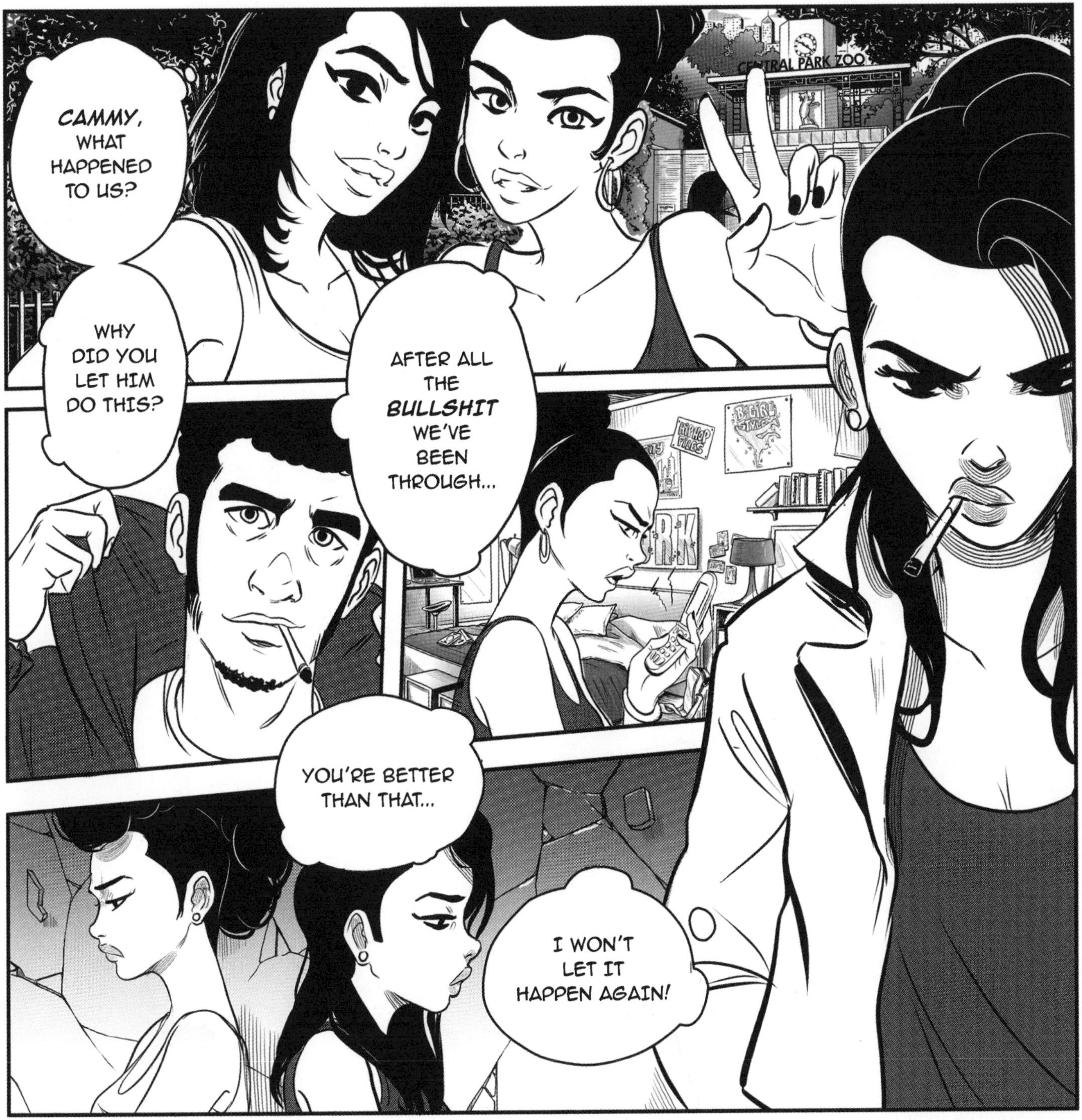

CENTRAL PARK ZOO
CAMMY, WHAT HAPPENED TO US?
WHY DID YOU LET HIM DO THIS?
AFTER ALL THE *BULLSHIT* WE'VE BEEN THROUGH...
HIPHOP FILES
B-GIRL
YOU'RE BETTER THAN THAT...
I WON'T LET IT HAPPEN AGAIN!

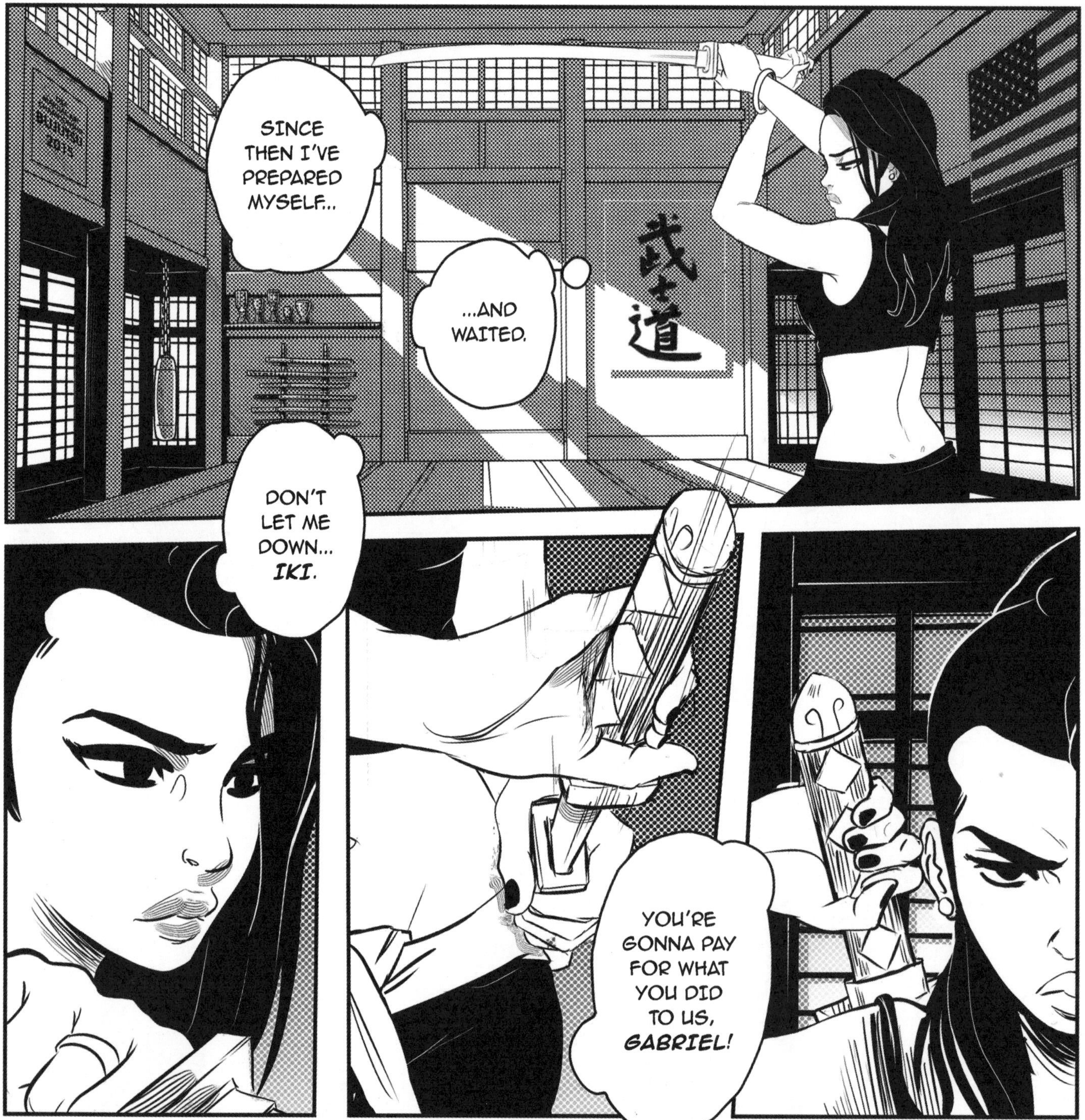
SINCE THEN I'VE PREPARED MYSELF...
...AND WAITED.
武士道
DON'T LET ME DOWN... *IKI*.
YOU'RE GONNA PAY FOR WHAT YOU DID TO US, *GABRIEL*!

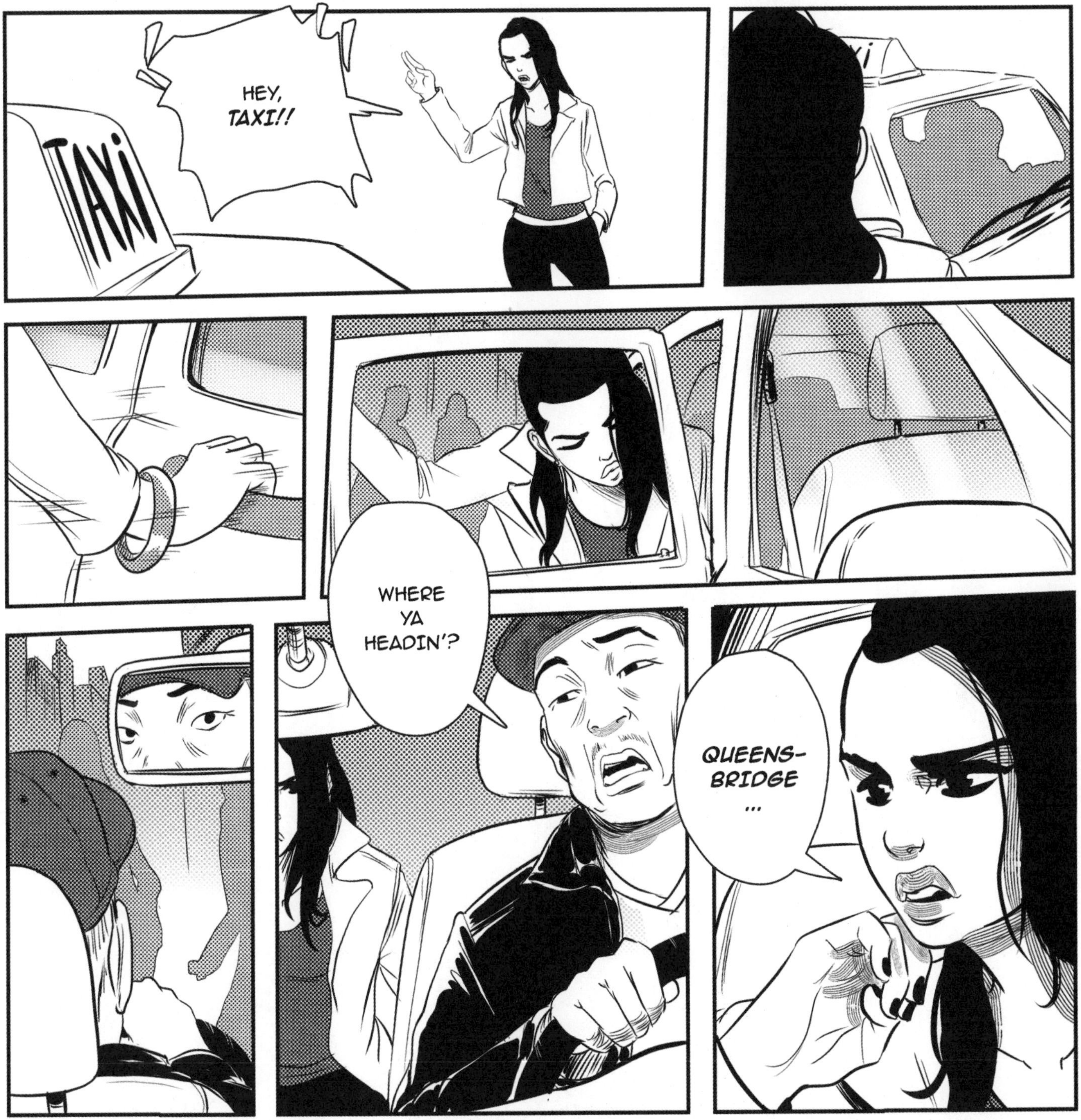
TAXI
HEY, TAXI!!
TAXI
WHERE YA HEADIN'?
QUEENS-BRIDGE ...

DYCKMAN ST

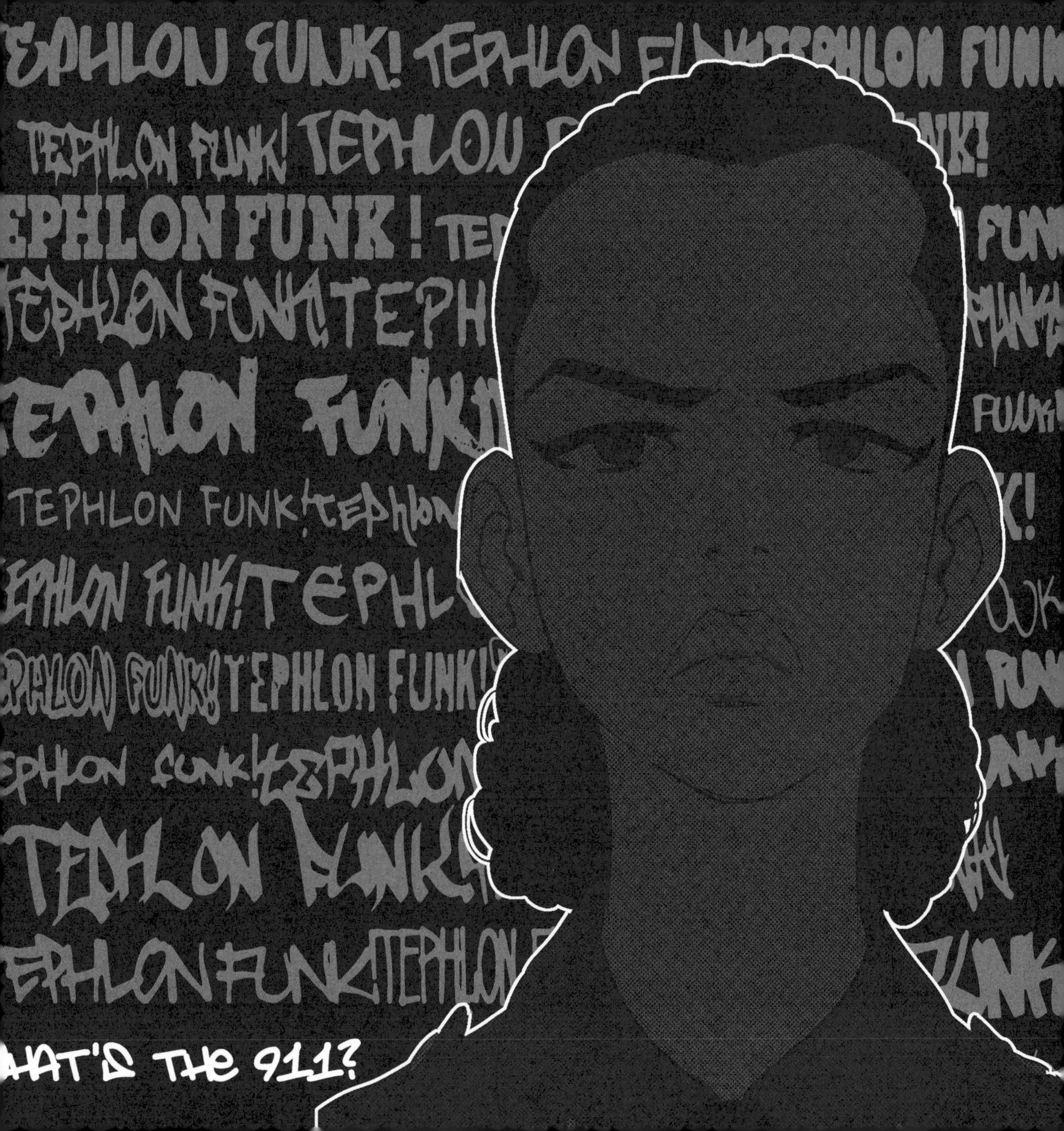
TEPHLON FUNK!
TEPHLON FUNK!
TEPHLON FUNK!
TEPHLON FUNK!
TEPHLON FUNK!
HAT'S THE 911?

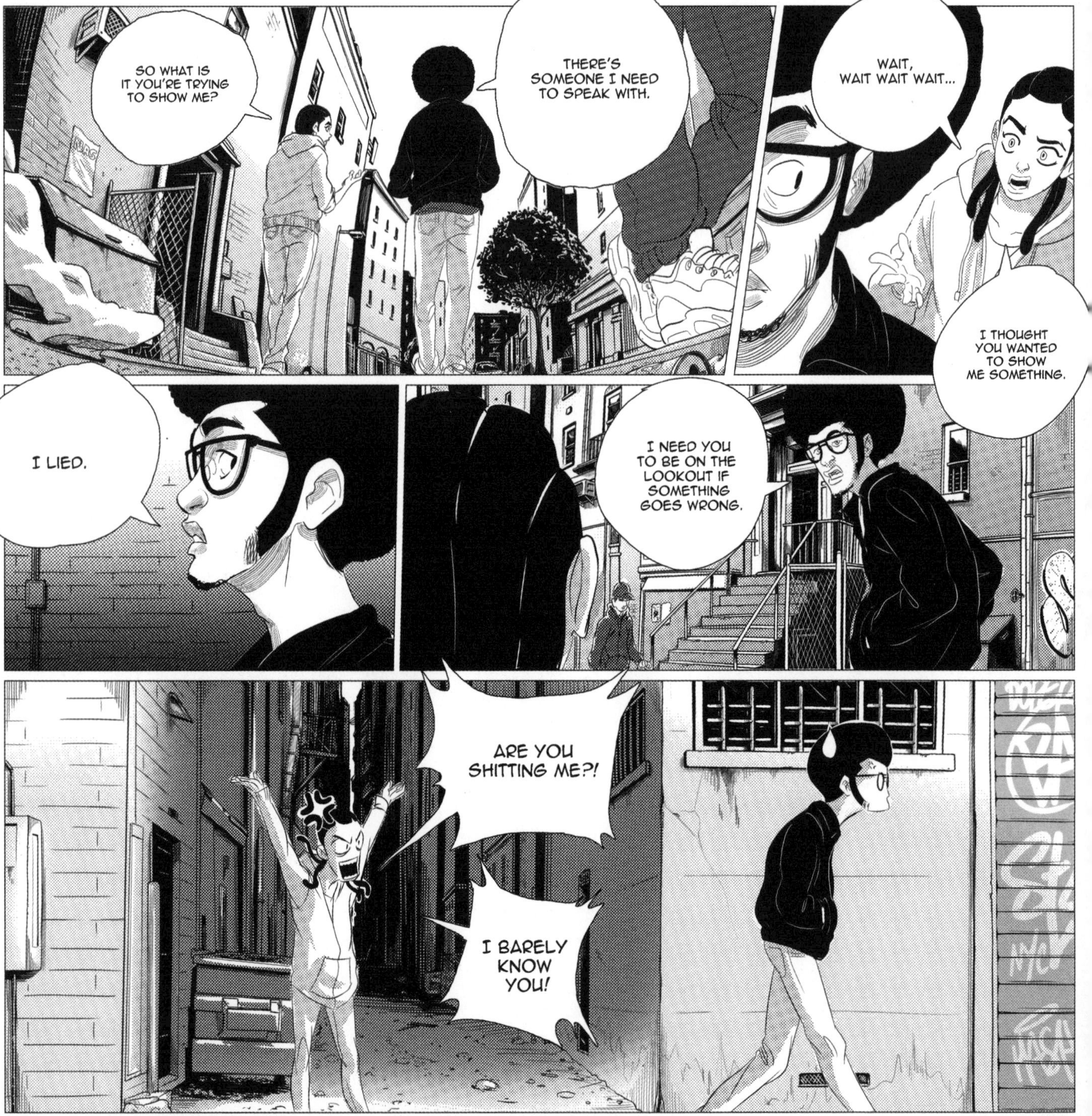
SO WHAT IS IT YOU'RE TRYING TO SHOW ME?
THERE'S SOMEONE I NEED TO SPEAK WITH.
WAIT, WAIT WAIT WAIT...
I THOUGHT YOU WANTED TO SHOW ME SOMETHING.
I LIED.
I NEED YOU TO BE ON THE LOOKOUT IF SOMETHING GOES WRONG.
ARE YOU SHITTING ME?!
I BARELY KNOW YOU!

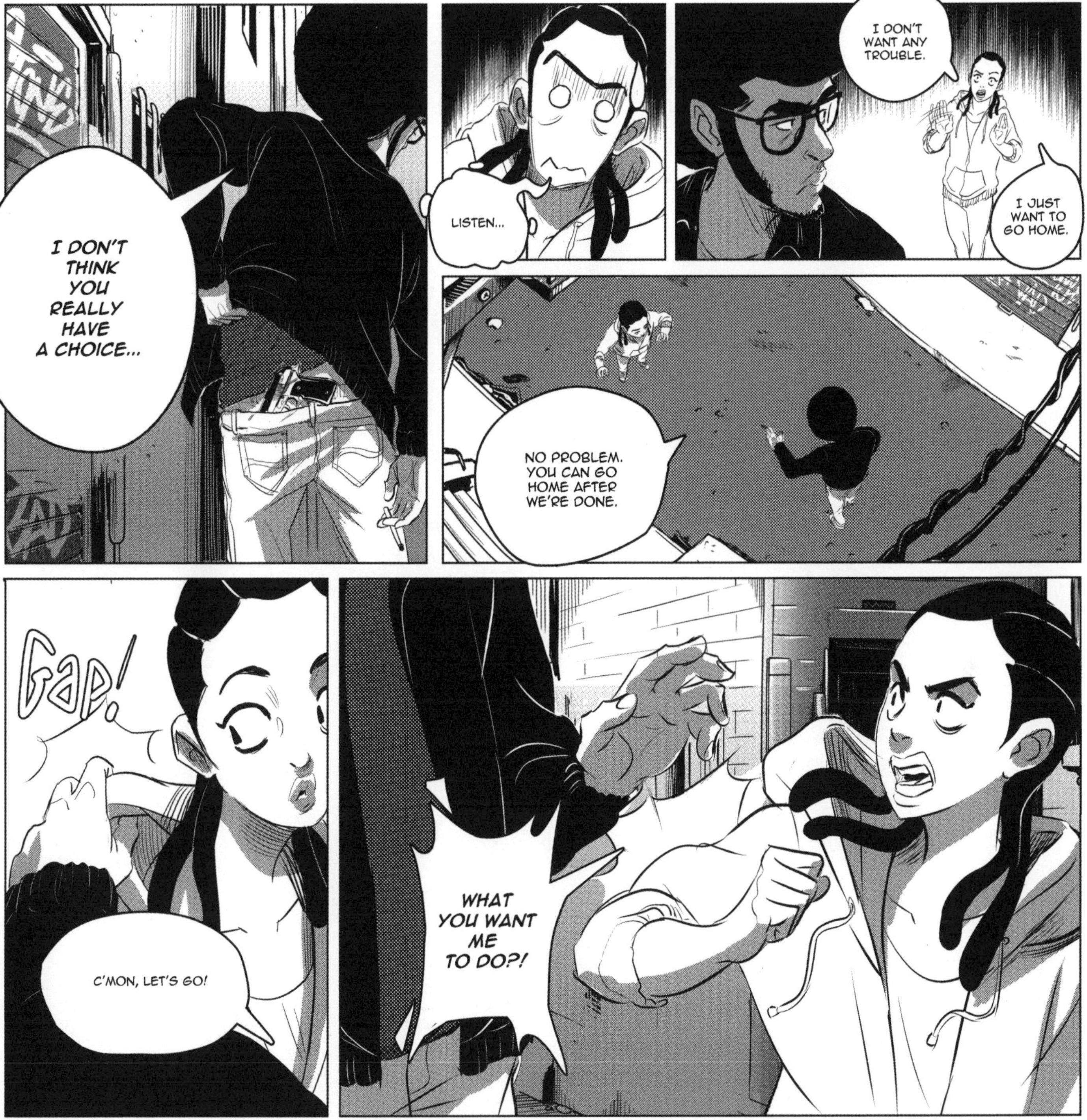
I DON'T THINK YOU REALLY HAVE A CHOICE...
LISTEN...
I DON'T WANT ANY TROUBLE.
I JUST WANT TO GO HOME.
NO PROBLEM. YOU CAN GO HOME AFTER WE'RE DONE.
GAP!
C'MON, LET'S GO!
WHAT YOU WANT ME TO DO?!

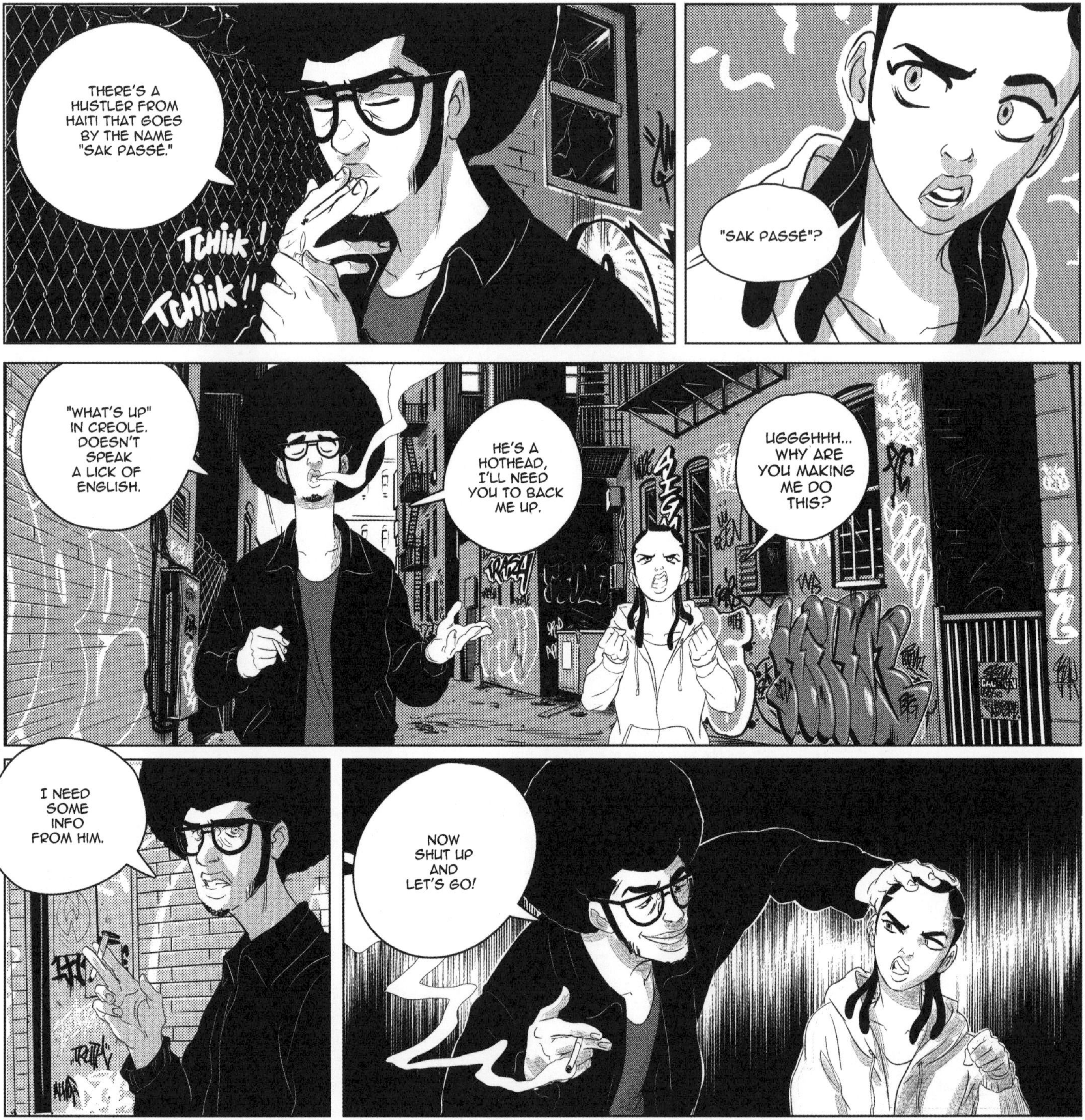
THERE'S A HUSTLER FROM HAITI THAT GOES BY THE NAME "SAK PASSÉ."
TCHIIK! TCHIIK!!
"SAK PASSÉ"?
"WHAT'S UP" IN CREOLE. DOESN'T SPEAK A LICK OF ENGLISH.
HE'S A HOTHEAD, I'LL NEED YOU TO BACK ME UP.
UGGGHHH... WHY ARE YOU MAKING ME DO THIS?
I NEED SOME INFO FROM HIM.
NOW SHUT UP AND LET'S GO!

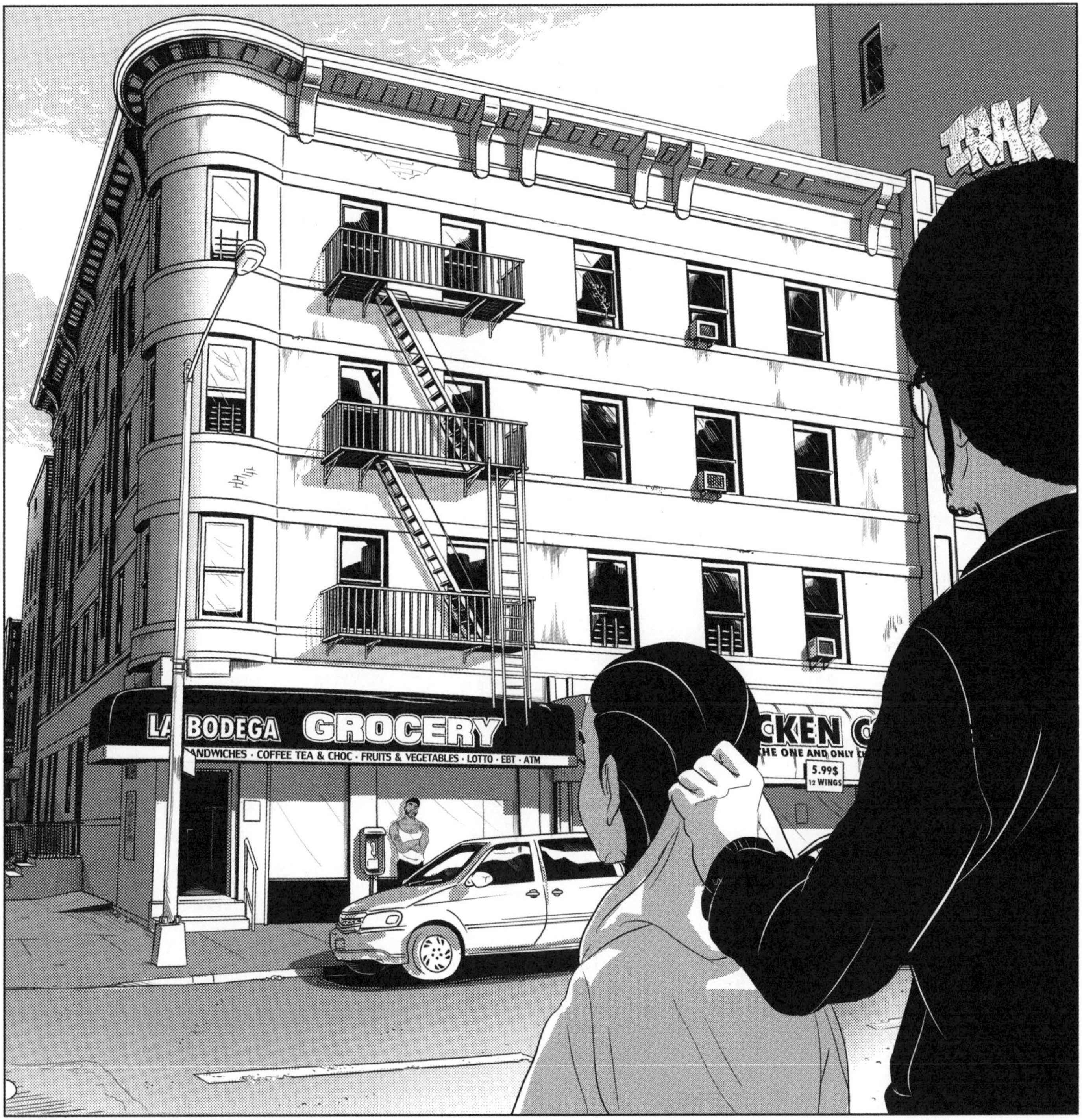
IRAK
LA BODEGA GROCERY
ANDWICHES · COFFEE TEA & CHOC · FRUITS & VEGETABLES · LOTTO · EBT · ATM
CKEN C
THE ONE AND ONLY
5.99$
12 WINGS

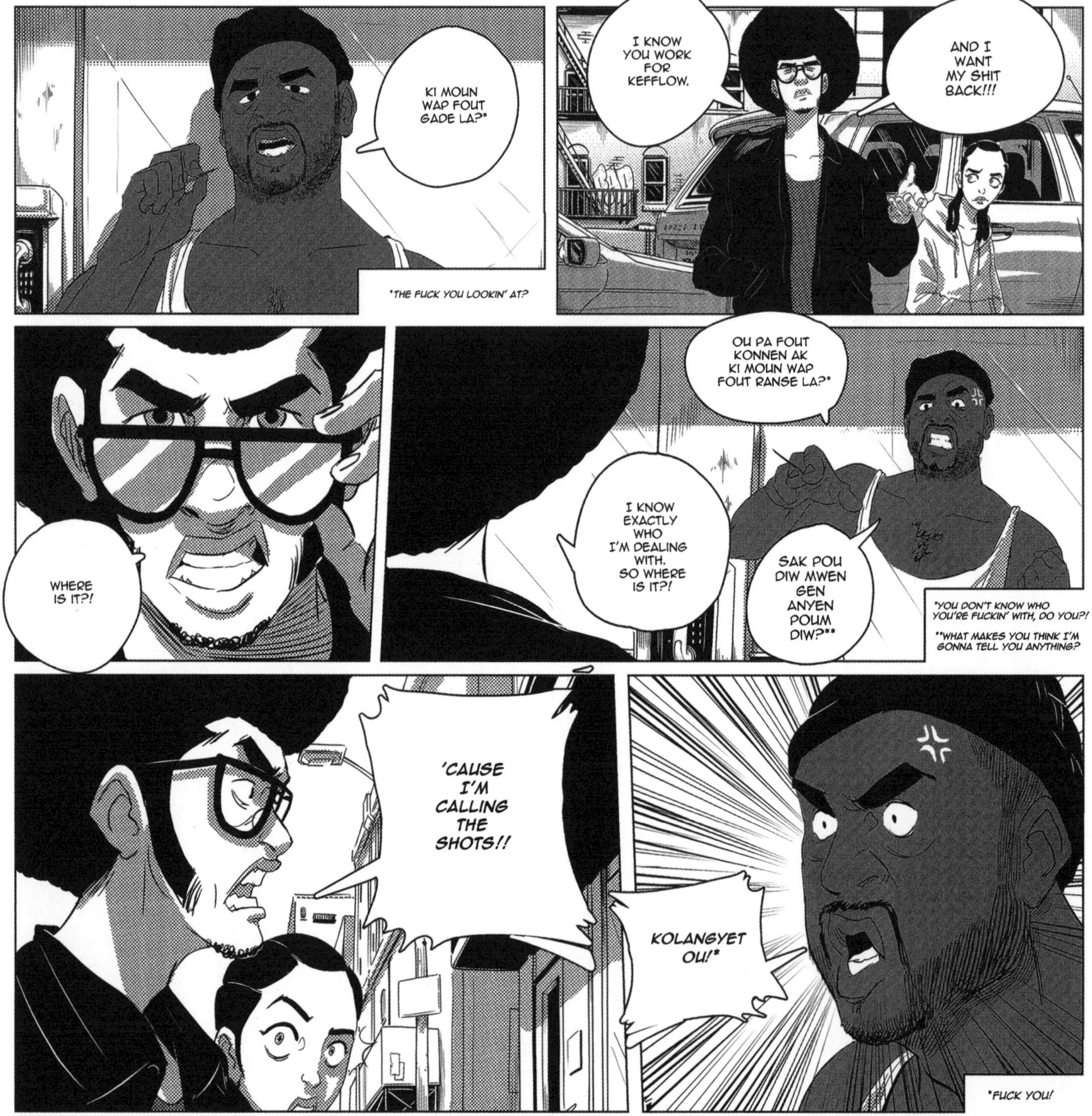
KI MOUN WAP FOUT GADE LA?*
*THE FUCK YOU LOOKIN' AT?
I KNOW YOU WORK FOR KEFFLOW.
AND I WANT MY SHIT BACK!!!
WHERE IS IT?!
OU PA FOUT KONNEN AK KI MOUN WAP FOUT RANSE LA?*
I KNOW EXACTLY WHO I'M DEALING WITH. SO WHERE IS IT?!
SAK POU DIW MWEN GEN ANYEN POUM DIW?**
*YOU DON'T KNOW WHO YOU'RE FUCKIN' WITH, DO YOU?!
**WHAT MAKES YOU THINK I'M GONNA TELL YOU ANYTHING?
'CAUSE I'M CALLING THE SHOTS!!
KOLANGYET OU!*
*FUCK YOU!

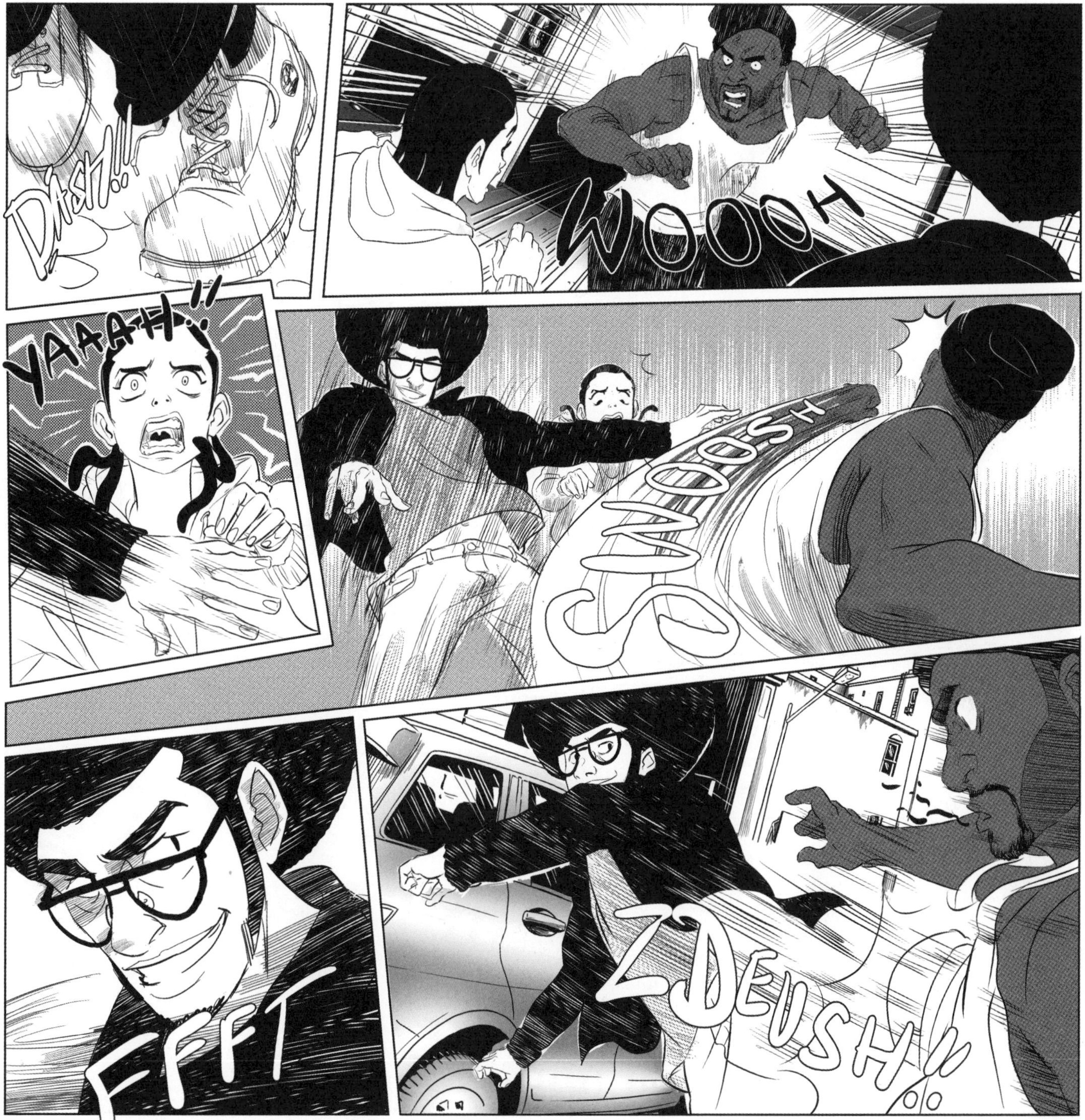

DASH!!!
WOOOH
YAAAH!!
WOOSH
FFFT
ZDEUSH!!

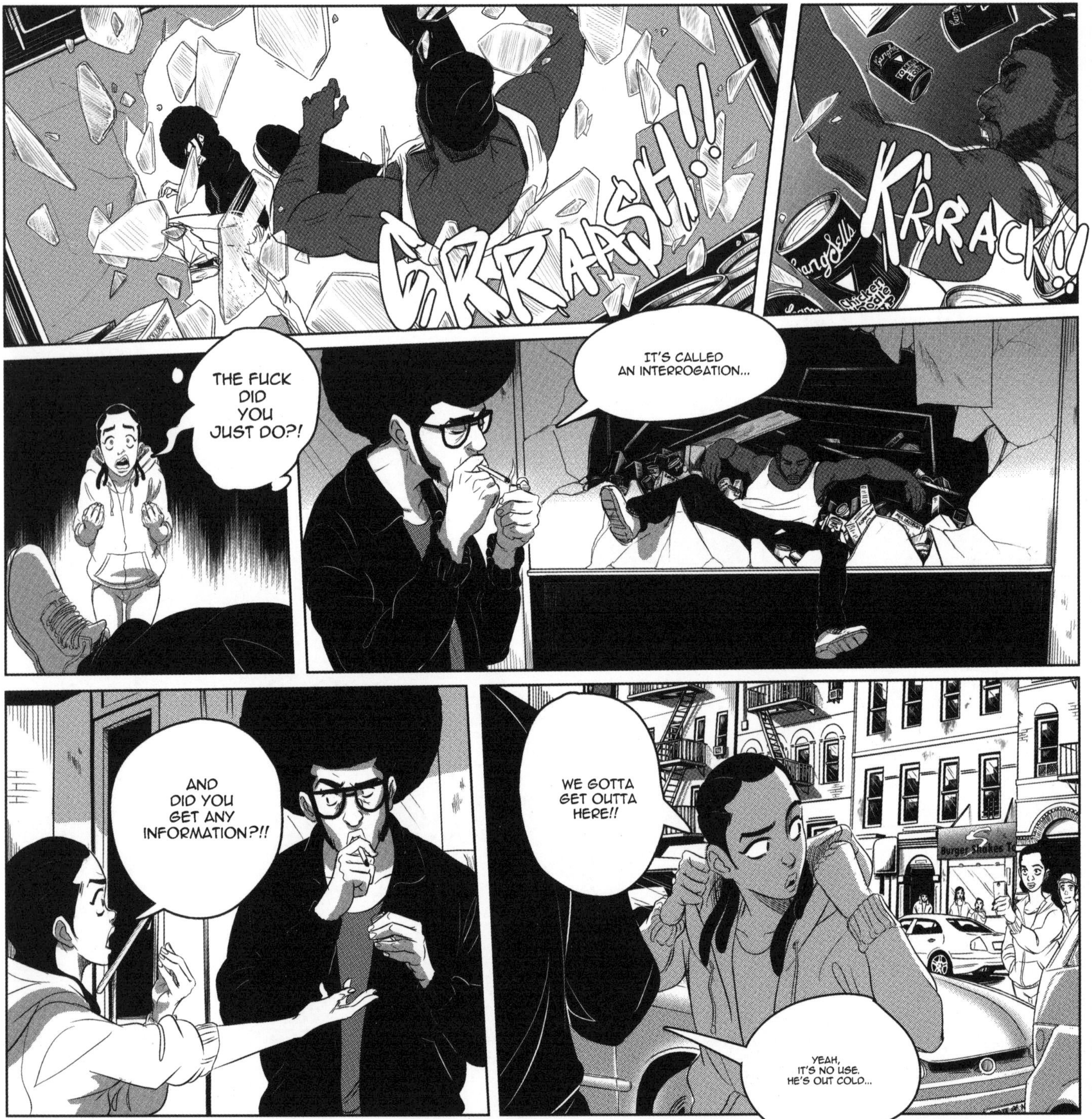
GRRAASH!!
KRRACK!!
THE FUCK DID YOU JUST DO?!
IT'S CALLED AN INTERROGATION...
AND DID YOU GET ANY INFORMATION?!!
WE GOTTA GET OUTTA HERE!!
YEAH, IT'S NO USE. HE'S OUT COLD...

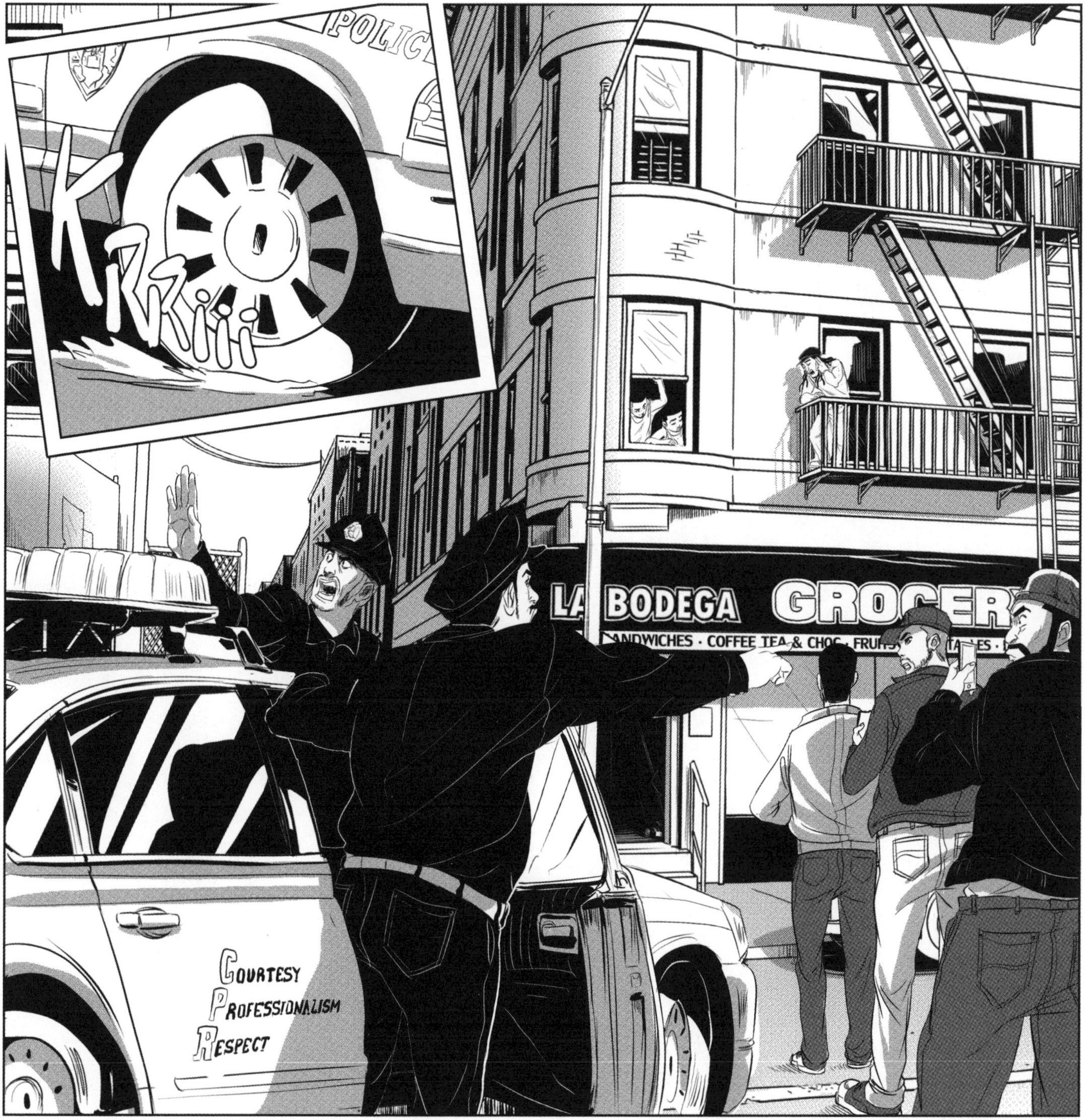
KRRRiiii
LA BODEGA
COURTESY
PROFESSIONALISM
RESPECT

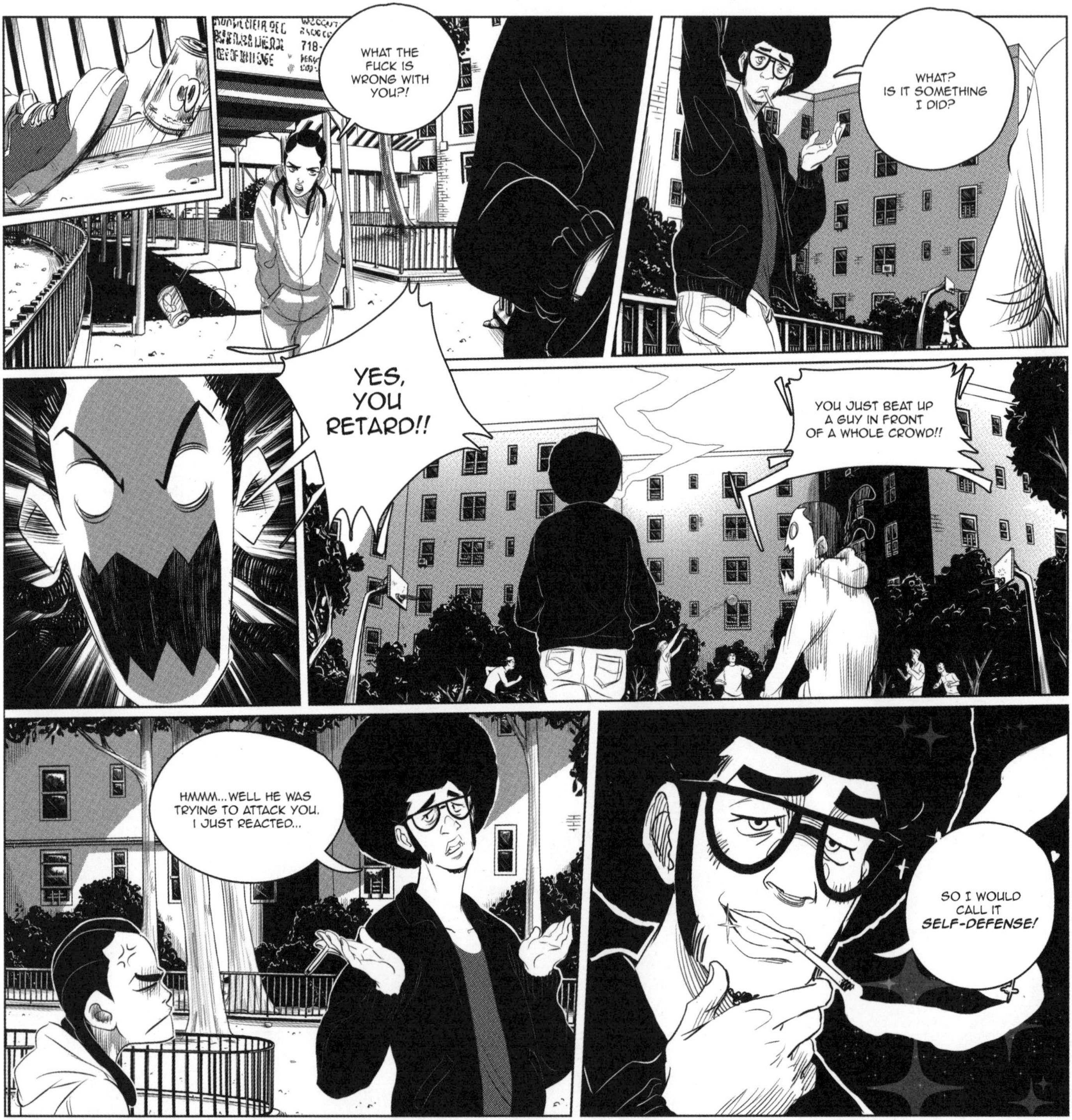
WHAT THE FUCK IS WRONG WITH YOU?!
WHAT? IS IT SOMETHING I DID?
YES, YOU RETARD!!
YOU JUST BEAT UP A GUY IN FRONT OF A WHOLE CROWD!!
HMMM...WELL HE WAS TRYING TO ATTACK YOU. I JUST REACTED...
SO I WOULD CALL IT *SELF-DEFENSE!*

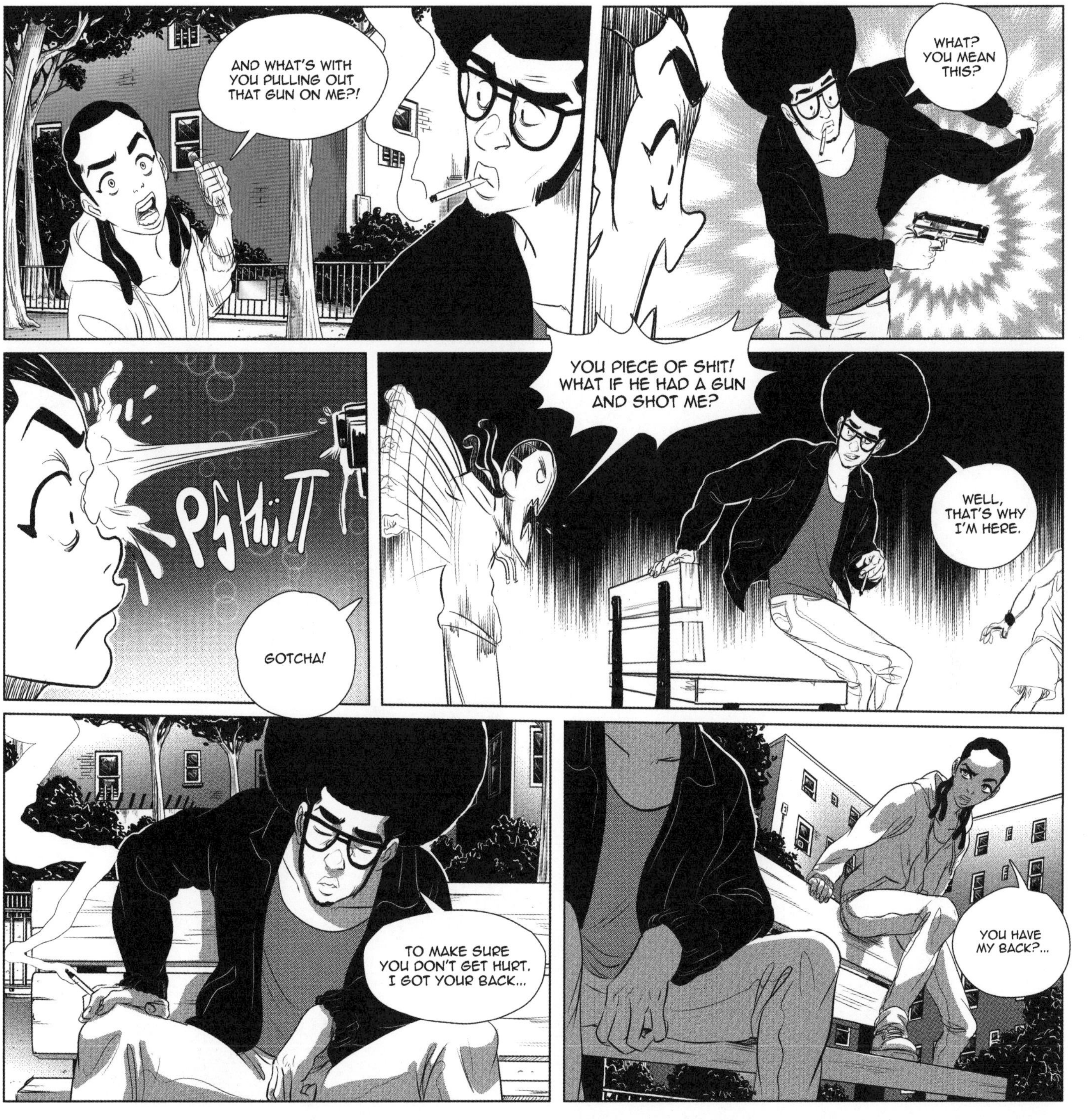

AND WHAT'S WITH YOU PULLING OUT THAT GUN ON ME?!
WHAT? YOU MEAN THIS?
PSHITT
GOTCHA!
YOU PIECE OF SHIT! WHAT IF HE HAD A GUN AND SHOT ME?
WELL, THAT'S WHY I'M HERE.
TO MAKE SURE YOU DON'T GET HURT. I GOT YOUR BACK...
YOU HAVE MY BACK?...

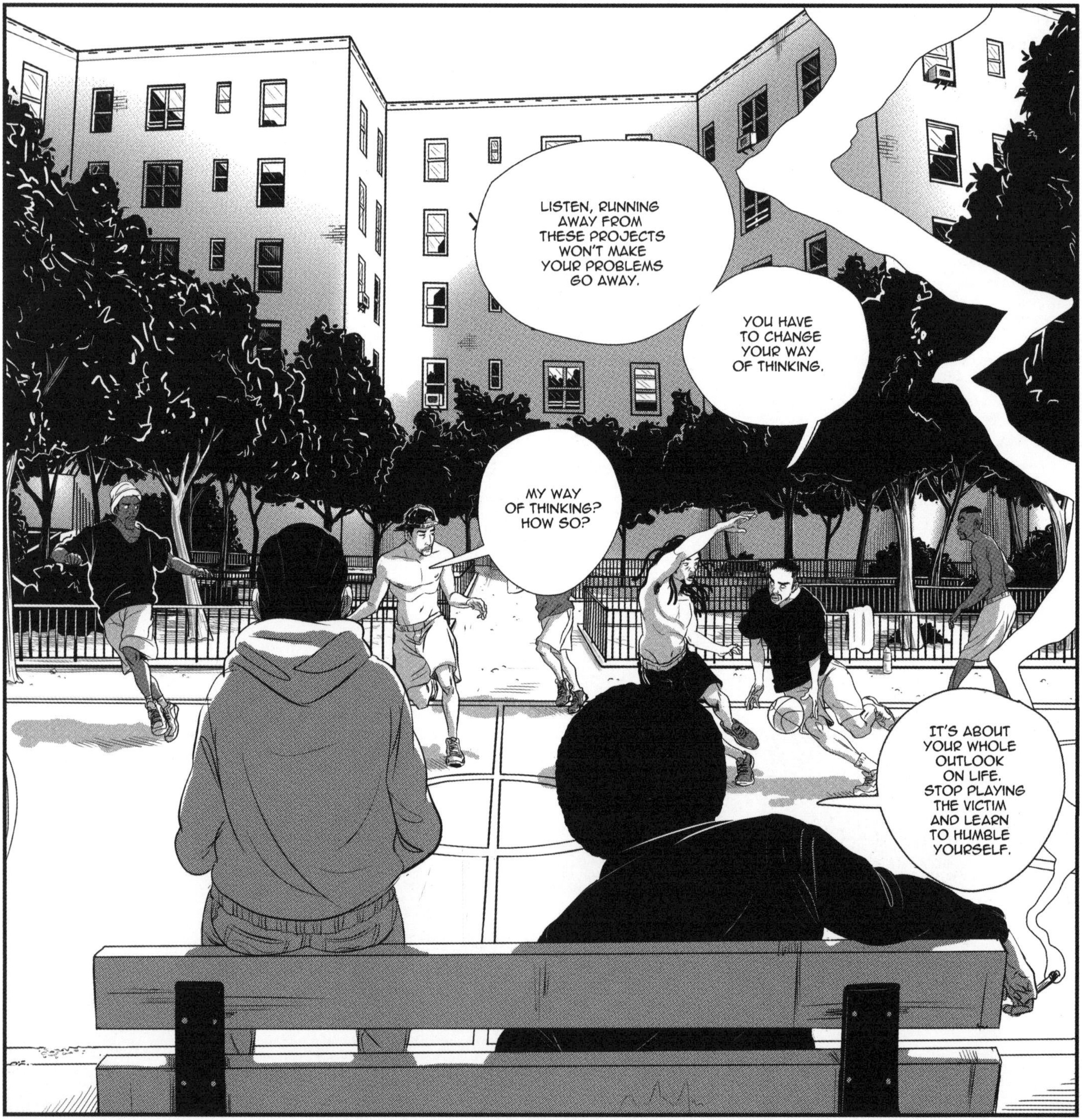
LISTEN, RUNNING AWAY FROM THESE PROJECTS WON'T MAKE YOUR PROBLEMS GO AWAY.
YOU HAVE TO CHANGE YOUR WAY OF THINKING.
MY WAY OF THINKING? HOW SO?
IT'S ABOUT YOUR WHOLE OUTLOOK ON LIFE. STOP PLAYING THE VICTIM AND LEARN TO HUMBLE YOURSELF.

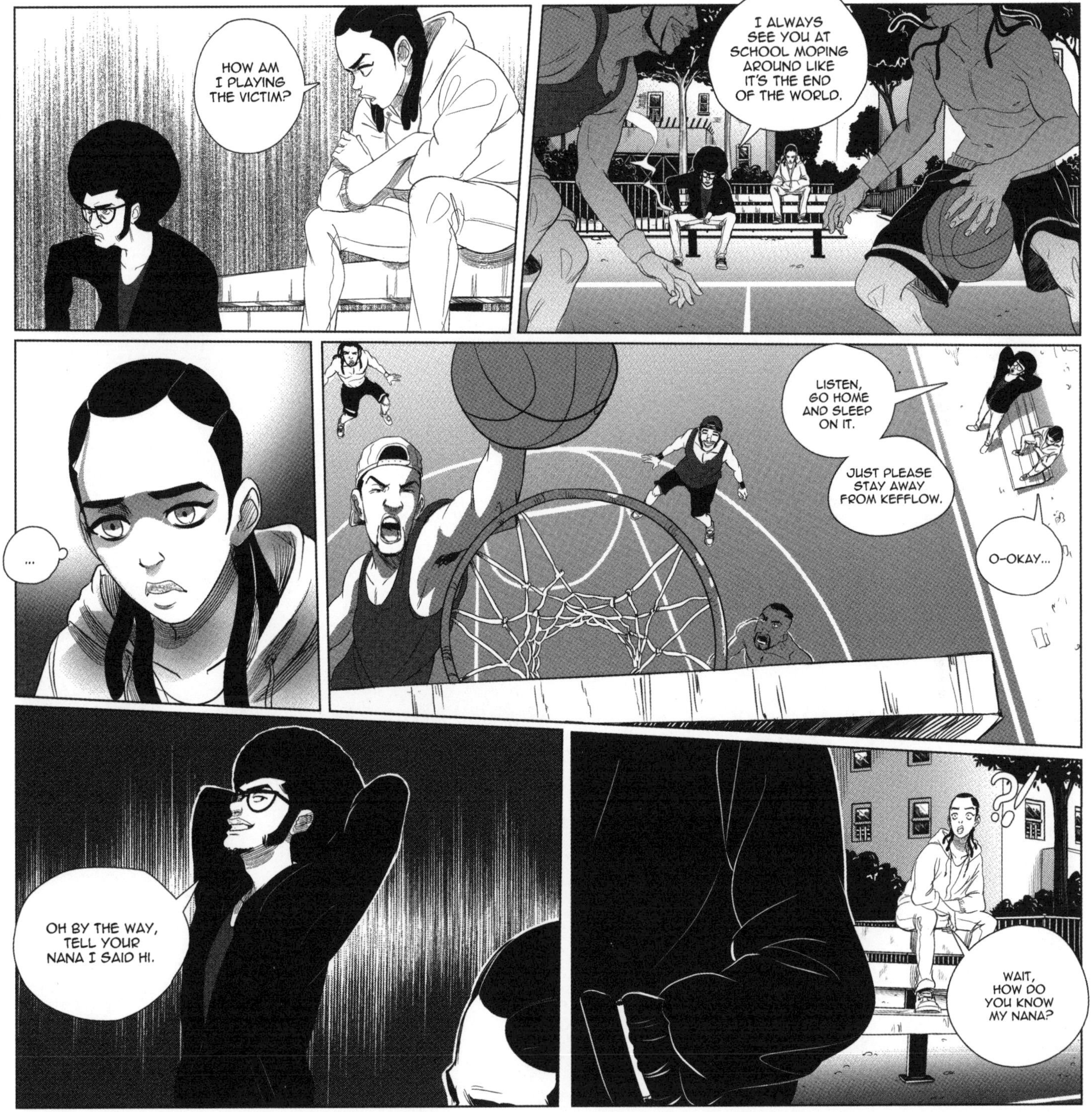
HOW AM I PLAYING THE VICTIM?
I ALWAYS SEE YOU AT SCHOOL MOPING AROUND LIKE IT'S THE END OF THE WORLD.
...
LISTEN, GO HOME AND SLEEP ON IT.
JUST PLEASE STAY AWAY FROM KEFFLOW.
O-OKAY...
OH BY THE WAY, TELL YOUR NANA I SAID HI.
WAIT, HOW DO YOU KNOW MY NANA?

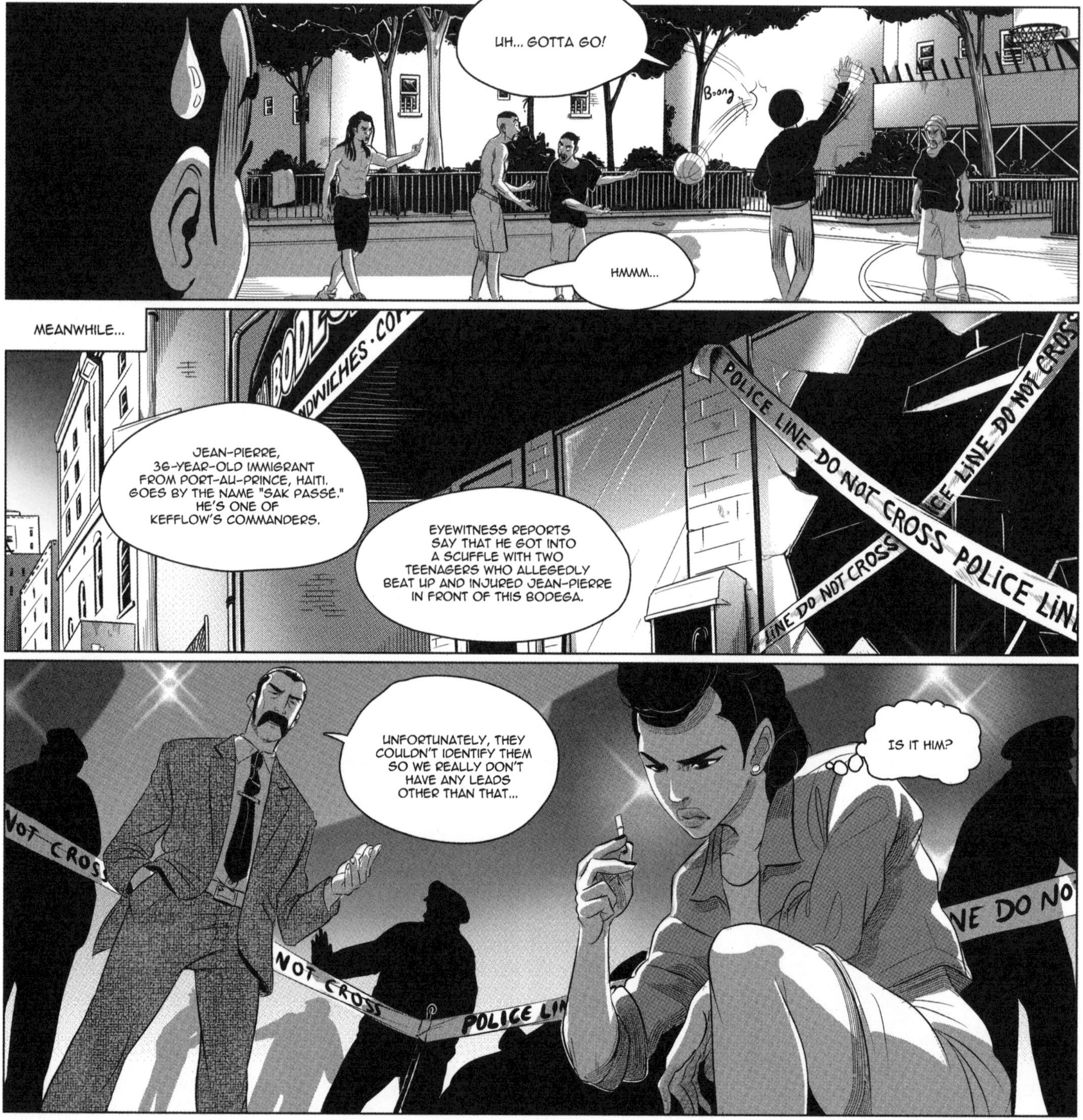
UH... GOTTA GO!
Boong
HMMM...
MEANWHILE...
JEAN-PIERRE, 36-YEAR-OLD IMMIGRANT FROM PORT-AU-PRINCE, HAITI. GOES BY THE NAME "SAK PASSÉ." HE'S ONE OF KEFFLOW'S COMMANDERS.
EYEWITNESS REPORTS SAY THAT HE GOT INTO A SCUFFLE WITH TWO TEENAGERS WHO ALLEGEDLY BEAT UP AND INJURED JEAN-PIERRE IN FRONT OF THIS BODEGA.
UNFORTUNATELY, THEY COULDN'T IDENTIFY THEM SO WE REALLY DON'T HAVE ANY LEADS OTHER THAN THAT...
IS IT HIM?

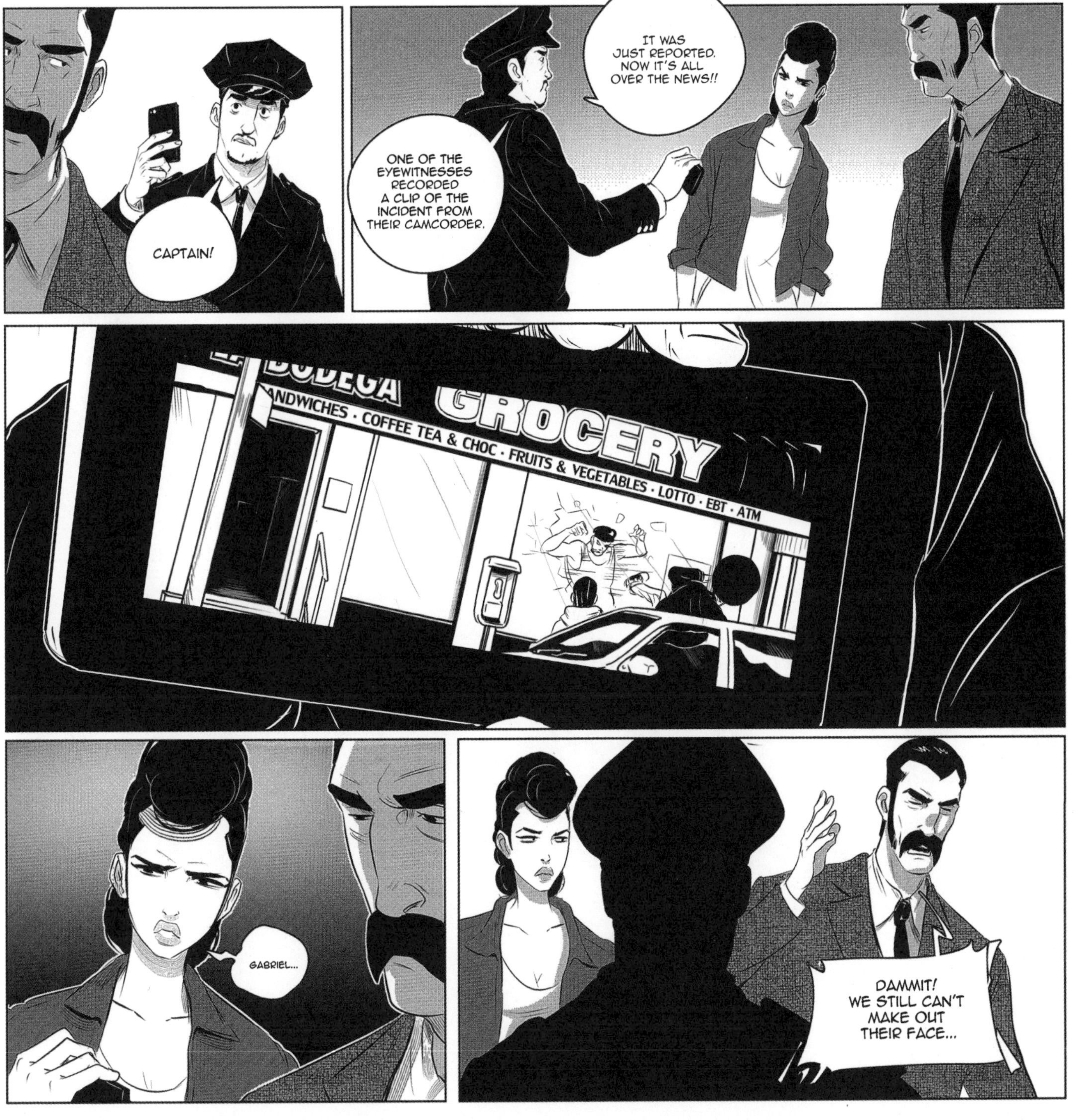
CAPTAIN!
IT WAS JUST REPORTED. NOW IT'S ALL OVER THE NEWS!!
ONE OF THE EYEWITNESSES RECORDED A CLIP OF THE INCIDENT FROM THEIR CAMCORDER.
BODEGA
GROCERY
ANDWICHES · COFFEE TEA & CHOC · FRUITS & VEGETABLES · LOTTO · EBT · ATM
GABRIEL...
DAMMIT! WE STILL CAN'T MAKE OUT THEIR FACE...

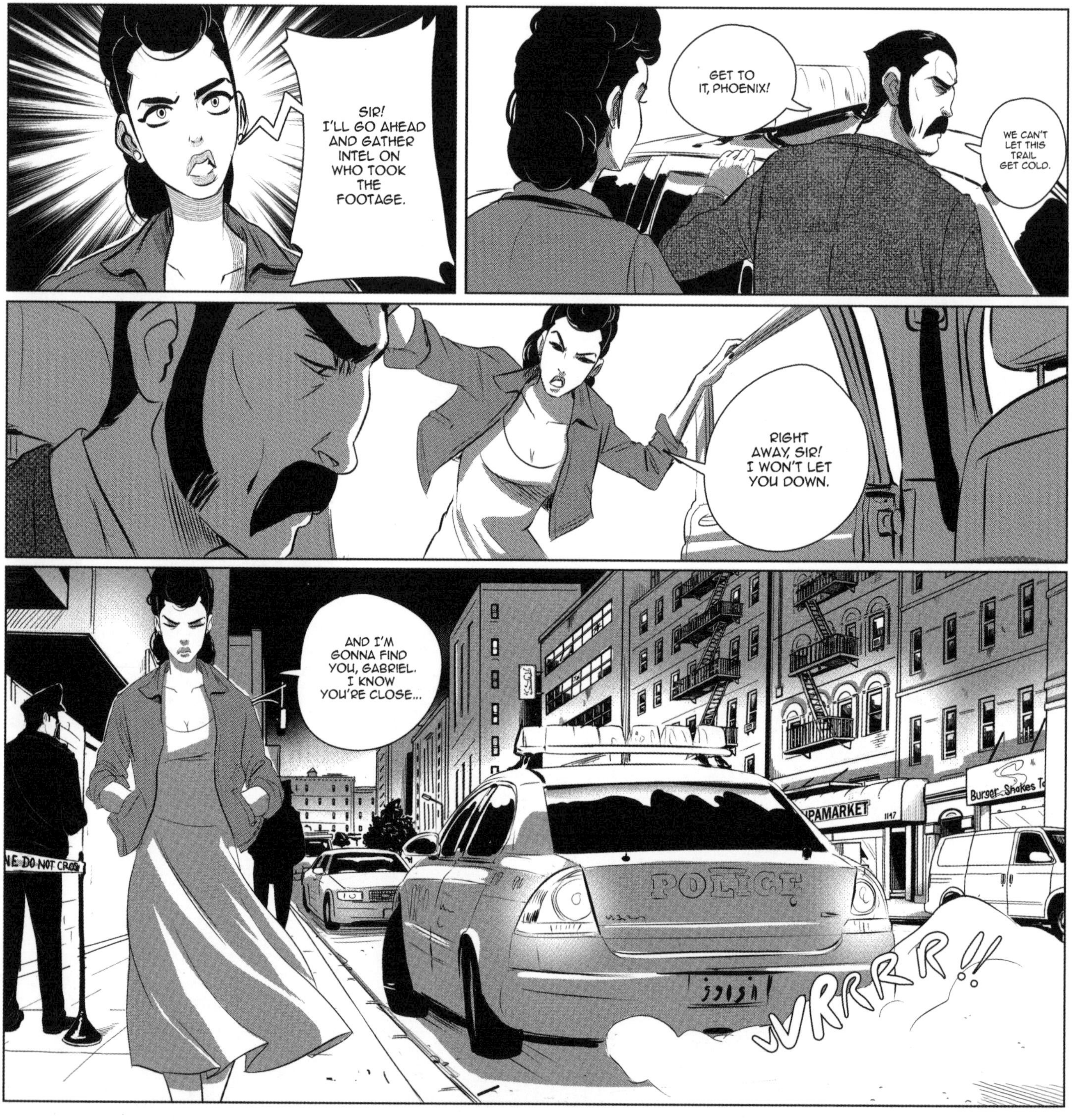
SIR! I'LL GO AHEAD AND GATHER INTEL ON WHO TOOK THE FOOTAGE.
GET TO IT, PHOENIX!
WE CAN'T LET THIS TRAIL GET COLD.
RIGHT AWAY, SIR! I WON'T LET YOU DOWN.
AND I'M GONNA FIND YOU, GABRIEL. I KNOW YOU'RE CLOSE...
NE DO NOT CROS
PAMARKET
Burger Shakes T
POLICE
VVRRRR!!

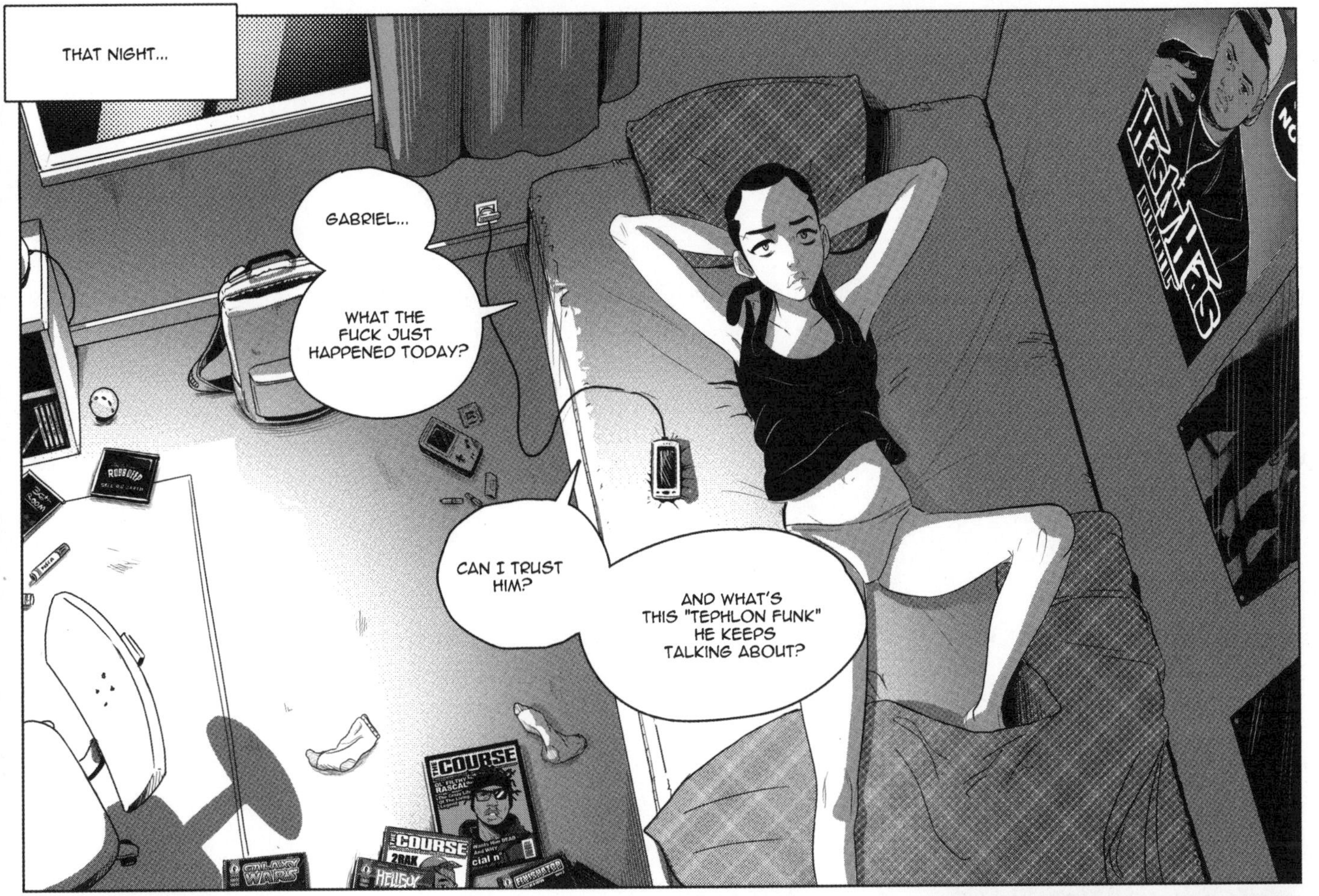
THAT NIGHT...
GABRIEL...
WHAT THE FUCK JUST HAPPENED TODAY?
CAN I TRUST HIM?
AND WHAT'S THIS "TEPHLON FUNK" HE KEEPS TALKING ABOUT?
THE COURSE
GALAXY WARS
THE COURSE
2BAK

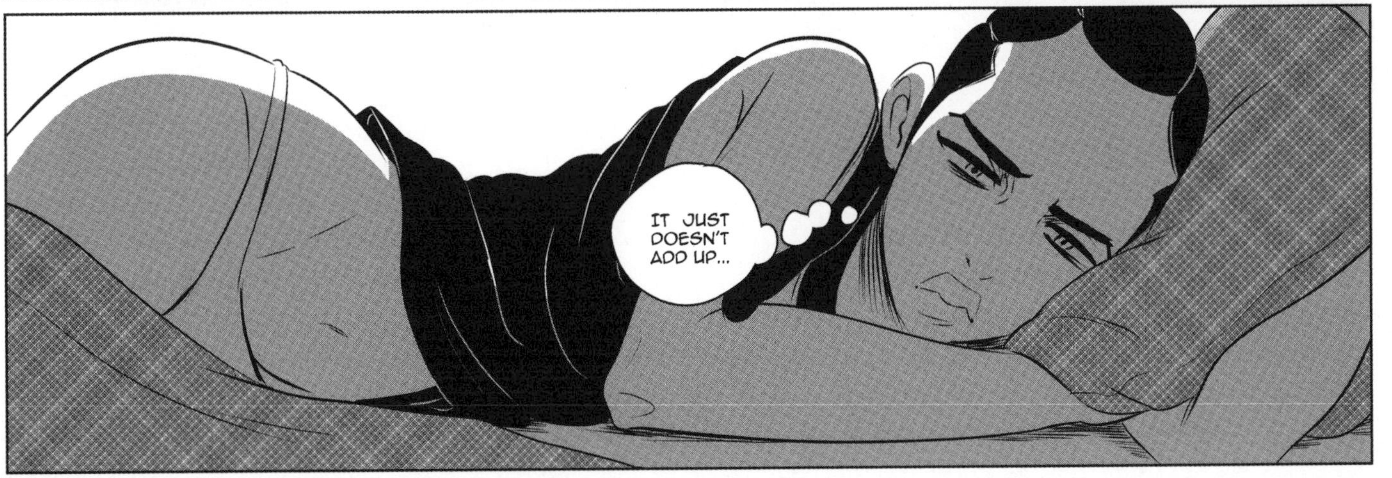
IT JUST DOESN'T ADD UP...

TEPHLON FUNK! TEPHLON FUNK!TEPHLON FUN

TEPHLON FUNK! TEPHLON FUNK!TEPHLON FUNK!

TEPHLON FUNK! TEPHLON FUNK! TEPHLON FUN

TEPHLON FUNK!TEPHLON FUNK! TEPHLON FUNK

TEPHLON FUNKTEPHLON FUNK! TEPHLON FUN

TEPHLON FUNK!TEPHLON FUNK! TEPHLON FUNK!

TEPHLON FUNK!TEPHLON FUNK! TEPHLON FUN

TEPHLON FUNK!TEPHLON FUNK! TEPHLON FUNK! TEPHLON FU

EPHLON FUNK!TEPHLON FUNK! TEPHLON FUNK

TEPHLON FUNKTEPHLON FUNK! TEPHLON FUNK

TEPHLON FUNKTEPHLON FUNKTEPHLON FUNK

TEPHLON FUNK TEPHLON FUNK TEPHLON FUN

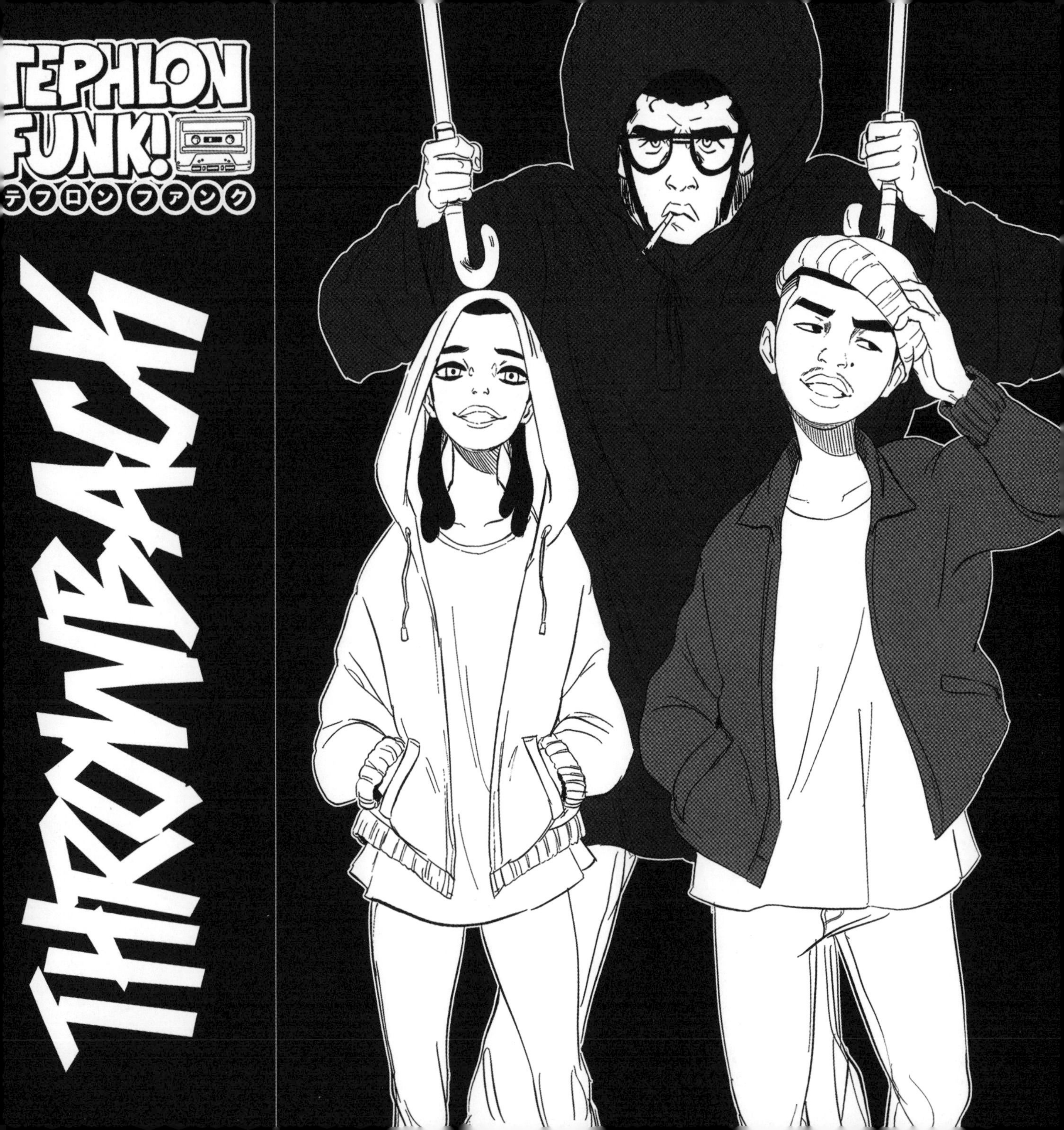
TEPHLON FUNK!
テフロン ファンク
THROWBACK

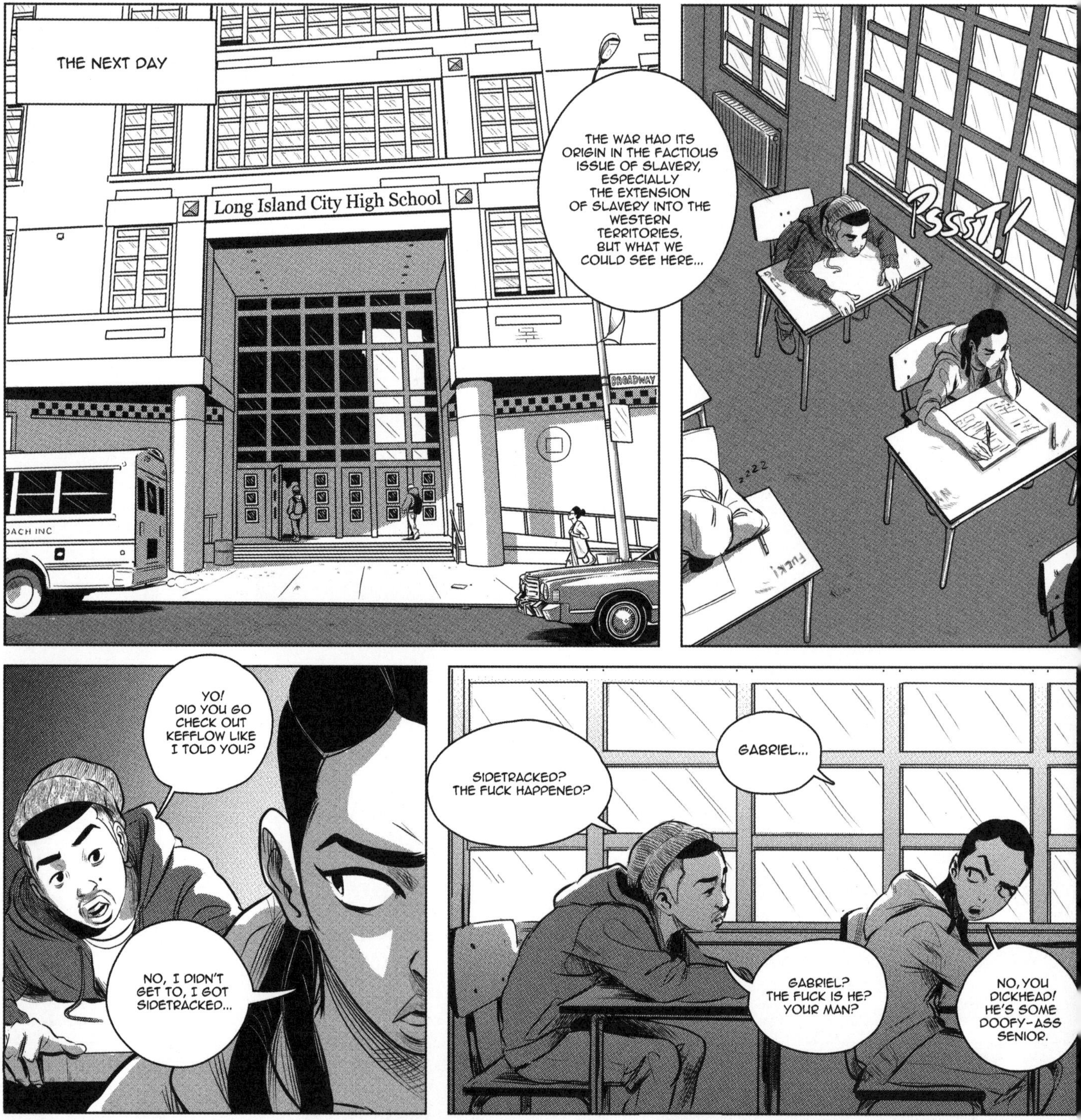
THE NEXT DAY
Long Island City High School
BROADWAY
THE WAR HAD ITS ORIGIN IN THE FACTIOUS ISSUE OF SLAVERY, ESPECIALLY THE EXTENSION OF SLAVERY INTO THE WESTERN TERRITORIES. BUT WHAT WE COULD SEE HERE...
PSSST!
YO! DID YOU GO CHECK OUT KEFFLOW LIKE I TOLD YOU?
NO, I DIDN'T GET TO, I GOT SIDETRACKED...
SIDETRACKED? THE FUCK HAPPENED?
GABRIEL...
GABRIEL? THE FUCK IS HE? YOUR MAN?
NO, YOU DICKHEAD! HE'S SOME DOOFY-ASS SENIOR.

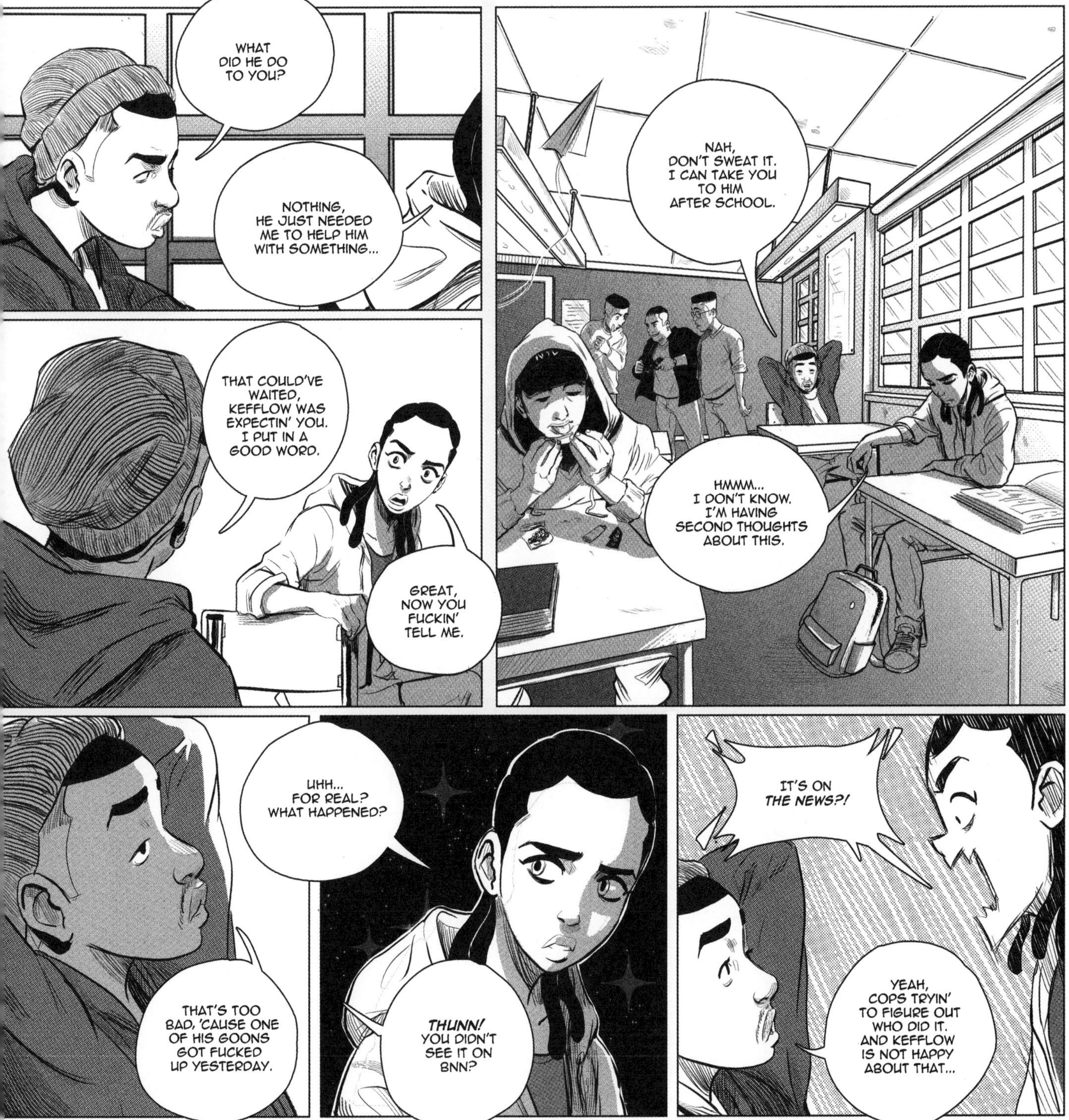
WHAT DID HE DO TO YOU?
NOTHING, HE JUST NEEDED ME TO HELP HIM WITH SOMETHING...
THAT COULD'VE WAITED, KEFFLOW WAS EXPECTIN' YOU. I PUT IN A GOOD WORD.
GREAT, NOW YOU FUCKIN' TELL ME.
NAH, DON'T SWEAT IT. I CAN TAKE YOU TO HIM AFTER SCHOOL.
HMMM... I DON'T KNOW. I'M HAVING SECOND THOUGHTS ABOUT THIS.
THAT'S TOO BAD, 'CAUSE ONE OF HIS GOONS GOT FUCKED UP YESTERDAY.
UHH... FOR REAL? WHAT HAPPENED?
THUNN! YOU DIDN'T SEE IT ON BNN?
IT'S ON *THE NEWS?!*
YEAH, COPS TRYIN' TO FIGURE OUT WHO DID IT. AND KEFFLOW IS NOT HAPPY ABOUT THAT...

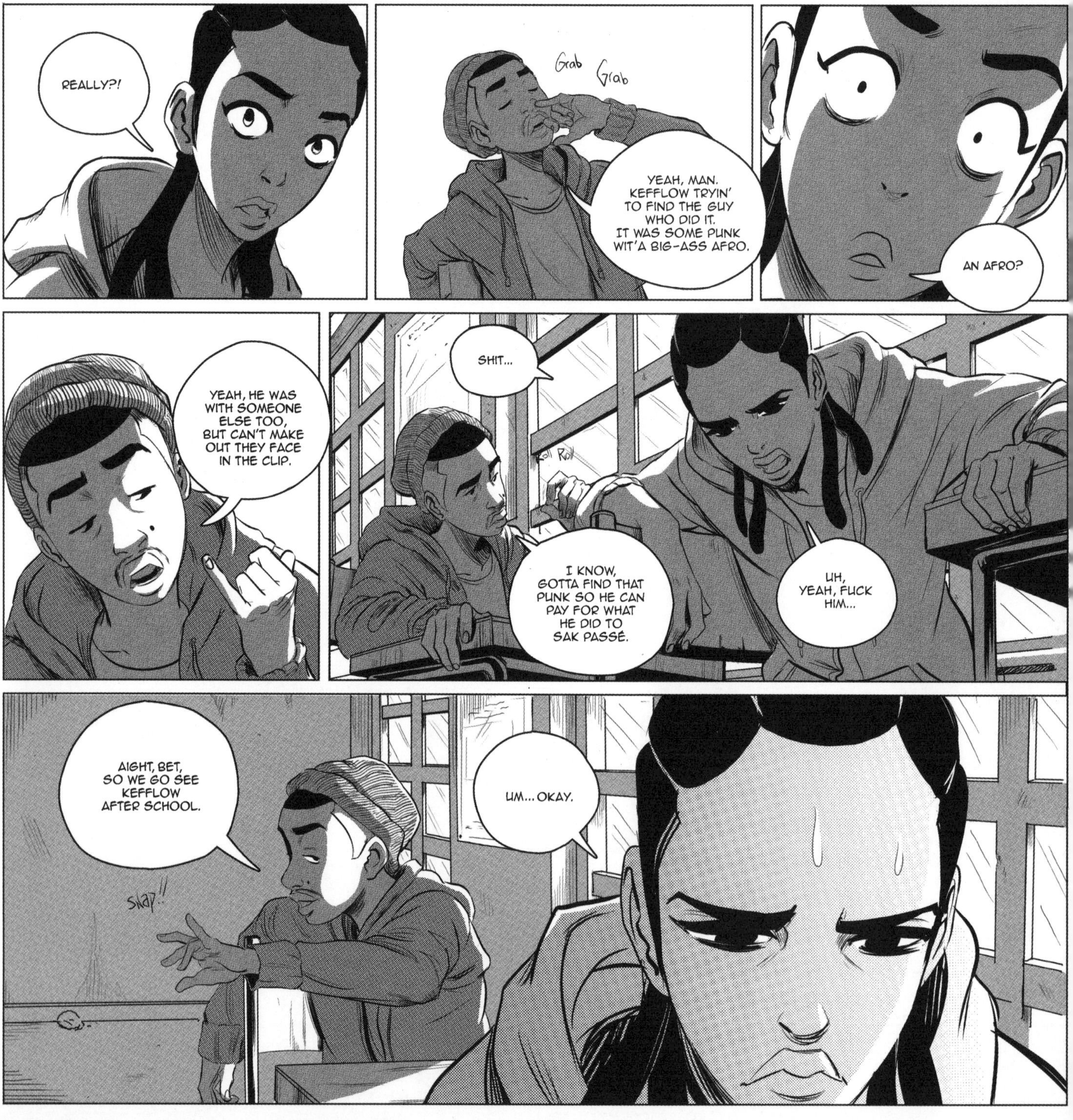
REALLY?!
Grab Grab
YEAH, MAN. KEFFLOW TRYIN' TO FIND THE GUY WHO DID IT. IT WAS SOME PUNK WIT'A BIG-ASS AFRO.
AN AFRO?
YEAH, HE WAS WITH SOMEONE ELSE TOO, BUT CAN'T MAKE OUT THEY FACE IN THE CLIP.
SHIT...
I KNOW, GOTTA FIND THAT PUNK SO HE CAN PAY FOR WHAT HE DID TO SAK PASSÉ.
UH, YEAH, FUCK HIM...
AIGHT, BET, SO WE GO SEE KEFFLOW AFTER SCHOOL.
UM... OKAY.
SNAP!!

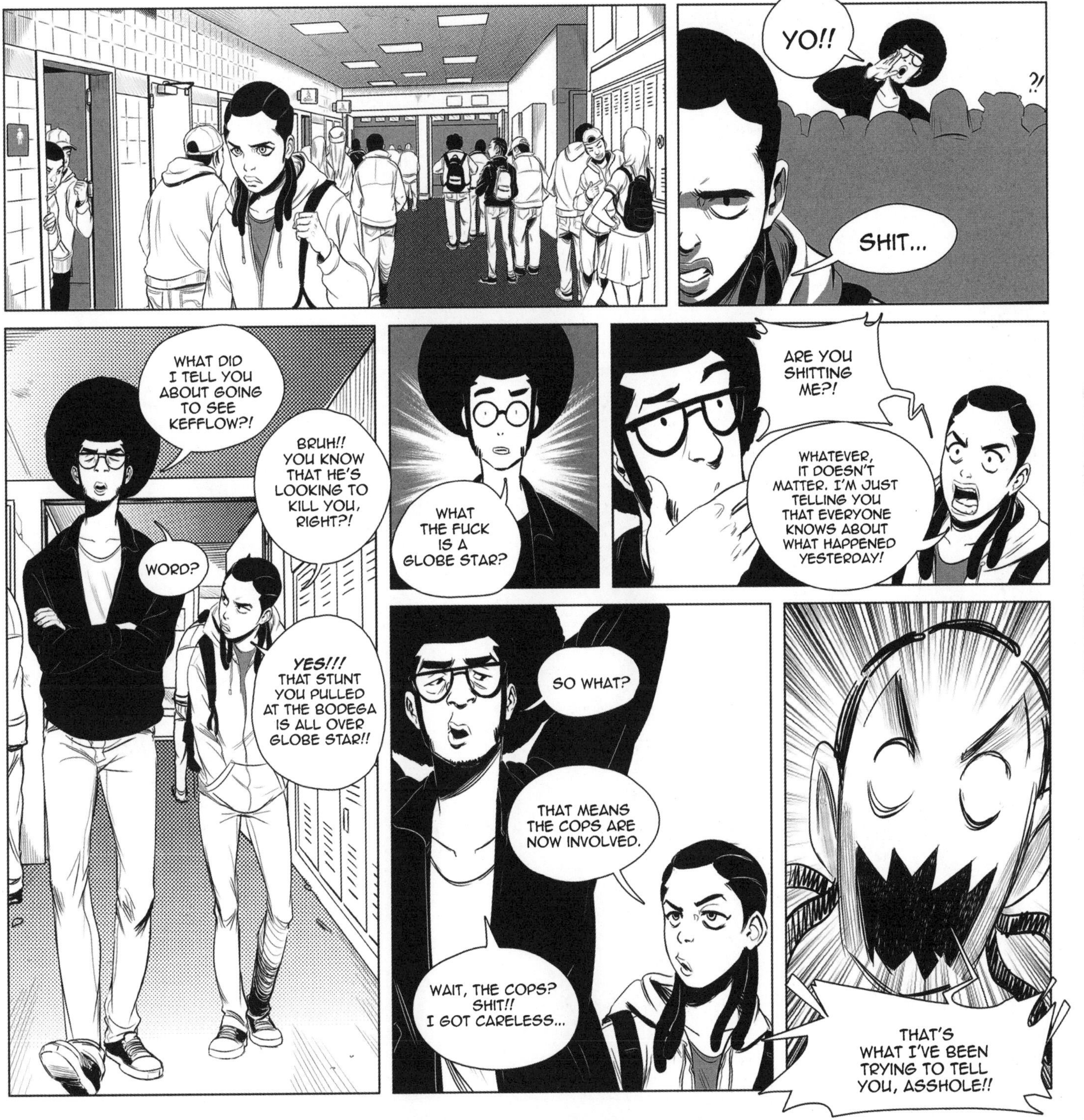
YO!!
?!
SHIT...
WHAT DID I TELL YOU ABOUT GOING TO SEE KEFFLOW?!
BRUH!! YOU KNOW THAT HE'S LOOKING TO KILL YOU, RIGHT?!
WORD?
YES!!! THAT STUNT YOU PULLED AT THE BODEGA IS ALL OVER GLOBE STAR!!
WHAT THE FUCK IS A GLOBE STAR?
ARE YOU SHITTING ME?!
WHATEVER, IT DOESN'T MATTER. I'M JUST TELLING YOU THAT EVERYONE KNOWS ABOUT WHAT HAPPENED YESTERDAY!
SO WHAT?
THAT MEANS THE COPS ARE NOW INVOLVED.
WAIT, THE COPS? SHIT!! I GOT CARELESS...
THAT'S WHAT I'VE BEEN TRYING TO TELL YOU, ASSHOLE!!

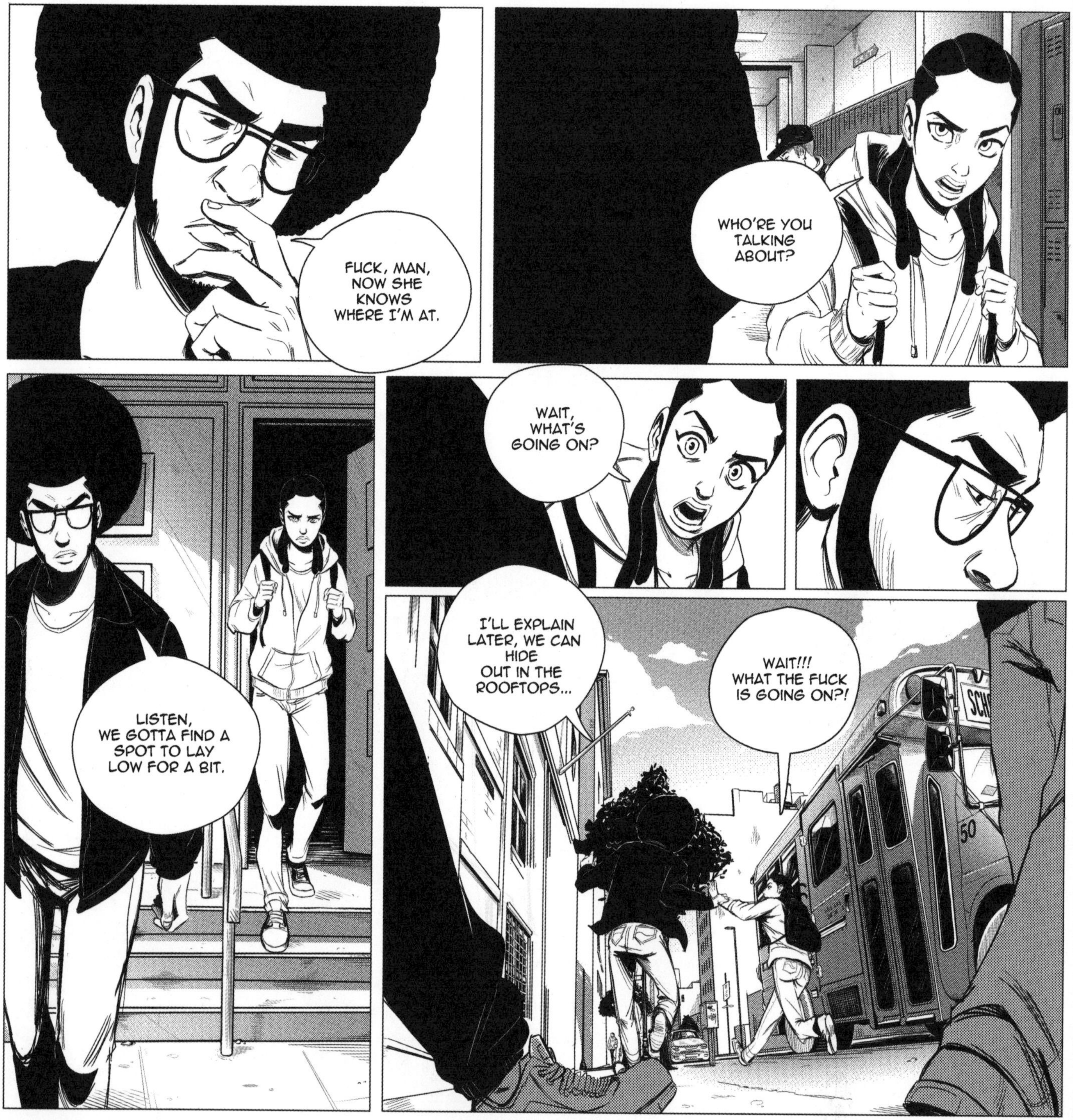
FUCK, MAN, NOW SHE KNOWS WHERE I'M AT.
WHO'RE YOU TALKING ABOUT?
LISTEN, WE GOTTA FIND A SPOT TO LAY LOW FOR A BIT.
WAIT, WHAT'S GOING ON?
I'LL EXPLAIN LATER, WE CAN HIDE OUT IN THE ROOFTOPS...
WAIT!!! WHAT THE FUCK IS GOING ON?!

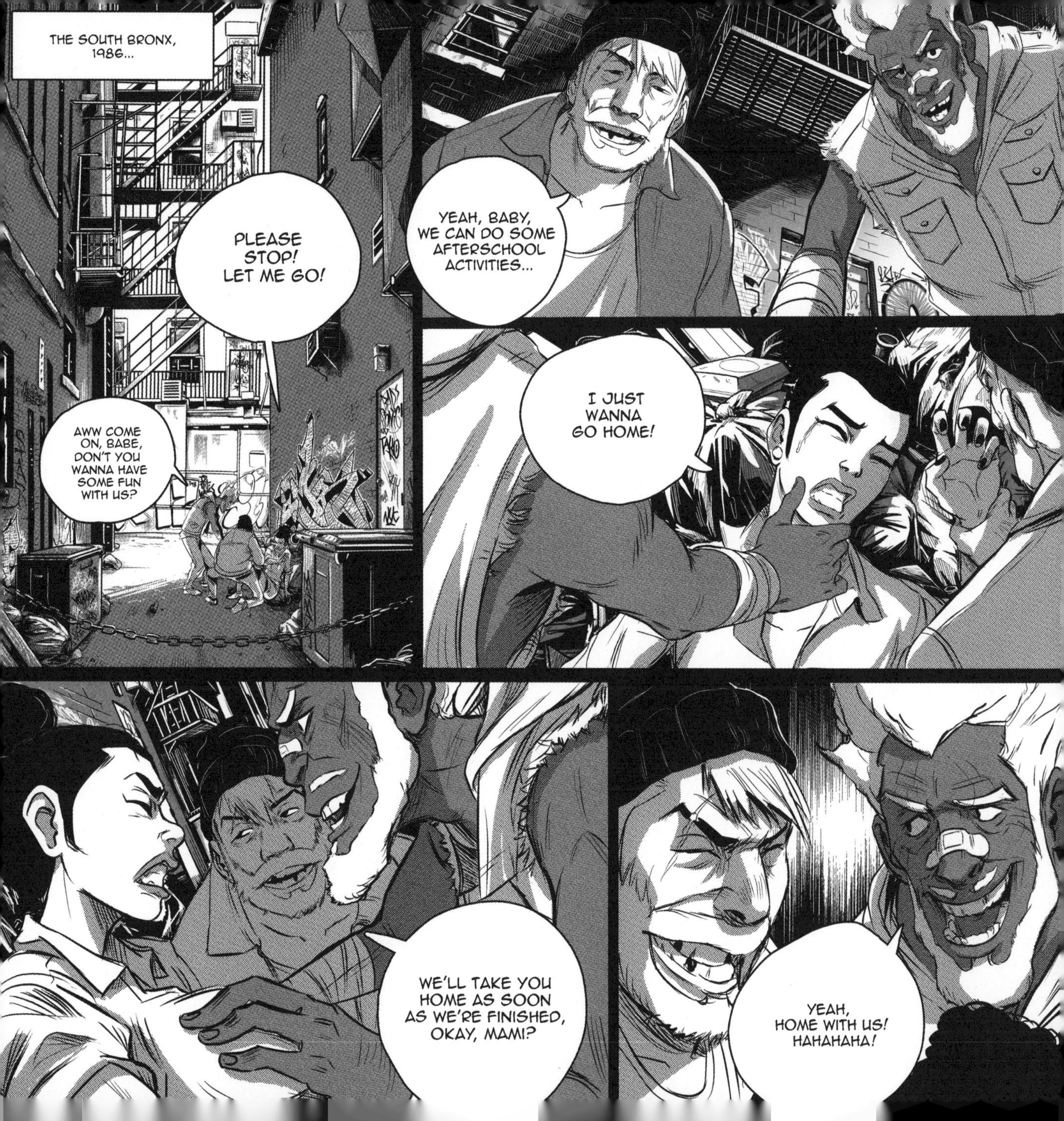
THE SOUTH BRONX, 1986...
PLEASE STOP! LET ME GO!
AWW COME ON, BABE, DON'T YOU WANNA HAVE SOME FUN WITH US?
YEAH, BABY, WE CAN DO SOME AFTERSCHOOL ACTIVITIES...
I JUST WANNA GO HOME!
WE'LL TAKE YOU HOME AS SOON AS WE'RE FINISHED, OKAY, MAMI?
YEAH, HOME WITH US! HAHAHAHA!

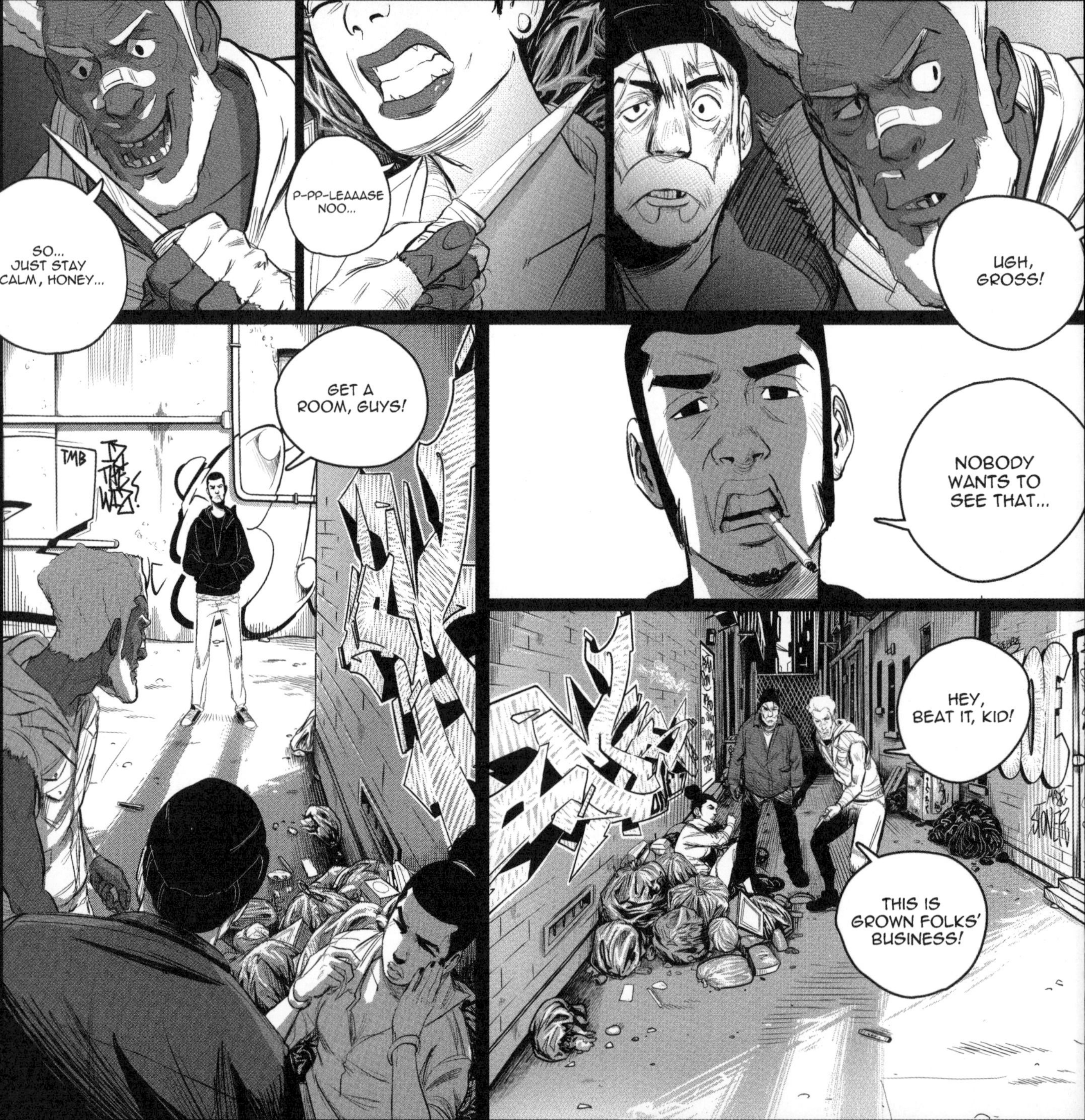
SO... JUST STAY CALM, HONEY...
P-PP-LEAAASE NOO...
UGH, GROSS!
GET A ROOM, GUYS!
NOBODY WANTS TO SEE THAT...
HEY, BEAT IT, KID!
THIS IS GROWN FOLKS' BUSINESS!

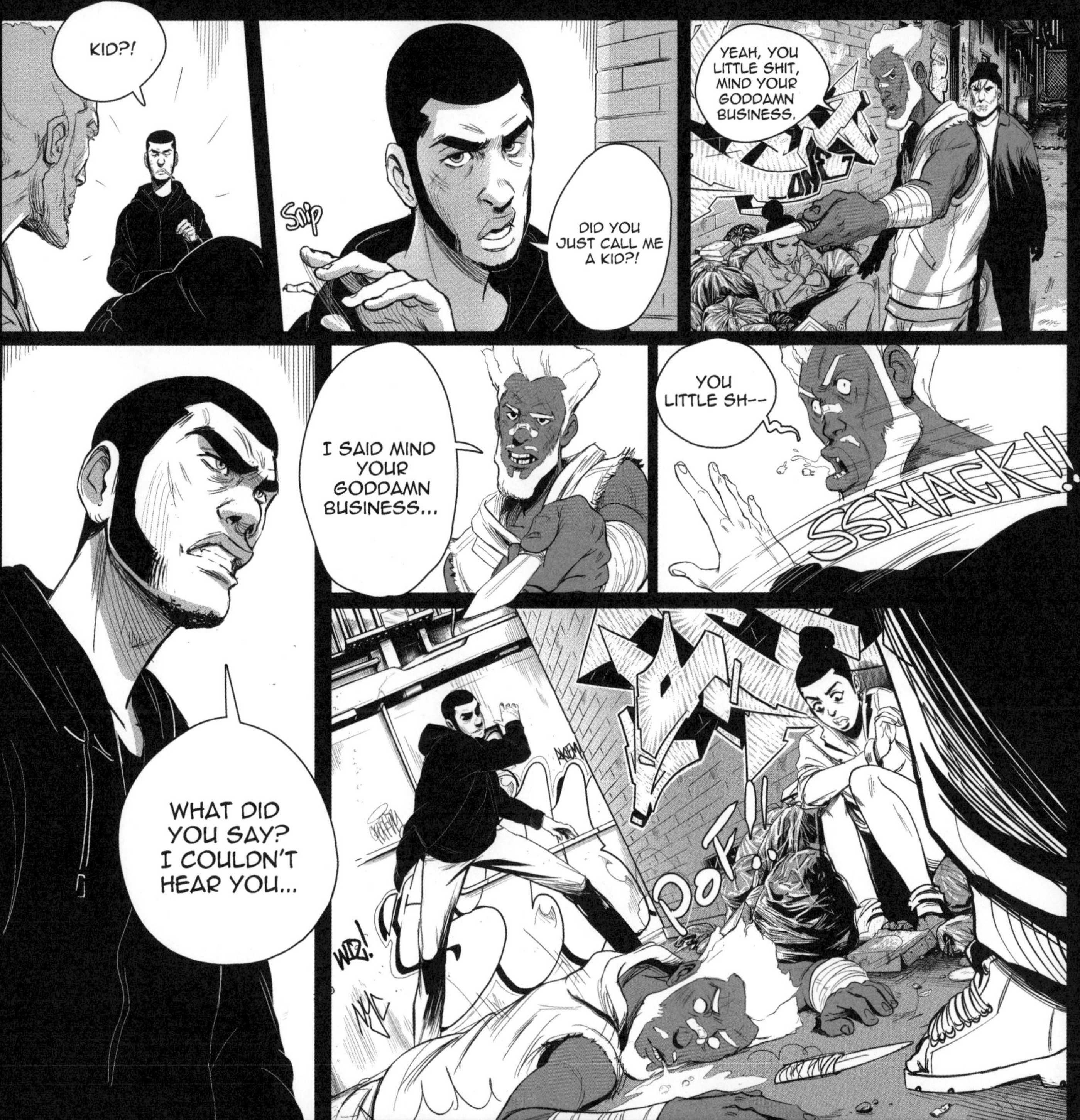
KID?!
Snip
DID YOU JUST CALL ME A KID?!
YEAH, YOU LITTLE SHIT, MIND YOUR GODDAMN BUSINESS.
I SAID MIND YOUR GODDAMN BUSINESS...
YOU LITTLE SH--
SSMACK!!
WHAT DID YOU SAY? I COULDN'T HEAR YOU...
POF!!

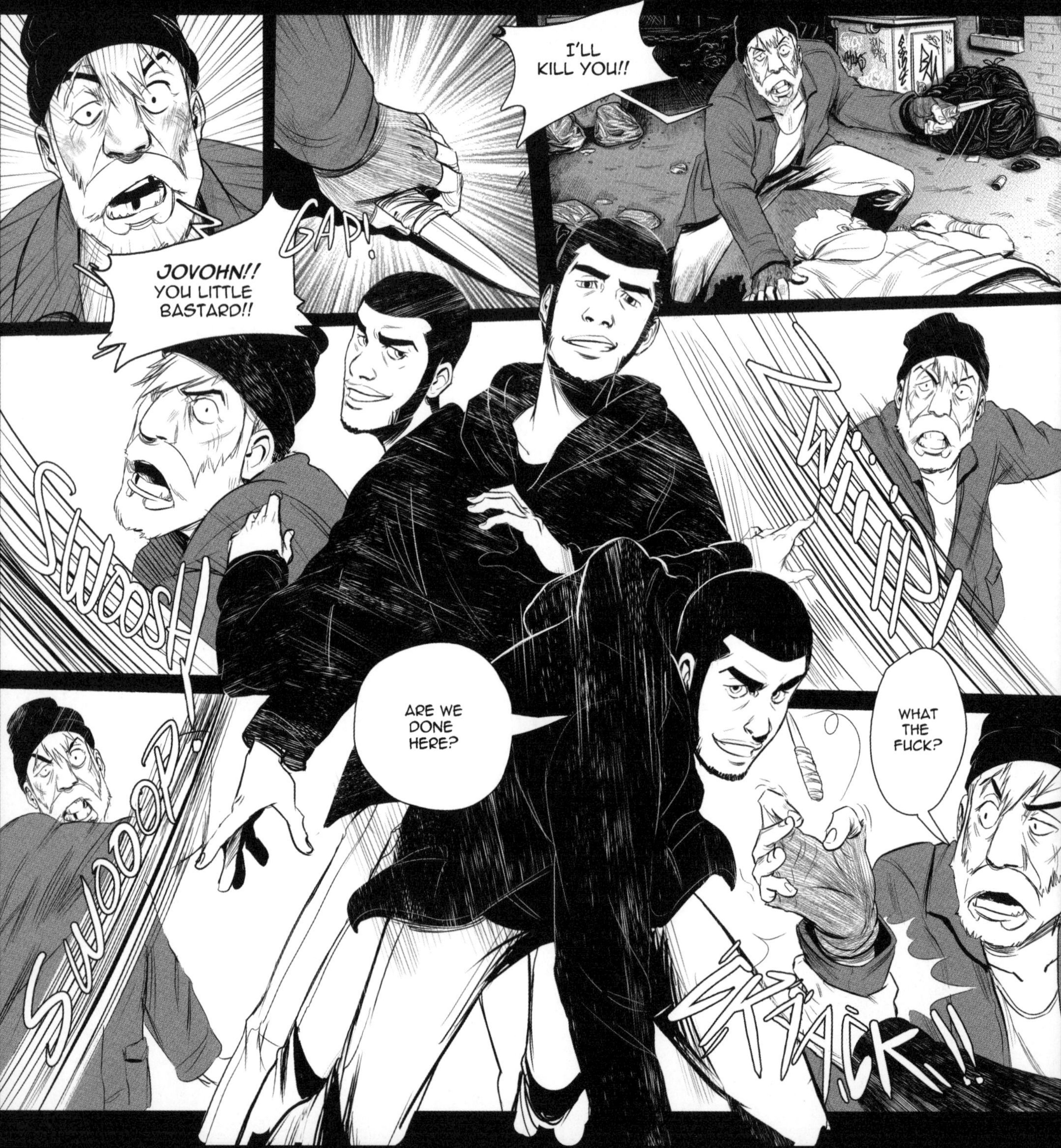

JOVOHN!! YOU LITTLE BASTARD!!
GAP!
I'LL KILL YOU!!
SWOOSH!
ZWIIIP!
WHAT THE FUCK?
SWOOOP!
ARE WE DONE HERE?
SKRACK!!

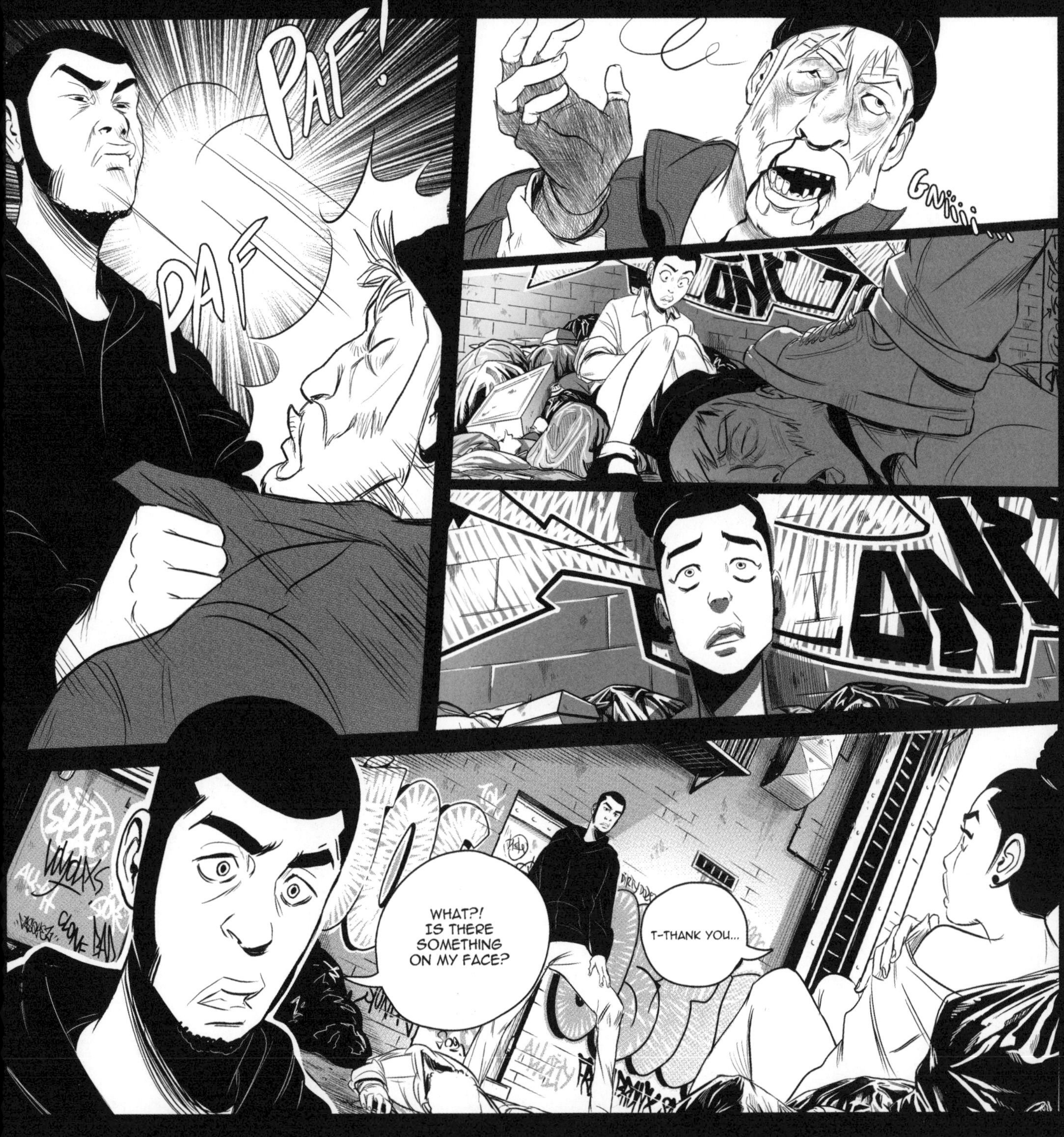
PAF!
PAF
GNiiii...
WHAT?! IS THERE SOMETHING ON MY FACE?
T-THANK YOU...

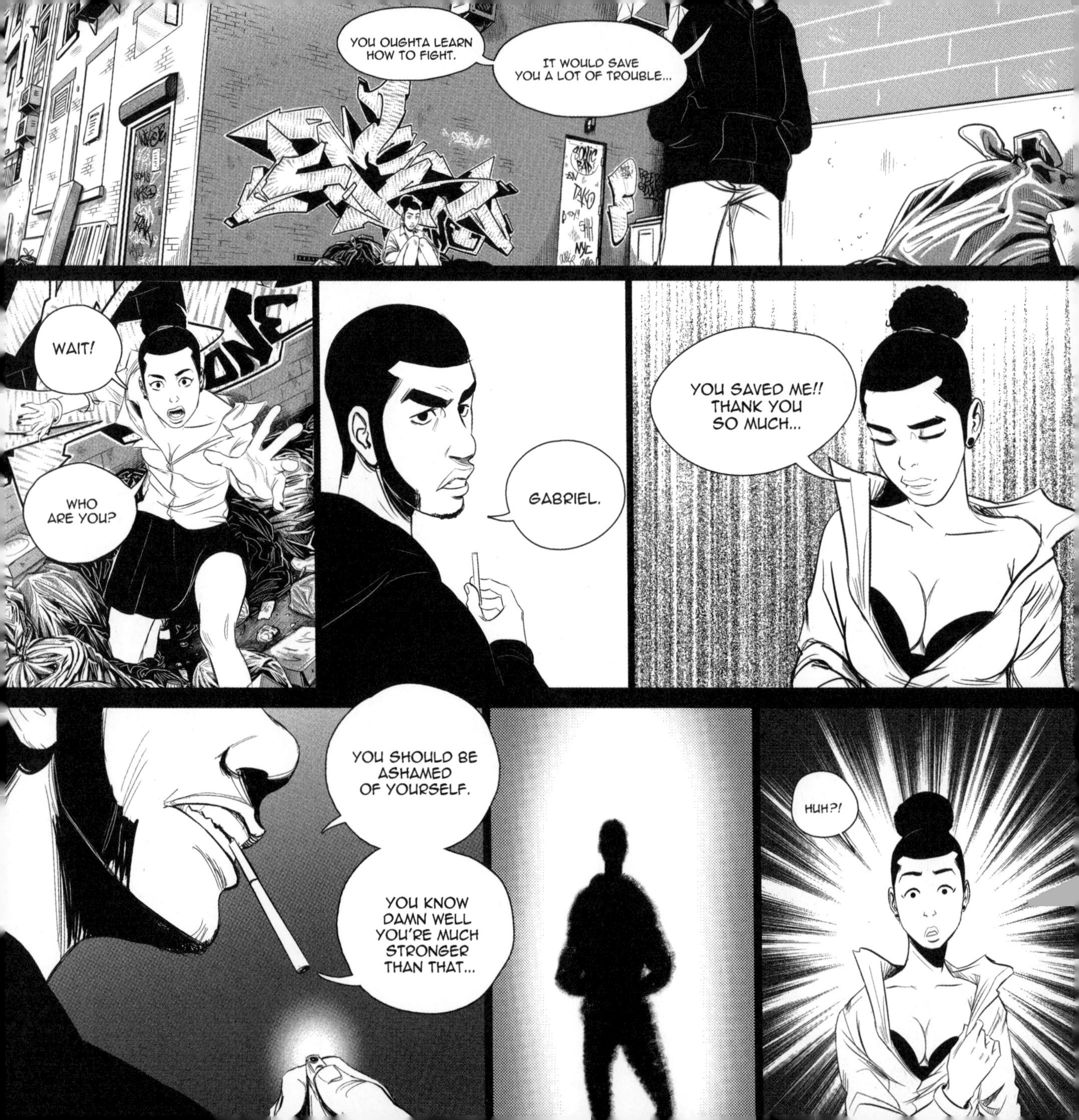
YOU OUGHTA LEARN HOW TO FIGHT.
IT WOULD SAVE YOU A LOT OF TROUBLE...
WAIT!
WHO ARE YOU?
GABRIEL.
YOU SAVED ME!! THANK YOU SO MUCH...
YOU SHOULD BE ASHAMED OF YOURSELF.
YOU KNOW DAMN WELL YOU'RE MUCH STRONGER THAN THAT...
HUH?!

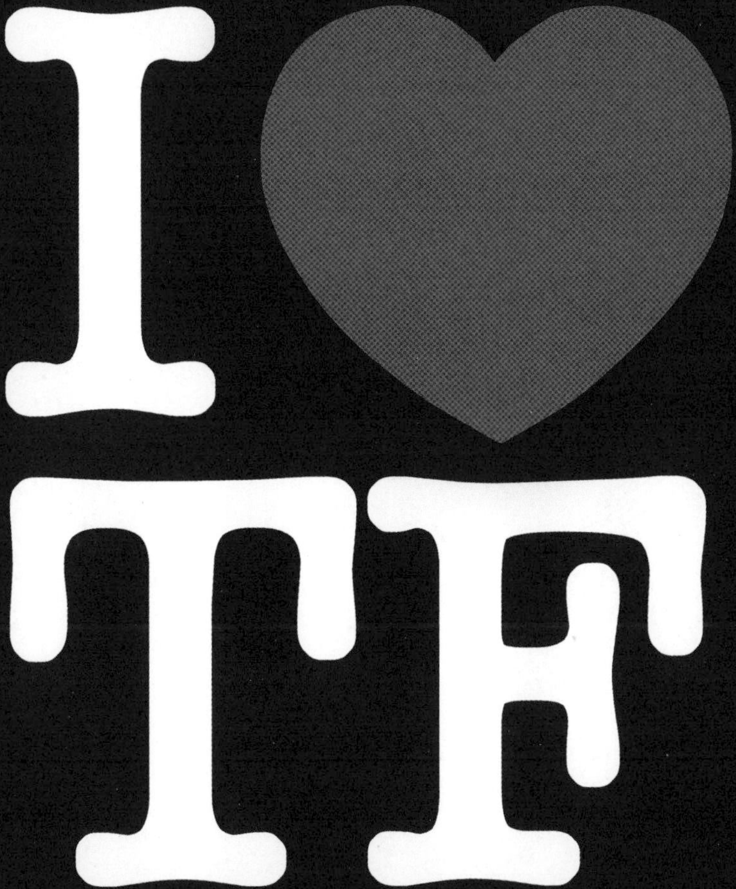
I ♥
TF

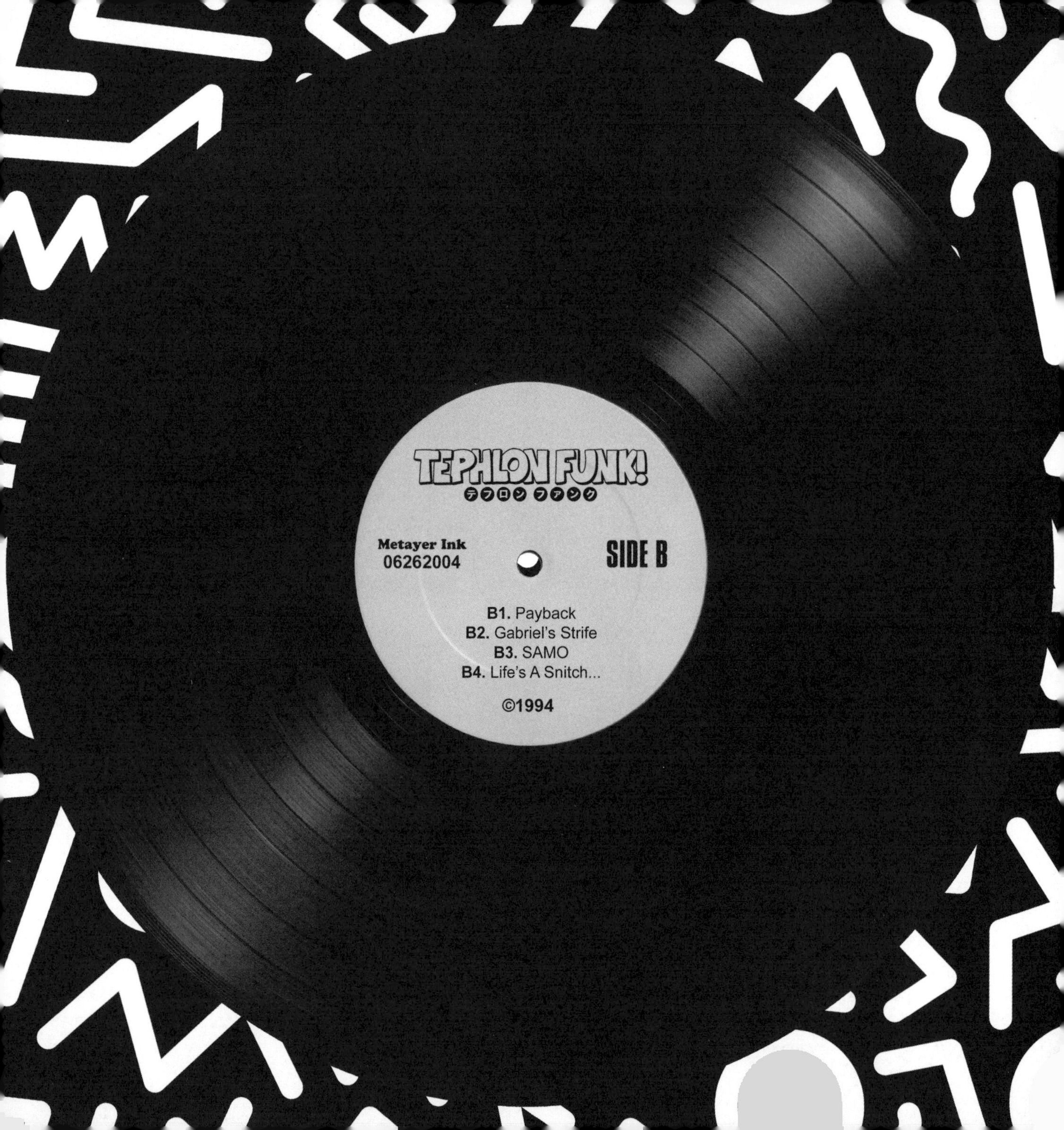
TEPHLON FUNK!
テフロン ファンク
Metayer Ink
06262004
SIDE B
B1. Payback
B2. Gabriel's Strife
B3. SAMO
B4. Life's A Snitch...
©1994

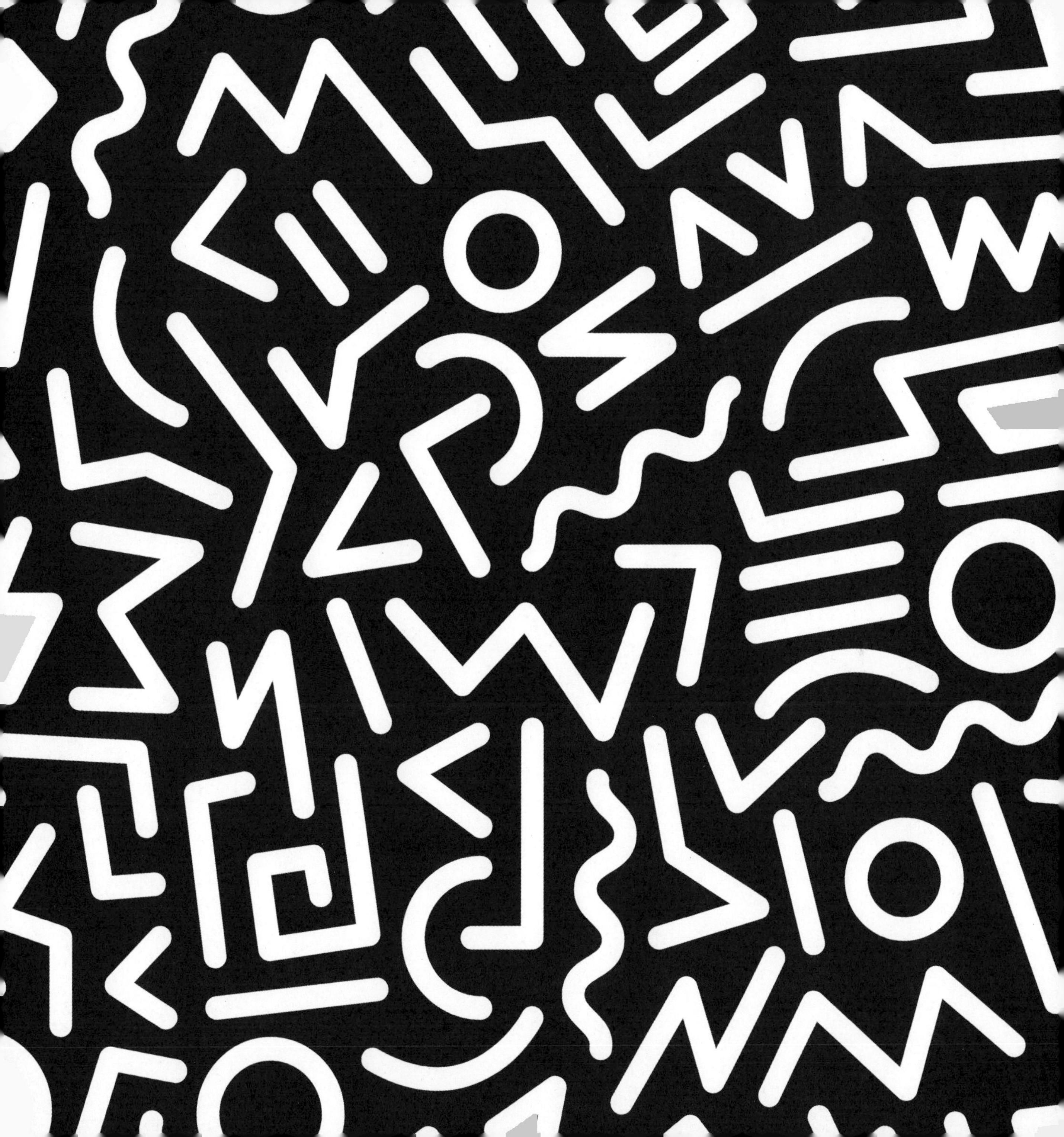

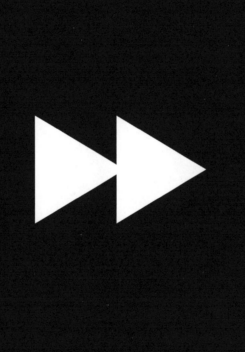

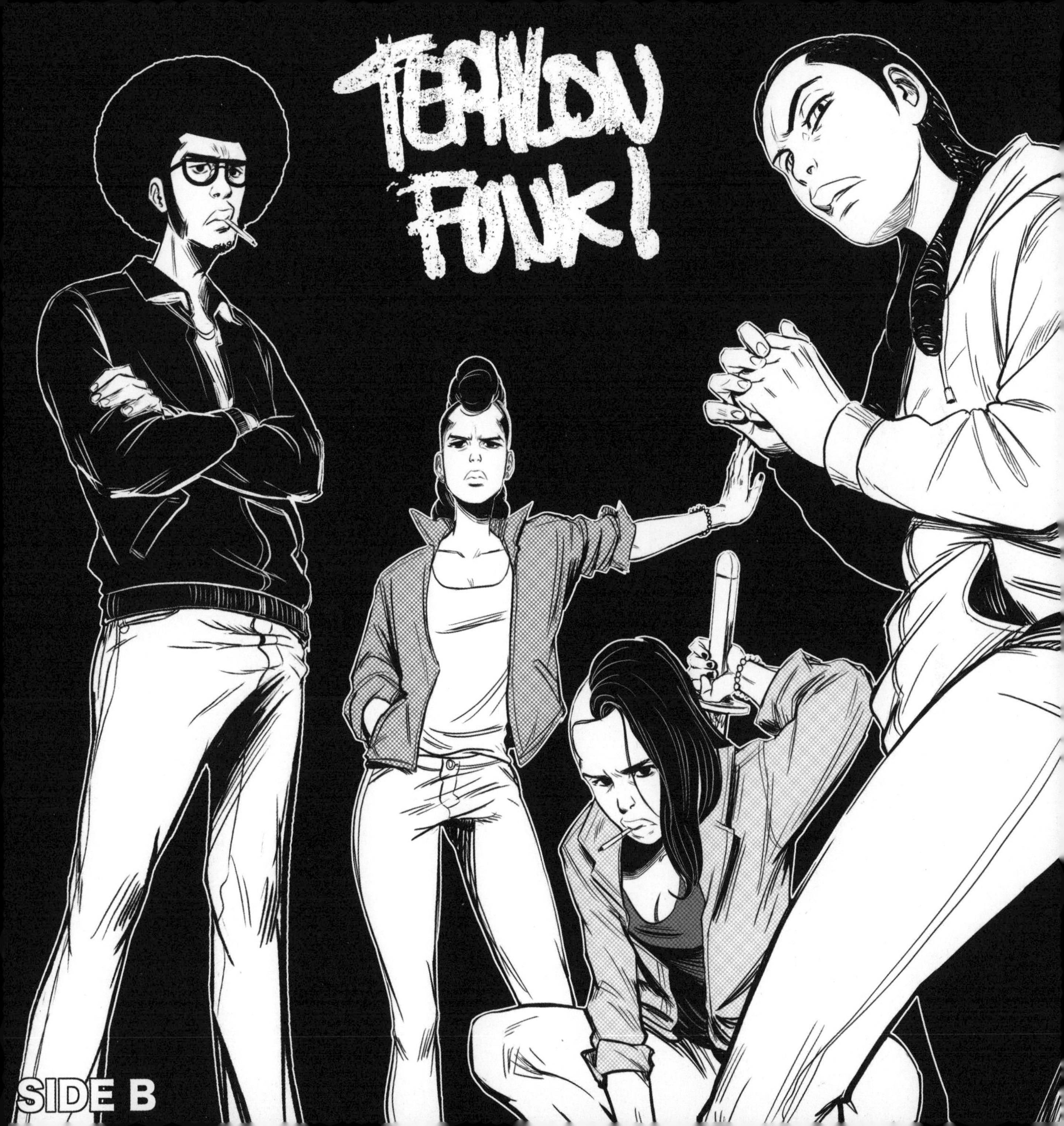
TEFLON FUNK!
SIDE B

1994

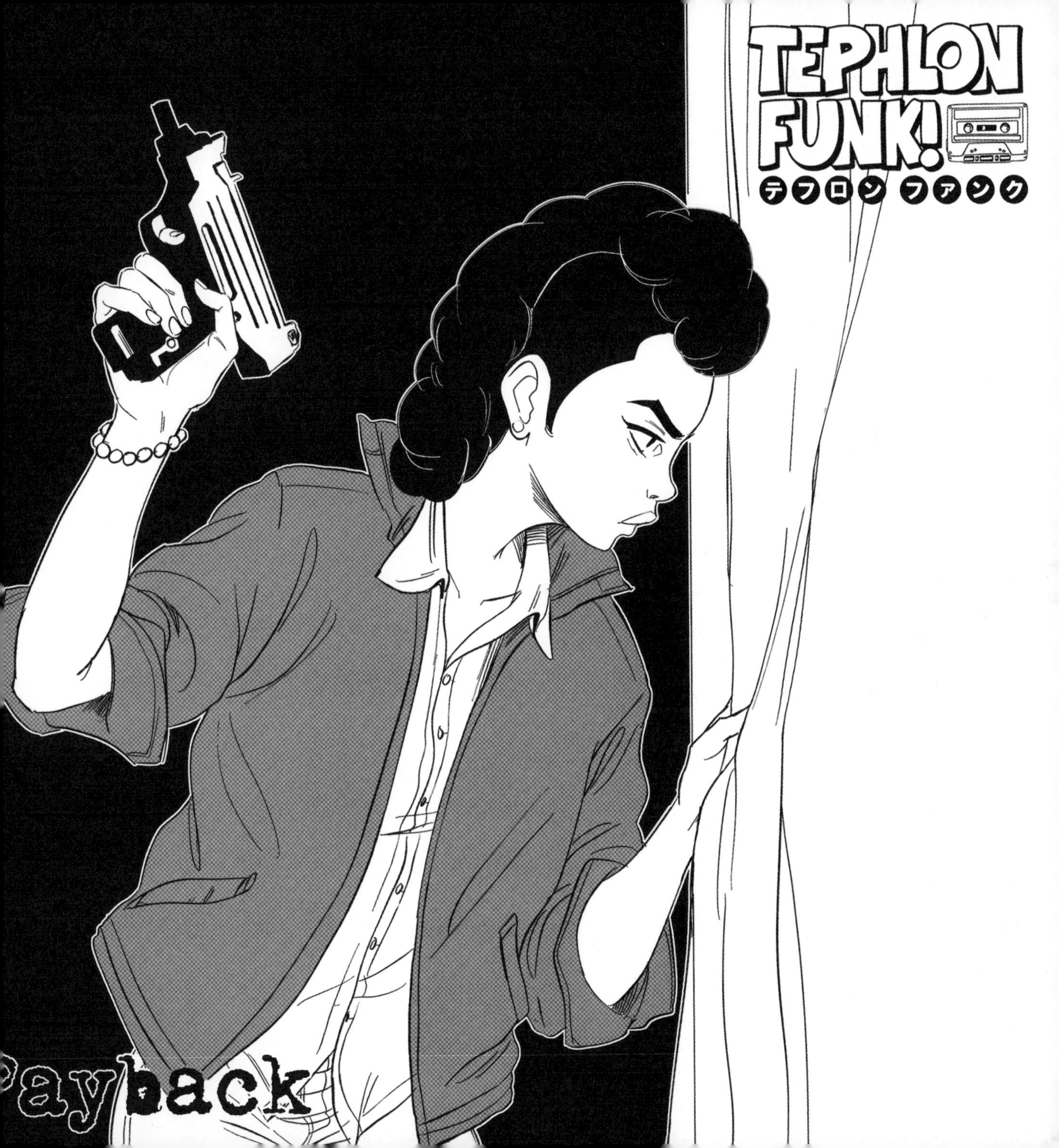
TEPHLON
FUNK!
テフロン ファンク
ayback

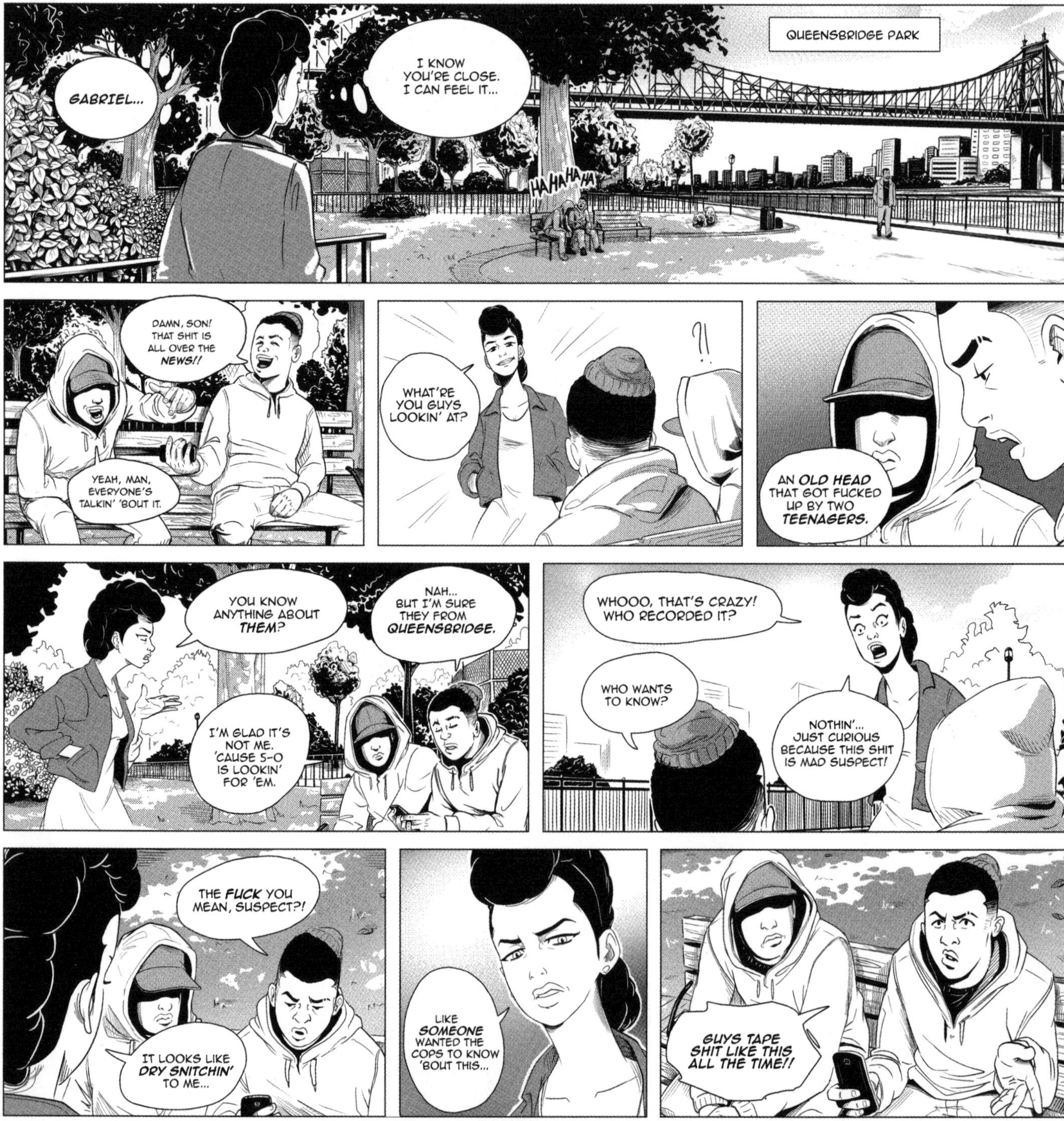
QUEENSBRIDGE PARK
GABRIEL...
I KNOW YOU'RE CLOSE. I CAN FEEL IT...
HAHAHAHA
DAMN, SON! THAT SHIT IS ALL OVER THE NEWS!!
YEAH, MAN, EVERYONE'S TALKIN' 'BOUT IT.
WHAT'RE YOU GUYS LOOKIN' AT?
?!
AN OLD HEAD THAT GOT FUCKED UP BY TWO TEENAGERS.
YOU KNOW ANYTHING ABOUT THEM?
NAH... BUT I'M SURE THEY FROM QUEENSBRIDGE.
I'M GLAD IT'S NOT ME. 'CAUSE 5-O IS LOOKIN' FOR 'EM.
WHOOO, THAT'S CRAZY! WHO RECORDED IT?
WHO WANTS TO KNOW?
NOTHIN'... JUST CURIOUS BECAUSE THIS SHIT IS MAD SUSPECT!
THE FUCK YOU MEAN, SUSPECT?!
IT LOOKS LIKE DRY SNITCHIN' TO ME...
LIKE SOMEONE WANTED THE COPS TO KNOW 'BOUT THIS...
GUYS TAPE SHIT LIKE THIS ALL THE TIME!!

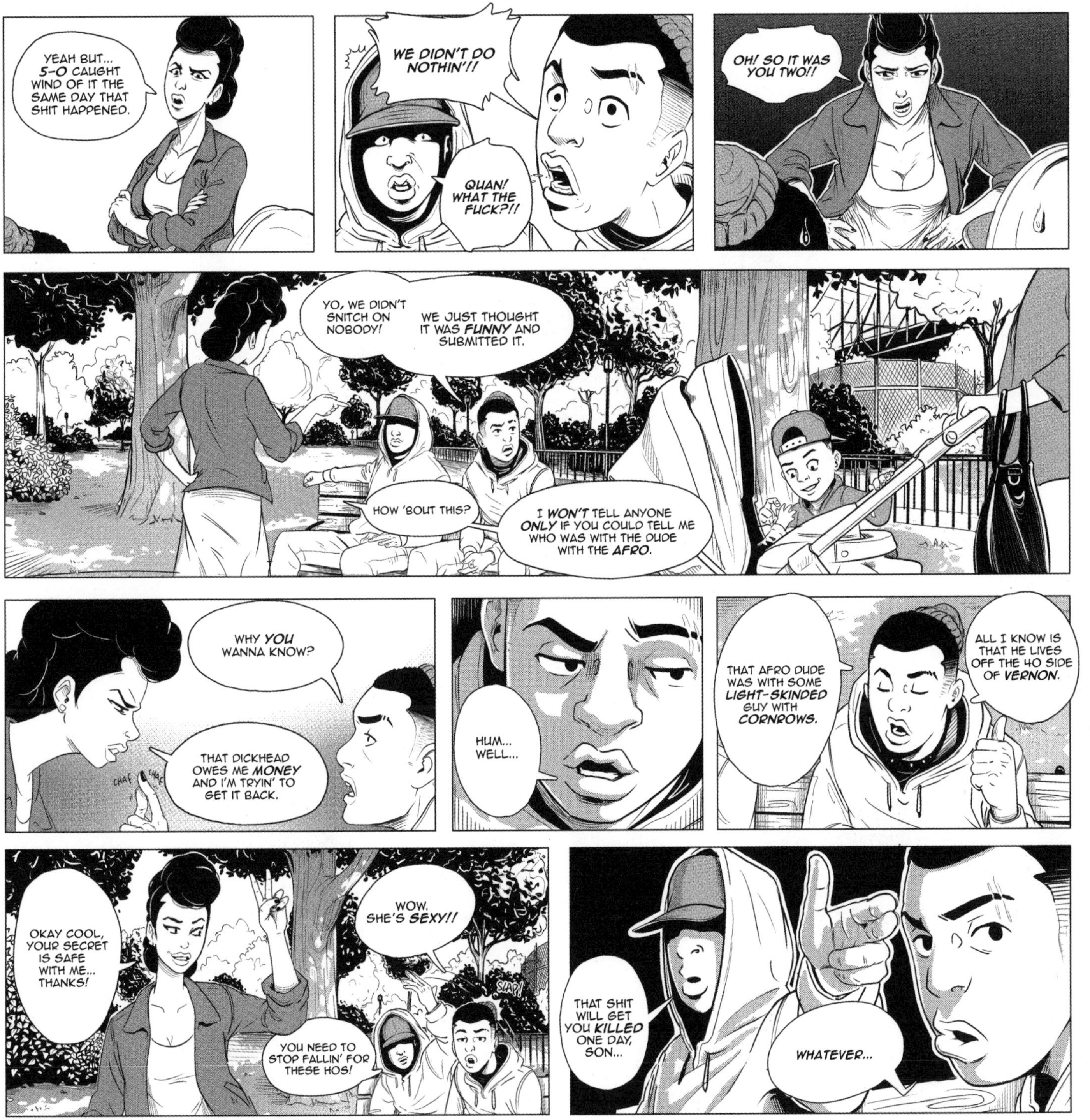
YEAH BUT... 5-O CAUGHT WIND OF IT THE SAME DAY THAT SHIT HAPPENED.
WE DIDN'T DO NOTHIN'!!
QUAN! WHAT THE FUCK?!!
OH! SO IT WAS YOU TWO!!
YO, WE DIDN'T SNITCH ON NOBODY!
WE JUST THOUGHT IT WAS FUNNY AND SUBMITTED IT.
HOW 'BOUT THIS?
I WON'T TELL ANYONE ONLY IF YOU COULD TELL ME WHO WAS WITH THE DUDE WITH THE AFRO.
WHY YOU WANNA KNOW?
THAT DICKHEAD OWES ME MONEY AND I'M TRYIN' TO GET IT BACK.
CHAF CHAF
HUM... WELL...
THAT AFRO DUDE WAS WITH SOME LIGHT-SKINDED GUY WITH CORNROWS.
ALL I KNOW IS THAT HE LIVES OFF THE 40 SIDE OF VERNON.
OKAY COOL, YOUR SECRET IS SAFE WITH ME... THANKS!
WOW. SHE'S SEXY!!
SLAP!
YOU NEED TO STOP FALLIN' FOR THESE HOS!
THAT SHIT WILL GET YOU KILLED ONE DAY, SON...
WHATEVER...

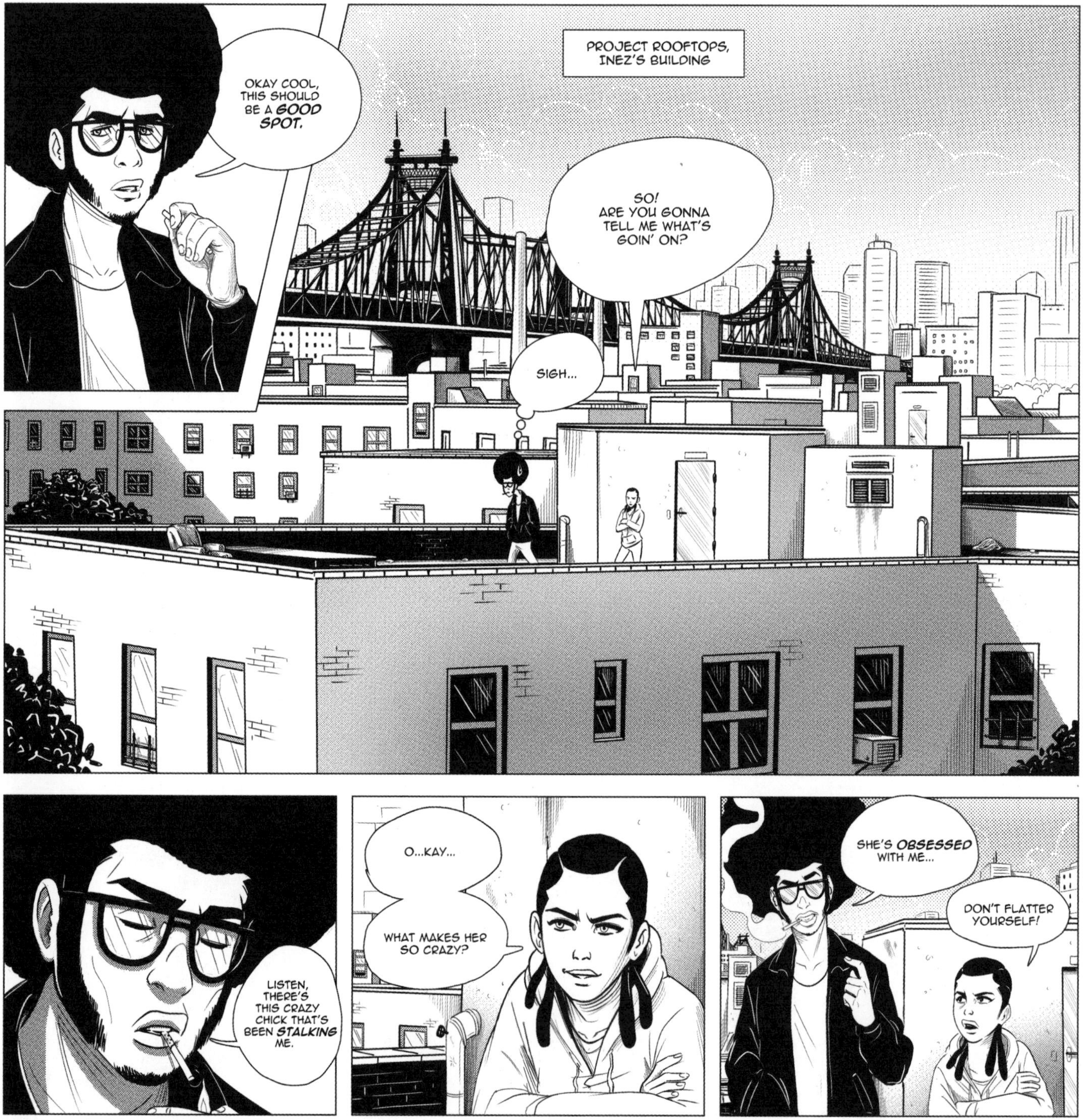
OKAY COOL, THIS SHOULD BE A GOOD SPOT.
PROJECT ROOFTOPS, INEZ'S BUILDING
SO! ARE YOU GONNA TELL ME WHAT'S GOIN' ON?
SIGH...
LISTEN, THERE'S THIS CRAZY CHICK THAT'S BEEN STALKING ME.
O...KAY...
WHAT MAKES HER SO CRAZY?
SHE'S OBSESSED WITH ME...
DON'T FLATTER YOURSELF!

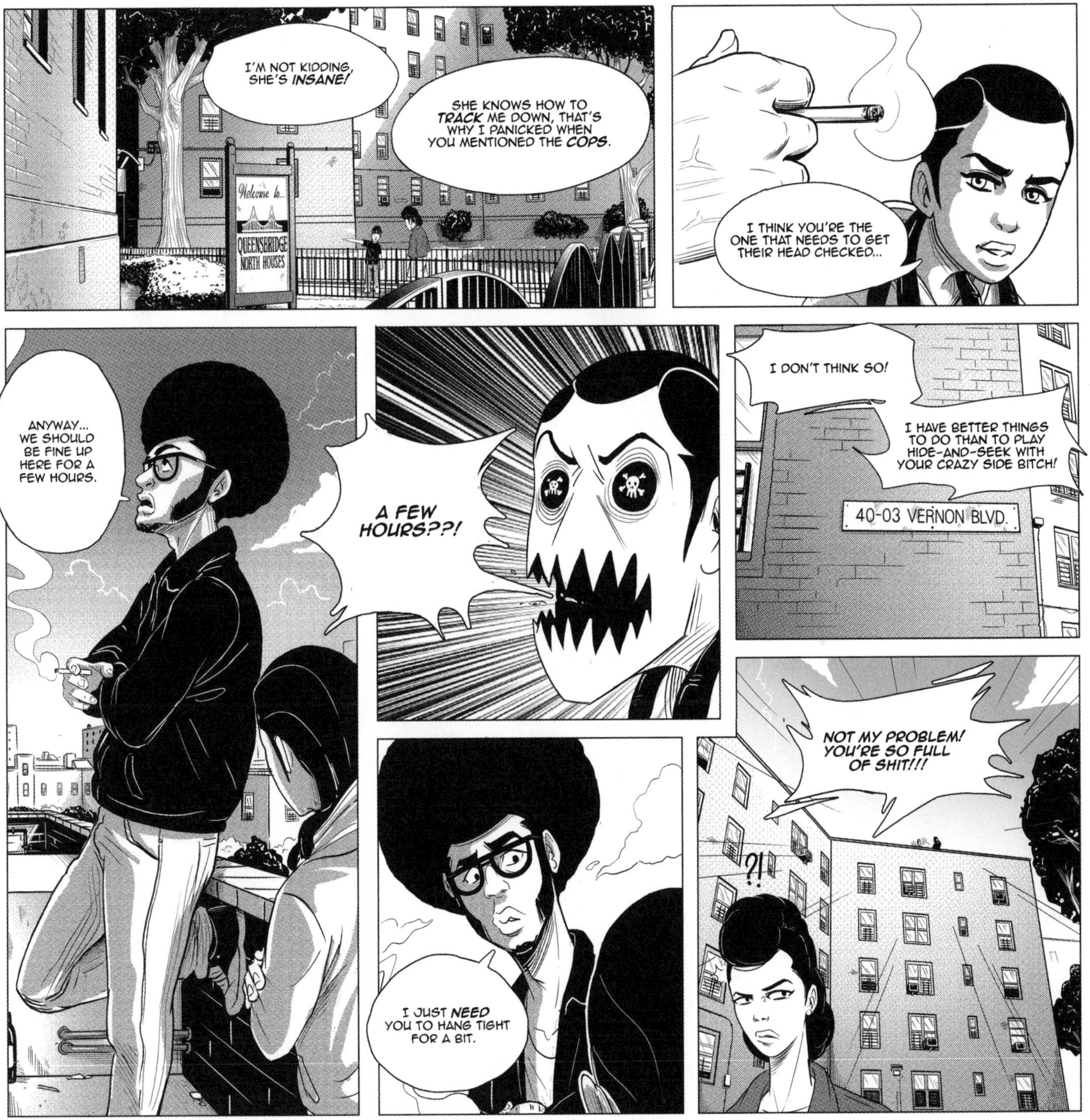
I'M NOT KIDDING, SHE'S INSANE!
SHE KNOWS HOW TO TRACK ME DOWN, THAT'S WHY I PANICKED WHEN YOU MENTIONED THE COPS.
Welcome to... QUEENSBRIDGE NORTH HOUSES
I THINK YOU'RE THE ONE THAT NEEDS TO GET THEIR HEAD CHECKED...
ANYWAY... WE SHOULD BE FINE UP HERE FOR A FEW HOURS.
A FEW HOURS??!
I DON'T THINK SO!
I HAVE BETTER THINGS TO DO THAN TO PLAY HIDE-AND-SEEK WITH YOUR CRAZY SIDE BITCH!
40-03 VERNON BLVD.
I JUST NEED YOU TO HANG TIGHT FOR A BIT.
NOT MY PROBLEM! YOU'RE SO FULL OF SHIT!!!
?!

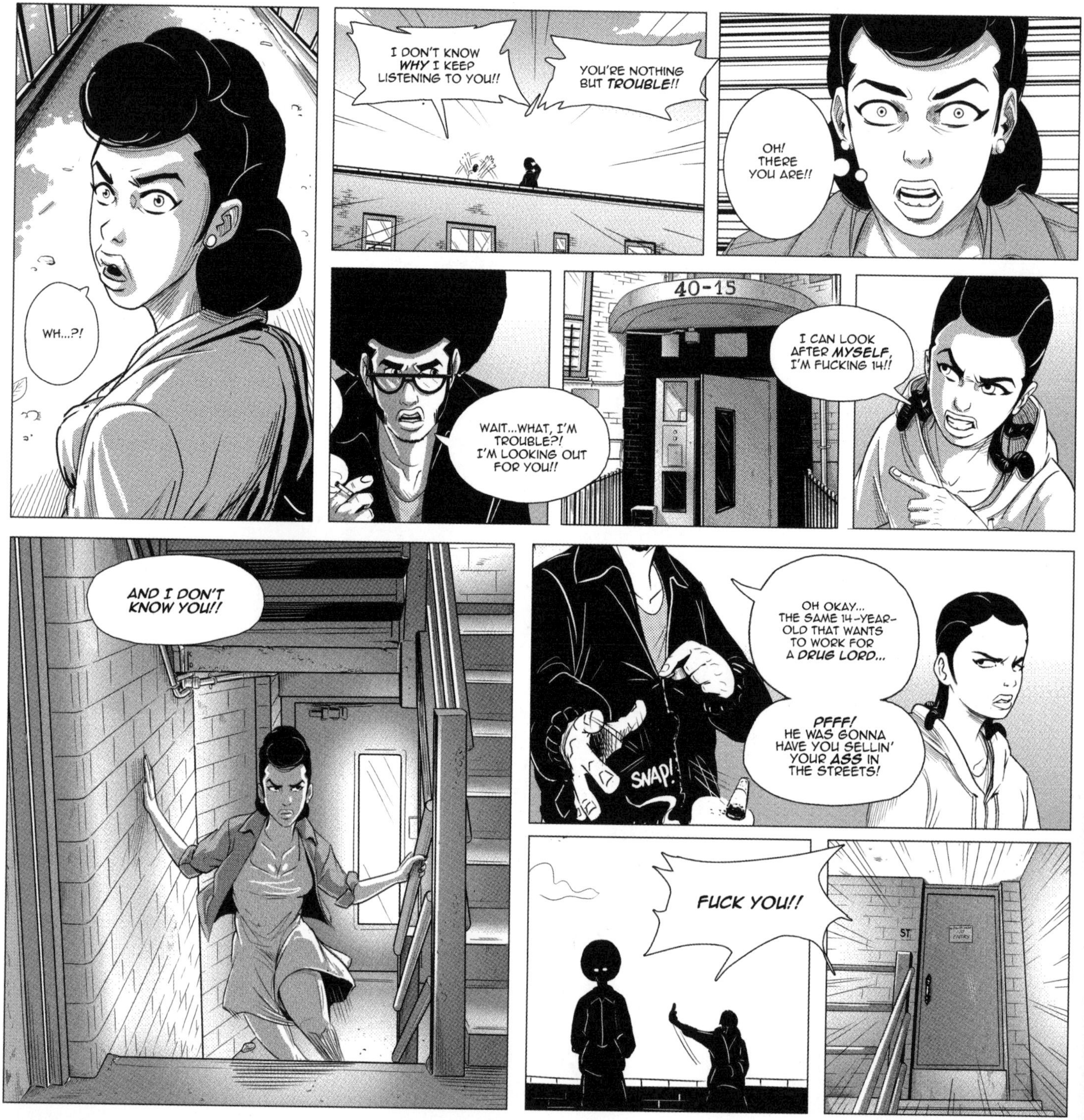
WH...?!
I DON'T KNOW *WHY* I KEEP LISTENING TO YOU!!
YOU'RE NOTHING BUT *TROUBLE*!!
OH! THERE YOU ARE!!
WAIT...WHAT, I'M TROUBLE?! I'M LOOKING OUT FOR YOU!!
40-15
I CAN LOOK AFTER *MYSELF*, I'M FUCKING 14!!
AND I DON'T KNOW YOU!!
OH OKAY... THE SAME 14-YEAR-OLD THAT WANTS TO WORK FOR A *DRUG LORD*...
SNAP!
PFFF! HE WAS GONNA HAVE YOU SELLIN' YOUR *ASS* IN THE STREETS!
FUCK YOU!!
ST

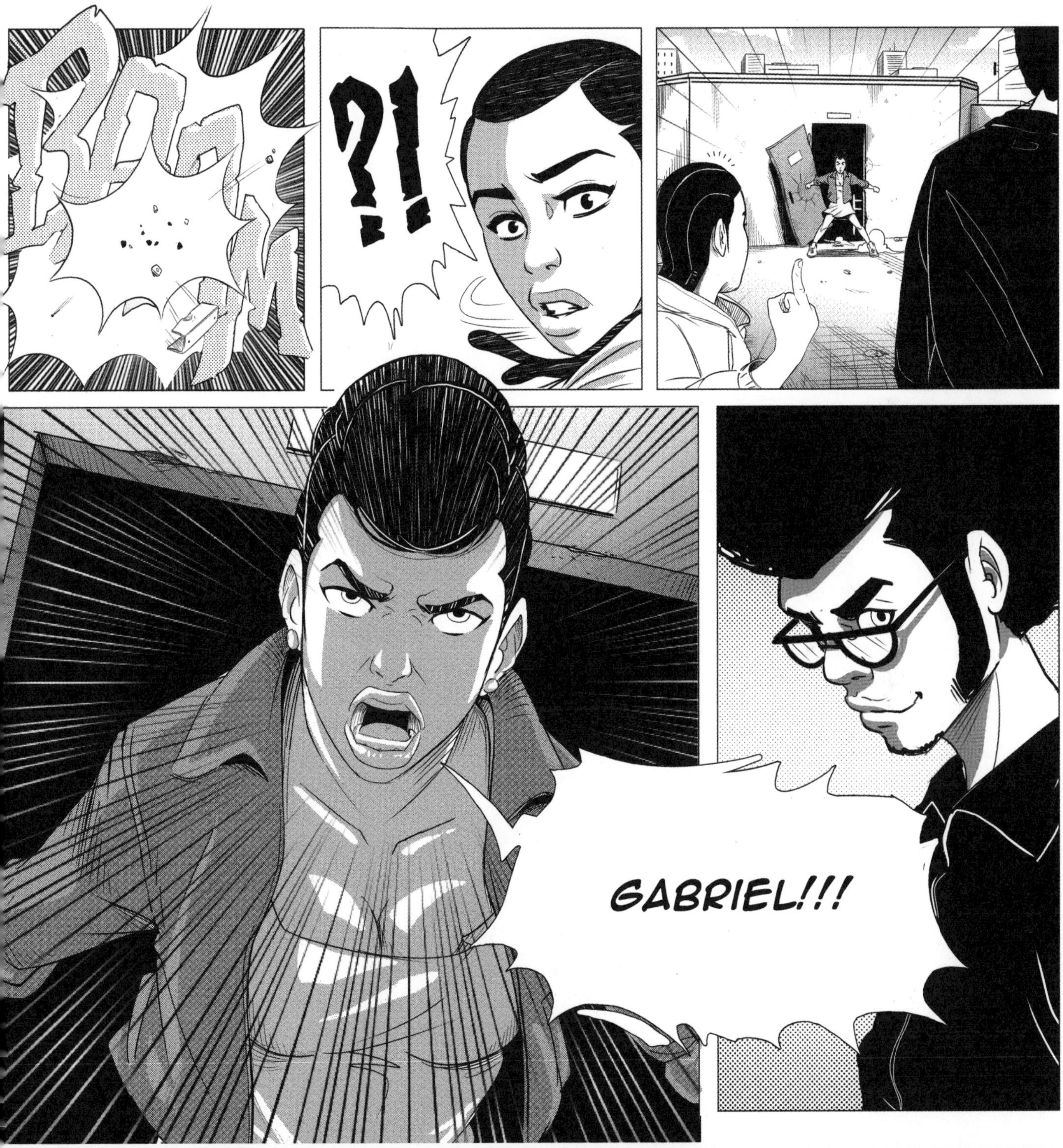
BOOM
?!
GABRIEL!!!

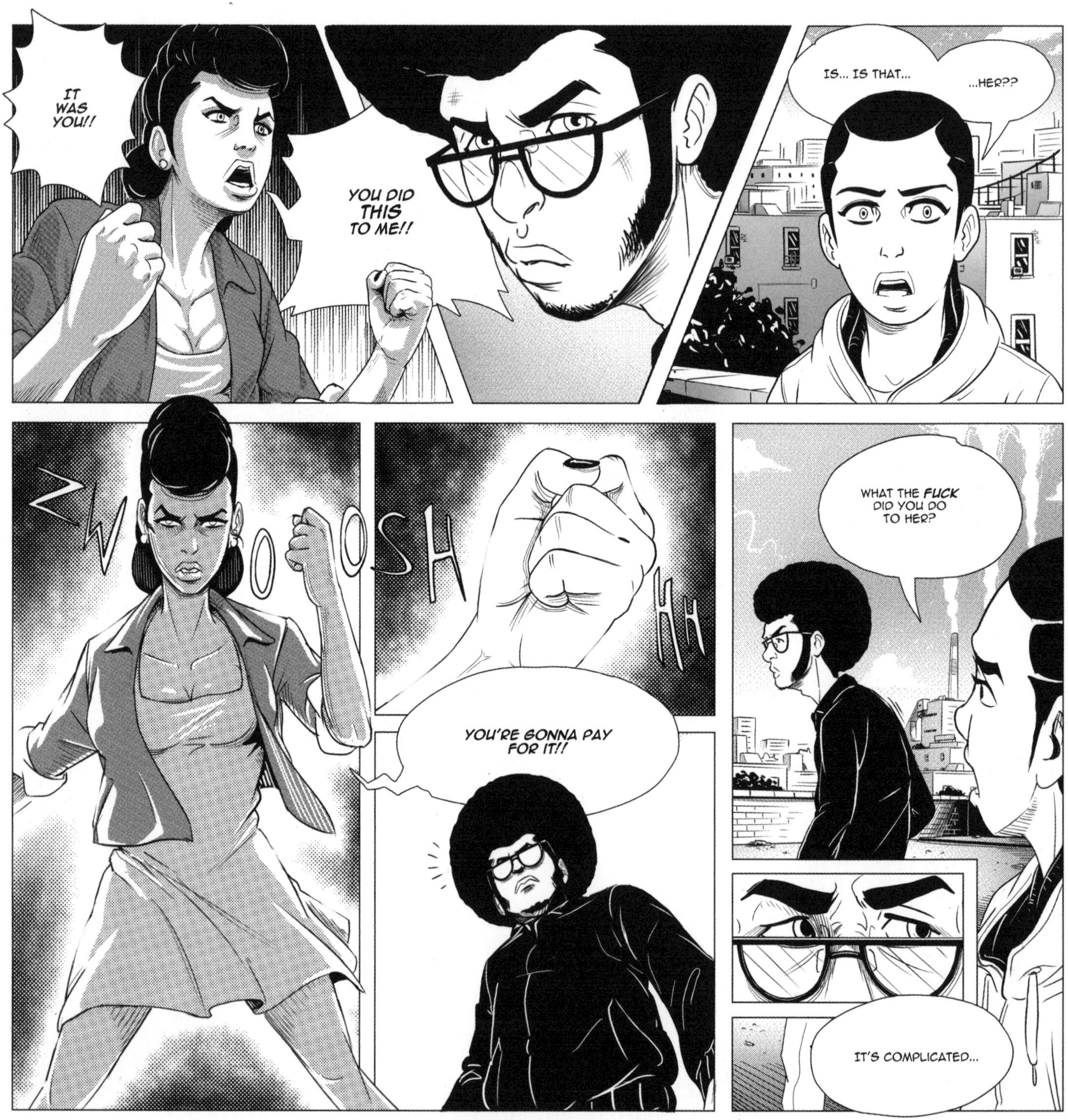
IT WAS YOU!!
YOU DID THIS TO ME!!
IS... IS THAT...
...HER??
ZWOOOSH
WHAT THE FUCK DID YOU DO TO HER?
YOU'RE GONNA PAY FOR IT!!
IT'S COMPLICATED...

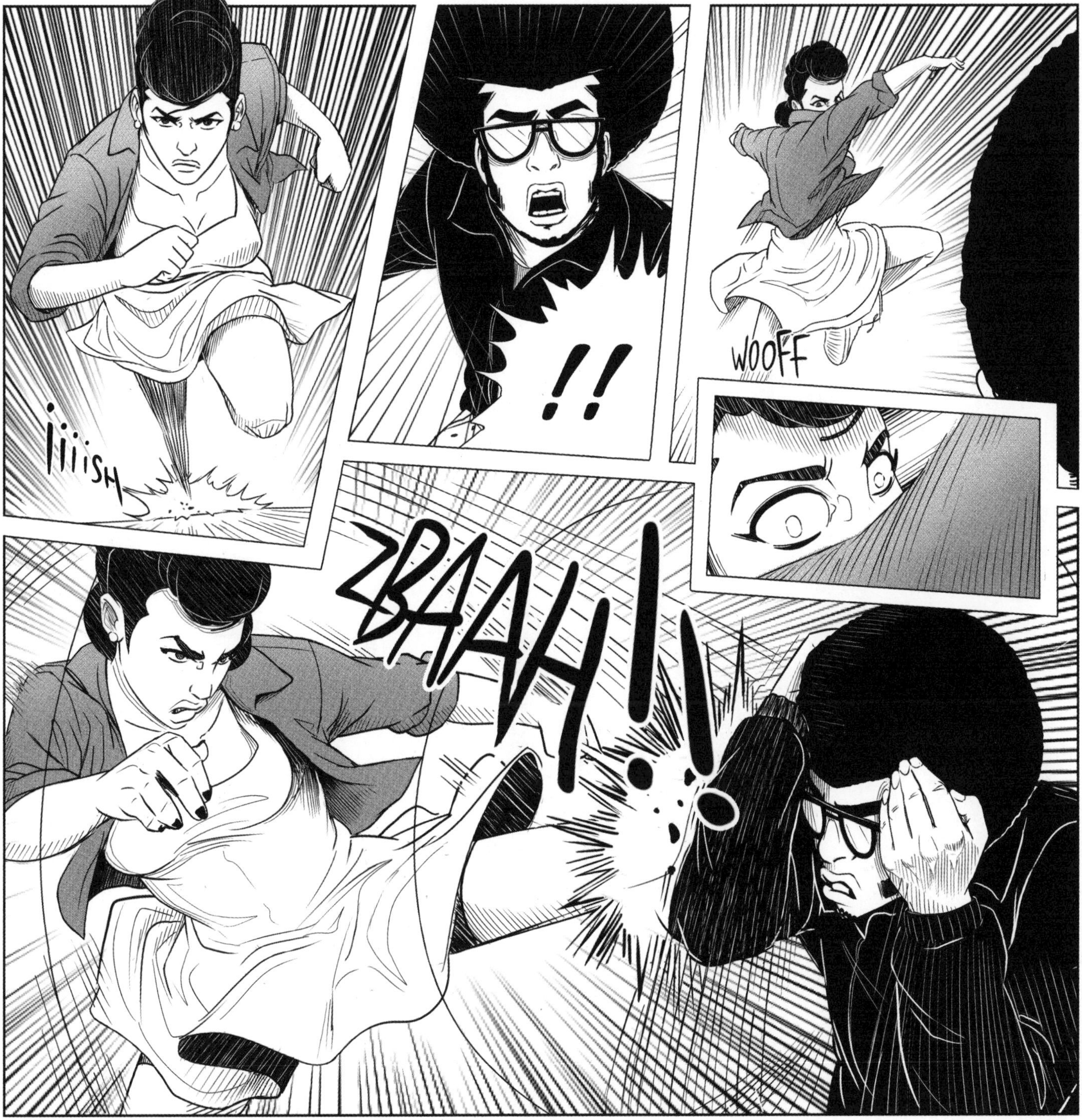

¡¡¡¡ISH
!!
WOOFF
ZBAAH!!

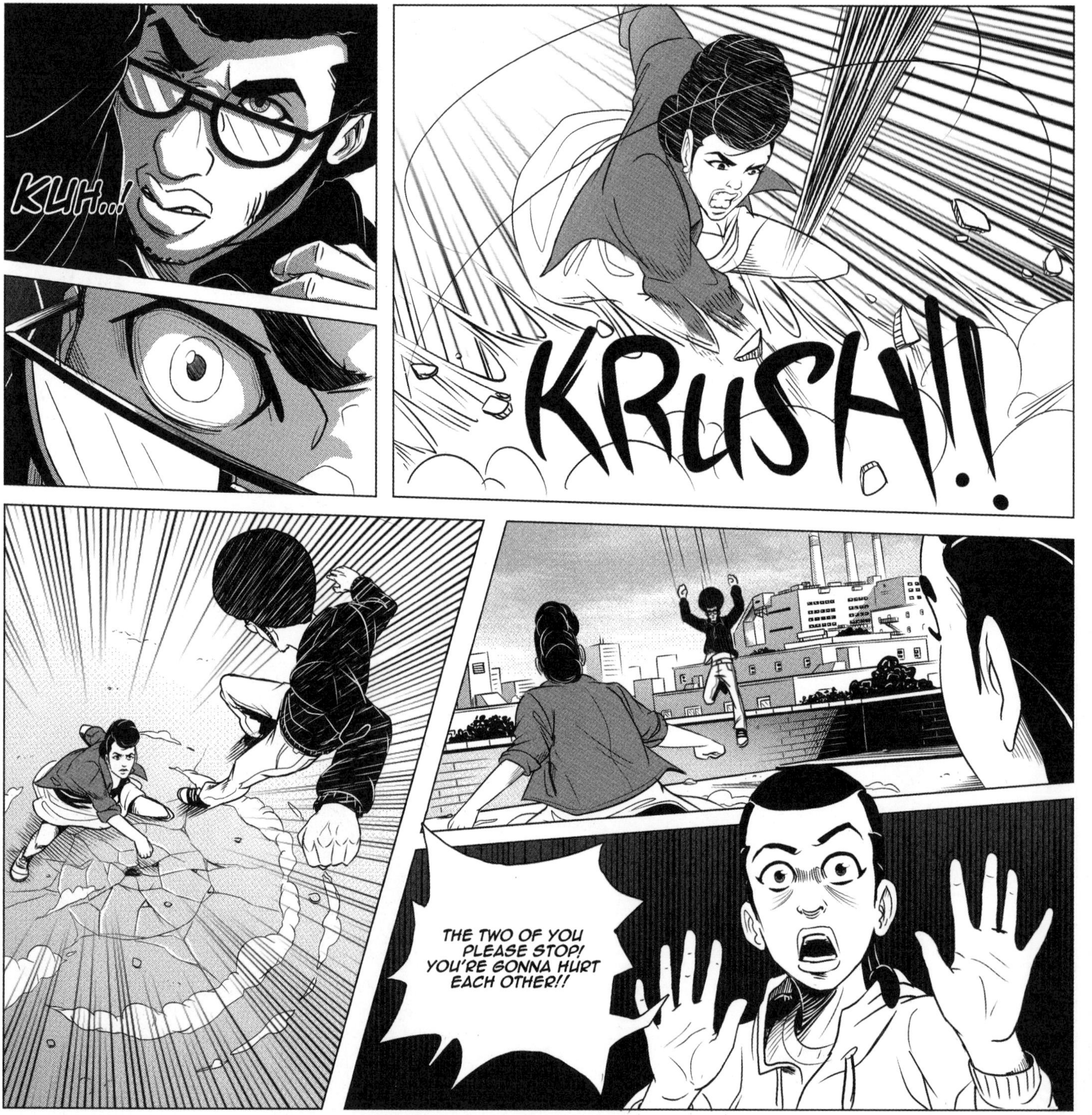
KUH..!
KRUSH!!
THE TWO OF YOU PLEASE STOP! YOU'RE GONNA HURT EACH OTHER!!

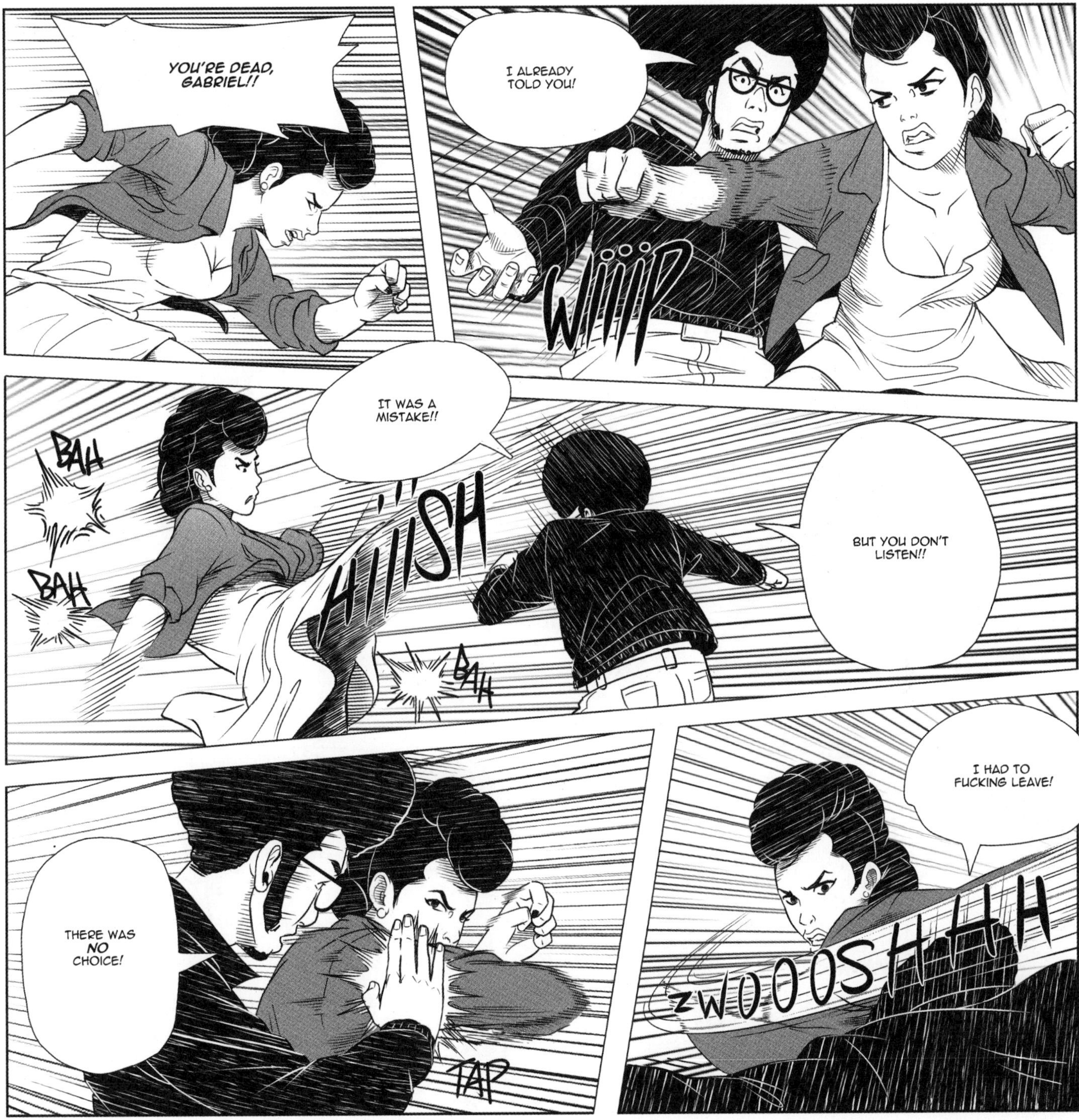
YOU'RE DEAD, GABRIEL!!
I ALREADY TOLD YOU!
WIIIP
IT WAS A MISTAKE!!
BAH
BAH
HIIISH
BAH
BUT YOU DON'T LISTEN!!
THERE WAS *NO* CHOICE!
TAP
I HAD TO FUCKING LEAVE!
ZWOOOSHHHH

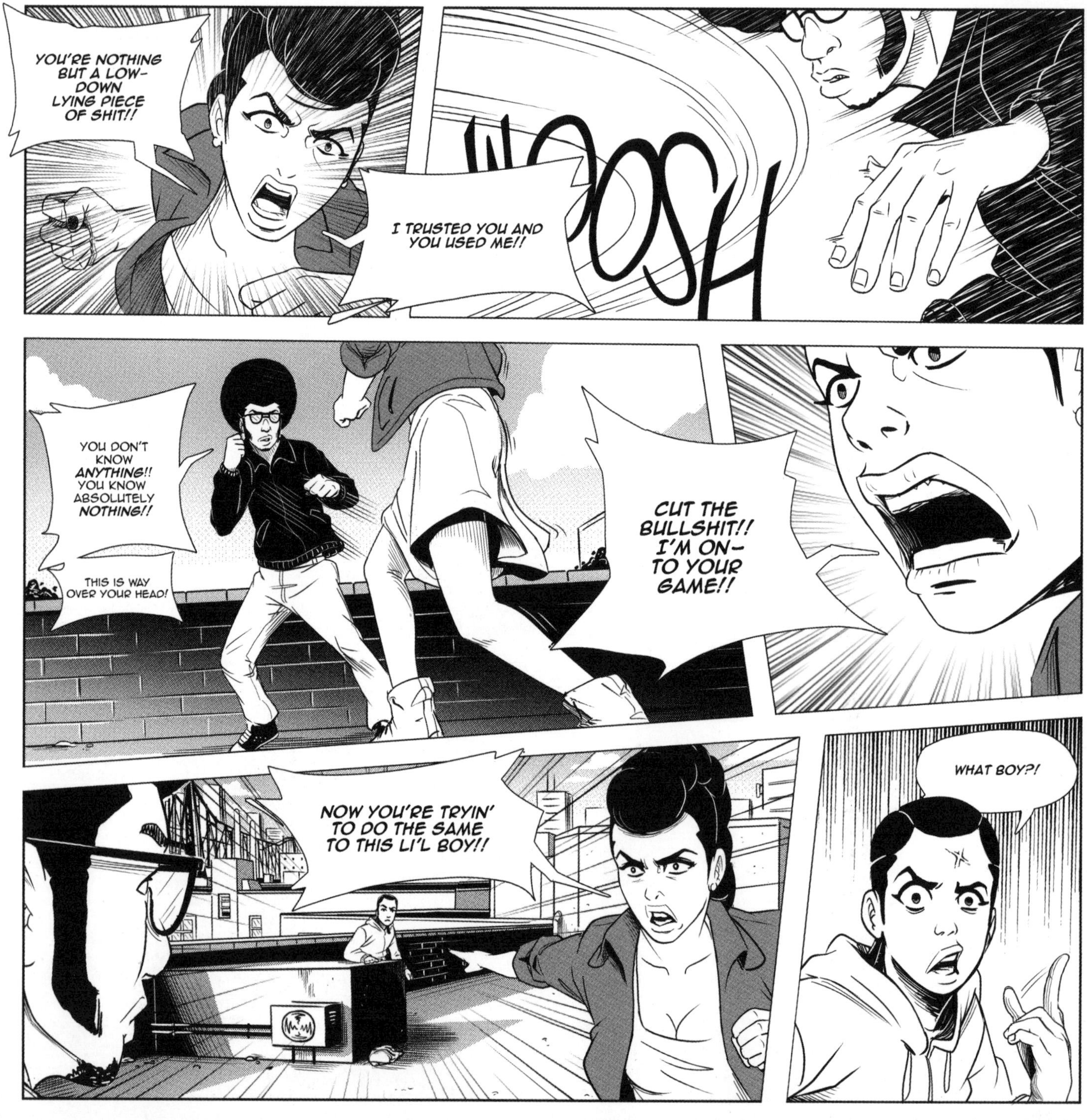
YOU'RE NOTHING BUT A LOW-DOWN LYING PIECE OF SHIT!!
I TRUSTED YOU AND YOU USED ME!!
WOOSH
YOU DON'T KNOW ANYTHING!! YOU KNOW ABSOLUTELY NOTHING!!
THIS IS WAY OVER YOUR HEAD!
CUT THE BULLSHIT!! I'M ON-TO YOUR GAME!!
NOW YOU'RE TRYIN' TO DO THE SAME TO THIS LI'L BOY!!
WHAT BOY?!

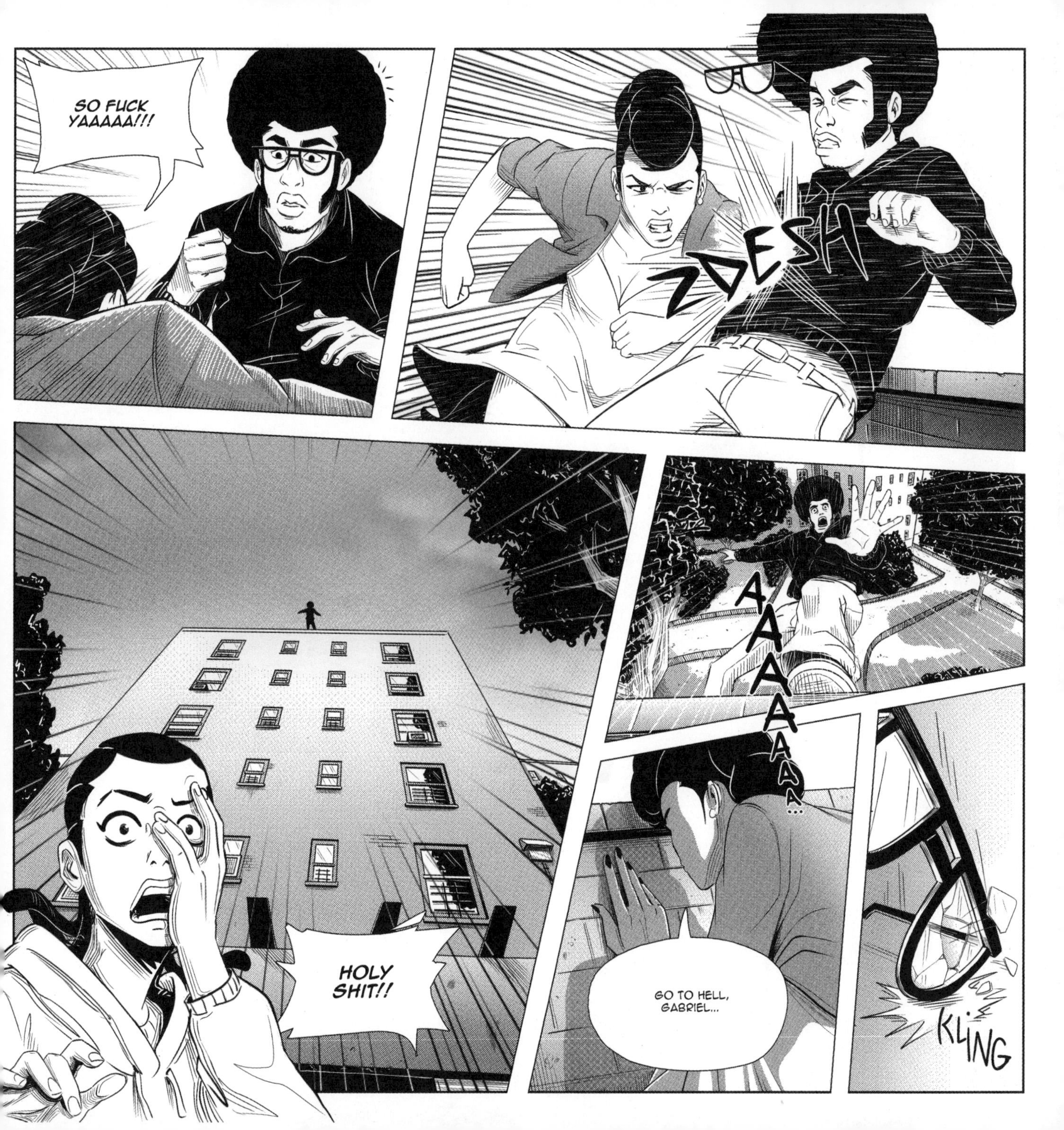
SO FUCK YAAAAA!!!
ZDESH
AAAAAAA...
HOLY SHIT!!
GO TO HELL, GABRIEL...
KLING

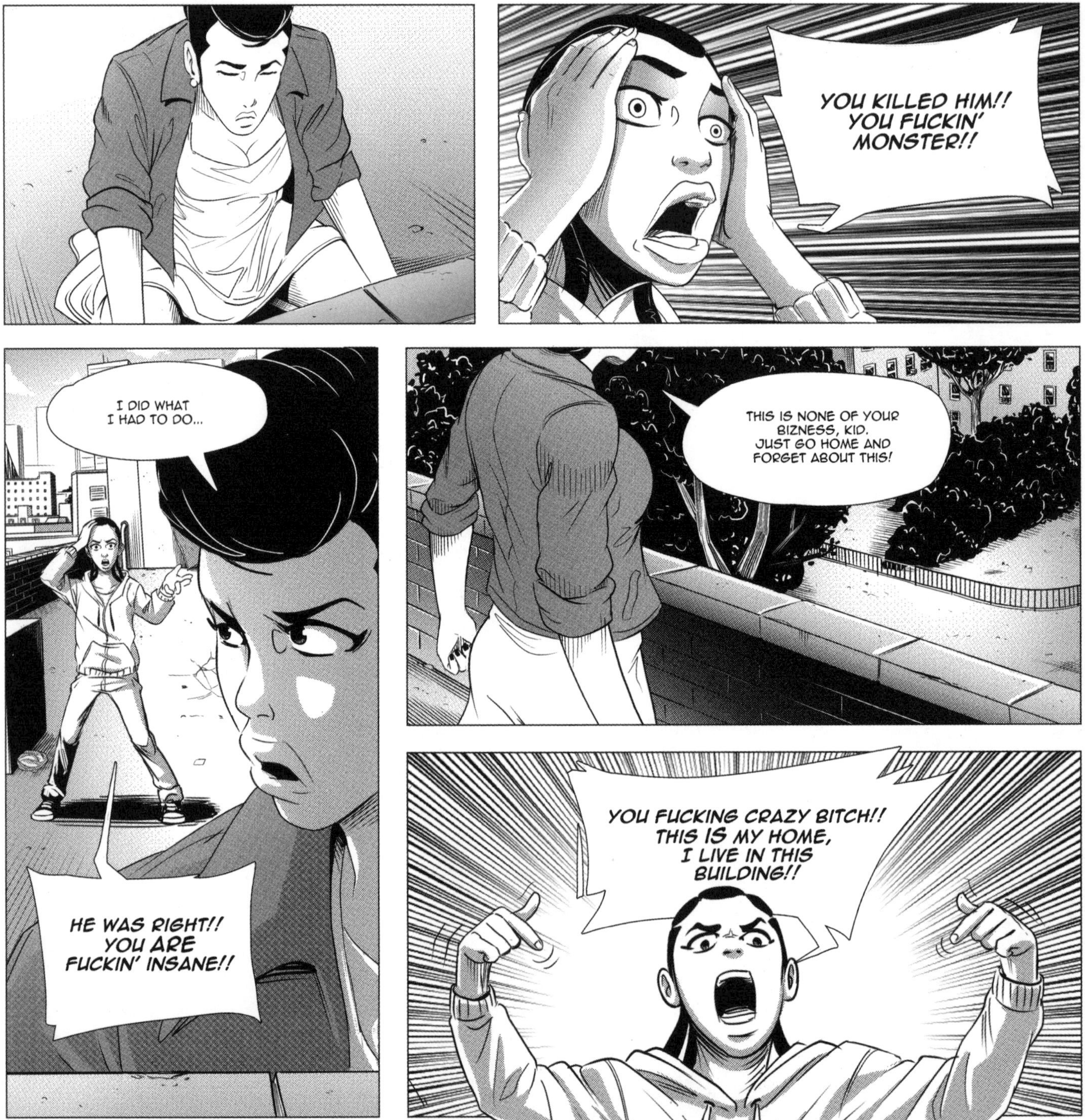
YOU KILLED HIM!! YOU FUCKIN' MONSTER!!
I DID WHAT I HAD TO DO...
HE WAS RIGHT!! YOU ARE FUCKIN' INSANE!!
THIS IS NONE OF YOUR BIZNESS, KID. JUST GO HOME AND FORGET ABOUT THIS!
YOU FUCKING CRAZY BITCH!! THIS IS MY HOME, I LIVE IN THIS BUILDING!!

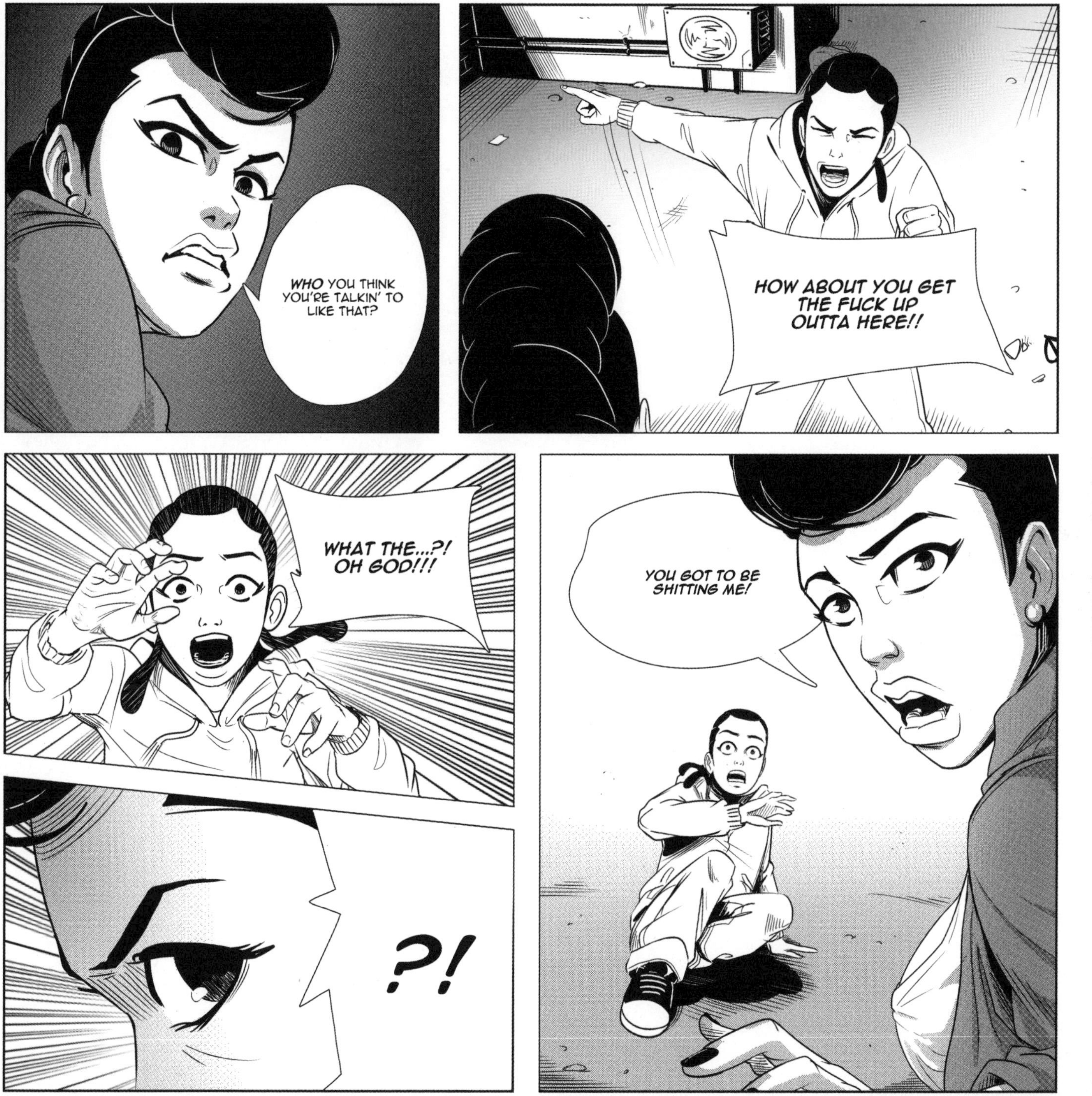
WHO YOU THINK YOU'RE TALKIN' TO LIKE THAT?
HOW ABOUT YOU GET THE FUCK UP OUTTA HERE!!
WHAT THE...?! OH GOD!!!
?!
YOU GOT TO BE SHITTING ME!

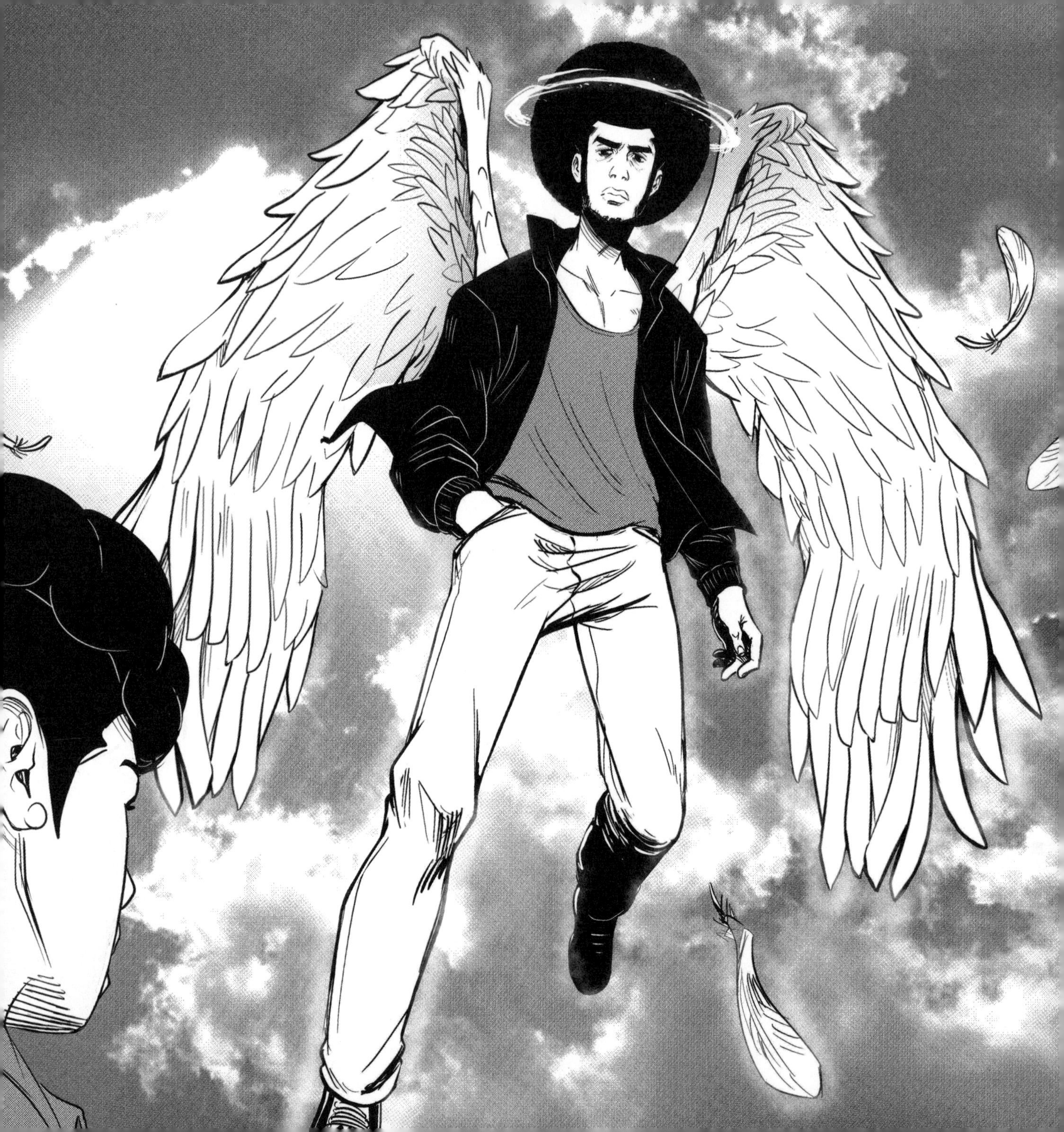

The Dopest...

TEPHLON FUNK!

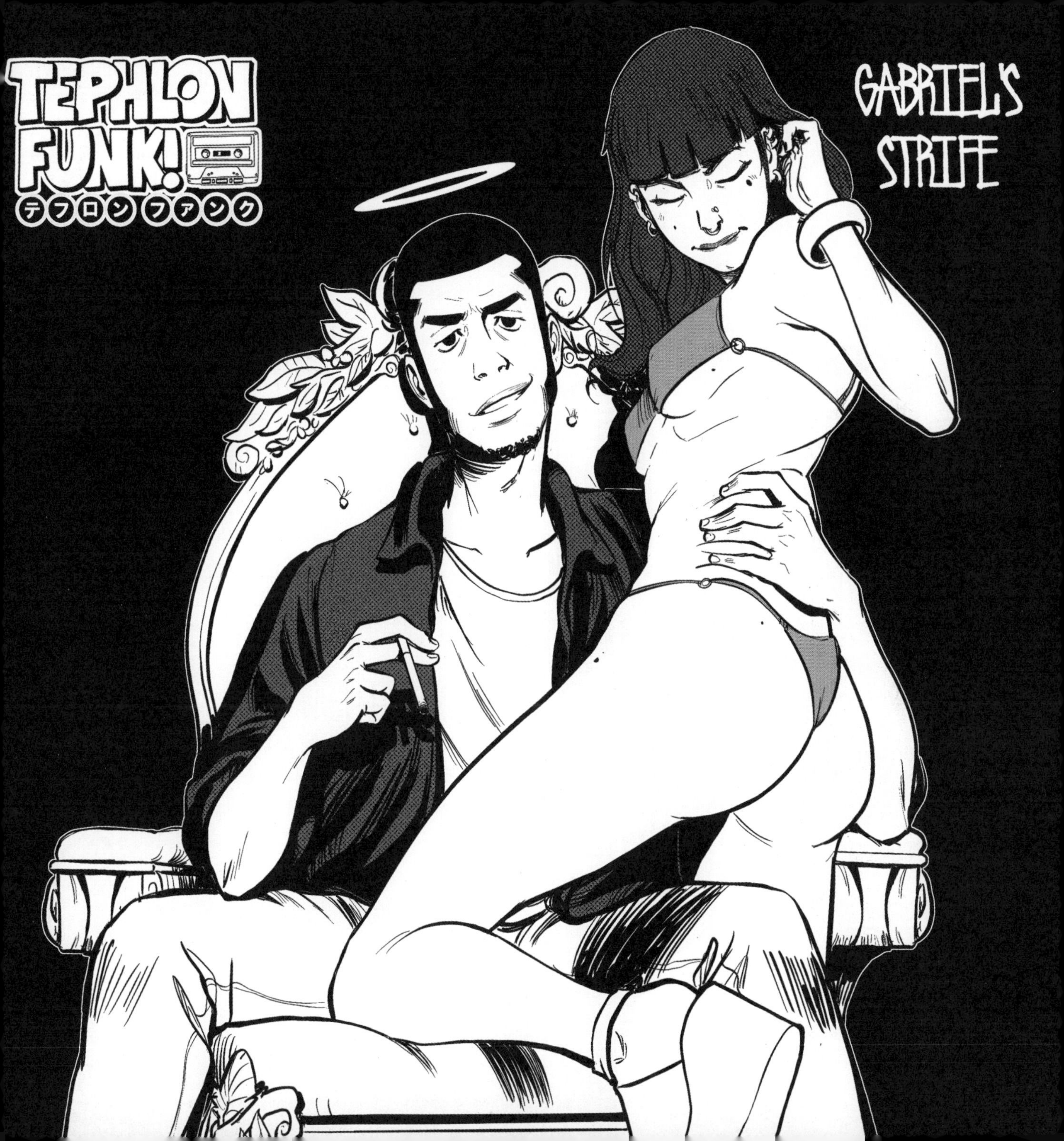
TEPHLON FUNK!
テフロン ファンク
GABRIEL'S STRIFE

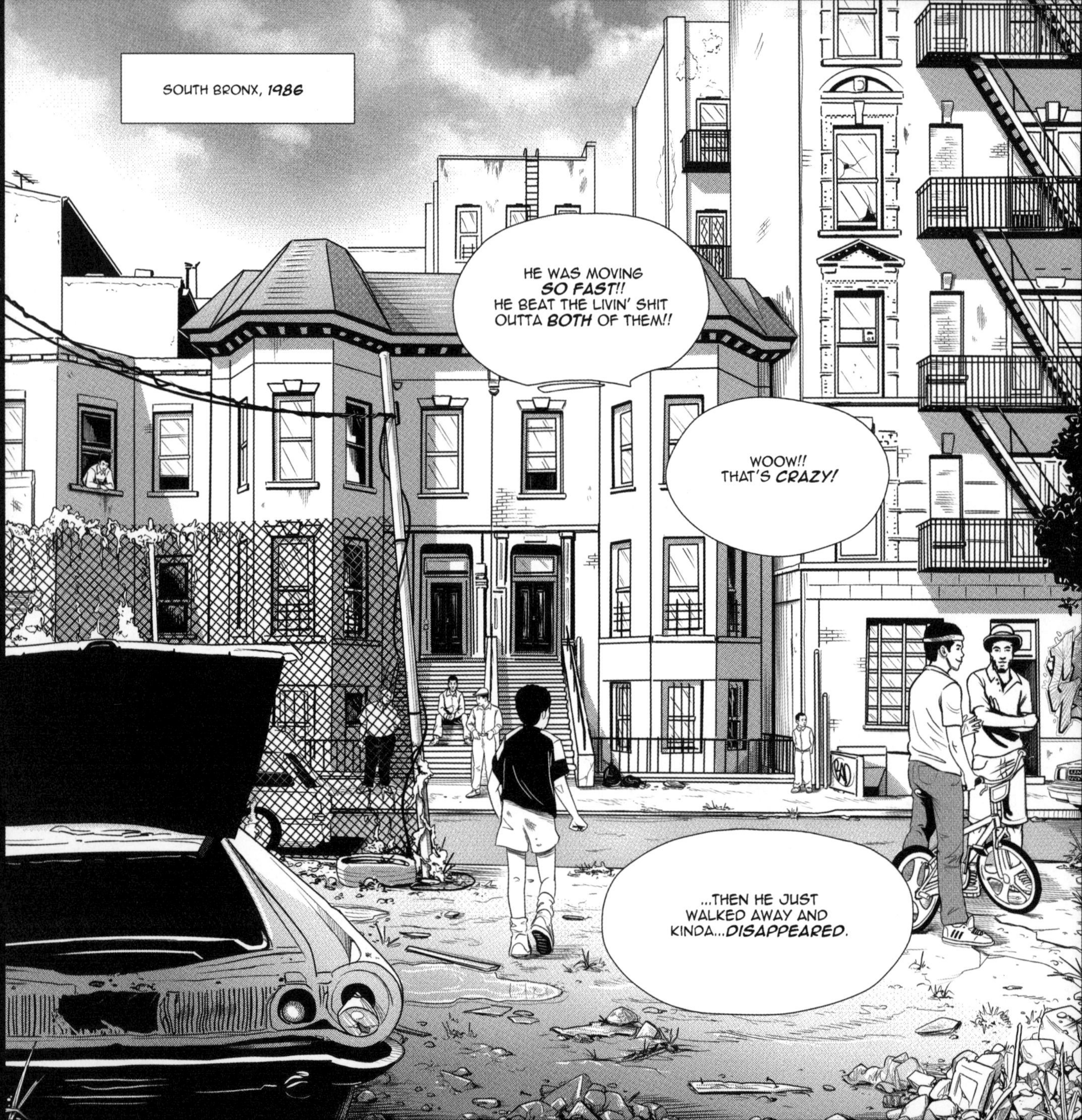
SOUTH BRONX, 1986
HE WAS MOVING SO FAST!! HE BEAT THE LIVIN' SHIT OUTTA BOTH OF THEM!!
WOOW!! THAT'S CRAZY!
...THEN HE JUST WALKED AWAY AND KINDA...DISAPPEARED.

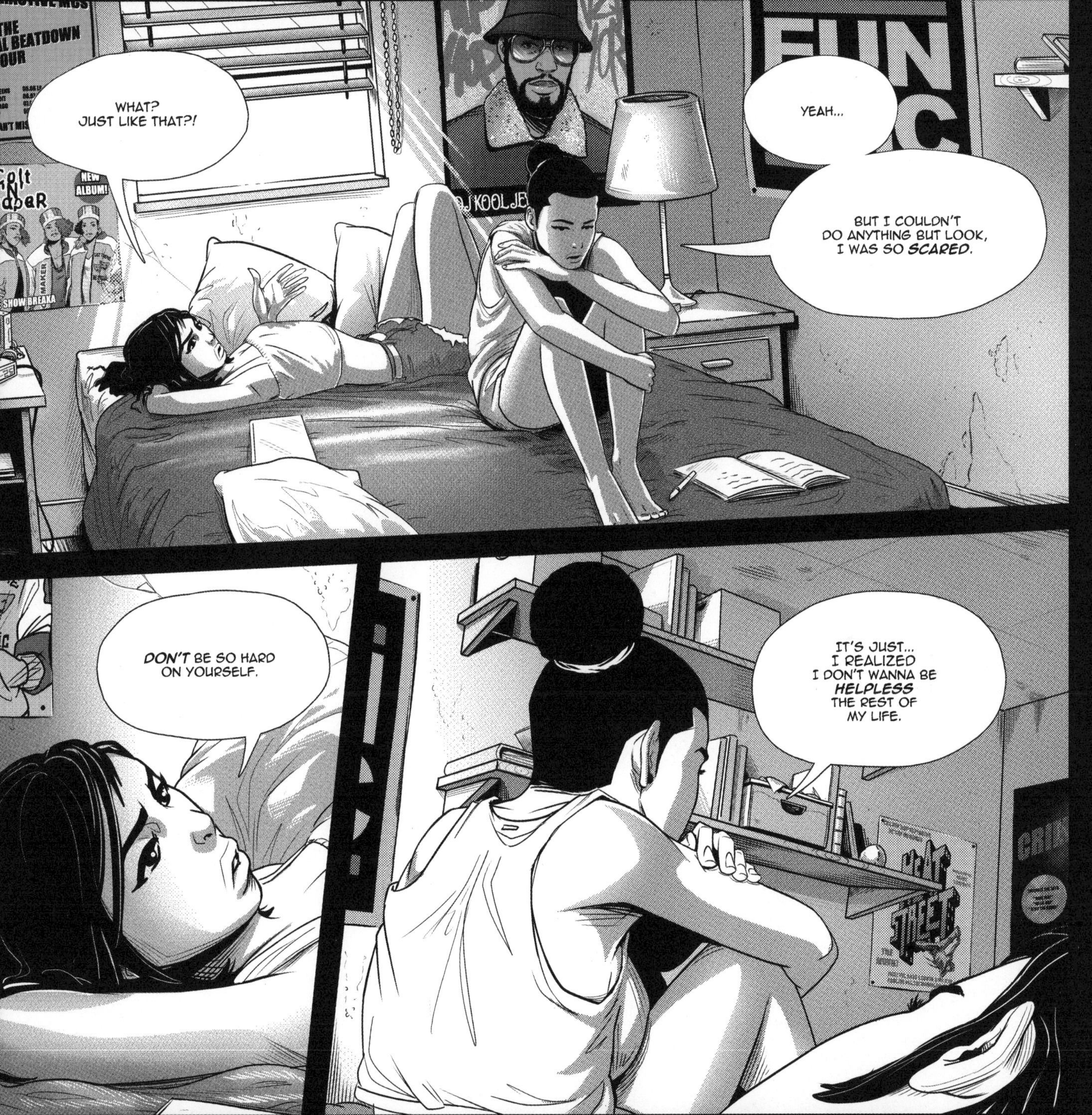
NEW ALBUM!
WHAT? JUST LIKE THAT?!
YEAH...
BUT I COULDN'T DO ANYTHING BUT LOOK, I WAS SO *SCARED*.
DON'T BE SO HARD ON YOURSELF.
IT'S JUST... I REALIZED I DON'T WANNA BE *HELPLESS* THE REST OF MY LIFE.

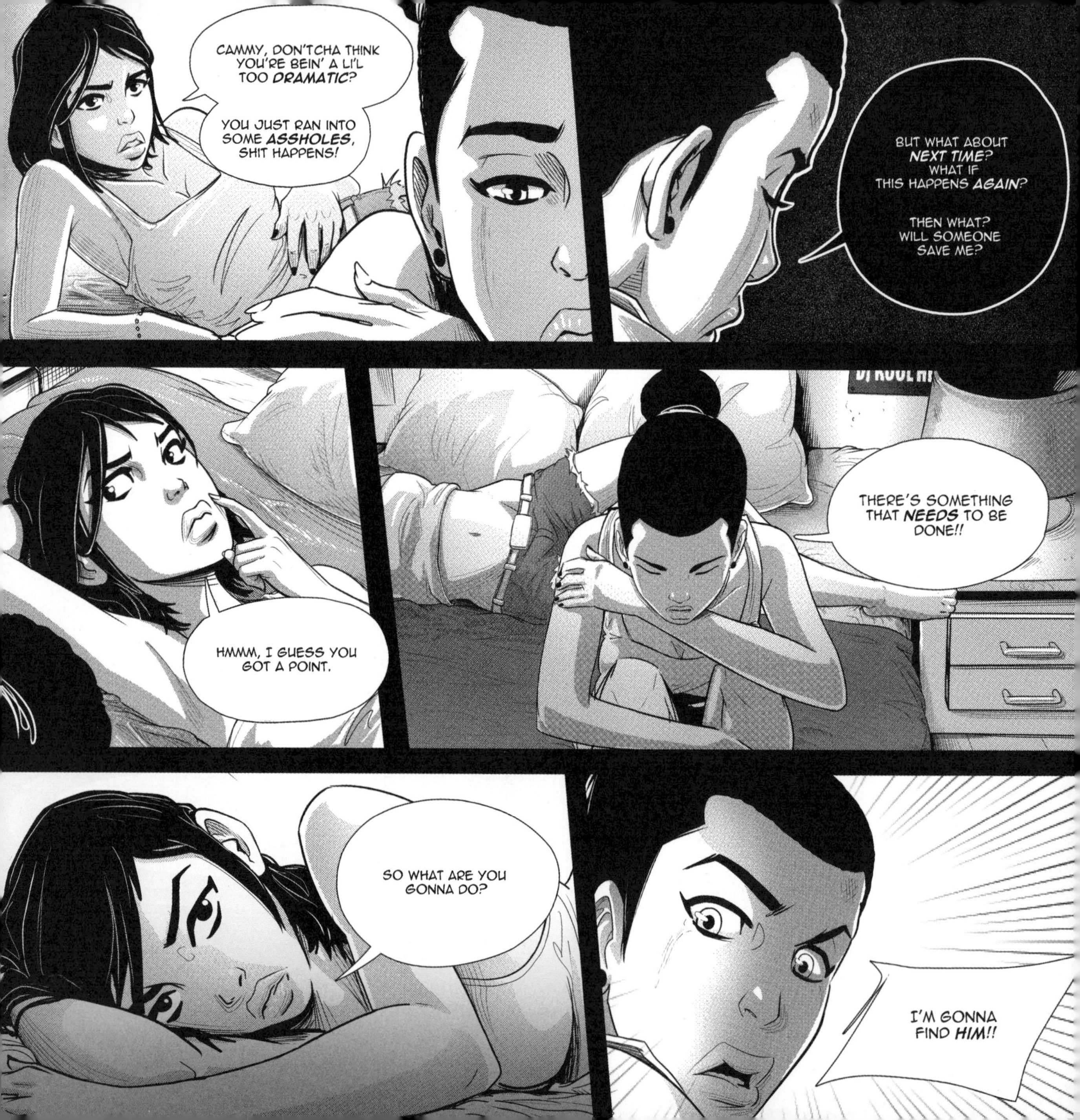
CAMMY, DON'TCHA THINK YOU'RE BEIN' A LI'L TOO DRAMATIC?
YOU JUST RAN INTO SOME ASSHOLES, SHIT HAPPENS!
BUT WHAT ABOUT NEXT TIME? WHAT IF THIS HAPPENS AGAIN?
THEN WHAT? WILL SOMEONE SAVE ME?
HMMM, I GUESS YOU GOT A POINT.
THERE'S SOMETHING THAT NEEDS TO BE DONE!!
SO WHAT ARE YOU GONNA DO?
I'M GONNA FIND HIM!!

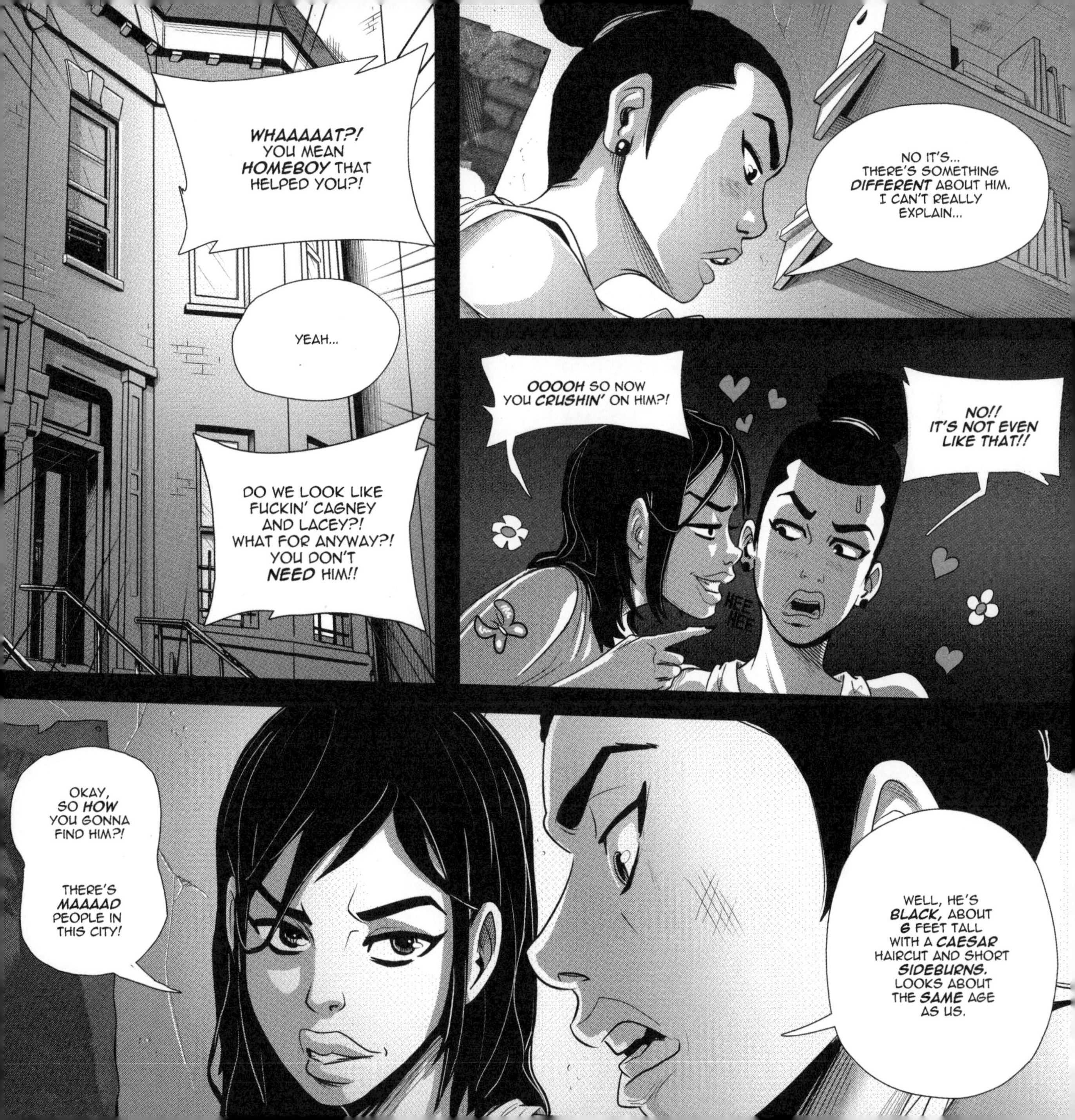
WHAAAAAT?! YOU MEAN HOMEBOY THAT HELPED YOU?!
NO IT'S... THERE'S SOMETHING DIFFERENT ABOUT HIM. I CAN'T REALLY EXPLAIN...
YEAH...
OOOOH SO NOW YOU CRUSHIN' ON HIM?!
NO!! IT'S NOT EVEN LIKE THAT!!
HEE HEE
DO WE LOOK LIKE FUCKIN' CAGNEY AND LACEY?! WHAT FOR ANYWAY?! YOU DON'T NEED HIM!!
OKAY, SO HOW YOU GONNA FIND HIM?!
THERE'S MAAAAD PEOPLE IN THIS CITY!
WELL, HE'S BLACK, ABOUT 6 FEET TALL WITH A CAESAR HAIRCUT AND SHORT SIDEBURNS. LOOKS ABOUT THE SAME AGE AS US.

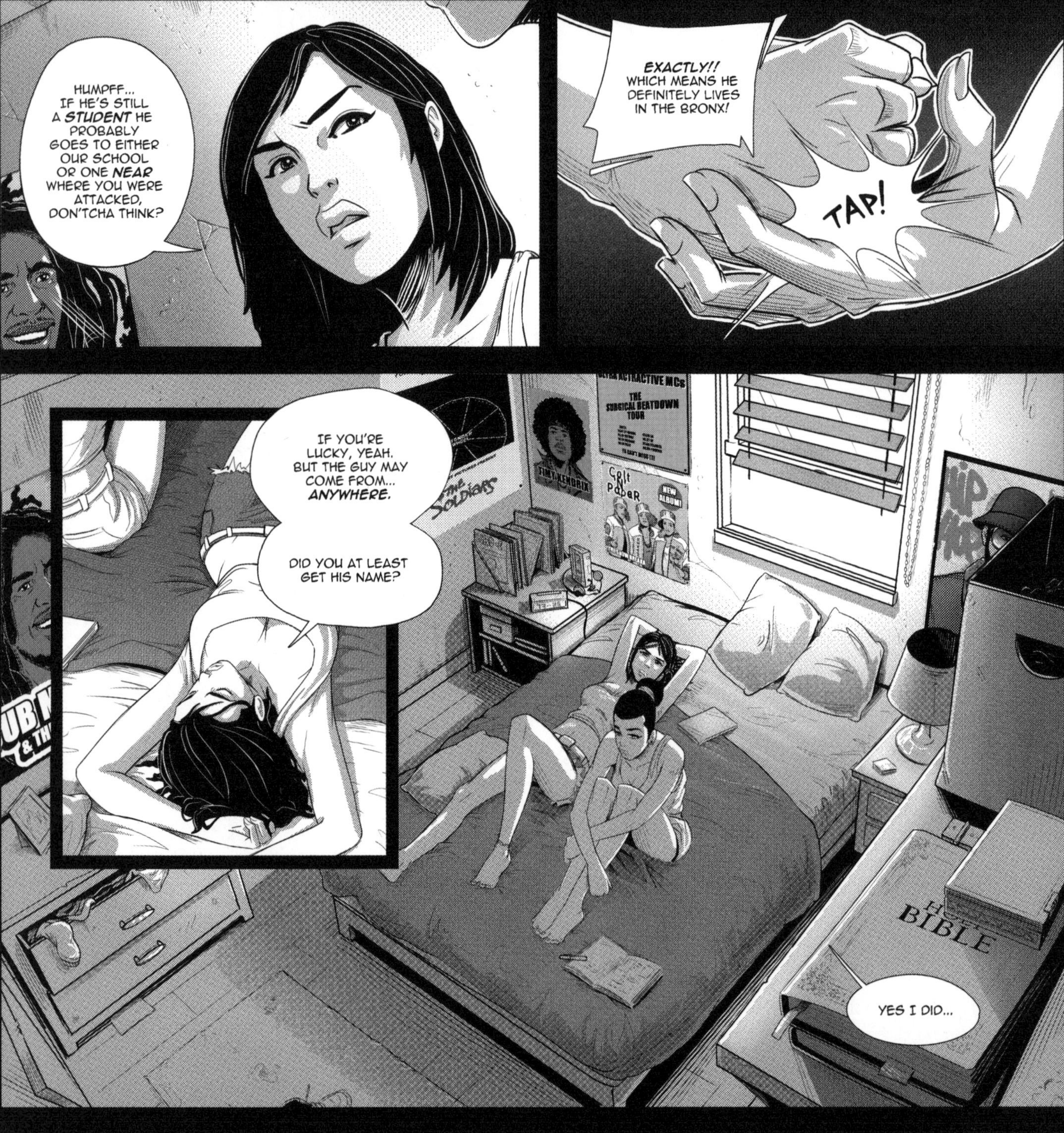
HUMPFF... IF HE'S STILL A **STUDENT** HE PROBABLY GOES TO EITHER OUR SCHOOL OR ONE **NEAR** WHERE YOU WERE ATTACKED, DON'TCHA THINK?
EXACTLY!! WHICH MEANS HE DEFINITELY LIVES IN THE BRONX!
TAP!
IF YOU'RE LUCKY, YEAH. BUT THE GUY MAY COME FROM... **ANYWHERE.**
DID YOU AT LEAST GET HIS NAME?
YES I DID...

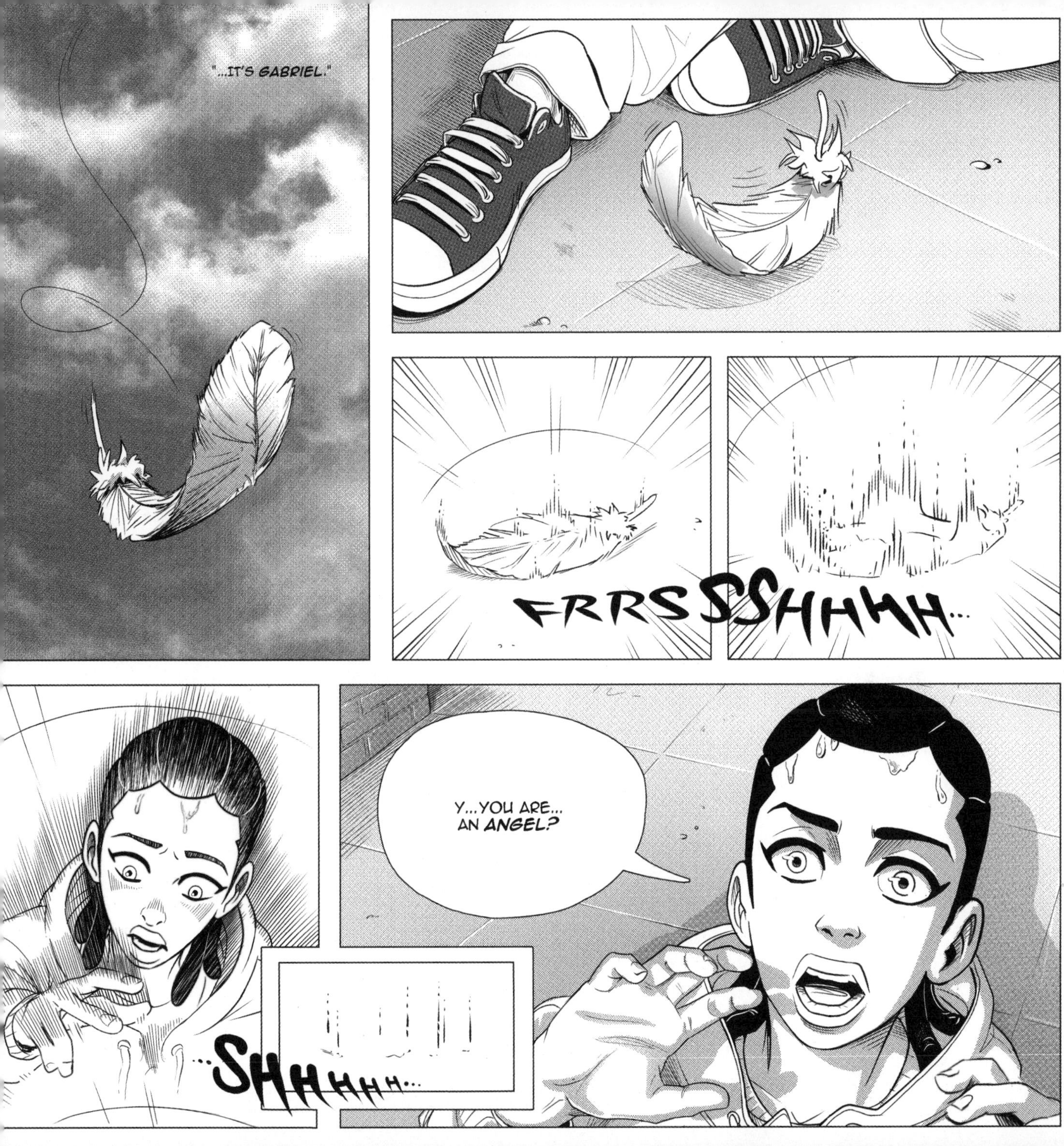

"...IT'S GABRIEL."
FRRSSSHHHH...
Y...YOU ARE... AN ANGEL?
...SHHHHH...

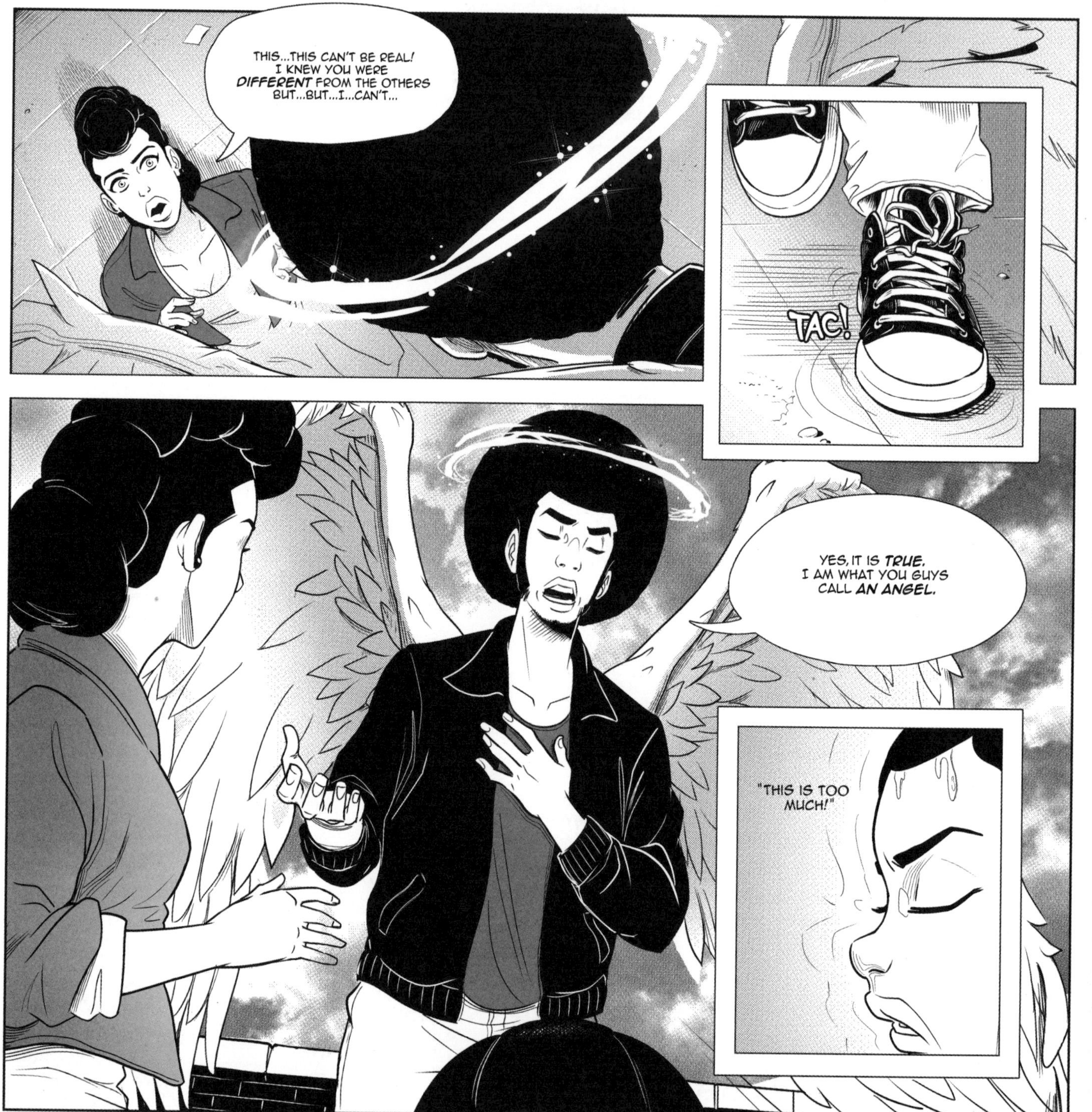
THIS...THIS CAN'T BE REAL! I KNEW YOU WERE *DIFFERENT* FROM THE OTHERS BUT...BUT...I...CAN'T...
TAC!
YES, IT IS *TRUE.* I AM WHAT YOU GUYS CALL *AN ANGEL.*
"THIS IS TOO MUCH!"

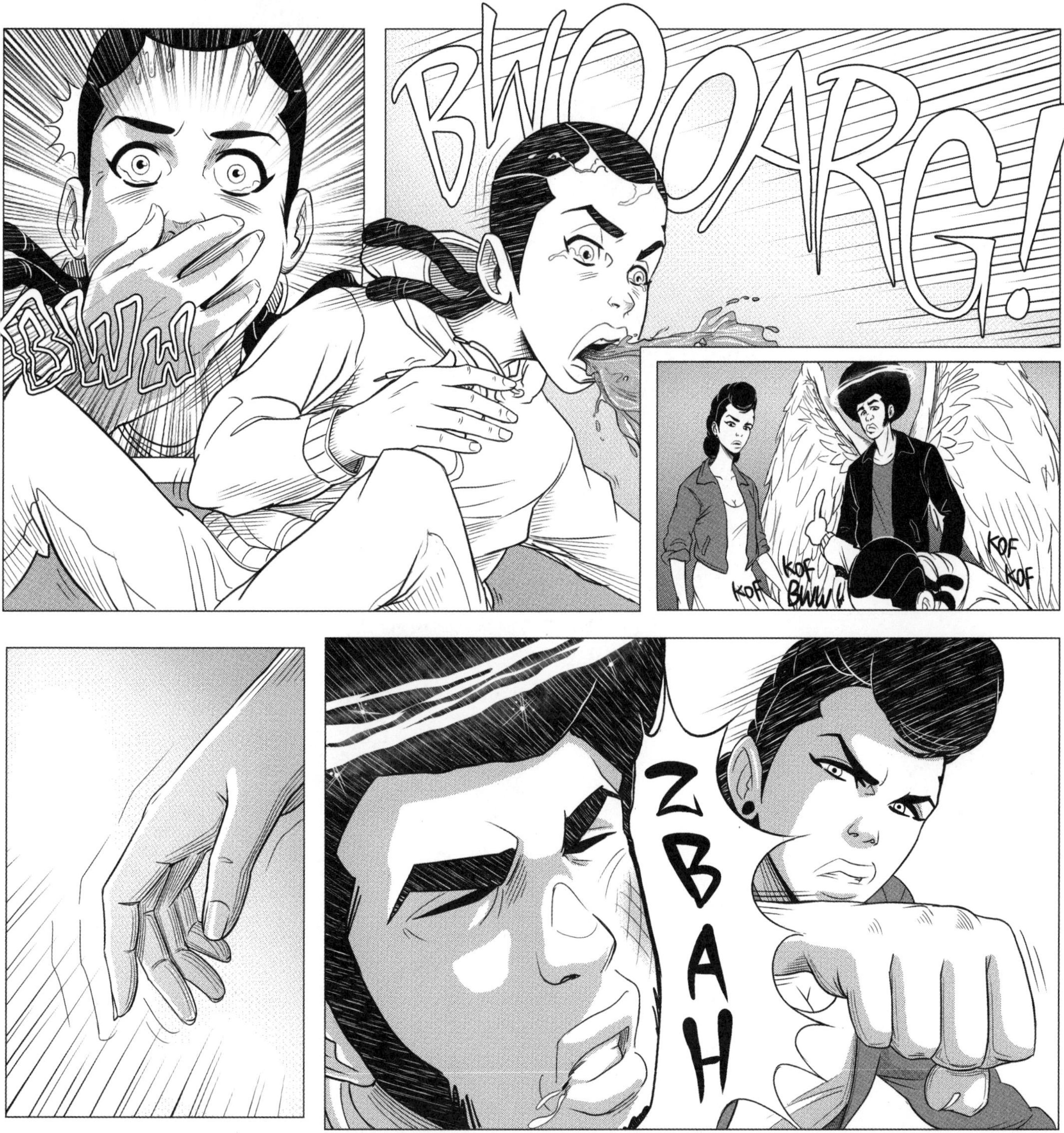

BWW
BWOOARG!
KOF
KOF
BWW
KOF
KOF
ZBAH

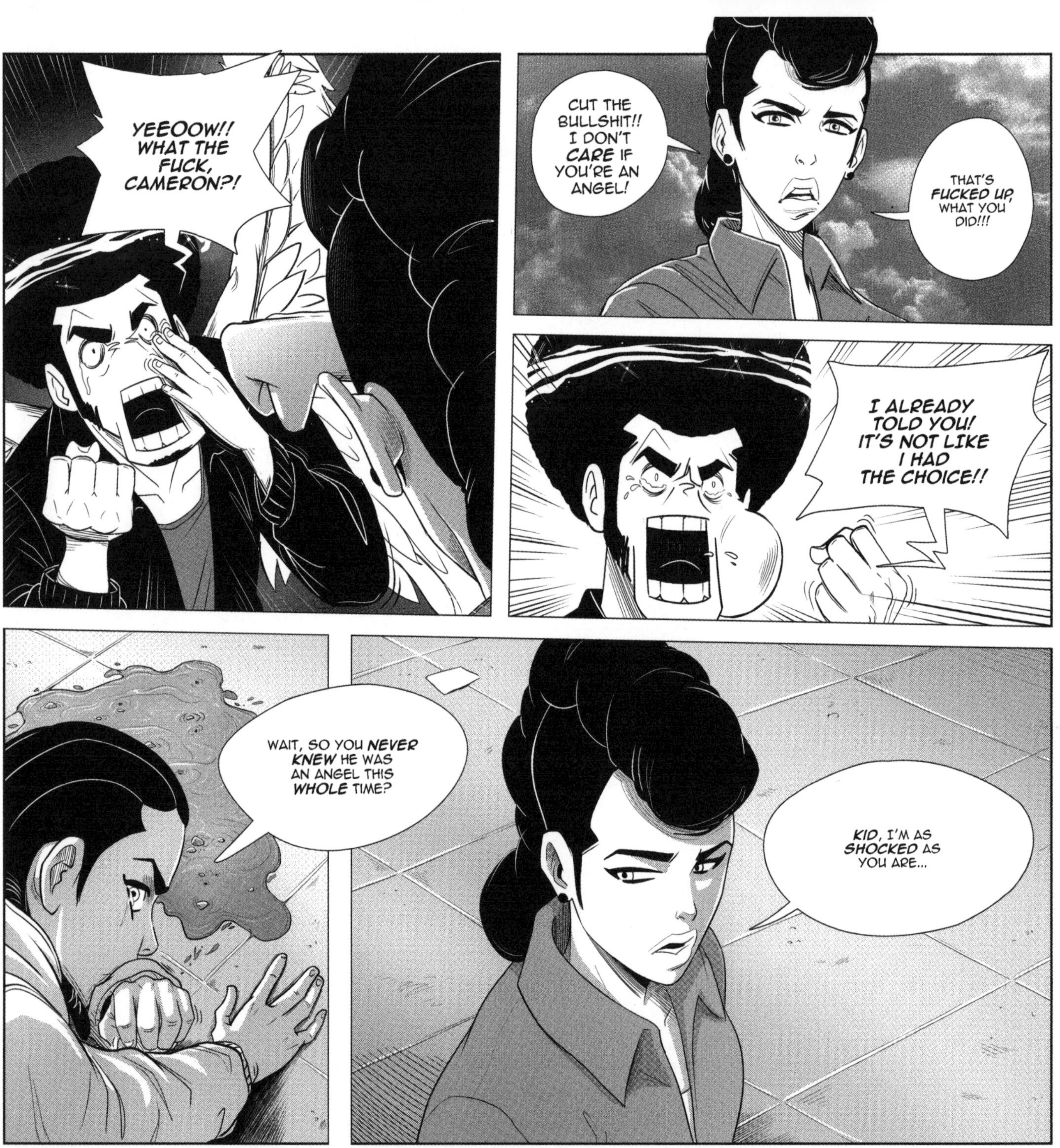
YEEOOW!! WHAT THE FUCK, CAMERON?!
CUT THE BULLSHIT!! I DON'T CARE IF YOU'RE AN ANGEL!
THAT'S FUCKED UP, WHAT YOU DID!!!
I ALREADY TOLD YOU! IT'S NOT LIKE I HAD THE CHOICE!!
WAIT, SO YOU NEVER KNEW HE WAS AN ANGEL THIS WHOLE TIME?
KID, I'M AS SHOCKED AS YOU ARE...

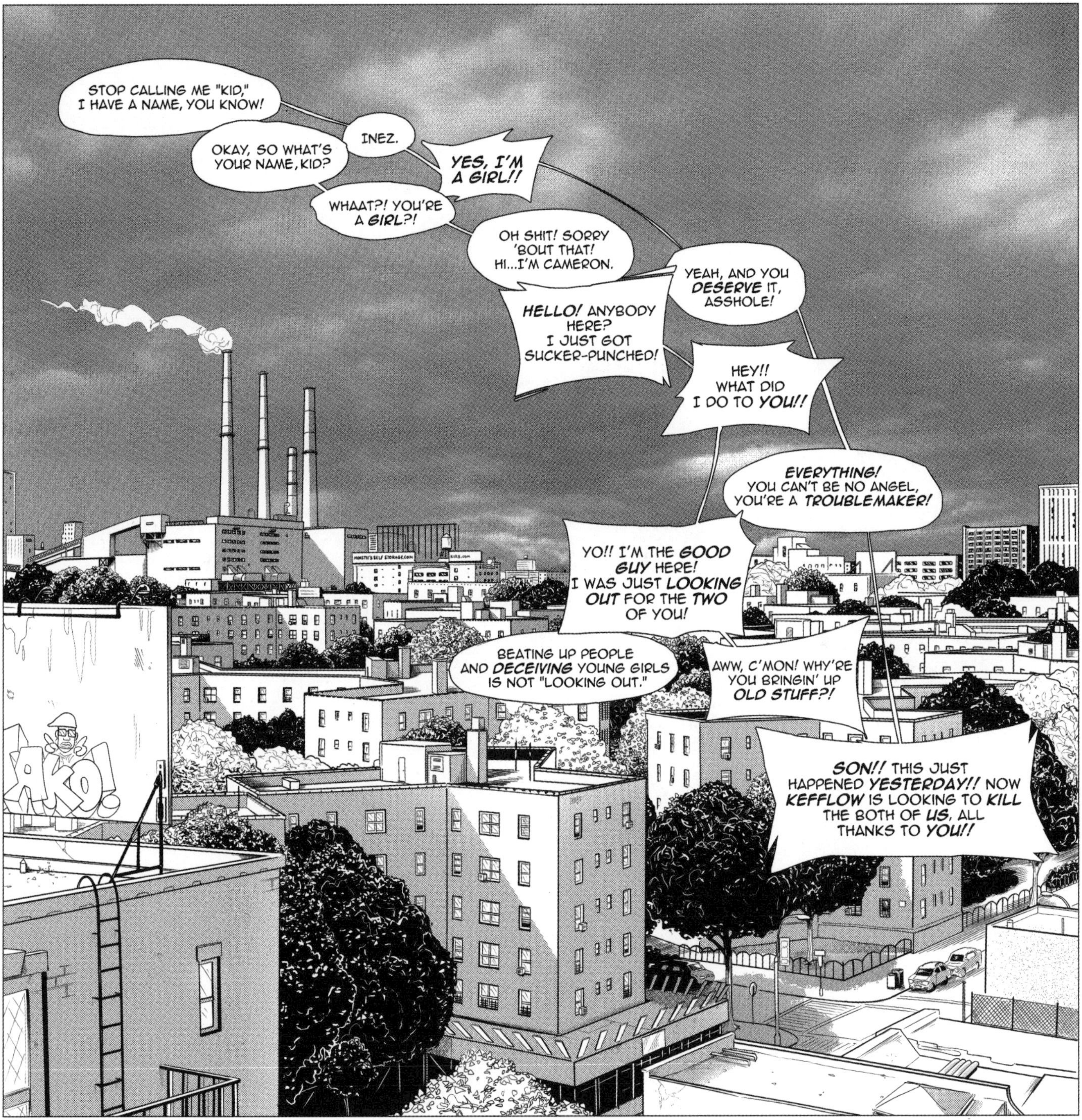
STOP CALLING ME "KID," I HAVE A NAME, YOU KNOW!
OKAY, SO WHAT'S YOUR NAME, KID?
INEZ.
WHAAT?! YOU'RE A *GIRL*?!
YES, I'M A GIRL!!
OH SHIT! SORRY 'BOUT THAT! HI...I'M CAMERON.
HELLO! ANYBODY HERE? I JUST GOT SUCKER-PUNCHED!
YEAH, AND YOU *DESERVE* IT, ASSHOLE!
HEY!! WHAT DID I DO TO *YOU!!*
EVERYTHING! YOU CAN'T BE NO ANGEL, YOU'RE A *TROUBLEMAKER!*
YO!! I'M THE *GOOD GUY* HERE! I WAS JUST *LOOKING OUT* FOR THE *TWO* OF YOU!
BEATING UP PEOPLE AND *DECEIVING* YOUNG GIRLS IS NOT "LOOKING OUT."
AWW, C'MON! WHY'RE YOU BRINGIN' UP *OLD STUFF?!*
SON!! THIS JUST HAPPENED *YESTERDAY!!* NOW *KEFFLOW* IS LOOKING TO *KILL* THE BOTH OF *US*, ALL THANKS TO *YOU!!*

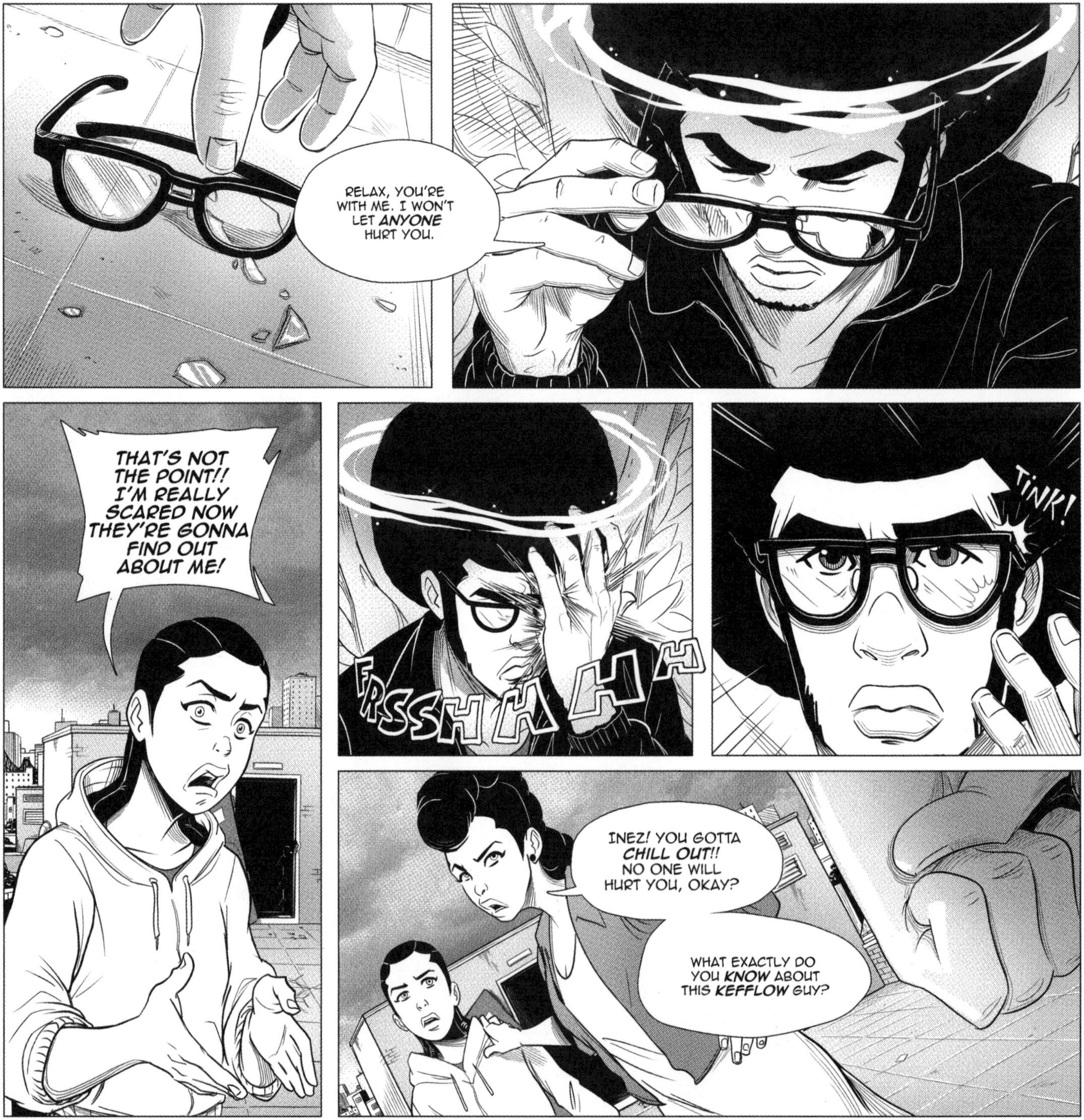

RELAX, YOU'RE WITH ME. I WON'T LET ANYONE HURT YOU.
THAT'S NOT THE POINT!! I'M REALLY SCARED NOW THEY'RE GONNA FIND OUT ABOUT ME!
FRSSHHHHH
TINK!
INEZ! YOU GOTTA CHILL OUT!! NO ONE WILL HURT YOU, OKAY?
WHAT EXACTLY DO YOU KNOW ABOUT THIS KEFFLOW GUY?

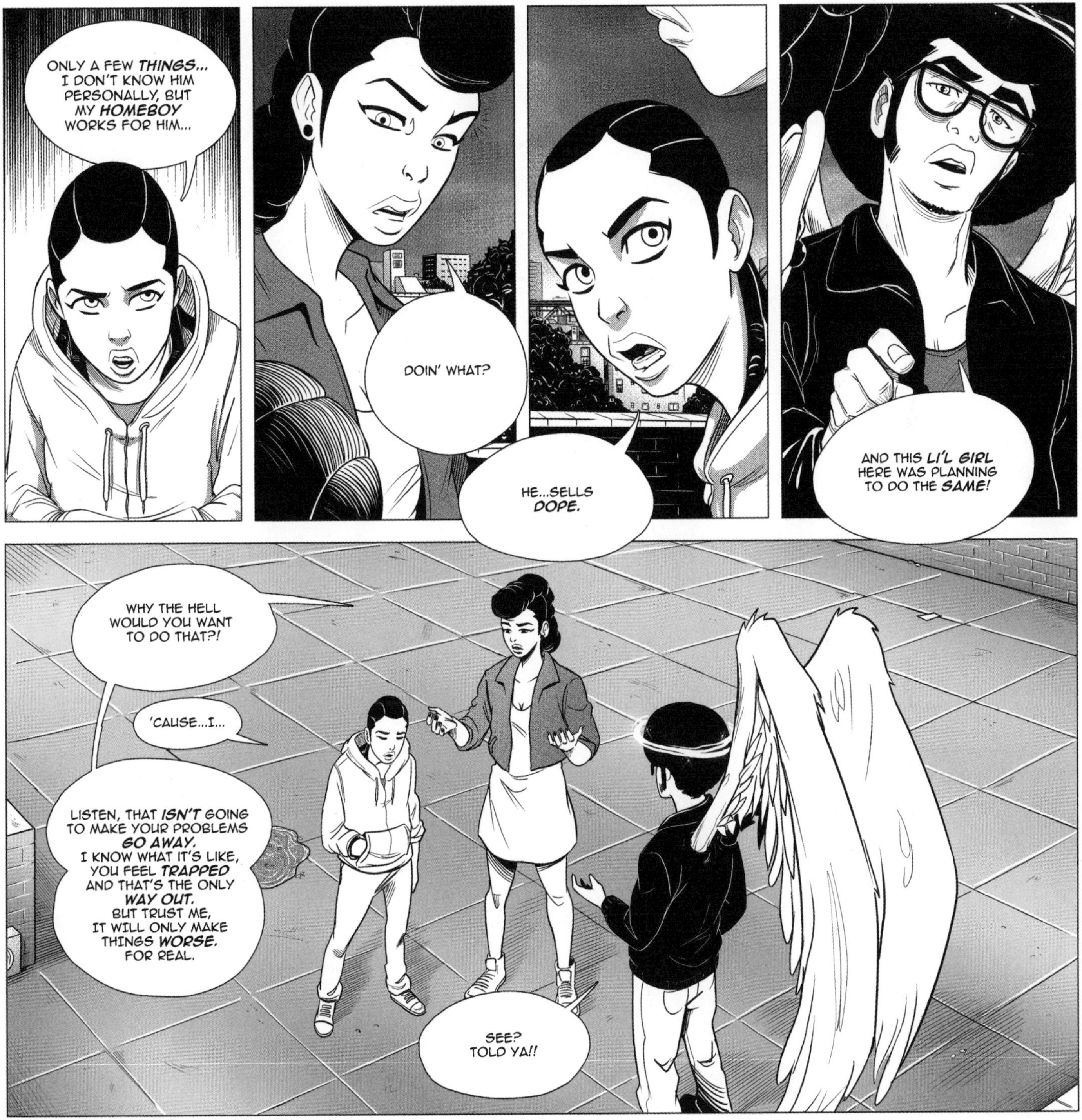

ONLY A FEW THINGS... I DON'T KNOW HIM PERSONALLY, BUT MY HOMEBOY WORKS FOR HIM...
DOIN' WHAT?
HE...SELLS DOPE.
AND THIS LI'L GIRL HERE WAS PLANNING TO DO THE SAME!
WHY THE HELL WOULD YOU WANT TO DO THAT?!
'CAUSE...I...
LISTEN, THAT ISN'T GOING TO MAKE YOUR PROBLEMS GO AWAY. I KNOW WHAT IT'S LIKE, YOU FEEL TRAPPED AND THAT'S THE ONLY WAY OUT. BUT TRUST ME, IT WILL ONLY MAKE THINGS WORSE. FOR REAL.
SEE? TOLD YA!!

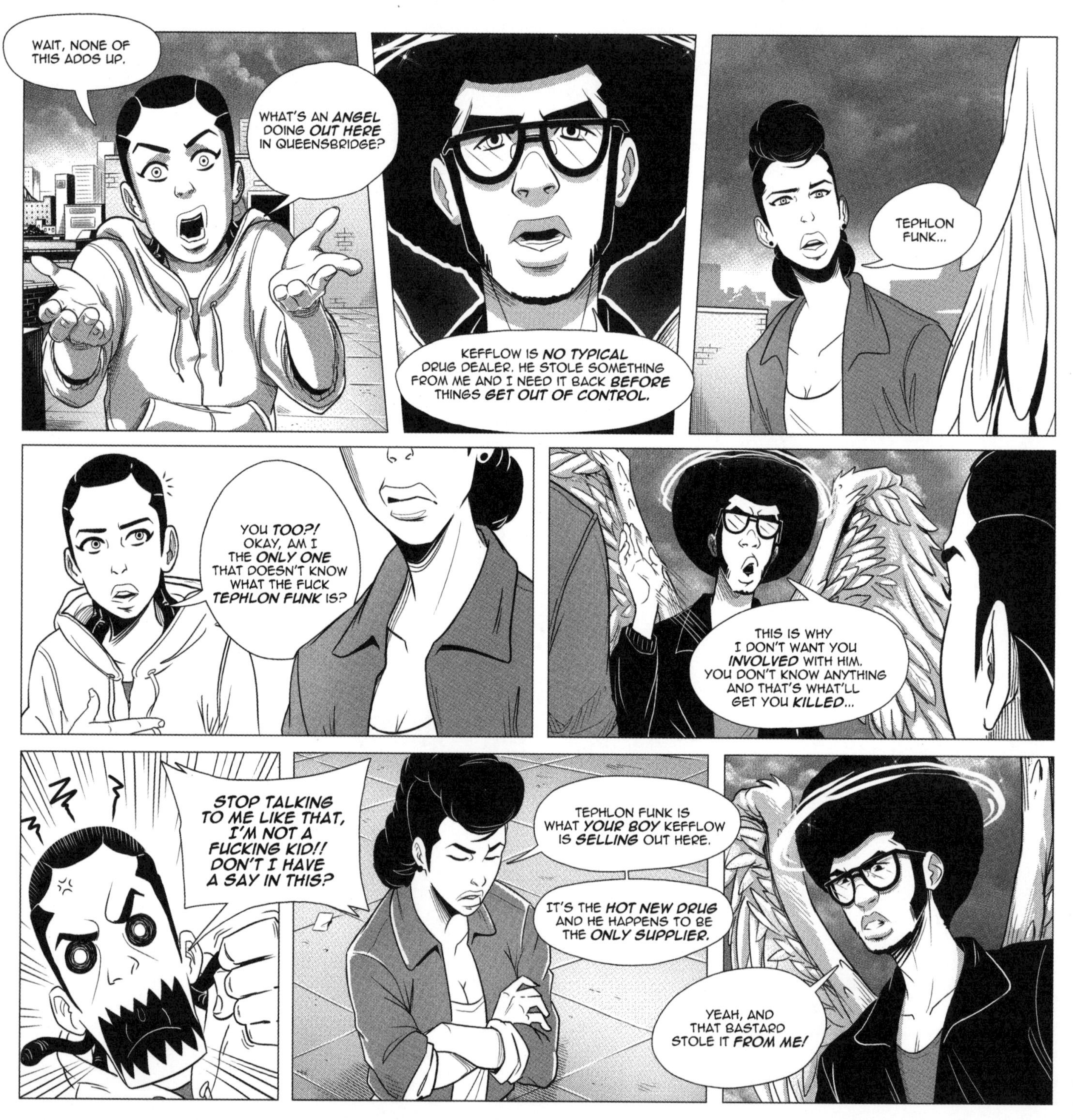
WAIT, NONE OF THIS ADDS UP.
WHAT'S AN ANGEL DOING OUT HERE IN QUEENSBRIDGE?
KEFFLOW IS NO TYPICAL DRUG DEALER. HE STOLE SOMETHING FROM ME AND I NEED IT BACK BEFORE THINGS GET OUT OF CONTROL.
TEPHLON FUNK...
YOU TOO?! OKAY, AM I THE ONLY ONE THAT DOESN'T KNOW WHAT THE FUCK TEPHLON FUNK IS?
THIS IS WHY I DON'T WANT YOU INVOLVED WITH HIM. YOU DON'T KNOW ANYTHING AND THAT'S WHAT'LL GET YOU KILLED...
STOP TALKING TO ME LIKE THAT, I'M NOT A FUCKING KID!! DON'T I HAVE A SAY IN THIS?
TEPHLON FUNK IS WHAT YOUR BOY KEFFLOW IS SELLING OUT HERE.
IT'S THE HOT NEW DRUG AND HE HAPPENS TO BE THE ONLY SUPPLIER.
YEAH, AND THAT BASTARD STOLE IT FROM ME!

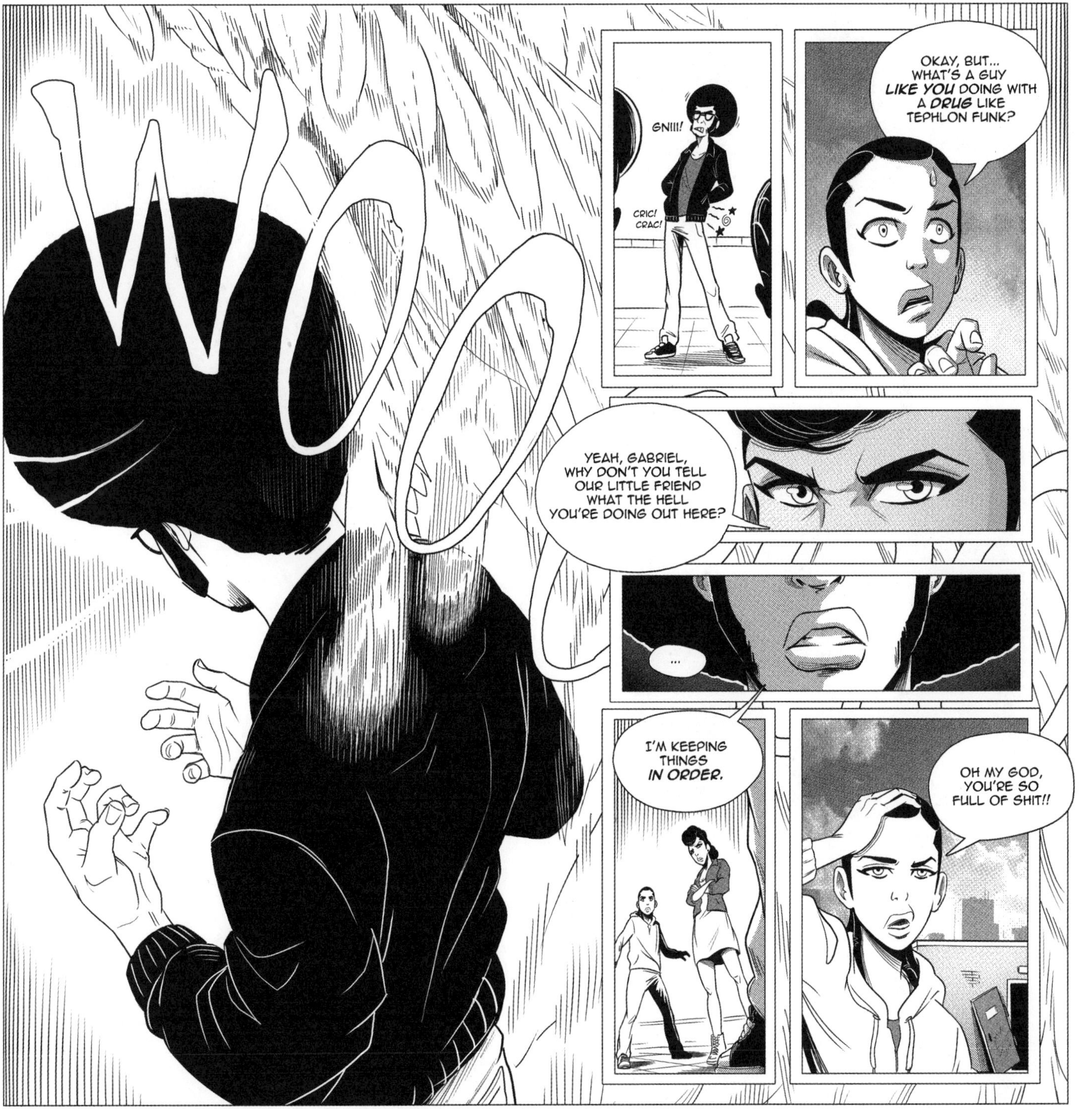
WOOO
GNIII!
CRIC! CRAC!
OKAY, BUT... WHAT'S A GUY LIKE YOU DOING WITH A DRUG LIKE TEPHLON FUNK?
YEAH, GABRIEL, WHY DON'T YOU TELL OUR LITTLE FRIEND WHAT THE HELL YOU'RE DOING OUT HERE?
...
I'M KEEPING THINGS IN ORDER.
OH MY GOD, YOU'RE SO FULL OF SHIT!!

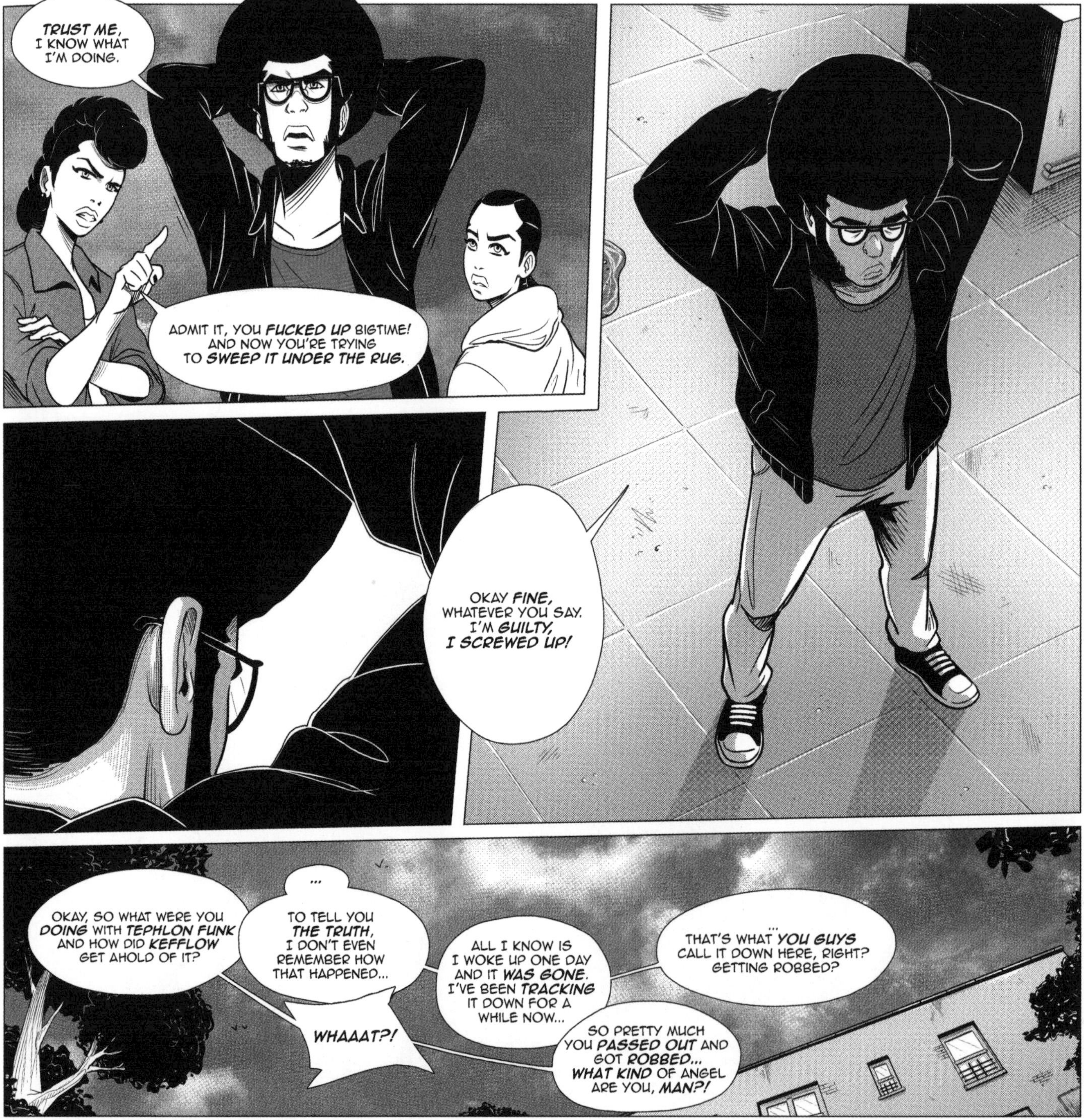
TRUST ME, I KNOW WHAT I'M DOING.
ADMIT IT, YOU FUCKED UP BIGTIME! AND NOW YOU'RE TRYING TO SWEEP IT UNDER THE RUG.
OKAY FINE, WHATEVER YOU SAY. I'M GUILTY, I SCREWED UP!
OKAY, SO WHAT WERE YOU DOING WITH TEPHLON FUNK AND HOW DID KEFFLOW GET AHOLD OF IT?
...
TO TELL YOU THE TRUTH, I DON'T EVEN REMEMBER HOW THAT HAPPENED...
WHAAAT?!
ALL I KNOW IS I WOKE UP ONE DAY AND IT WAS GONE. I'VE BEEN TRACKING IT DOWN FOR A WHILE NOW...
... THAT'S WHAT YOU GUYS CALL IT DOWN HERE, RIGHT? GETTING ROBBED?
SO PRETTY MUCH YOU PASSED OUT AND GOT ROBBED... WHAT KIND OF ANGEL ARE YOU, MAN?!

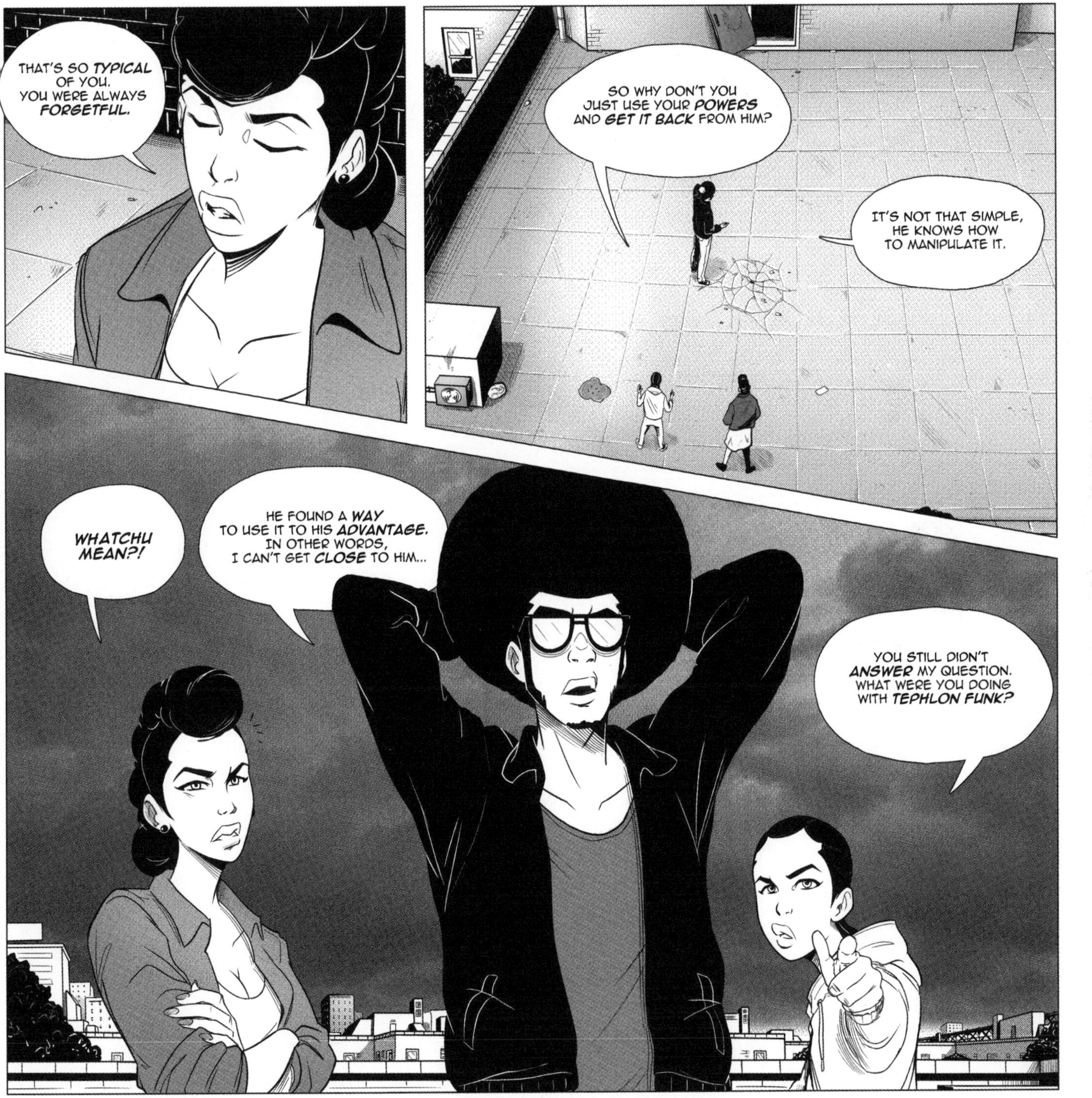
THAT'S SO TYPICAL OF YOU. YOU WERE ALWAYS FORGETFUL.
SO WHY DON'T YOU JUST USE YOUR POWERS AND GET IT BACK FROM HIM?
IT'S NOT THAT SIMPLE, HE KNOWS HOW TO MANIPULATE IT.
WHATCHU MEAN?!
HE FOUND A WAY TO USE IT TO HIS ADVANTAGE. IN OTHER WORDS, I CAN'T GET CLOSE TO HIM...
YOU STILL DIDN'T ANSWER MY QUESTION. WHAT WERE YOU DOING WITH TEPHLON FUNK?

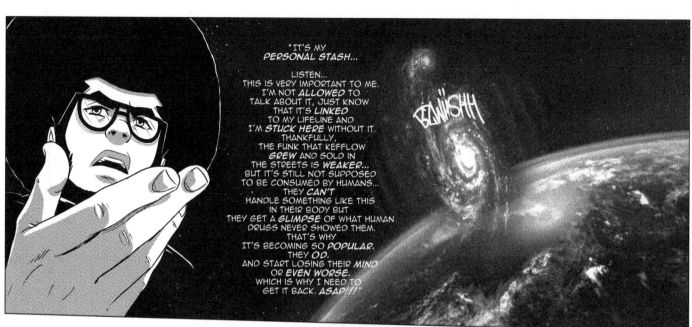

"IT'S MY *PERSONAL STASH...*

LISTEN...
THIS IS VERY IMPORTANT TO ME.
I'M NOT *ALLOWED* TO
TALK ABOUT IT, JUST KNOW
THAT IT'S *LINKED*
TO MY LIFELINE AND
I'M *STUCK HERE* WITHOUT IT.
THANKFULLY,
THE FUNK THAT KEFFLOW
GREW AND SOLD IN
THE STREETS IS *WEAKER...*
BUT IT'S STILL NOT SUPPOSED
TO BE CONSUMED BY HUMANS...
THEY *CAN'T*
HANDLE SOMETHING LIKE THIS
IN THEIR BODY BUT
THEY GET A *GLIMPSE* OF WHAT HUMAN
DRUGS NEVER SHOWED THEM.
THAT'S WHY
IT'S BECOMING SO *POPULAR.*
THEY *OD.*
AND START LOSING THEIR *MIND*
OR *EVEN WORSE.*
WHICH IS WHY I NEED TO
GET IT BACK. *ASAP!!!*"

SZWÜSHH

NOW I SEE...

LOOKS LIKE YOU ARE GONNA NEED *HELP.*

I *KNOW* WHAT I'M DOING...

YEAH RIGHT, YOU'RE A HOT MESS. YOU'RE *DEFINITELY* GONNA NEED OUR HELP. SO WHAT NOW?

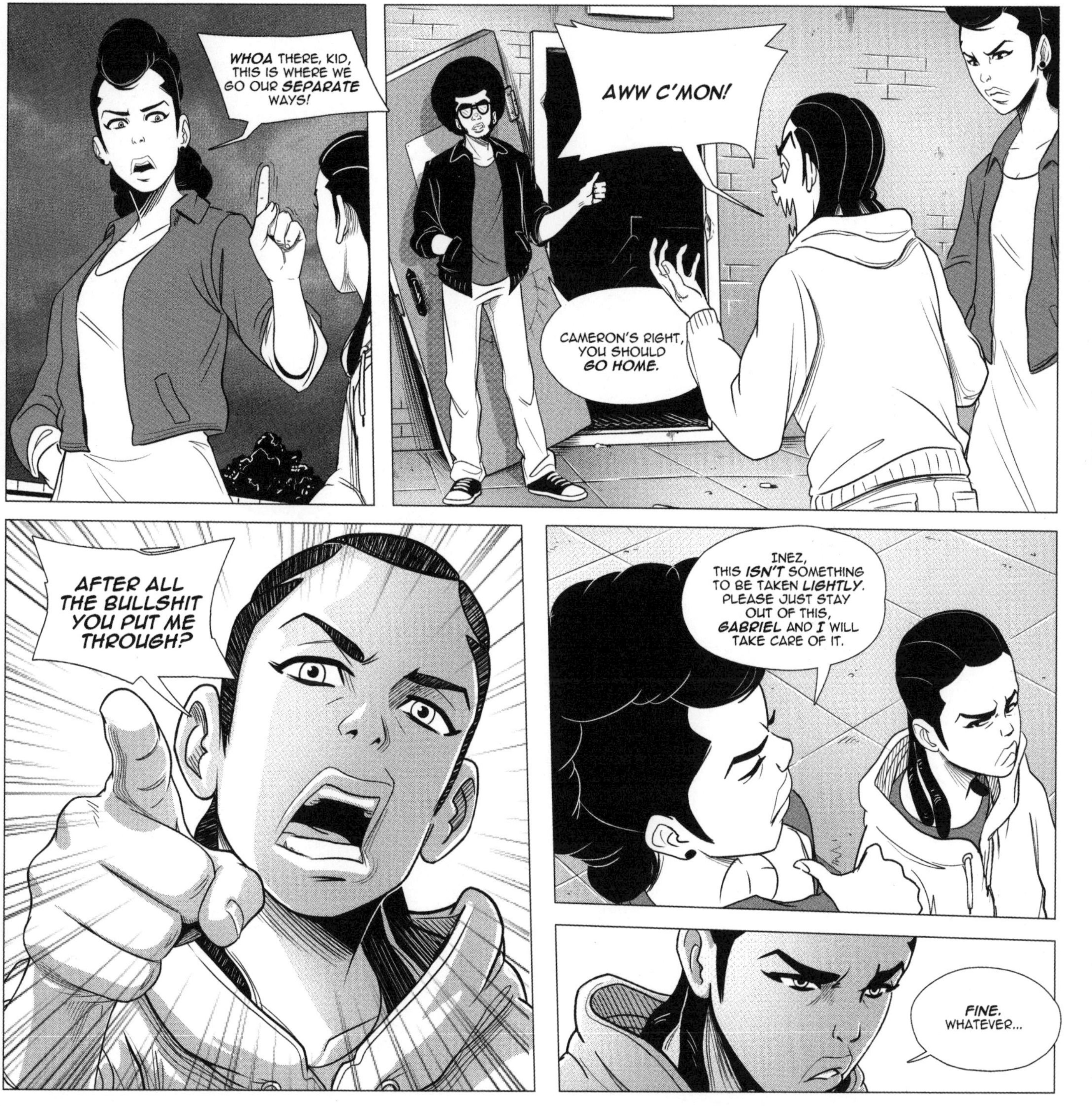

WHOA THERE, KID, THIS IS WHERE WE GO OUR SEPARATE WAYS!
AWW C'MON!
CAMERON'S RIGHT, YOU SHOULD GO HOME.
AFTER ALL THE BULLSHIT YOU PUT ME THROUGH?
INEZ, THIS ISN'T SOMETHING TO BE TAKEN LIGHTLY. PLEASE JUST STAY OUT OF THIS, GABRIEL AND I WILL TAKE CARE OF IT.
FINE. WHATEVER...

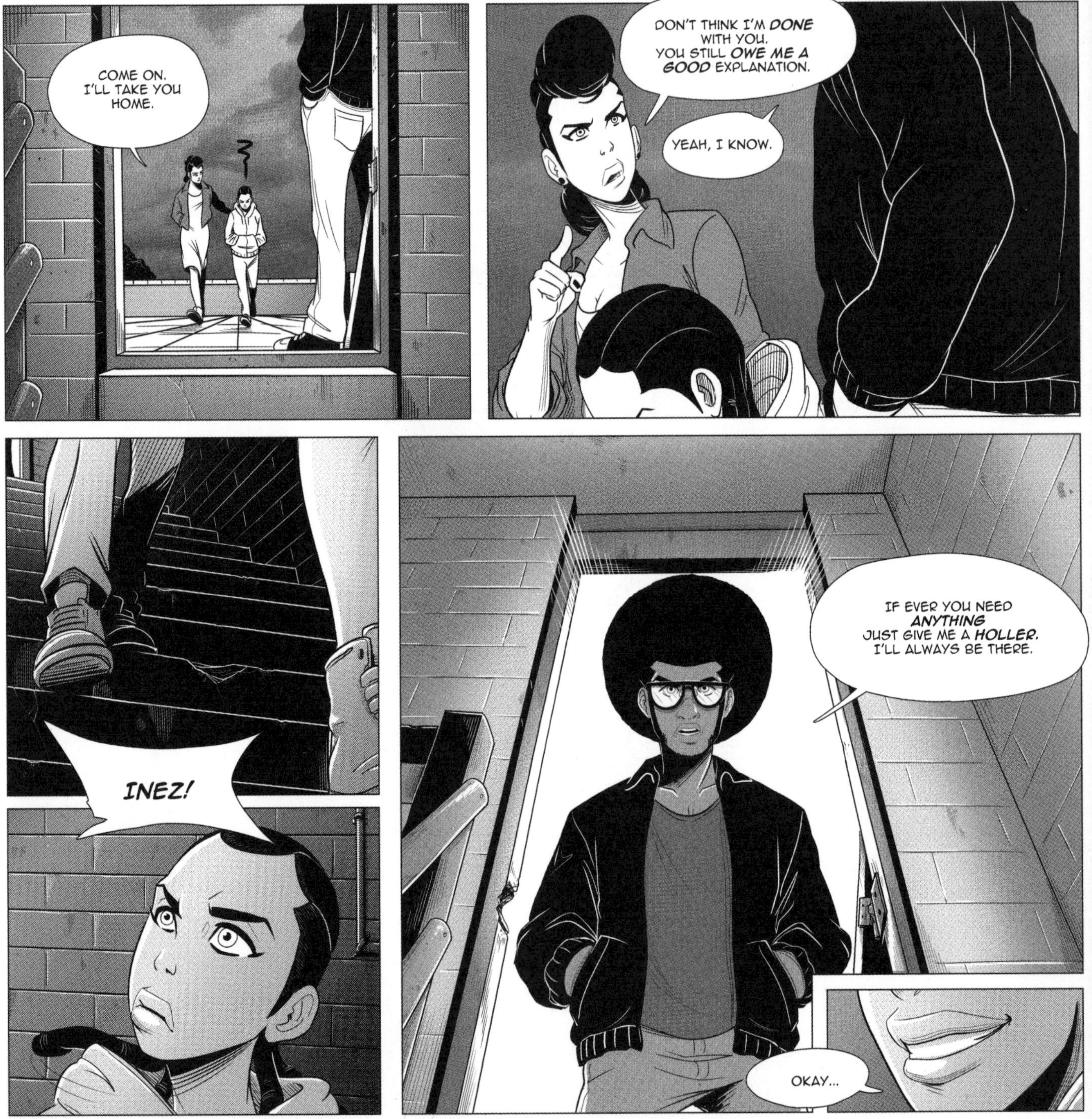
COME ON. I'LL TAKE YOU HOME.
DON'T THINK I'M DONE WITH YOU. YOU STILL OWE ME A GOOD EXPLANATION.
YEAH, I KNOW.
INEZ!
IF EVER YOU NEED ANYTHING JUST GIVE ME A HOLLER. I'LL ALWAYS BE THERE.
OKAY...

TEPHLON FUNK

NYC

IS FOR THE CHILDREN

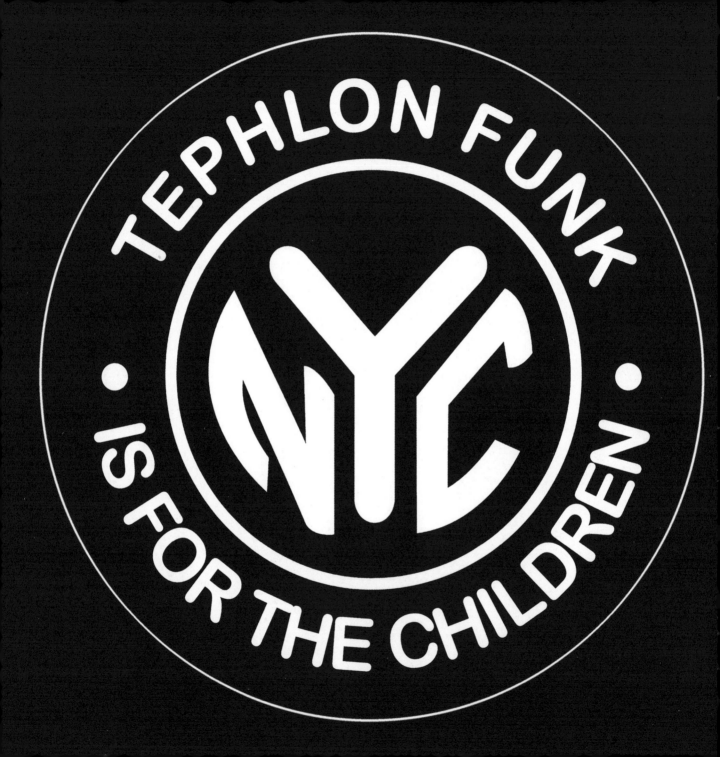

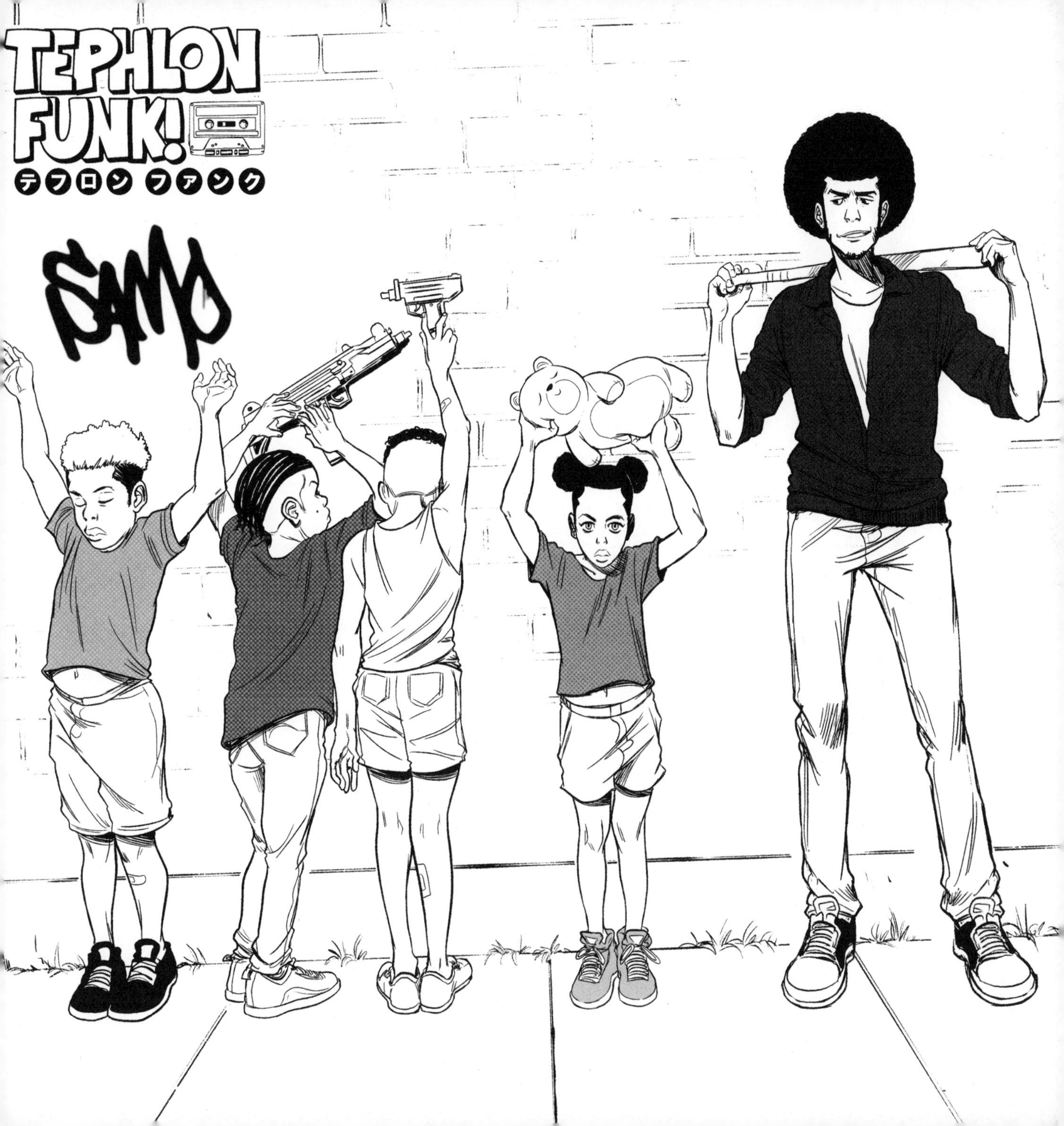
TEPHLON FUNK!
テフロン ファンク
SAMO

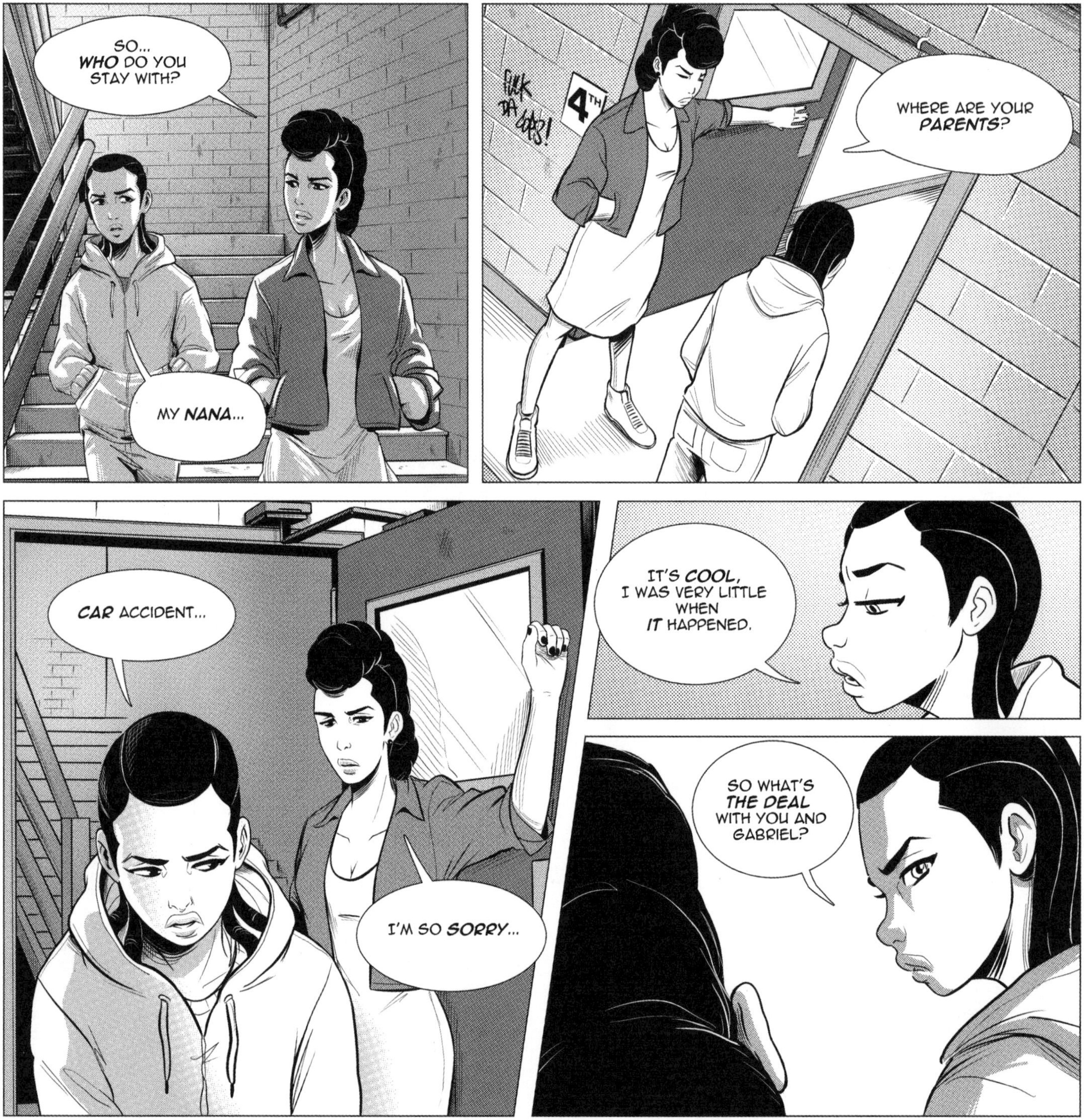
SO... **WHO** DO YOU STAY WITH?
MY **NANA**...
FUCK DA COPS!
4TH
WHERE ARE YOUR **PARENTS**?
CAR ACCIDENT...
I'M SO **SORRY**...
IT'S **COOL**, I WAS VERY LITTLE WHEN **IT** HAPPENED.
SO WHAT'S **THE DEAL** WITH YOU AND GABRIEL?

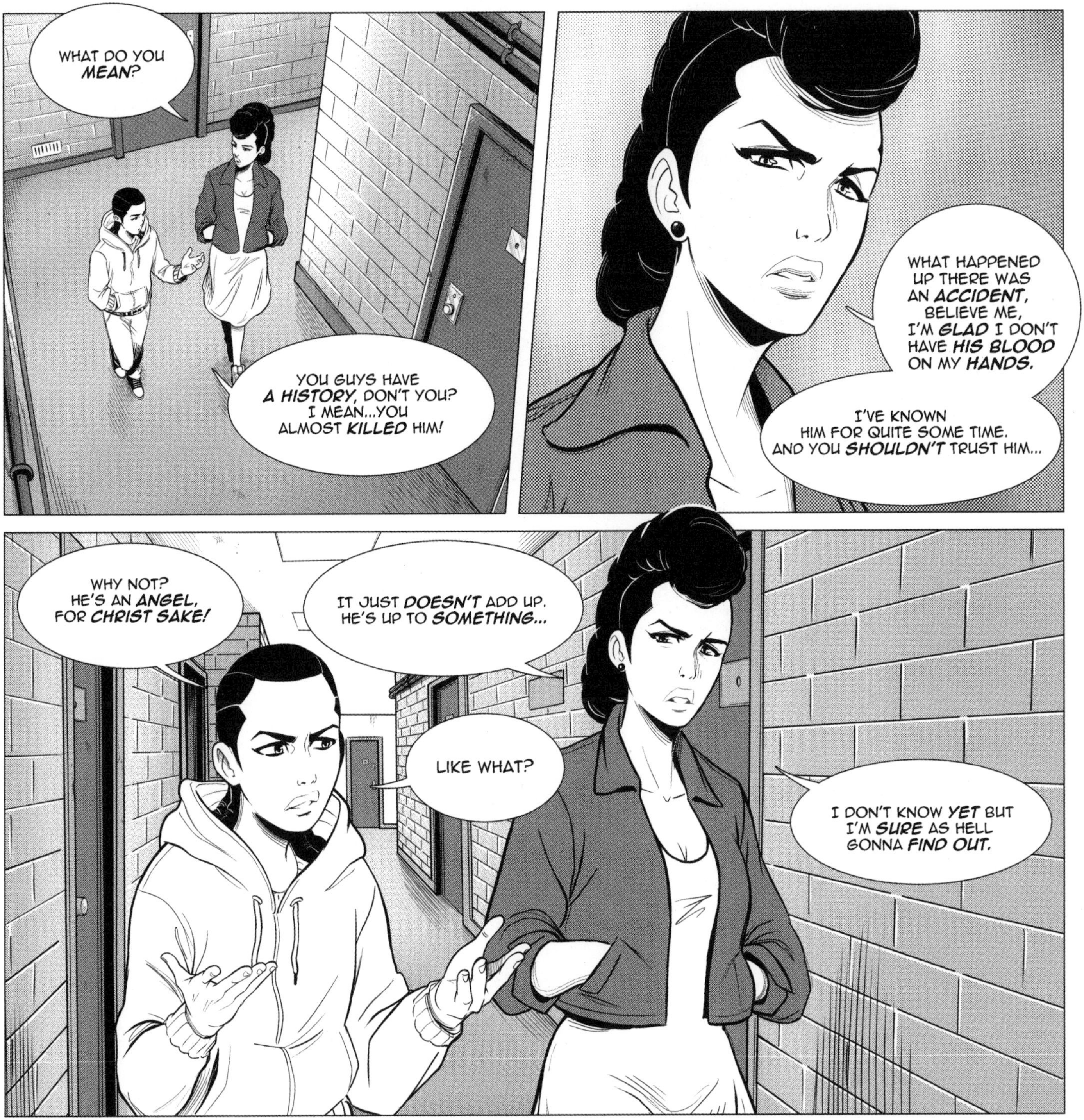
WHAT DO YOU MEAN?
YOU GUYS HAVE A HISTORY, DON'T YOU? I MEAN...YOU ALMOST KILLED HIM!
WHAT HAPPENED UP THERE WAS AN ACCIDENT, BELIEVE ME, I'M GLAD I DON'T HAVE HIS BLOOD ON MY HANDS.
I'VE KNOWN HIM FOR QUITE SOME TIME. AND YOU SHOULDN'T TRUST HIM...
WHY NOT? HE'S AN ANGEL, FOR CHRIST SAKE!
IT JUST DOESN'T ADD UP. HE'S UP TO SOMETHING...
LIKE WHAT?
I DON'T KNOW YET BUT I'M SURE AS HELL GONNA FIND OUT.

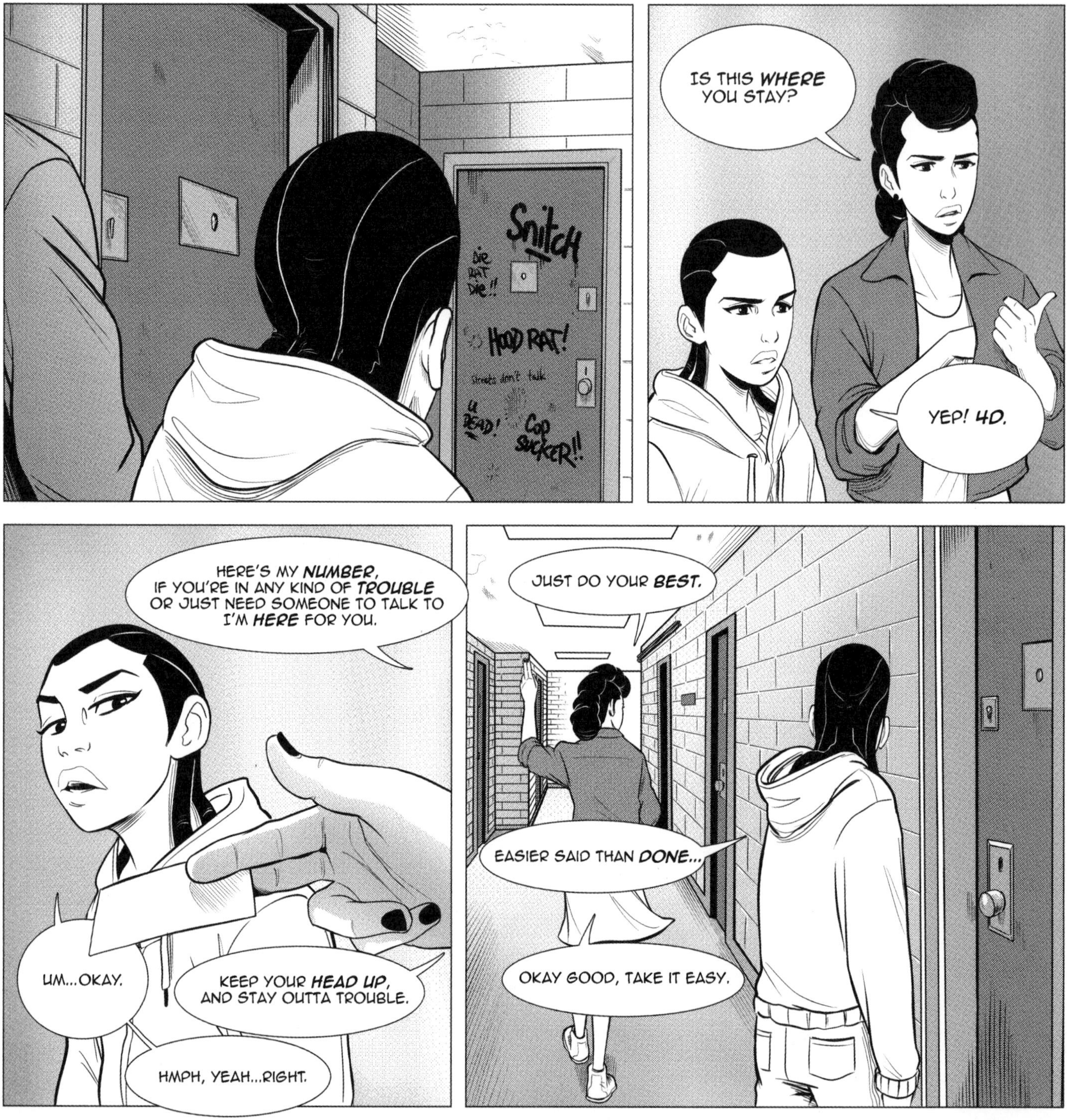
Snitch
Die RAT Die!!
HOOD RAT!
streets don't talk
U DEAD!
COP SUCKER!!
IS THIS WHERE YOU STAY?
YEP! 4D.
HERE'S MY NUMBER, IF YOU'RE IN ANY KIND OF TROUBLE OR JUST NEED SOMEONE TO TALK TO I'M HERE FOR YOU.
UM...OKAY.
KEEP YOUR HEAD UP, AND STAY OUTTA TROUBLE.
HMPH, YEAH...RIGHT.
JUST DO YOUR BEST.
EASIER SAID THAN DONE...
OKAY GOOD, TAKE IT EASY.

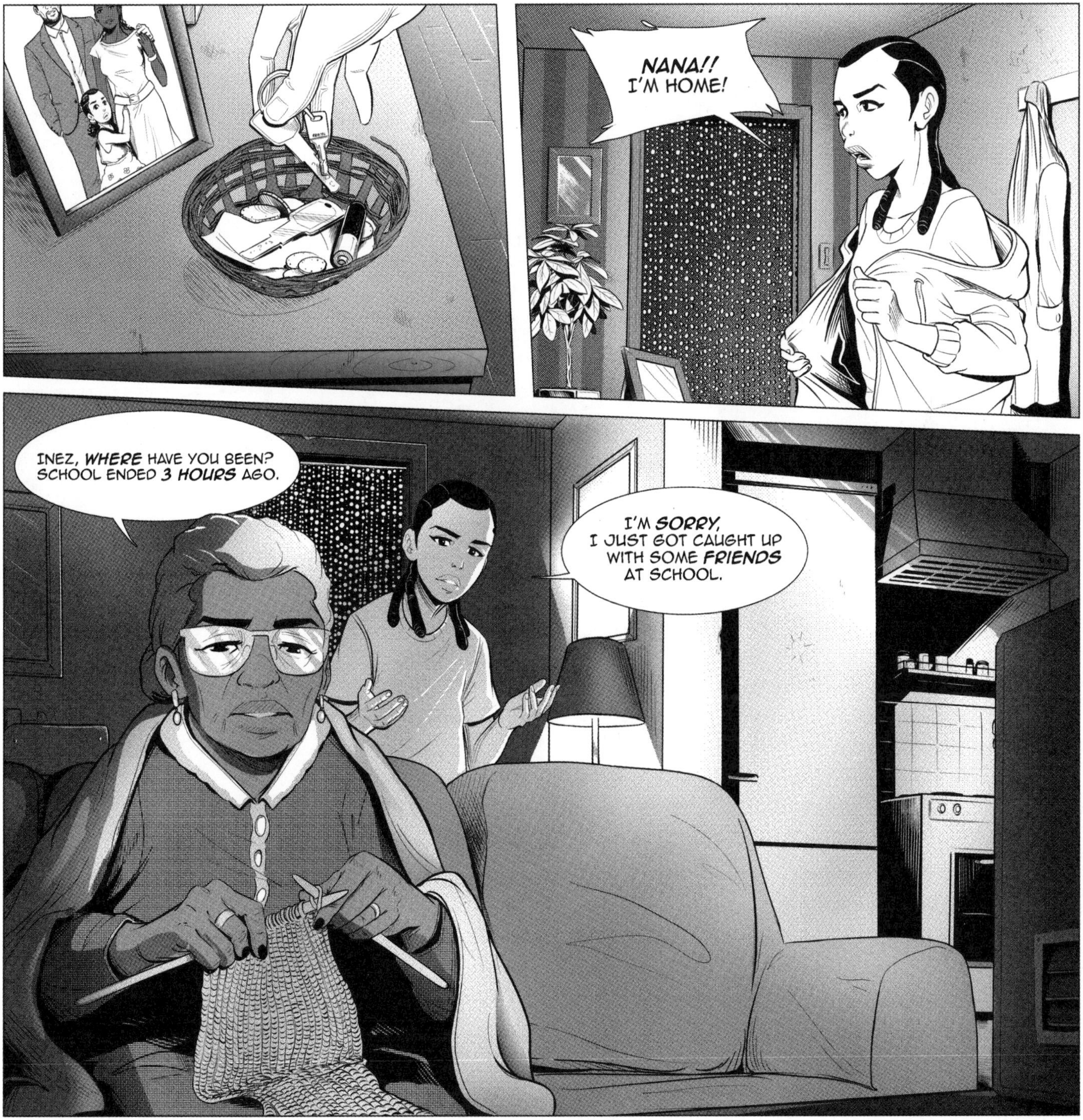
NANA!! I'M HOME!
INEZ, WHERE HAVE YOU BEEN? SCHOOL ENDED 3 HOURS AGO.
I'M SORRY, I JUST GOT CAUGHT UP WITH SOME FRIENDS AT SCHOOL.

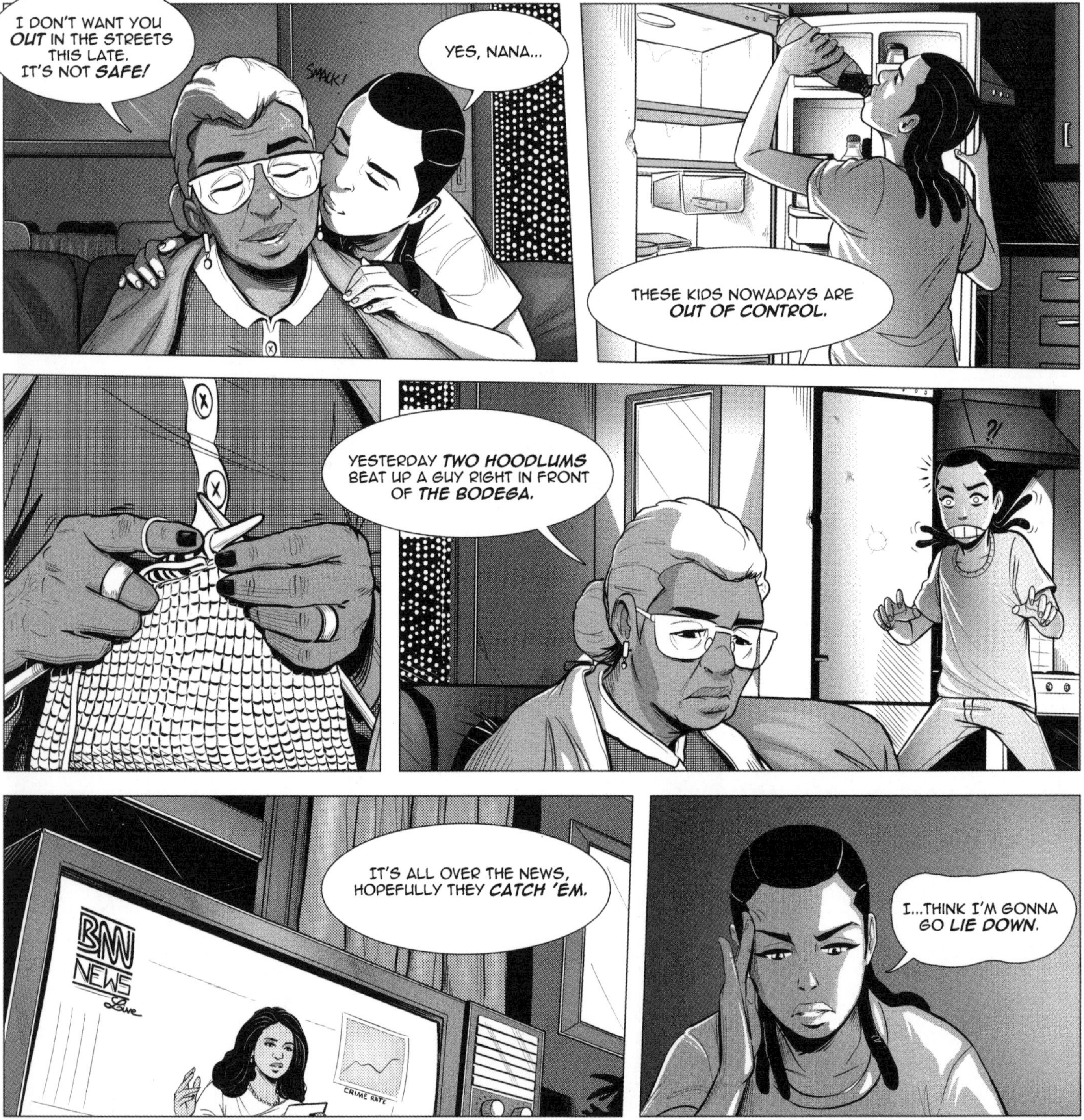
I DON'T WANT YOU OUT IN THE STREETS THIS LATE. IT'S NOT SAFE!
SMACK!
YES, NANA...
THESE KIDS NOWADAYS ARE OUT OF CONTROL.
YESTERDAY TWO HOODLUMS BEAT UP A GUY RIGHT IN FRONT OF THE BODEGA.
?!
IT'S ALL OVER THE NEWS, HOPEFULLY THEY CATCH 'EM.
BNN NEWS Live
CRIME RATE
I...THINK I'M GONNA GO LIE DOWN.

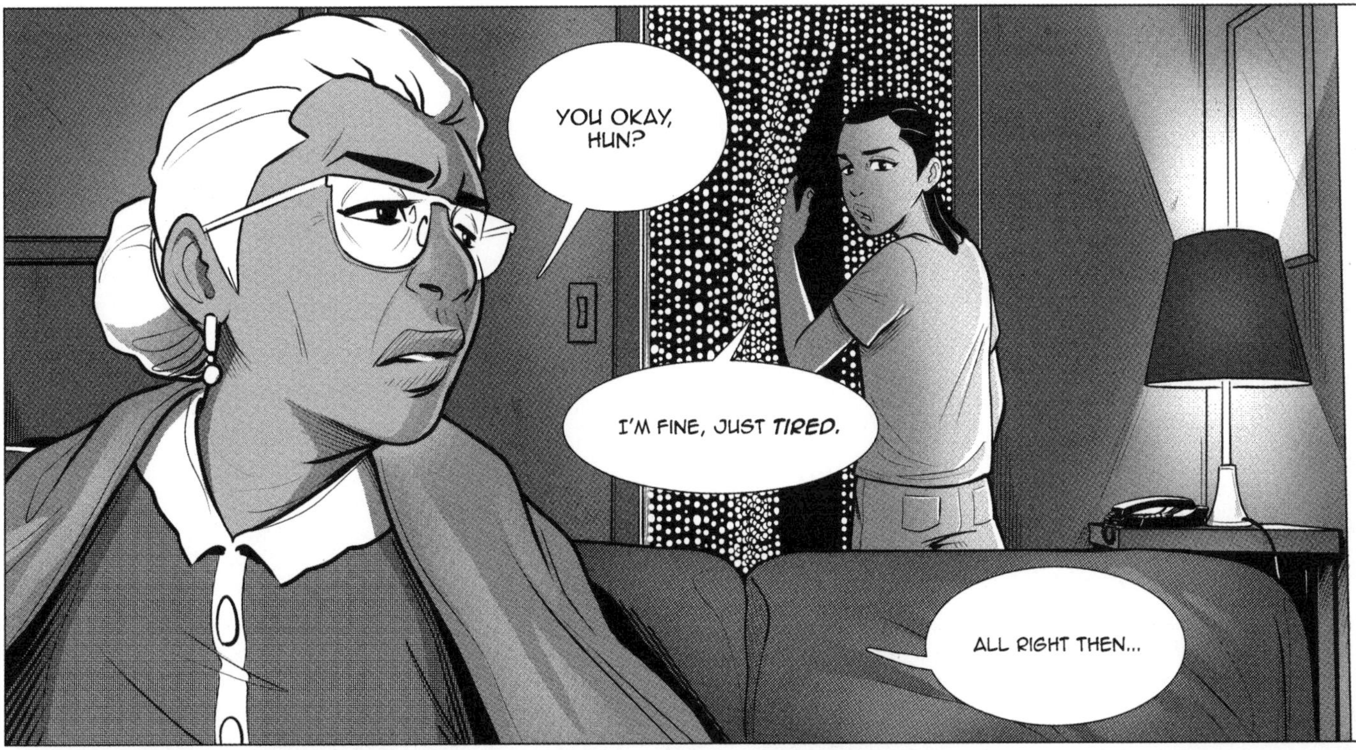
YOU OKAY, HUN?
I'M FINE, JUST *TIRED.*
ALL RIGHT THEN...

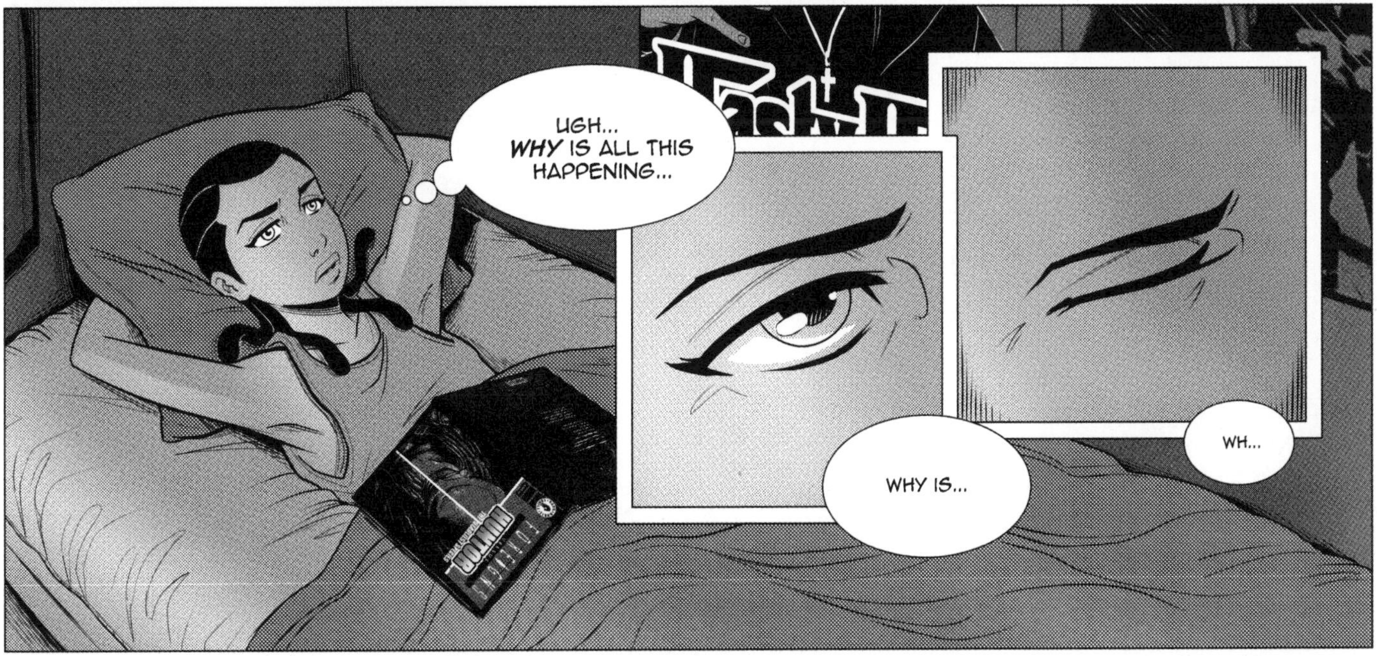
UGH... *WHY* IS ALL THIS HAPPENING...
WHY IS...
WH...

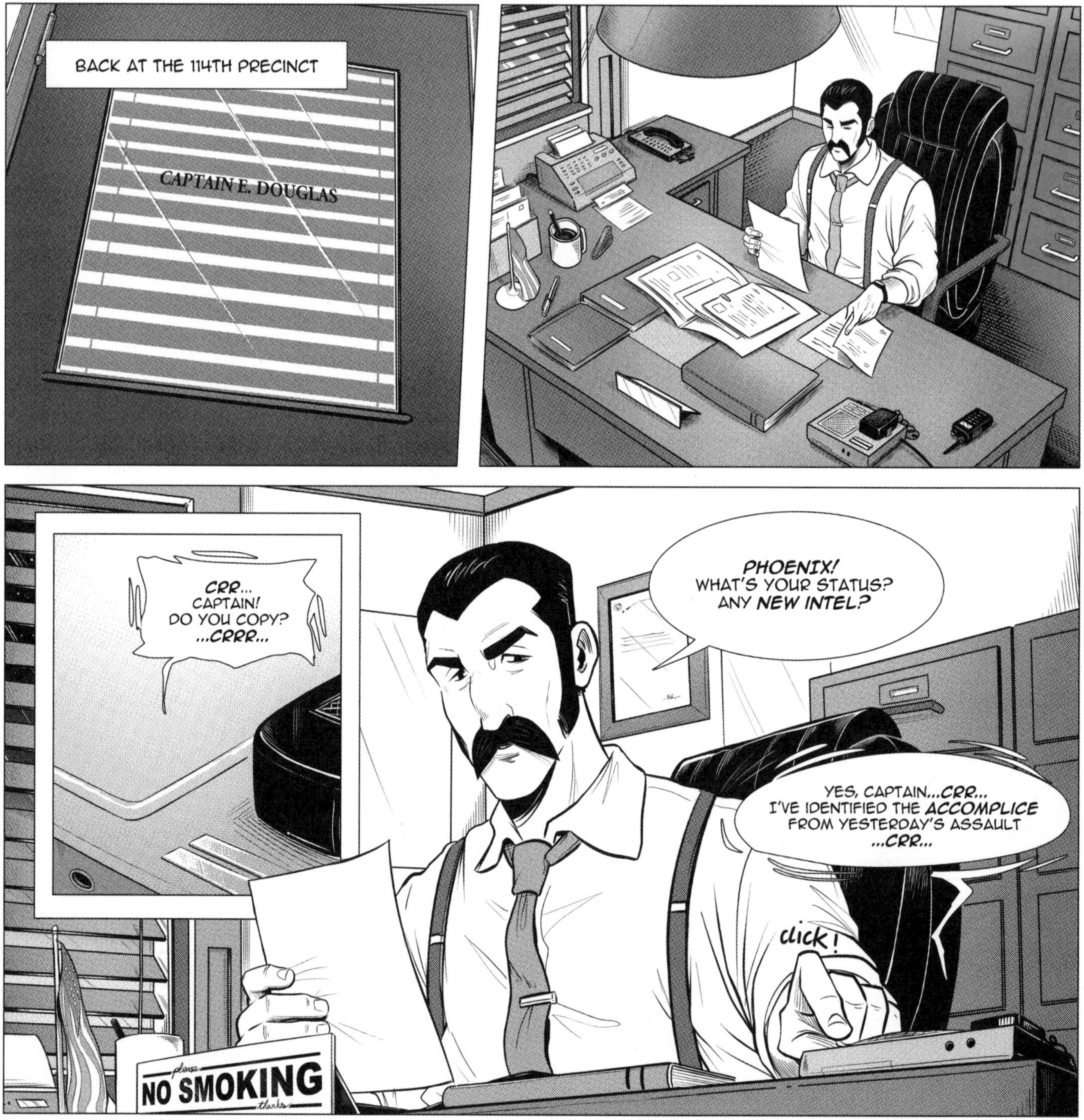
BACK AT THE 114TH PRECINCT
CAPTAIN E. DOUGLAS
CRR... CAPTAIN! DO YOU COPY? ...CRRR...
PHOENIX! WHAT'S YOUR STATUS? ANY NEW INTEL?
YES, CAPTAIN... CRR... I'VE IDENTIFIED THE ACCOMPLICE FROM YESTERDAY'S ASSAULT ...CRR...
click!
please NO SMOKING thanks

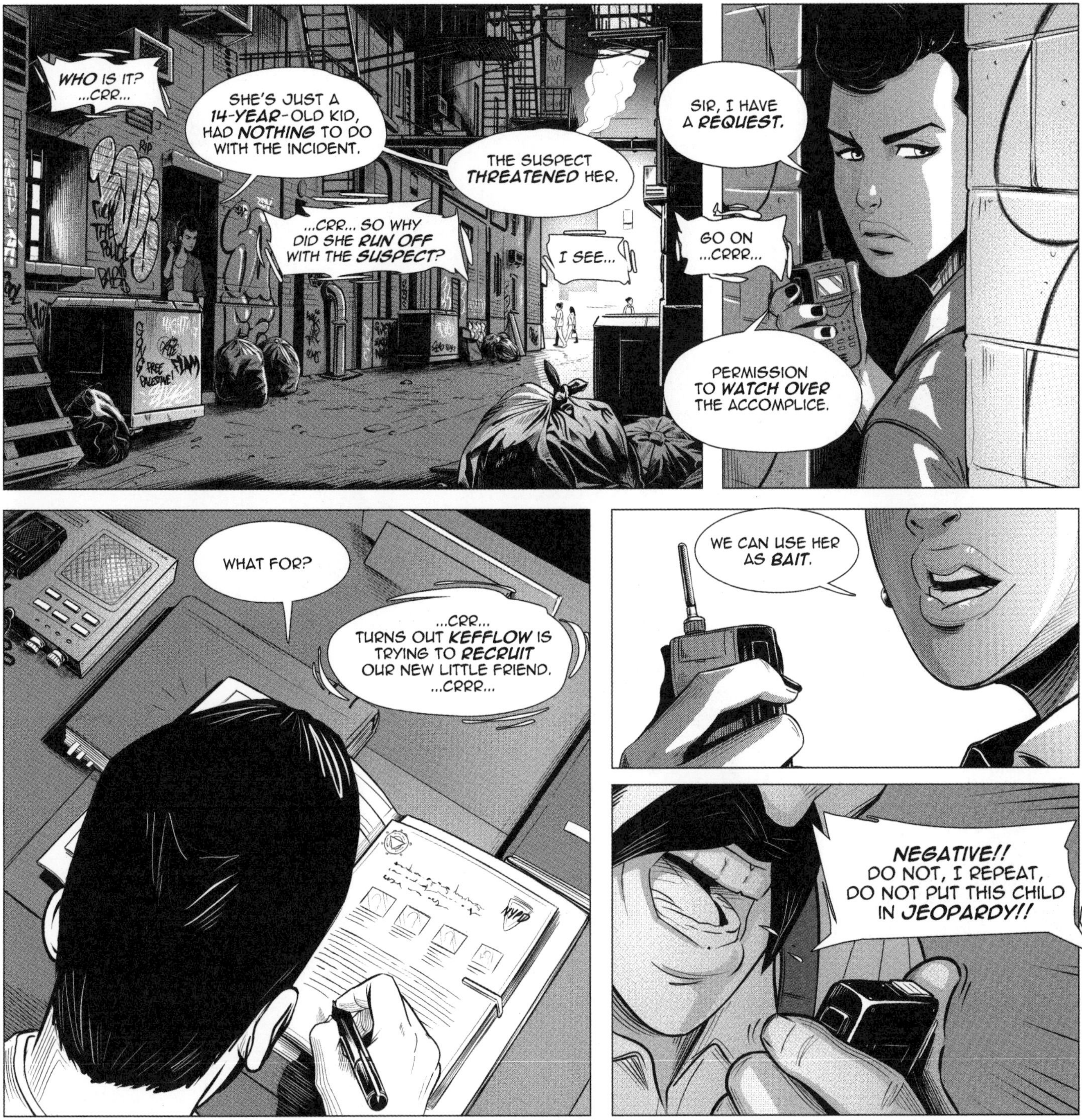
WHO IS IT? ...CRR...
SHE'S JUST A 14-YEAR-OLD KID, HAD NOTHING TO DO WITH THE INCIDENT.
THE SUSPECT THREATENED HER.
...CRR... SO WHY DID SHE RUN OFF WITH THE SUSPECT?
I SEE...
SIR, I HAVE A REQUEST.
GO ON ...CRRR...
PERMISSION TO WATCH OVER THE ACCOMPLICE.
WHAT FOR?
...CRR... TURNS OUT KEFFLOW IS TRYING TO RECRUIT OUR NEW LITTLE FRIEND. ...CRRR...
WE CAN USE HER AS BAIT.
NEGATIVE!! DO NOT, I REPEAT, DO NOT PUT THIS CHILD IN JEOPARDY!!

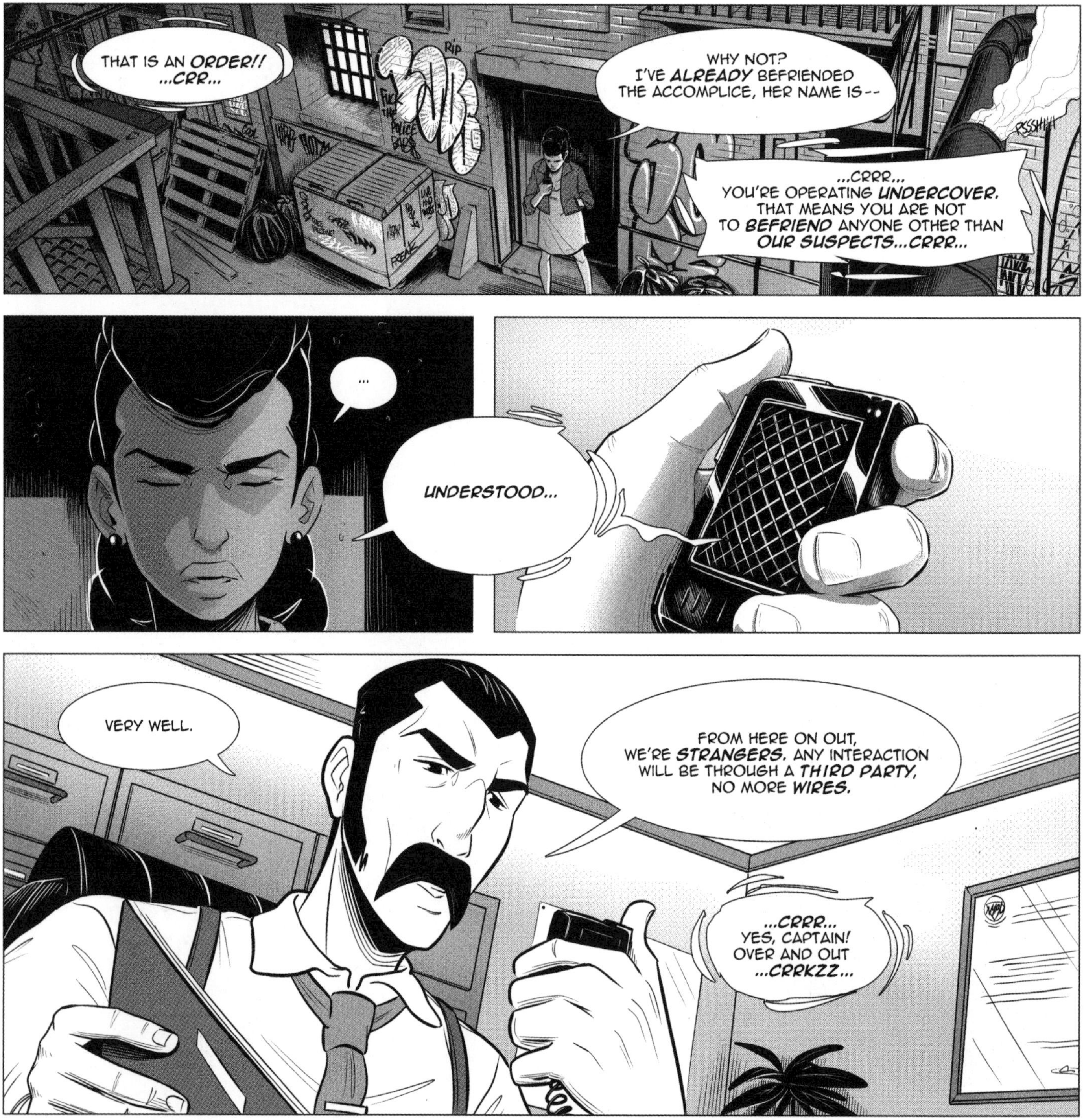

THAT IS AN *ORDER!!* ...*CRR*...
WHY NOT? I'VE *ALREADY* BEFRIENDED THE ACCOMPLICE, HER NAME IS--
...CRRR... YOU'RE OPERATING *UNDERCOVER.* THAT MEANS YOU ARE NOT TO *BEFRIEND* ANYONE OTHER THAN *OUR SUSPECTS...CRRR...*
...
UNDERSTOOD...
VERY WELL.
FROM HERE ON OUT, WE'RE *STRANGERS.* ANY INTERACTION WILL BE THROUGH A *THIRD PARTY,* NO MORE *WIRES.*
...CRRR... YES, CAPTAIN! OVER AND OUT *...CRRKZZ...*

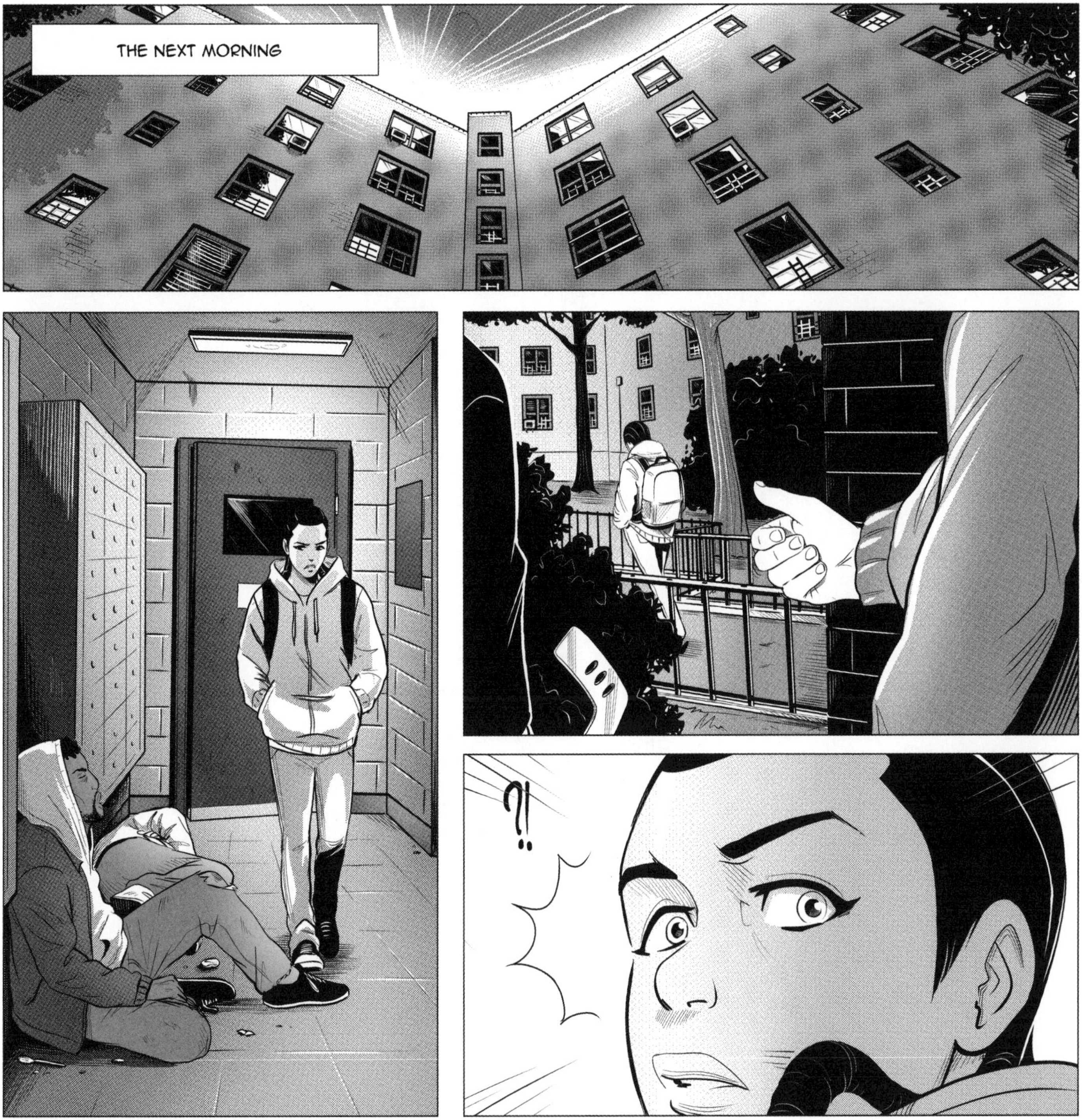
THE NEXT MORNING
?!

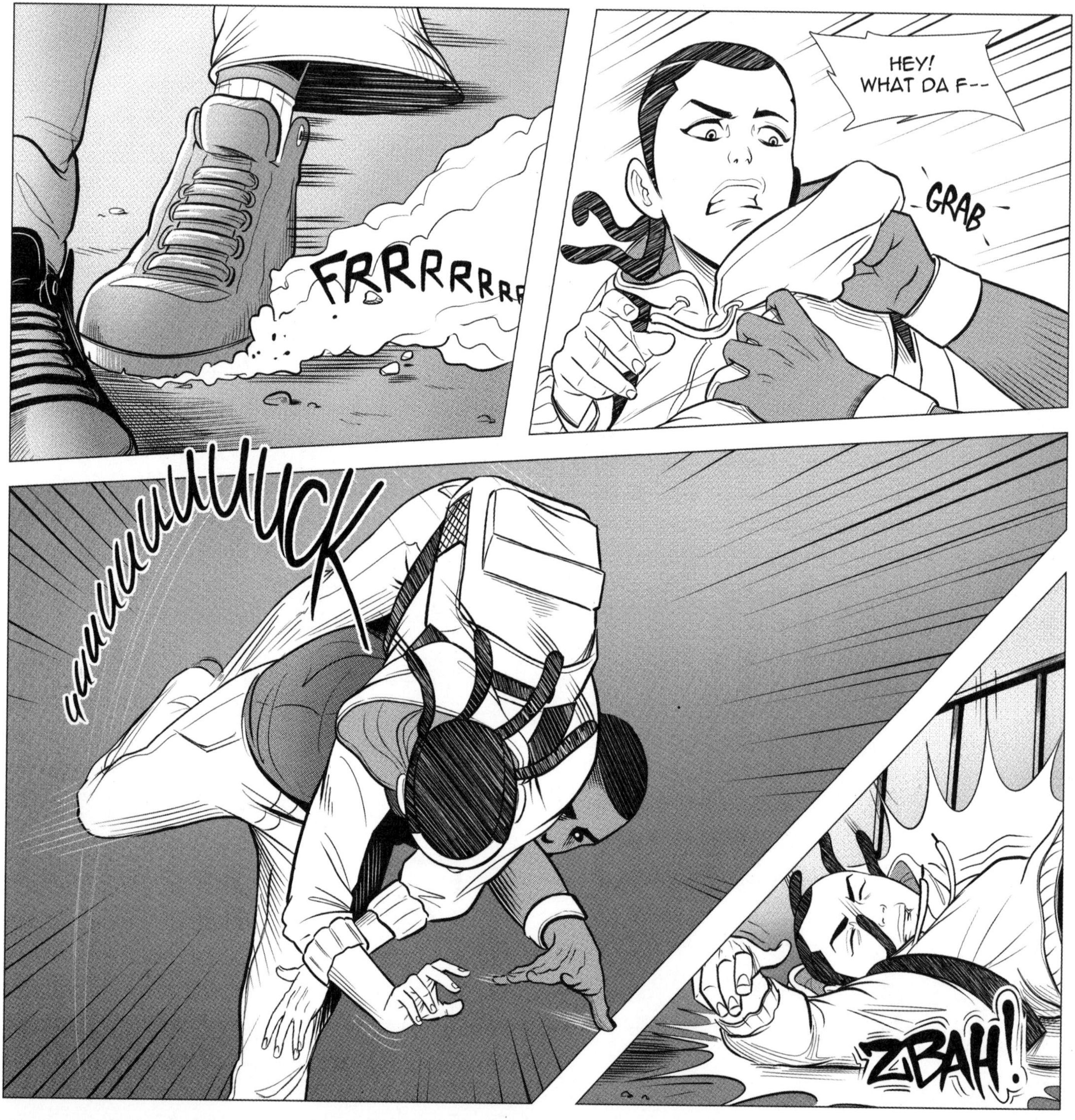
FRRRRRRRR
HEY!
WHAT DA F--
GRAB
uuuuuuuuuUCK
ZBAH!

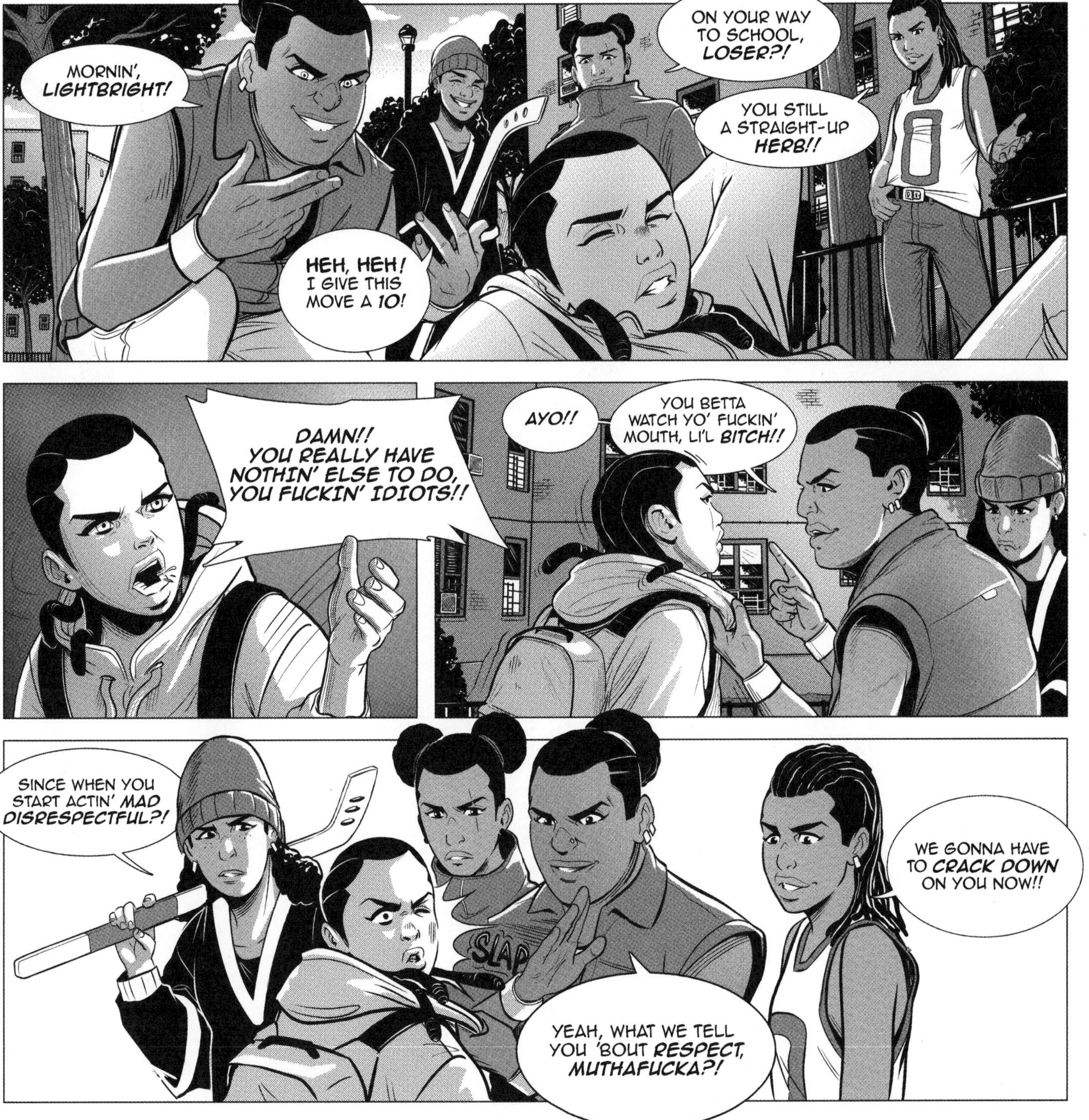
MORNIN', LIGHTBRIGHT!
HEH, HEH! I GIVE THIS MOVE A 10!
ON YOUR WAY TO SCHOOL, LOSER?!
YOU STILL A STRAIGHT-UP HERB!!
DAMN!! YOU REALLY HAVE NOTHIN' ELSE TO DO, YOU FUCKIN' IDIOTS!!
AYO!!
YOU BETTA WATCH YO' FUCKIN' MOUTH, LI'L BITCH!!
SINCE WHEN YOU START ACTIN' MAD DISRESPECTFUL?!
SLAP
YEAH, WHAT WE TELL YOU 'BOUT RESPECT, MUTHAFUCKA?!
WE GONNA HAVE TO CRACK DOWN ON YOU NOW!!

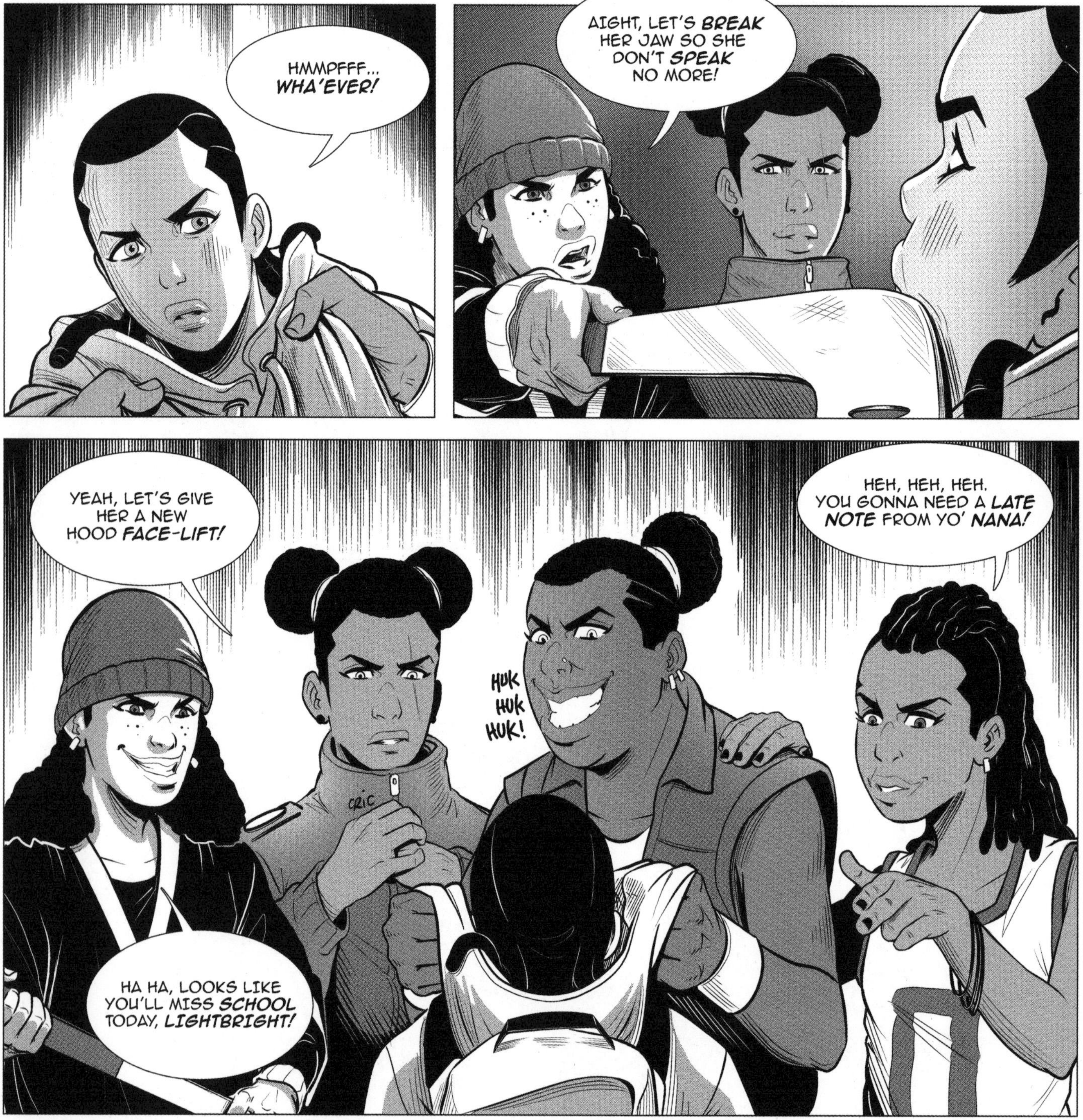

HMMPFFF... WHA'EVER!
AIGHT, LET'S BREAK HER JAW SO SHE DON'T SPEAK NO MORE!
YEAH, LET'S GIVE HER A NEW HOOD FACE-LIFT!
HUK HUK HUK!
HEH, HEH, HEH. YOU GONNA NEED A LATE NOTE FROM YO' NANA!
HA HA, LOOKS LIKE YOU'LL MISS SCHOOL TODAY, LIGHTBRIGHT!

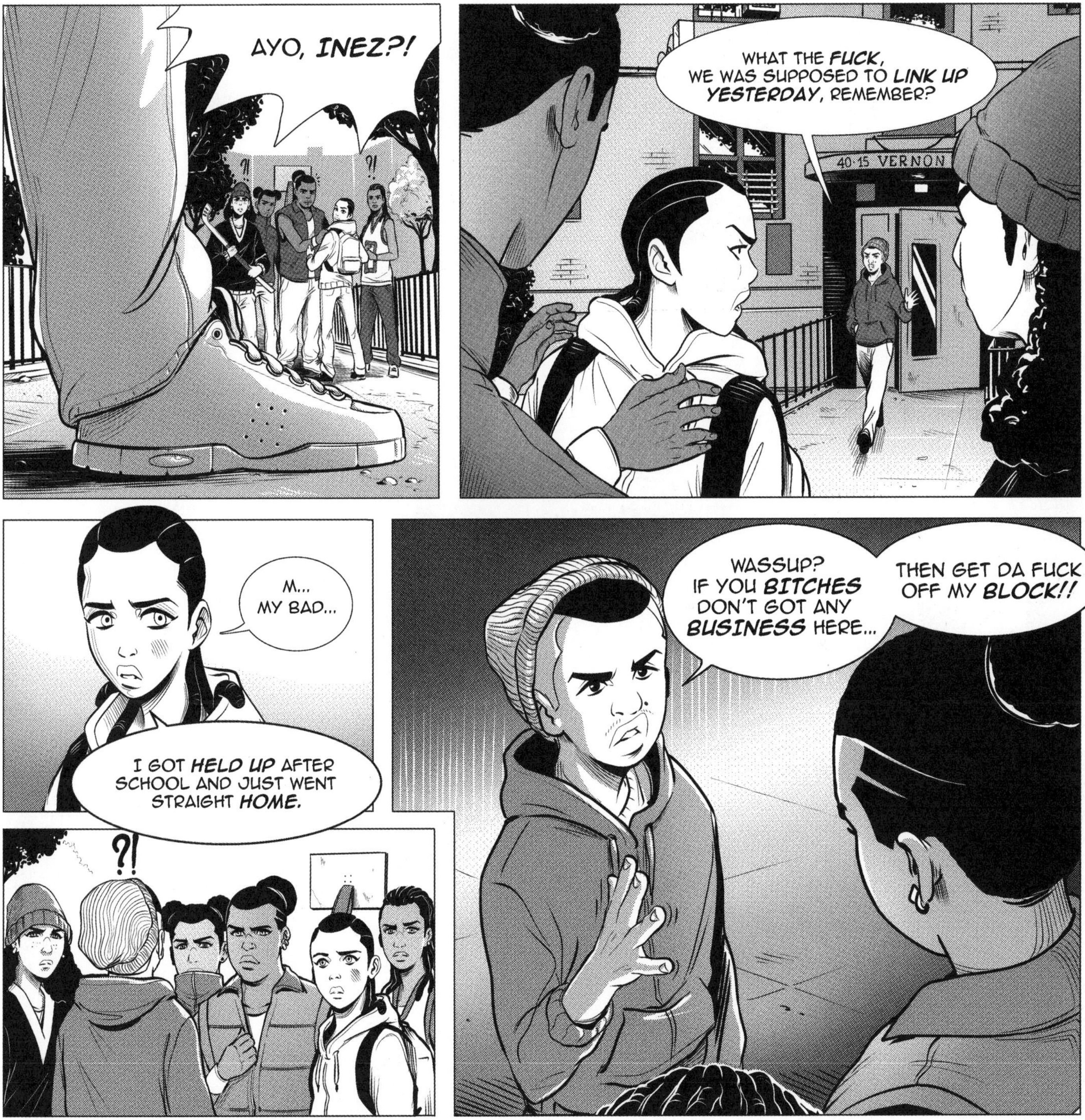
AYO, INEZ?!
?!
?!
WHAT THE FUCK, WE WAS SUPPOSED TO LINK UP YESTERDAY, REMEMBER?
40-15 VERNON
M... MY BAD...
I GOT HELD UP AFTER SCHOOL AND JUST WENT STRAIGHT HOME.
?!
WASSUP? IF YOU BITCHES DON'T GOT ANY BUSINESS HERE...
THEN GET DA FUCK OFF MY BLOCK!!

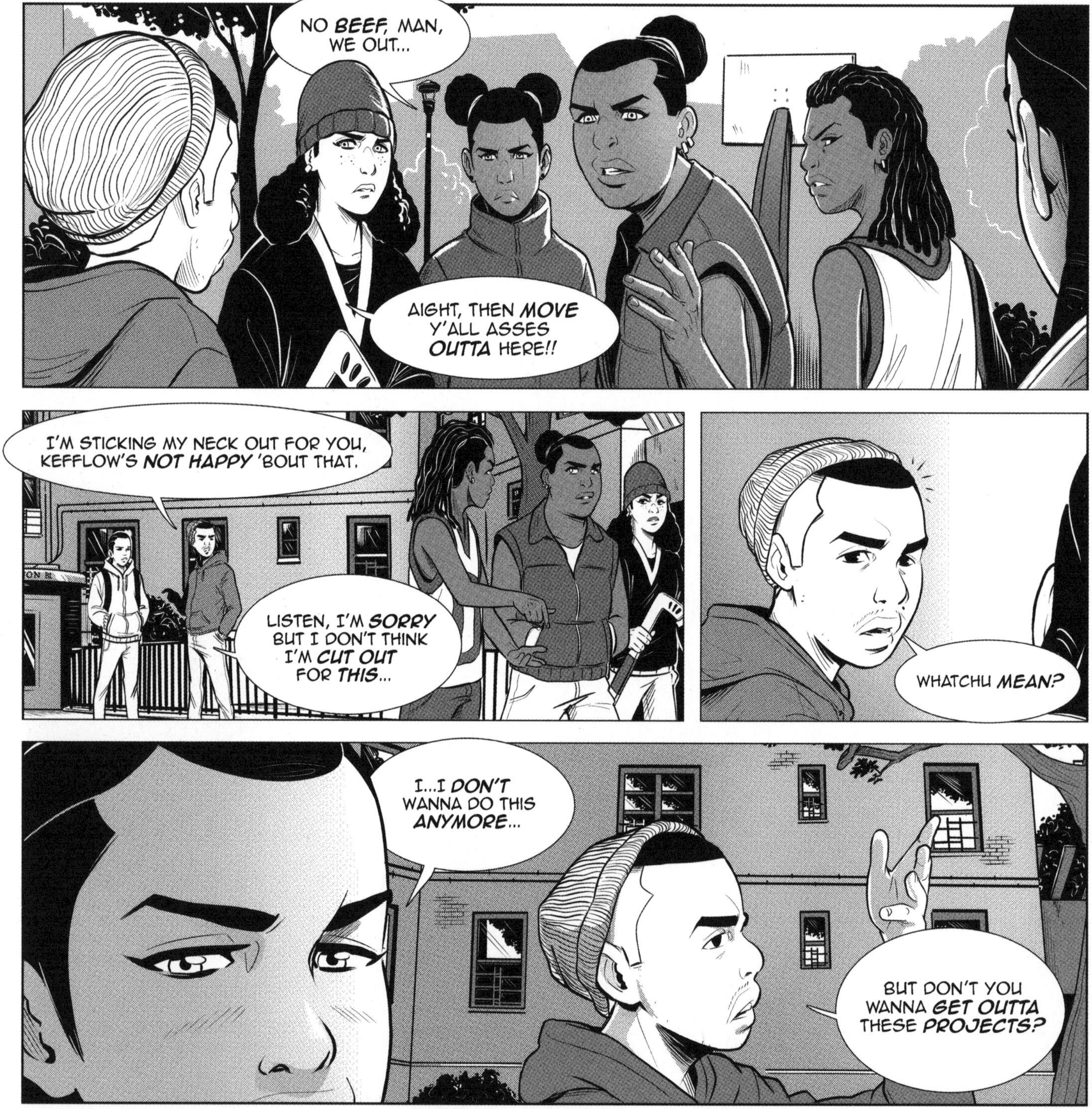
NO BEEF, MAN, WE OUT...
AIGHT, THEN MOVE Y'ALL ASSES OUTTA HERE!!
I'M STICKING MY NECK OUT FOR YOU, KEFFLOW'S NOT HAPPY 'BOUT THAT.
LISTEN, I'M SORRY BUT I DON'T THINK I'M CUT OUT FOR THIS...
WHATCHU MEAN?
I...I DON'T WANNA DO THIS ANYMORE...
BUT DON'T YOU WANNA GET OUTTA THESE PROJECTS?

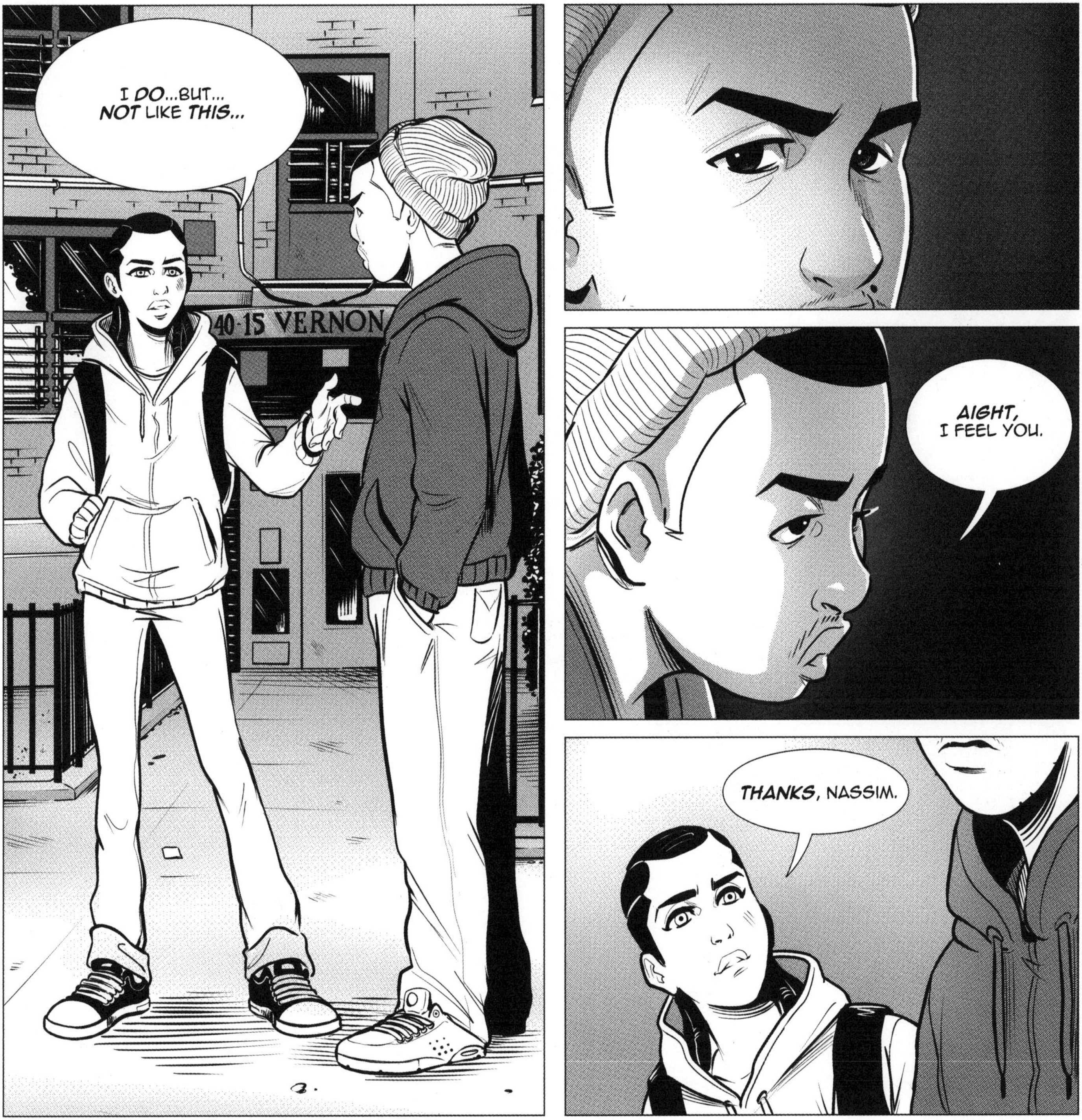
I DO...BUT...
NOT LIKE THIS...
40-15 VERNON
AIGHT,
I FEEL YOU.
THANKS, NASSIM.

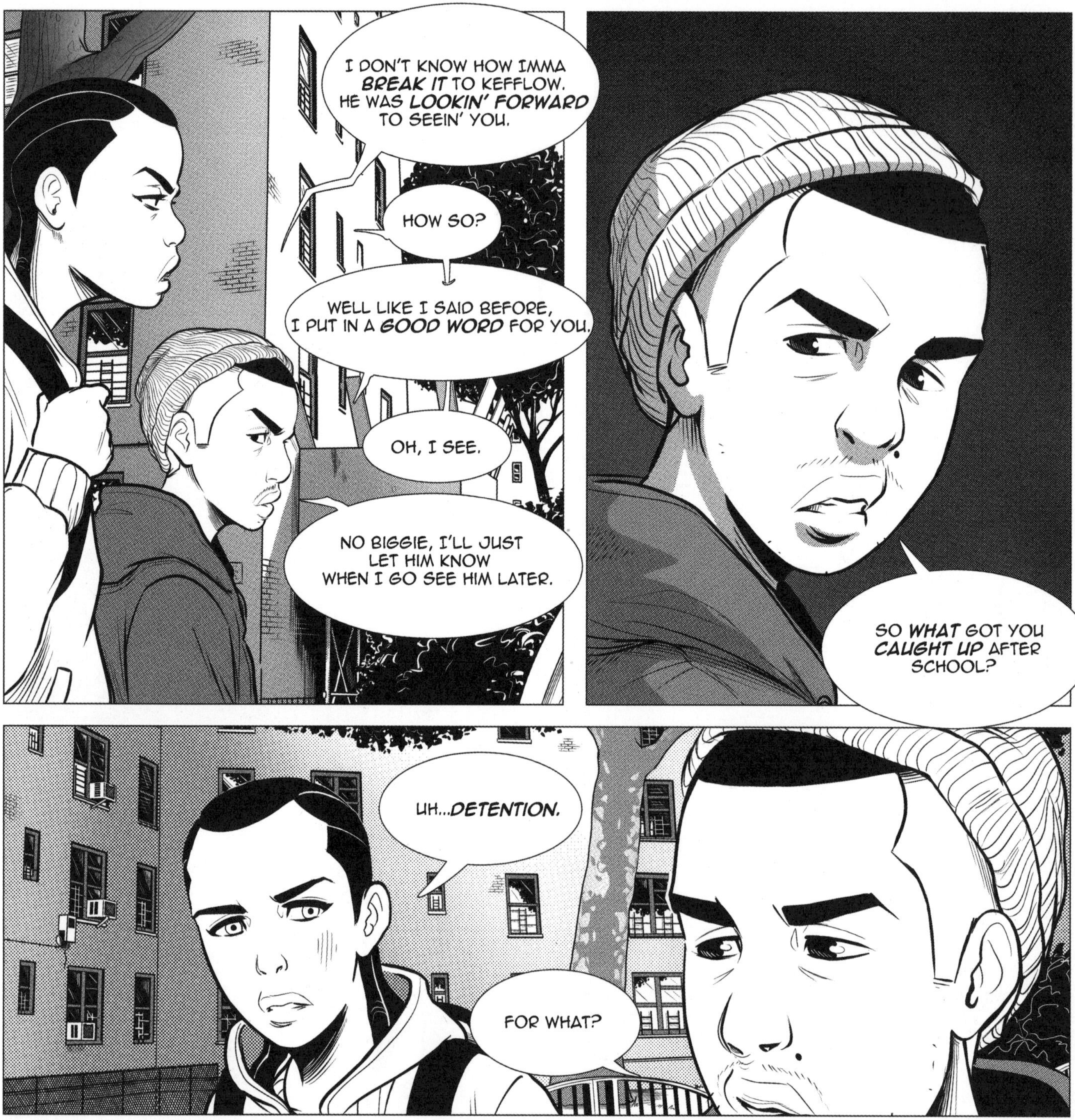
I DON'T KNOW HOW IMMA BREAK IT TO KEFFLOW. HE WAS LOOKIN' FORWARD TO SEEIN' YOU.
HOW SO?
WELL LIKE I SAID BEFORE, I PUT IN A GOOD WORD FOR YOU.
OH, I SEE.
NO BIGGIE, I'LL JUST LET HIM KNOW WHEN I GO SEE HIM LATER.
SO WHAT GOT YOU CAUGHT UP AFTER SCHOOL?
UH...DETENTION.
FOR WHAT?

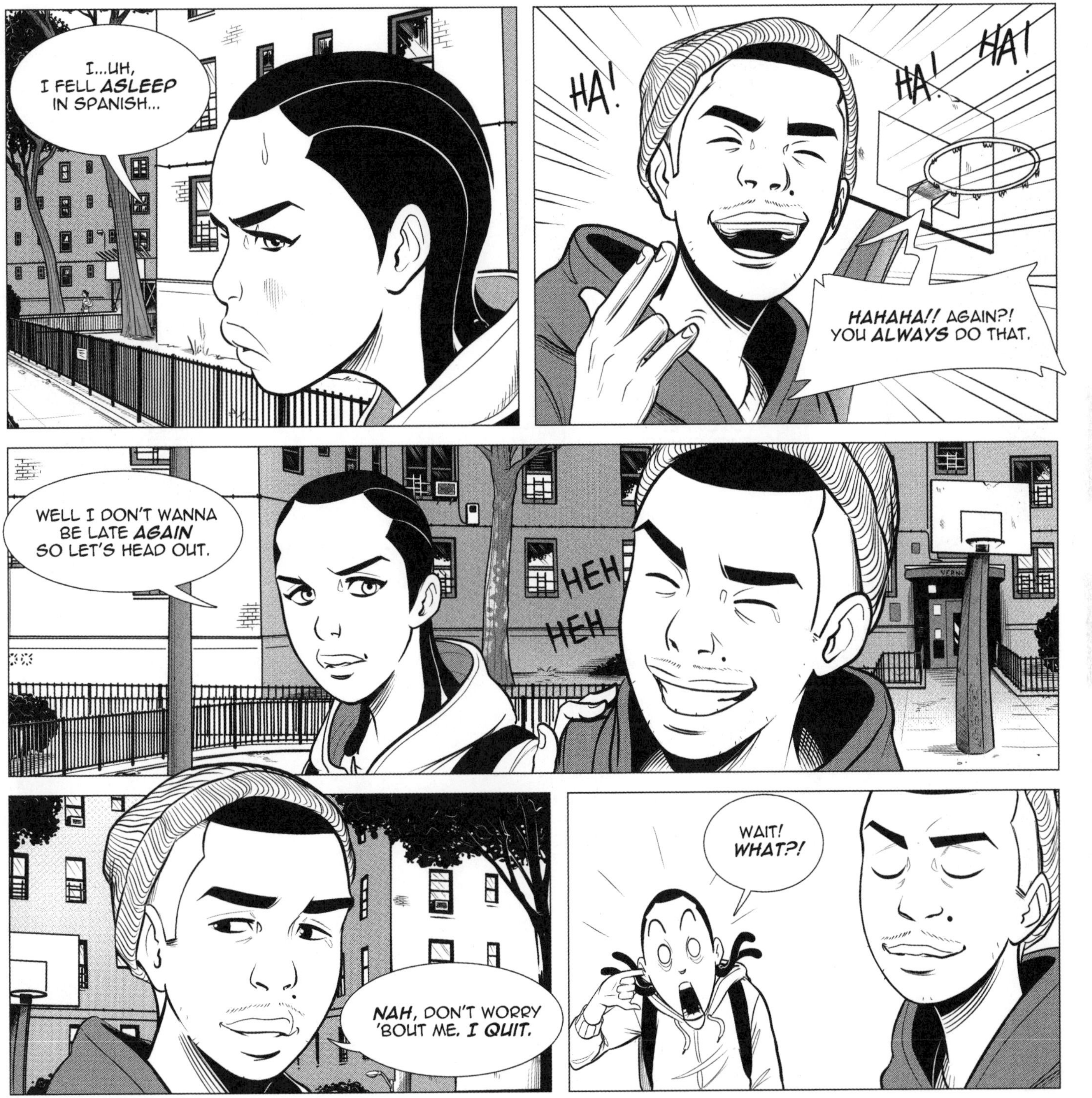

I...UH, I FELL **ASLEEP** IN SPANISH...
HA! HA! HA!
HAHAHA!! AGAIN?! YOU **ALWAYS** DO THAT.
WELL I DON'T WANNA BE LATE **AGAIN** SO LET'S HEAD OUT.
HEH HEH
NAH, DON'T WORRY 'BOUT ME. **I QUIT.**
WAIT! **WHAT?!**

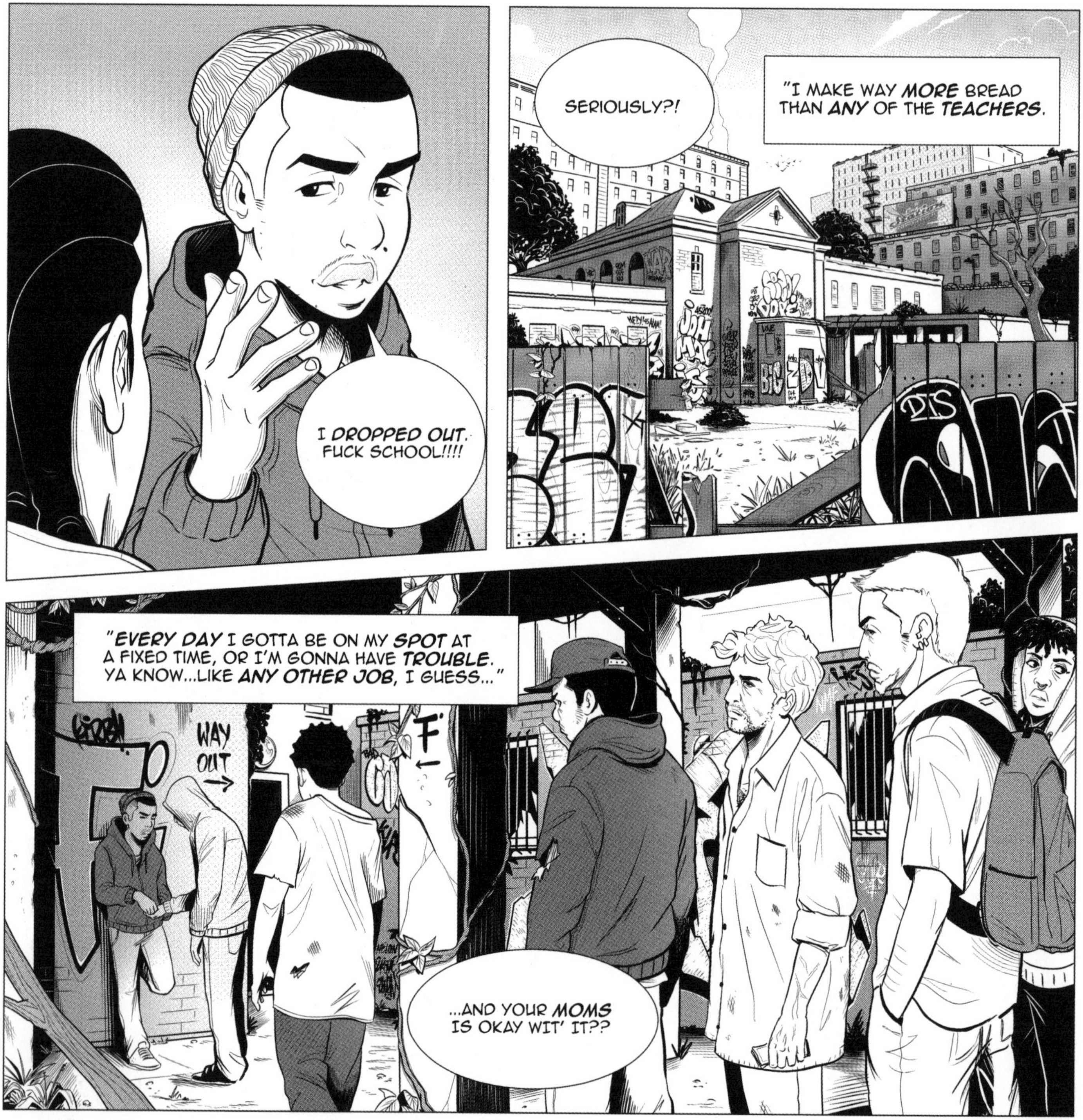
I DROPPED OUT. FUCK SCHOOL!!!!
SERIOUSLY?!
"I MAKE WAY MORE BREAD THAN ANY OF THE TEACHERS.
"EVERY DAY I GOTTA BE ON MY SPOT AT A FIXED TIME, OR I'M GONNA HAVE TROUBLE. YA KNOW...LIKE ANY OTHER JOB, I GUESS..."
WAY OUT
...AND YOUR MOMS IS OKAY WIT' IT??

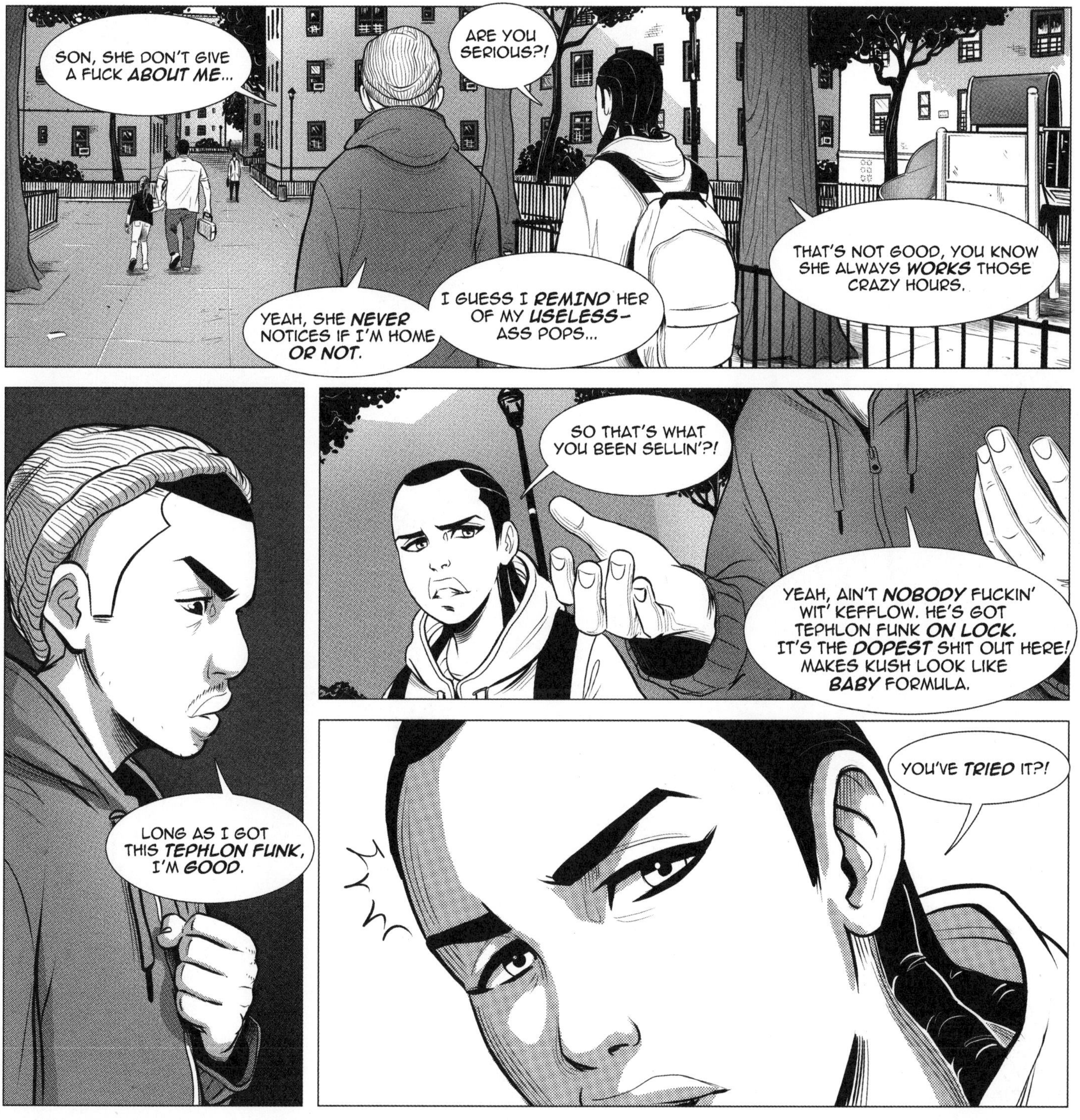

SON, SHE DON'T GIVE A FUCK ABOUT ME...
ARE YOU SERIOUS?!
YEAH, SHE NEVER NOTICES IF I'M HOME OR NOT.
I GUESS I REMIND HER OF MY USELESS-ASS POPS...
THAT'S NOT GOOD, YOU KNOW SHE ALWAYS WORKS THOSE CRAZY HOURS.
LONG AS I GOT THIS TEPHLON FUNK, I'M GOOD.
SO THAT'S WHAT YOU BEEN SELLIN'?!
YEAH, AIN'T NOBODY FUCKIN' WIT' KEFFLOW. HE'S GOT TEPHLON FUNK ON LOCK. IT'S THE DOPEST SHIT OUT HERE! MAKES KUSH LOOK LIKE BABY FORMULA.
YOU'VE TRIED IT?!

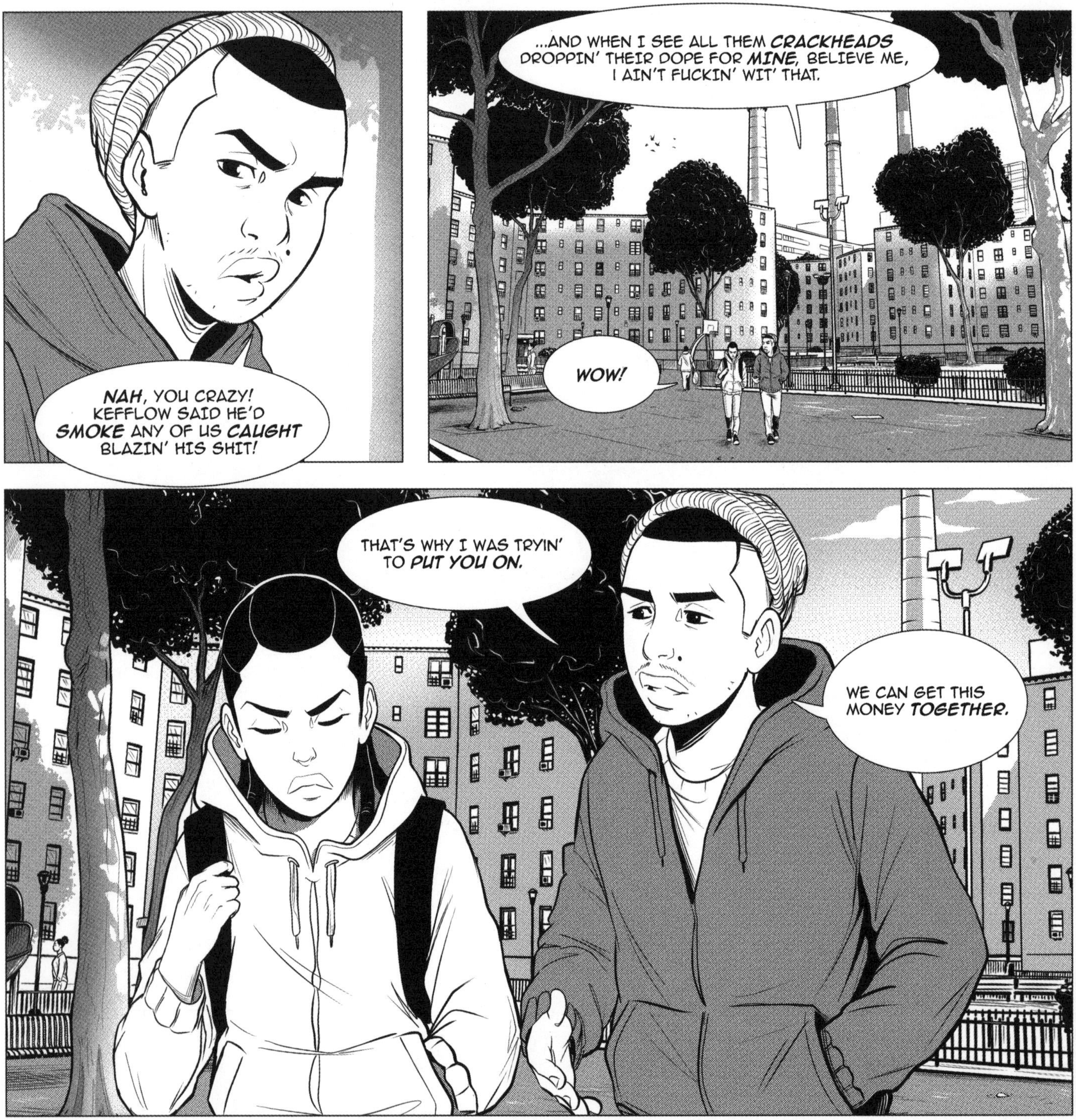
NAH, YOU CRAZY! KEFFLOW SAID HE'D SMOKE ANY OF US CAUGHT BLAZIN' HIS SHIT!
...AND WHEN I SEE ALL THEM CRACKHEADS DROPPIN' THEIR DOPE FOR MINE, BELIEVE ME, I AIN'T FUCKIN' WIT' THAT.
WOW!
THAT'S WHY I WAS TRYIN' TO PUT YOU ON.
WE CAN GET THIS MONEY TOGETHER.

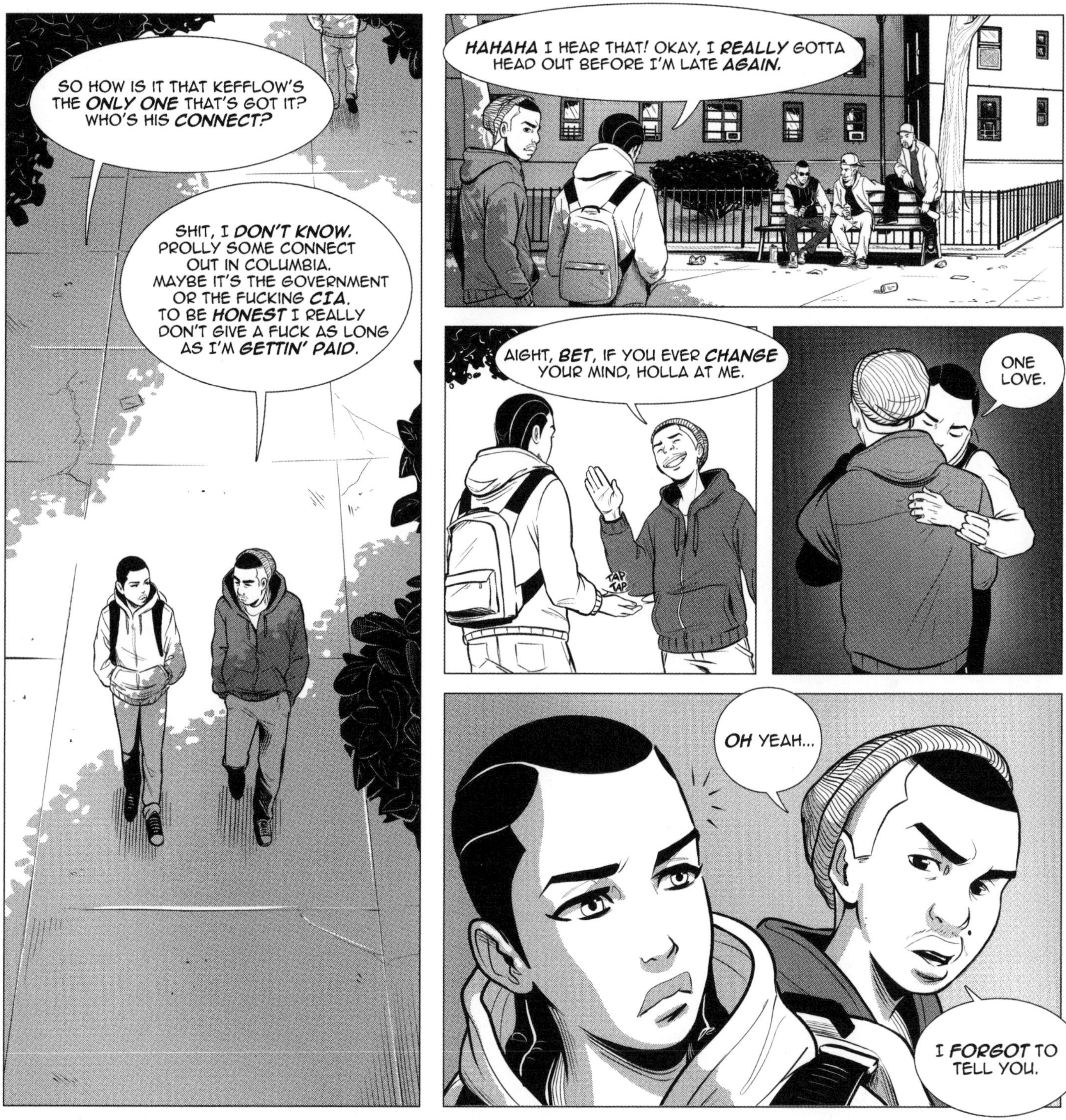
SO HOW IS IT THAT KEFFLOW'S THE ONLY ONE THAT'S GOT IT? WHO'S HIS CONNECT?
SHIT, I DON'T KNOW. PROLLY SOME CONNECT OUT IN COLUMBIA. MAYBE IT'S THE GOVERNMENT OR THE FUCKING CIA. TO BE HONEST I REALLY DON'T GIVE A FUCK AS LONG AS I'M GETTIN' PAID.
HAHAHA I HEAR THAT! OKAY, I REALLY GOTTA HEAD OUT BEFORE I'M LATE AGAIN.
AIGHT, BET, IF YOU EVER CHANGE YOUR MIND, HOLLA AT ME.
TAP TAP
ONE LOVE.
OH YEAH...
I FORGOT TO TELL YOU.

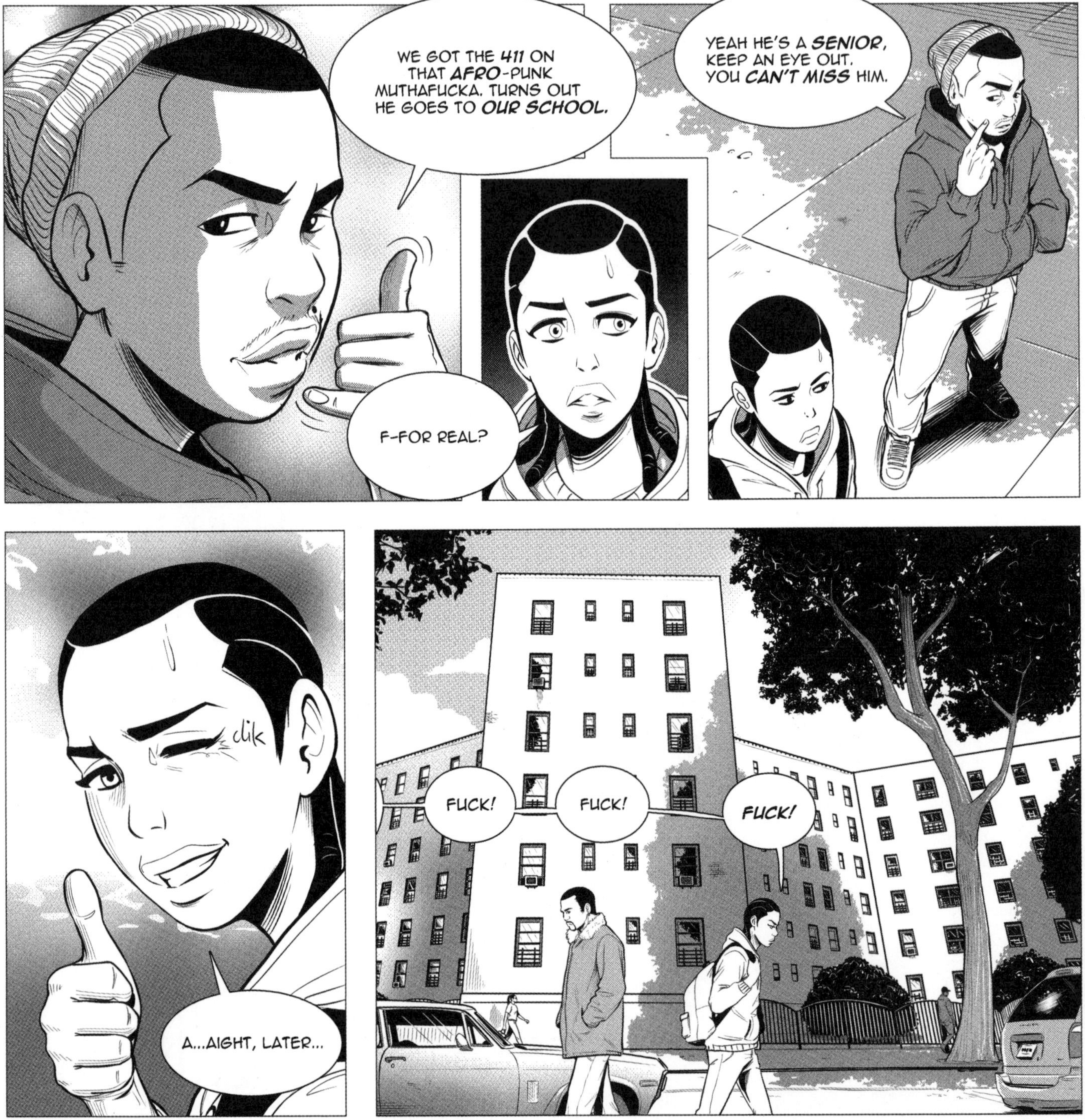
WE GOT THE 411 ON THAT AFRO-PUNK MUTHAFUCKA. TURNS OUT HE GOES TO OUR SCHOOL.
F-FOR REAL?
YEAH HE'S A SENIOR, KEEP AN EYE OUT. YOU CAN'T MISS HIM.
clik
A...AIGHT, LATER...
FUCK!
FUCK!
FUCK!

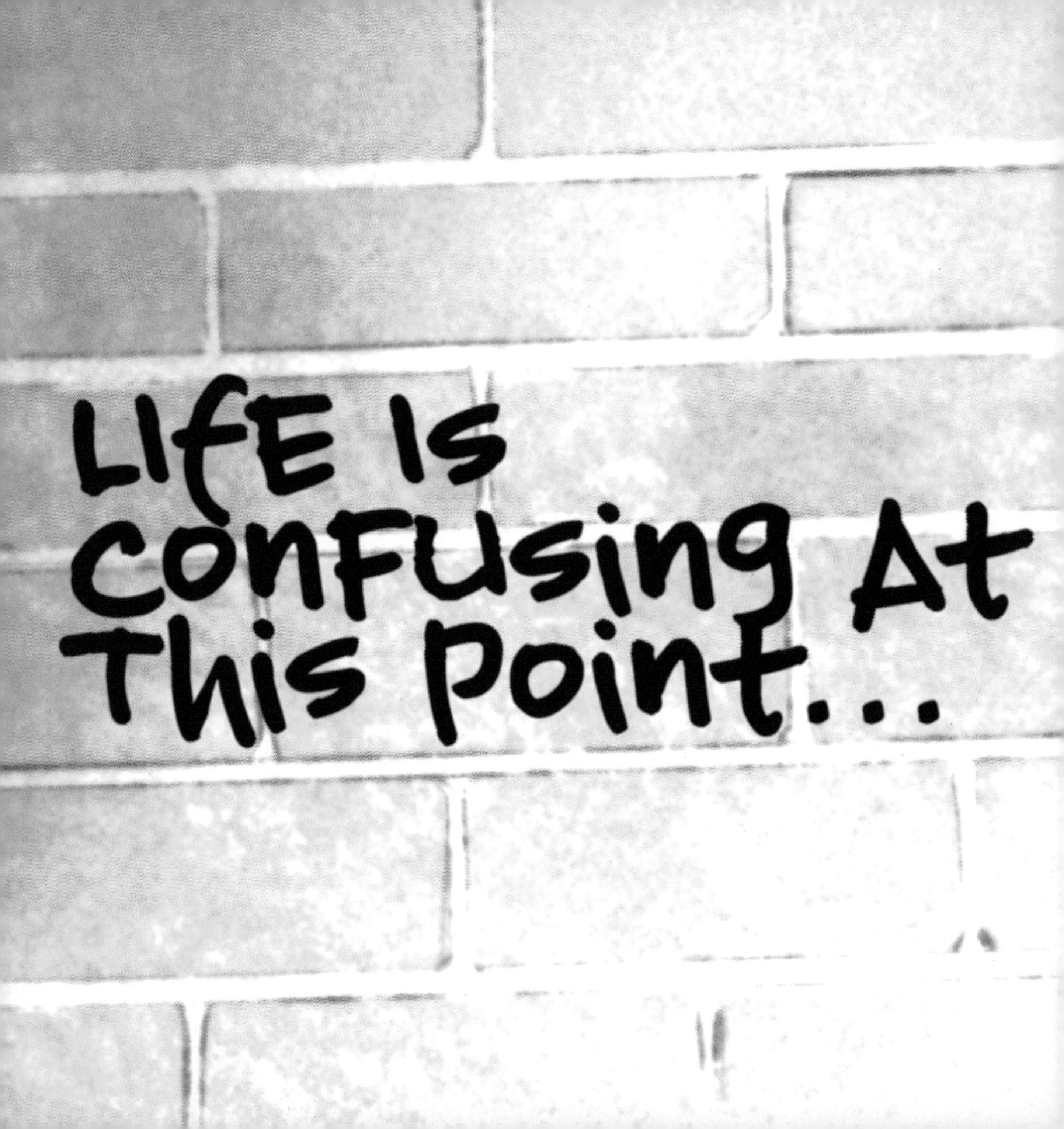
LIFE IS
CONFUSING AT
THIS POINT...

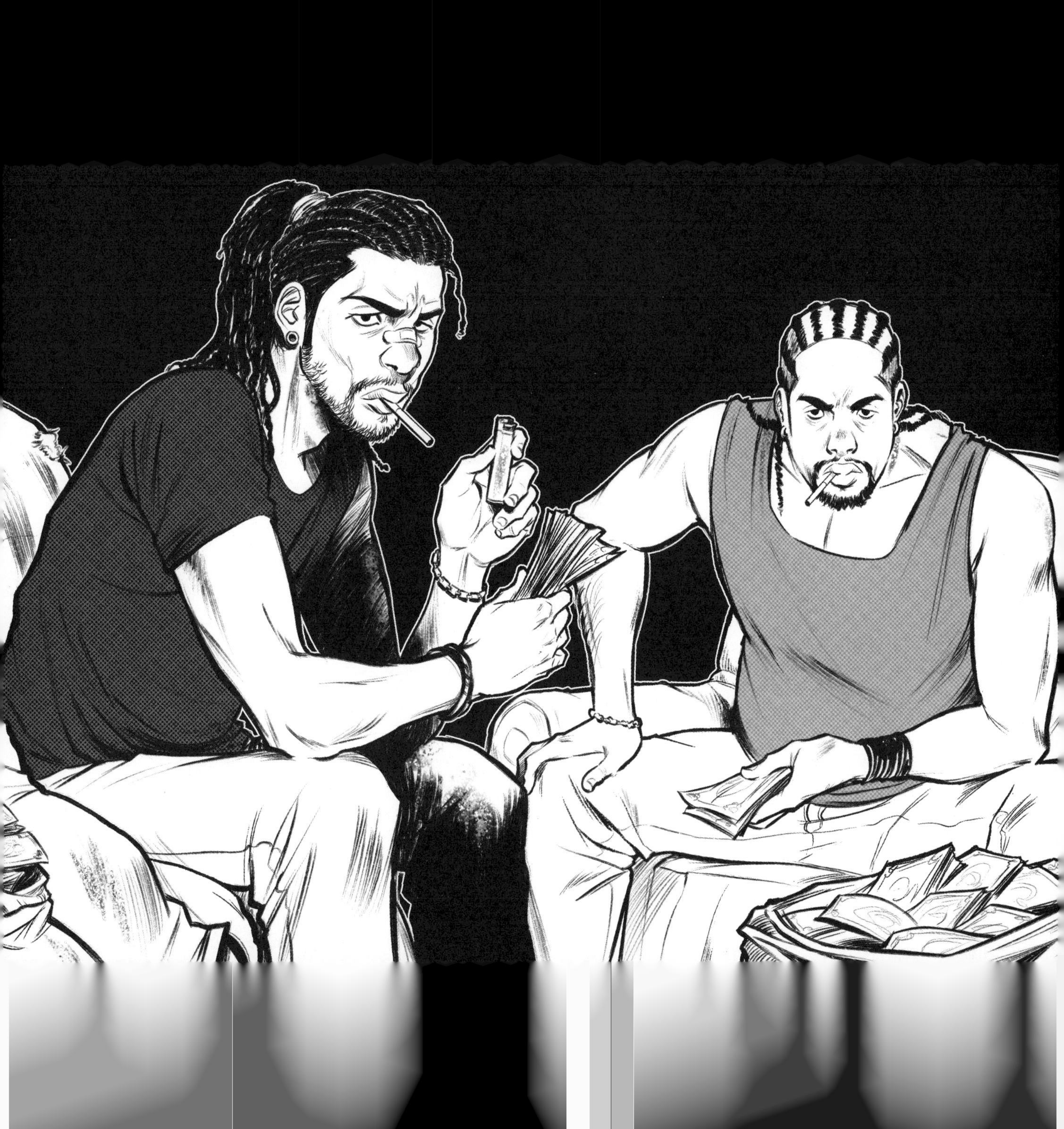

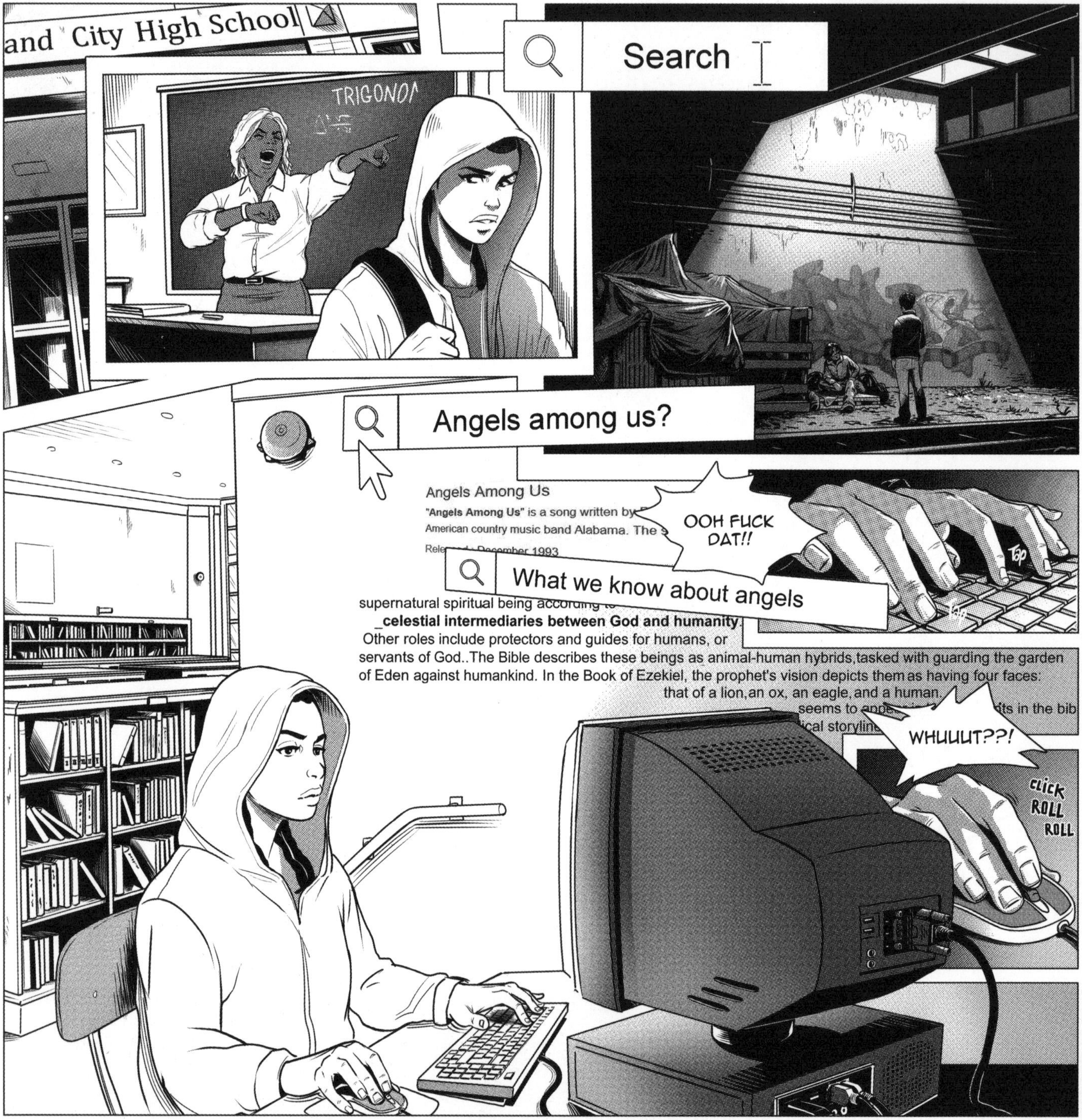
and City High School
Search
Angels among us?
Angels Among Us
"Angels Among Us" is a song written by
American country music band Alabama. The
OOH FUCK DAT!!
What we know about angels
TAP
supernatural spiritual being according to
_celestial intermediaries between God and humanity.
Other roles include protectors and guides for humans, or
servants of God..The Bible describes these beings as animal-human hybrids,tasked with guarding the garden
of Eden against humankind. In the Book of Ezekiel, the prophet's vision depicts them as having four faces:
that of a lion,an ox, an eagle,and a human.
WHUUUT??!
CLICK
ROLL
ROLL

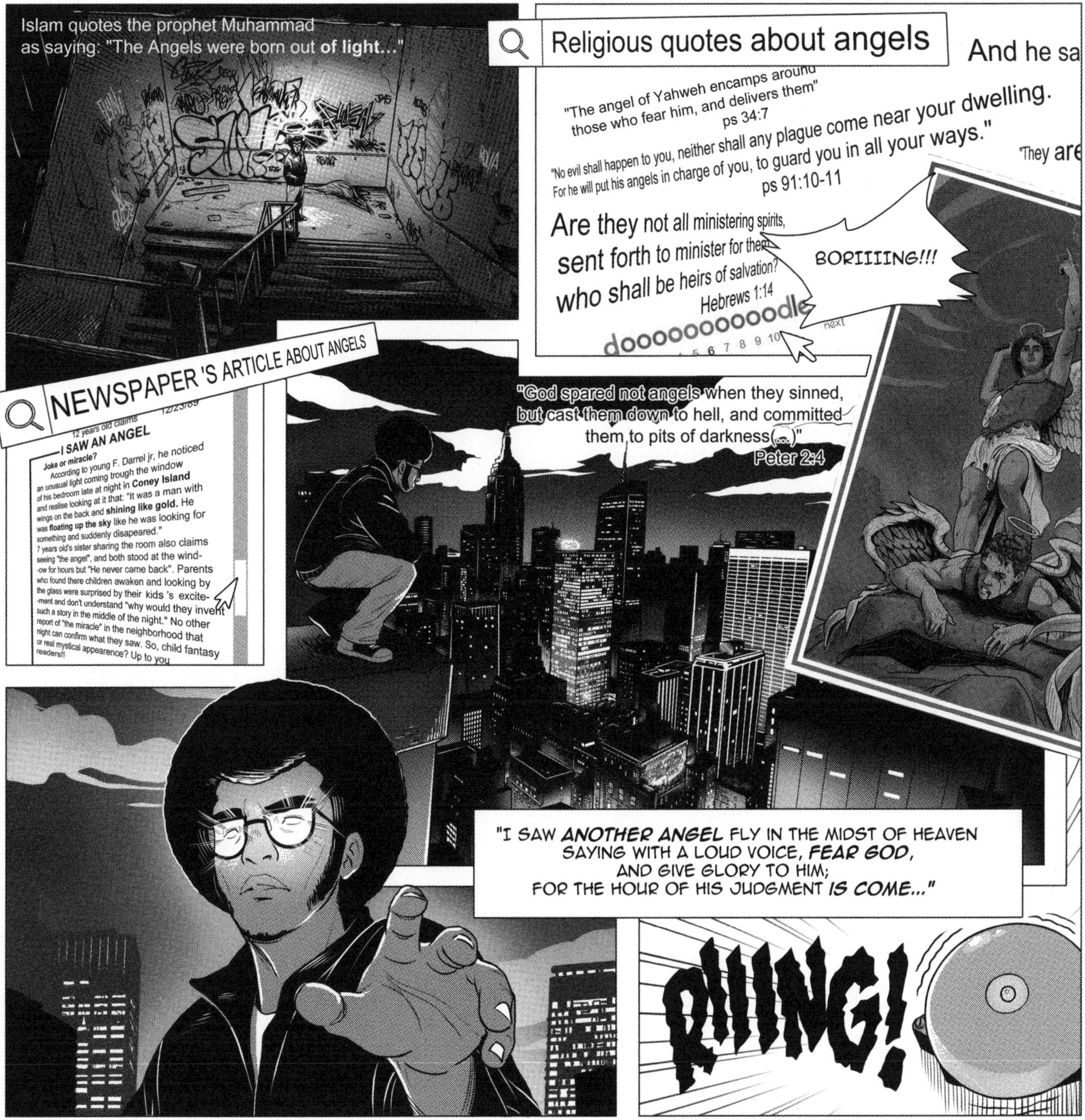
Islam quotes the prophet Muhammad as saying: "The Angels were born out of light..."
Religious quotes about angels
And he sa
"The angel of Yahweh encamps around those who fear him, and delivers them" ps 34:7
"No evil shall happen to you, neither shall any plague come near your dwelling. For he will put his angels in charge of you, to guard you in all your ways." ps 91:10-11
"They are
Are they not all ministering spirits, sent forth to minister for them who shall be heirs of salvation? Hebrews 1:14
BORIIIING!!!
doooooooooodle
6 7 8 9 10
next
NEWSPAPER 'S ARTICLE ABOUT ANGELS
12/23/89
12 years old claims
I SAW AN ANGEL
Joke or miracle?
According to young F. Darrel jr, he noticed an unusual light coming trough the window of his bedroom late at night in Coney Island and realise looking at it that: "It was a man with wings on the back and shining like gold. He was floating up the sky like he was looking for something and suddenly disapeared."
7 years old's sister sharing the room also claims seeing "the angel", and both stood at the wind--ow for hours but "He never came back". Parents who found there children awaken and looking by the glass were surprised by their kids 's excite--ment and don't understand "why would they invent such a story in the middle of the night." No other report of "the miracle" in the neighborhood that night can confirm what they saw. So, child fantasy or real mystical appearence? Up to you readers!!
"God spared not angels when they sinned, but cast them down to hell, and committed them to pits of darkness(...)" Peter 2:4
"I SAW ANOTHER ANGEL FLY IN THE MIDST OF HEAVEN SAYING WITH A LOUD VOICE, FEAR GOD, AND GIVE GLORY TO HIM; FOR THE HOUR OF HIS JUDGMENT IS COME..."
RIIING!

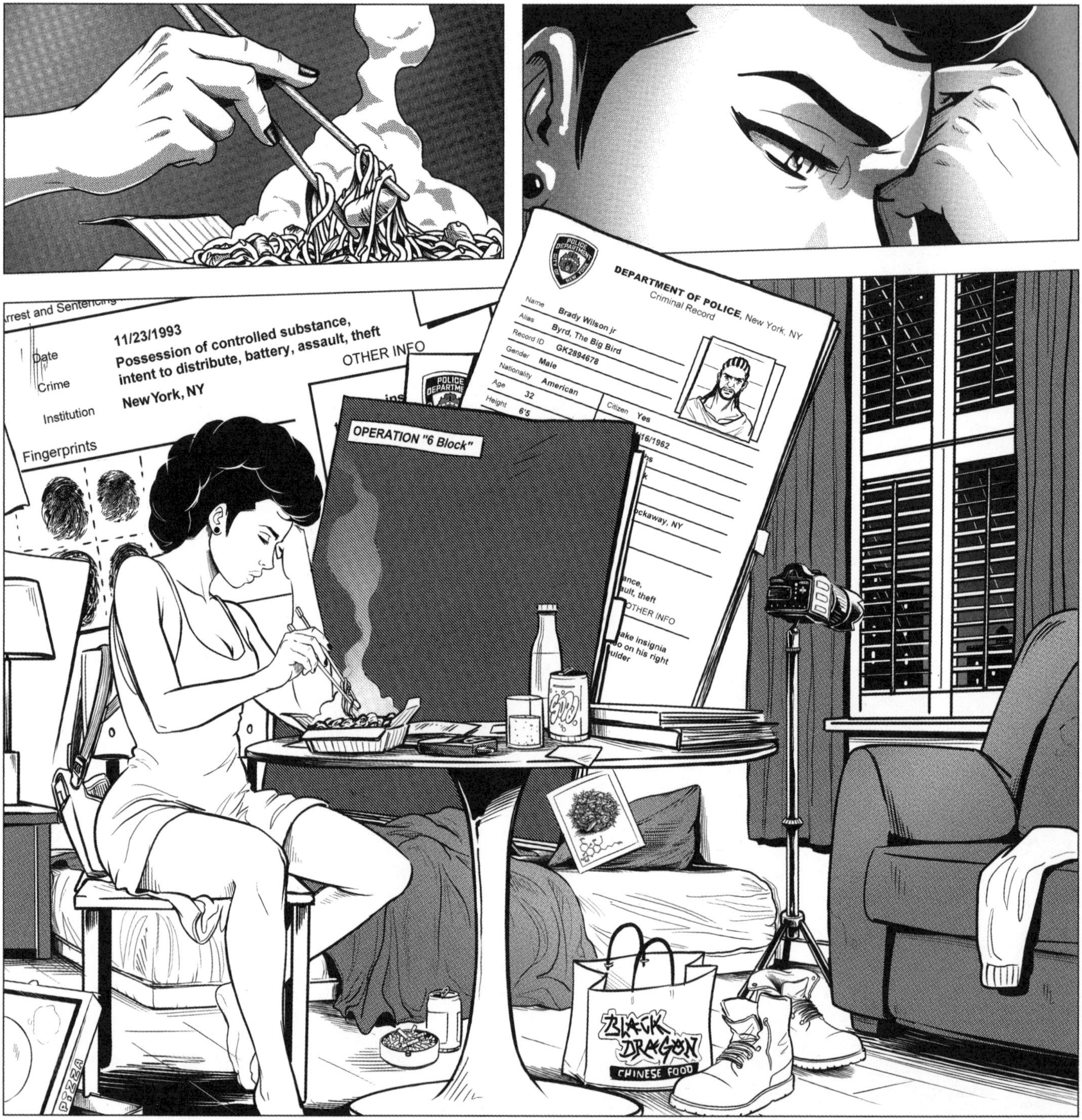

Arrest and Sentencing
Date 11/23/1993
Crime Possession of controlled substance, intent to distribute, battery, assault, theft
Institution New York, NY
OTHER INFO
Fingerprints
OPERATION "6 Block"
DEPARTMENT OF POLICE, New York, NY
Criminal Record
Name Brady Wilson jr
Alias Byrd, The Big Bird
Record ID GK2894678
Gender Male
Nationality American
Age 32
Height 6'5
Citizen Yes
BLACK DRAGON
CHINESE FOOD
PIZZA

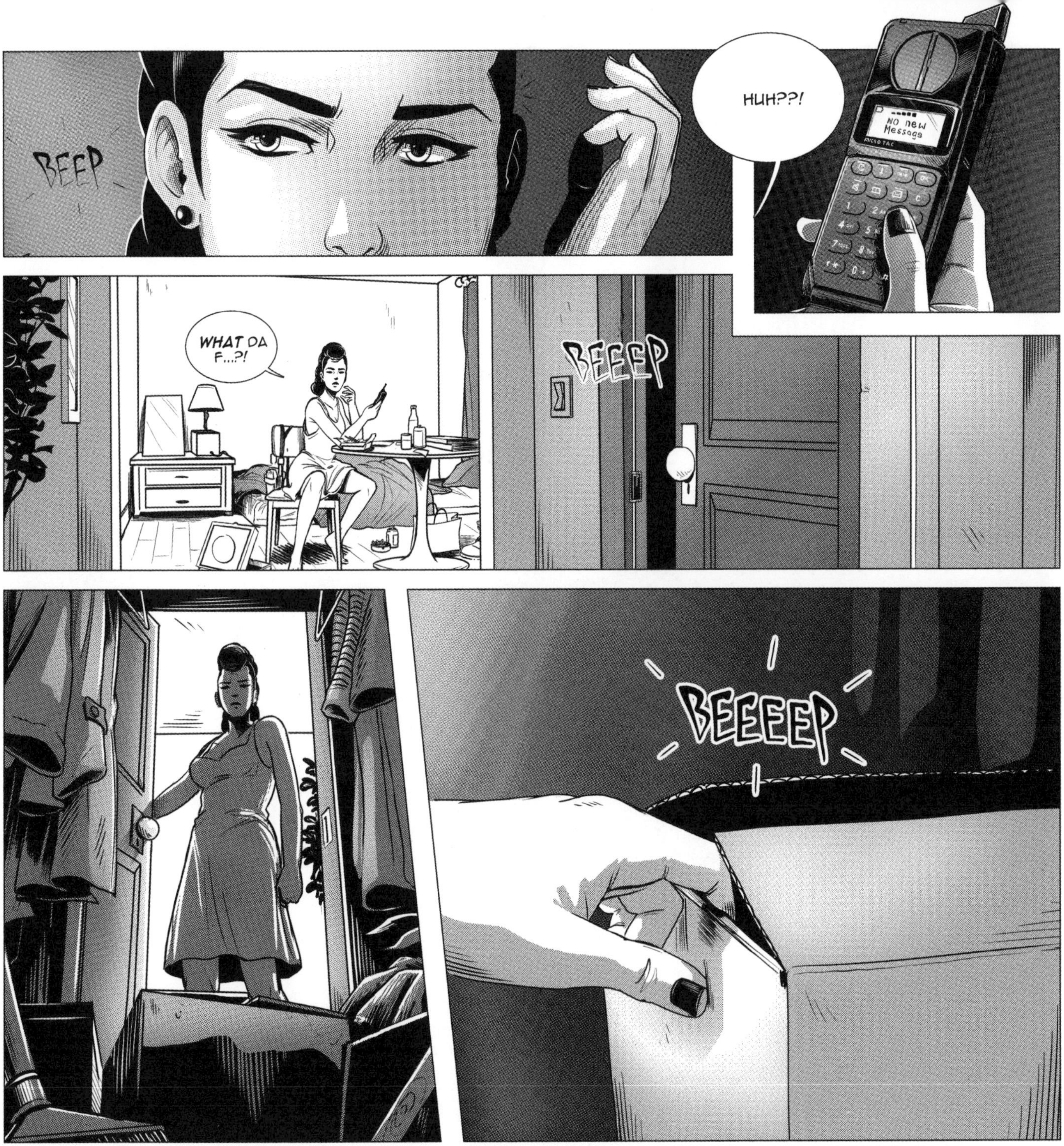
BEEP
HUH??!
NO new Message
MICRO TAC
WHAT DA F...?!
BEEEP
BEEEEP

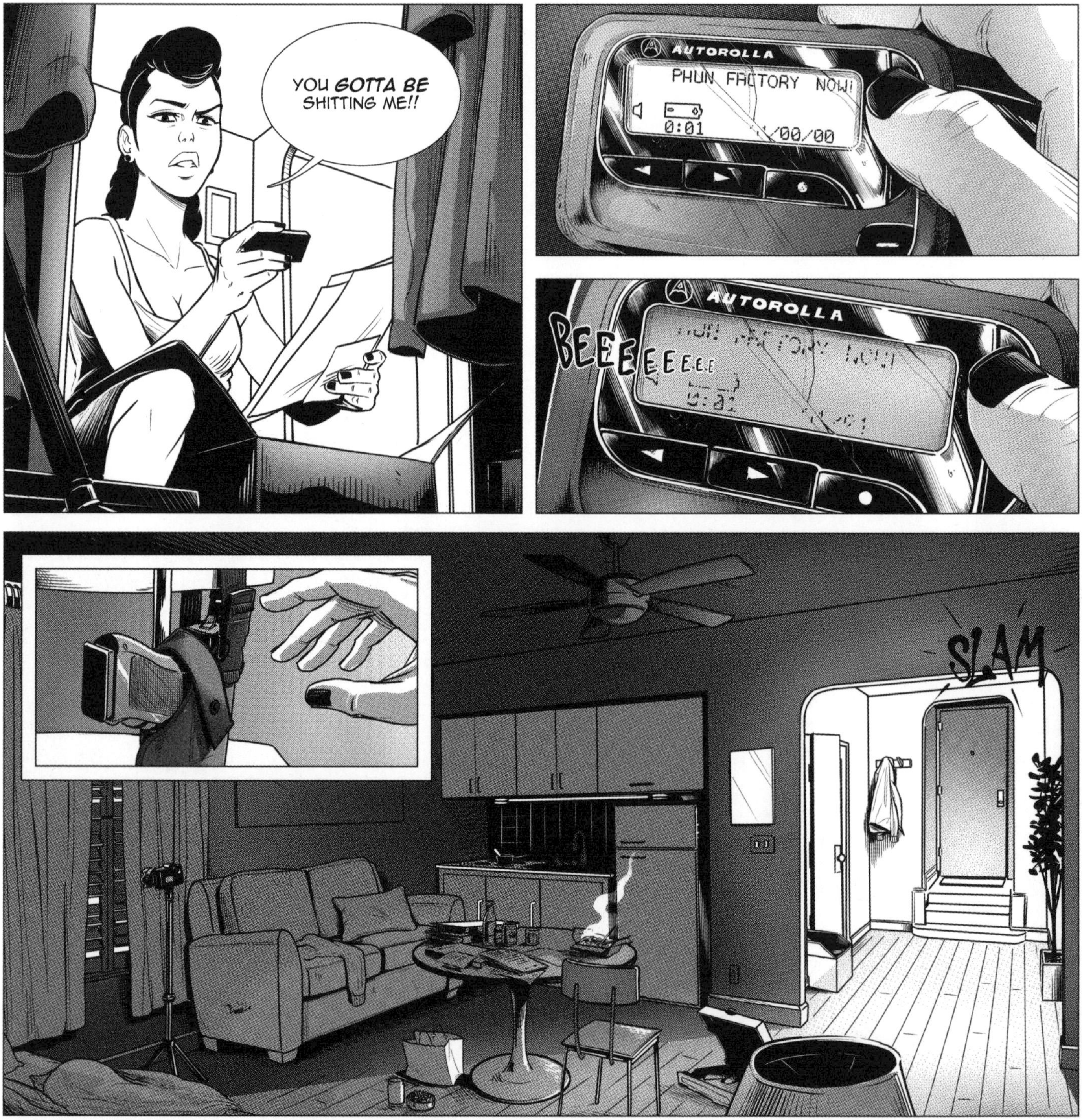
YOU GOTTA BE SHITTING ME!!
AUTOROLLA
PHUN FACTORY NOW!
0:01
AUTOROLLA
BEEEEEEEEE
SLAM

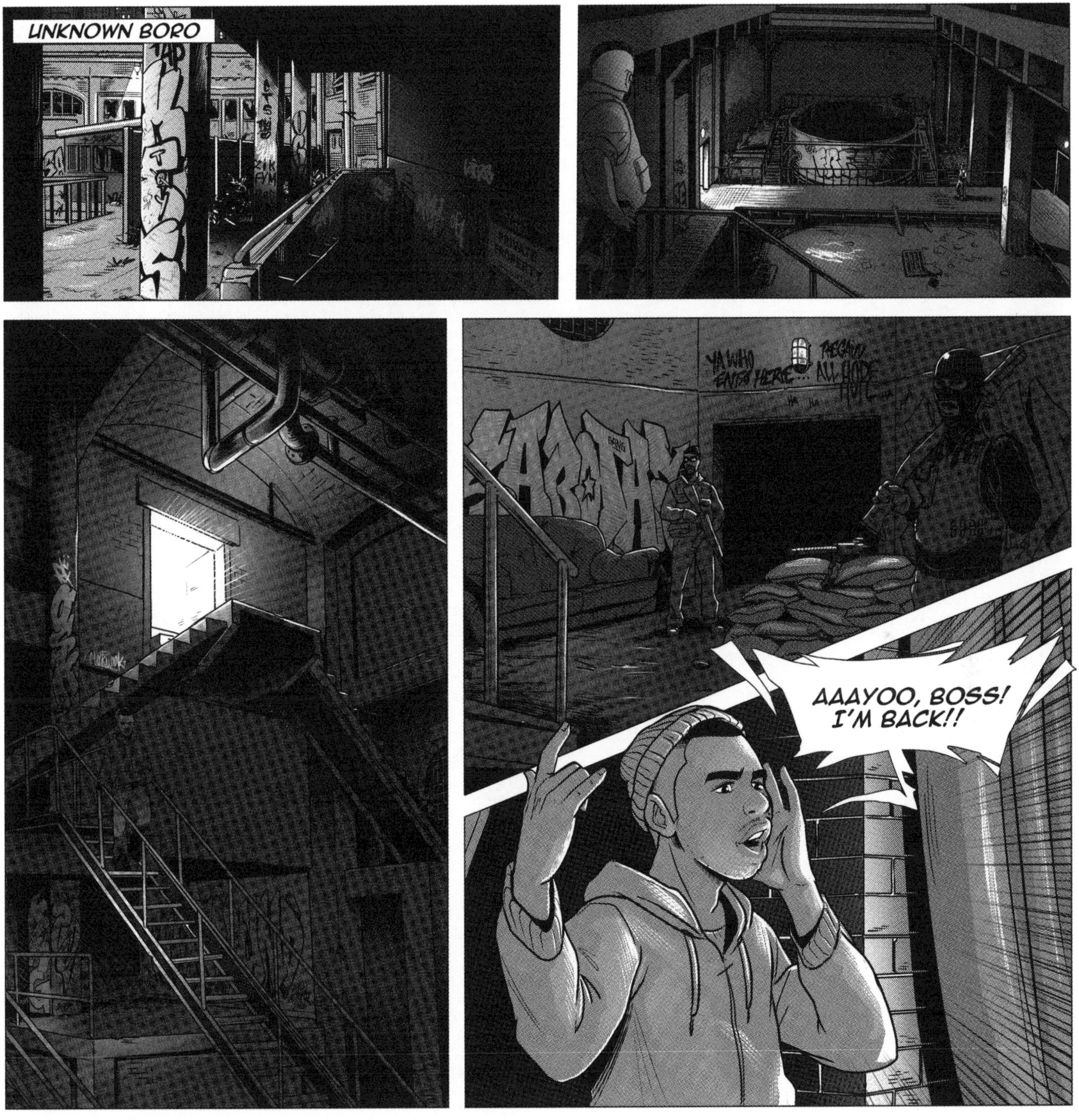
UNKNOWN BORO
AAAYOO, BOSS! I'M BACK!!

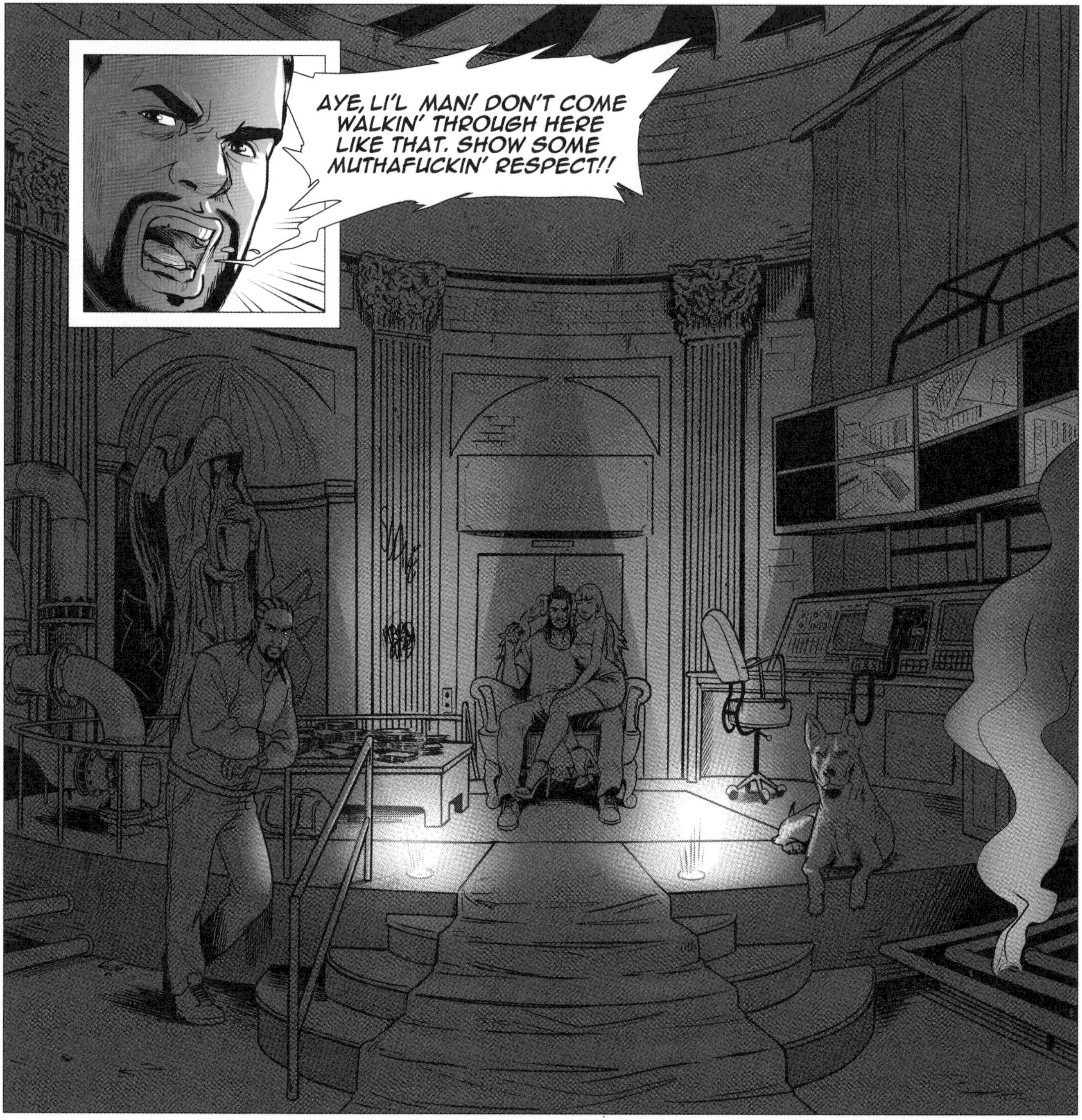
AYE, LI'L MAN! DON'T COME WALKIN' THROUGH HERE LIKE THAT. SHOW SOME MUTHAFUCKIN' RESPECT!!

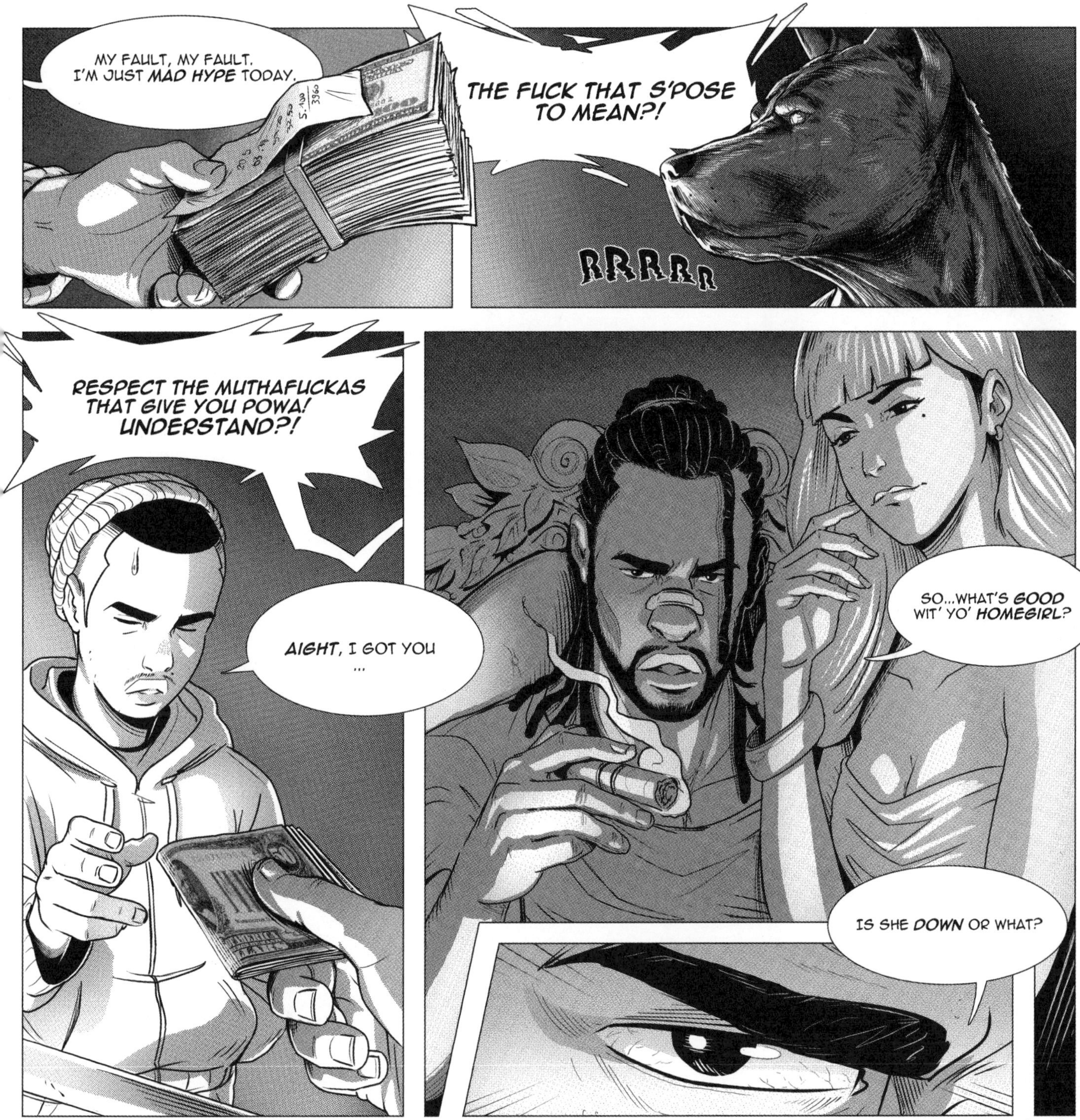
MY FAULT, MY FAULT. I'M JUST MAD HYPE TODAY.
THE FUCK THAT S'POSE TO MEAN?!
RRRRRR
RESPECT THE MUTHAFUCKAS THAT GIVE YOU POWA! UNDERSTAND?!
AIGHT, I GOT YOU ...
SO...WHAT'S GOOD WIT' YO' HOMEGIRL?
IS SHE DOWN OR WHAT?

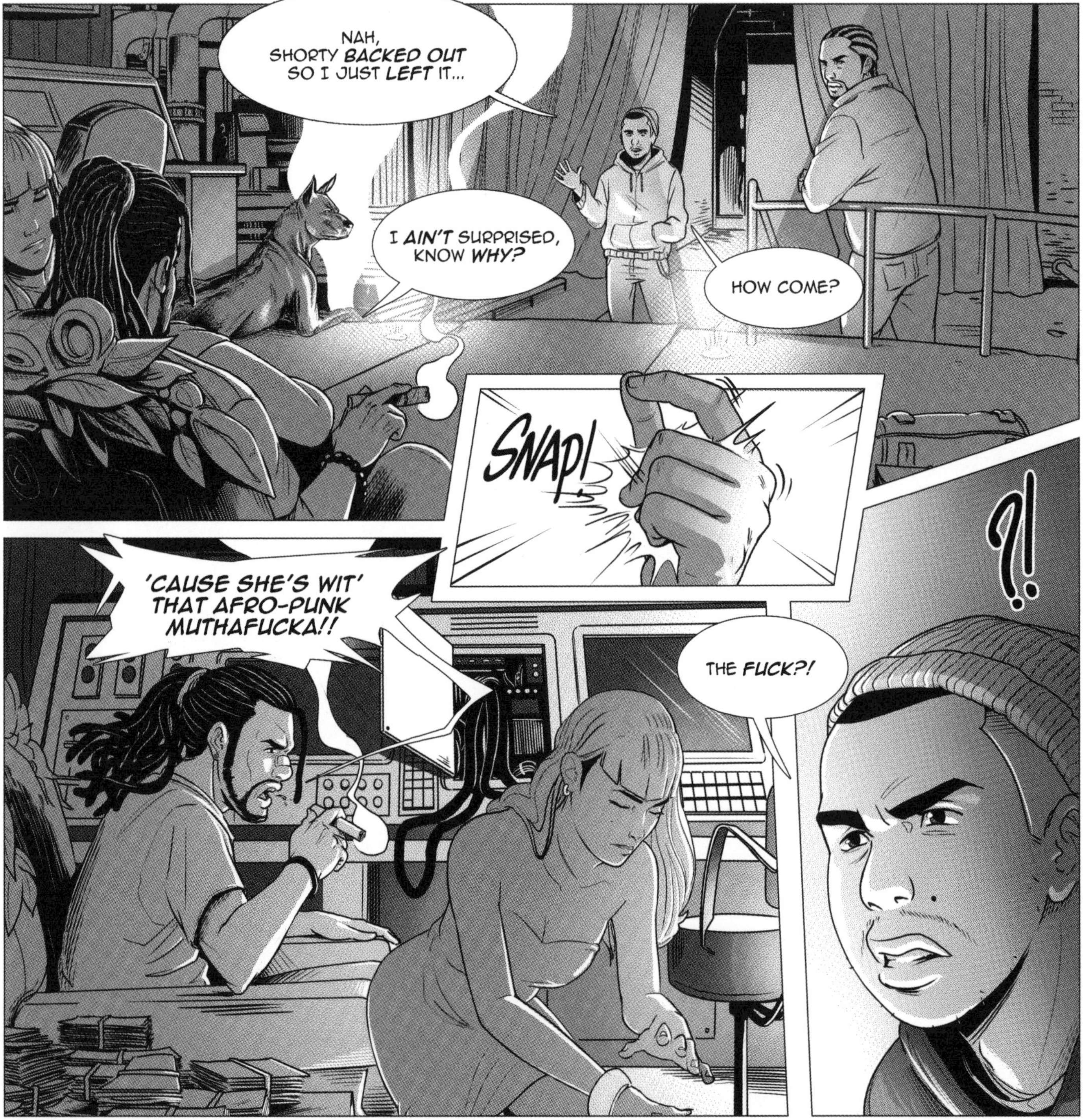
NAH, SHORTY BACKED OUT SO I JUST LEFT IT...
I AIN'T SURPRISED, KNOW WHY?
HOW COME?
SNAP!
'CAUSE SHE'S WIT' THAT AFRO-PUNK MUTHAFUCKA!!
THE FUCK?!
?!

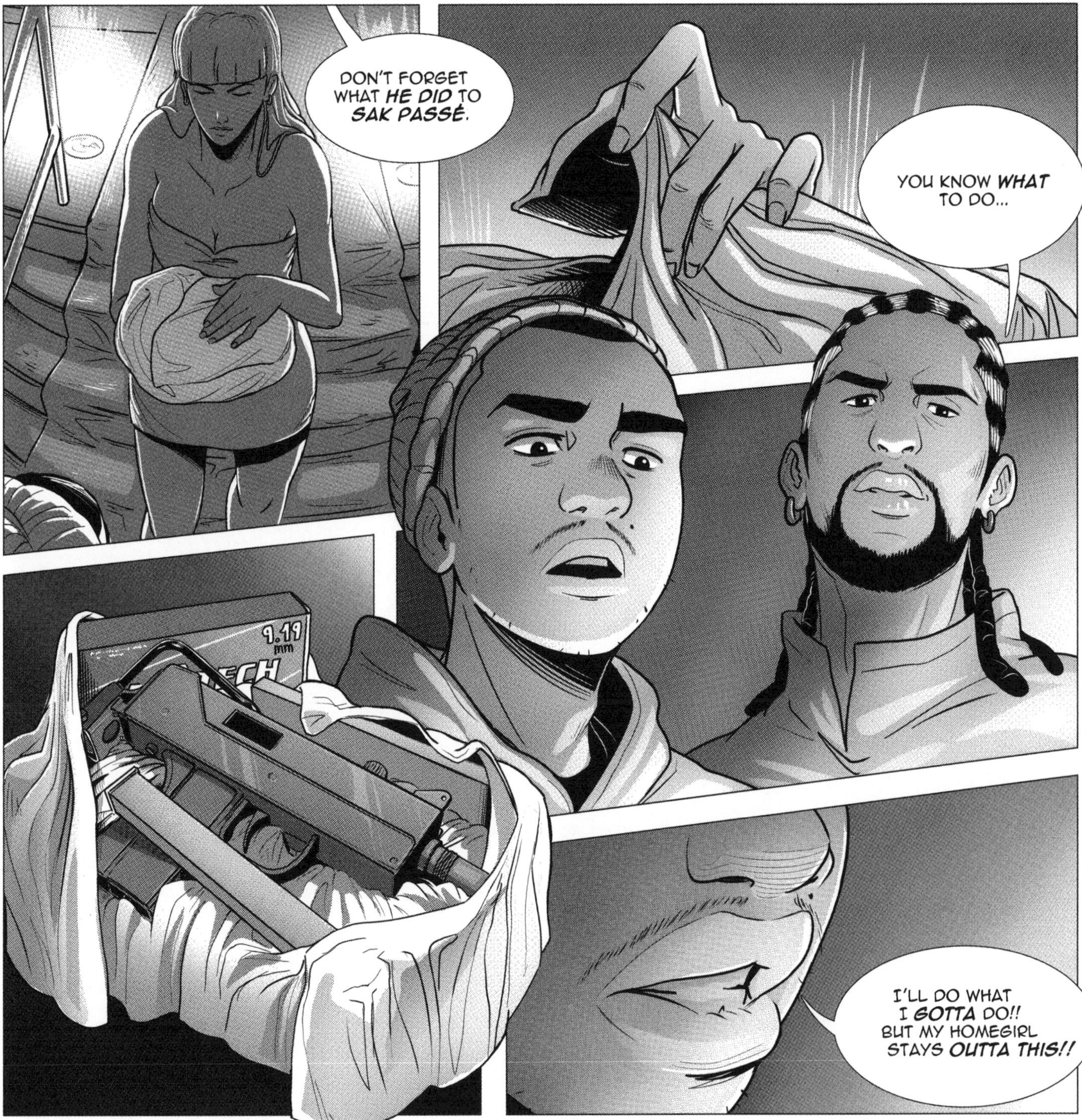
DON'T FORGET WHAT *HE DID* TO *SAK PASSÉ*.
YOU KNOW *WHAT* TO DO...
I'LL DO WHAT *I GOTTA* DO!! BUT MY HOMEGIRL STAYS *OUTTA THIS!!*
9.19 mm

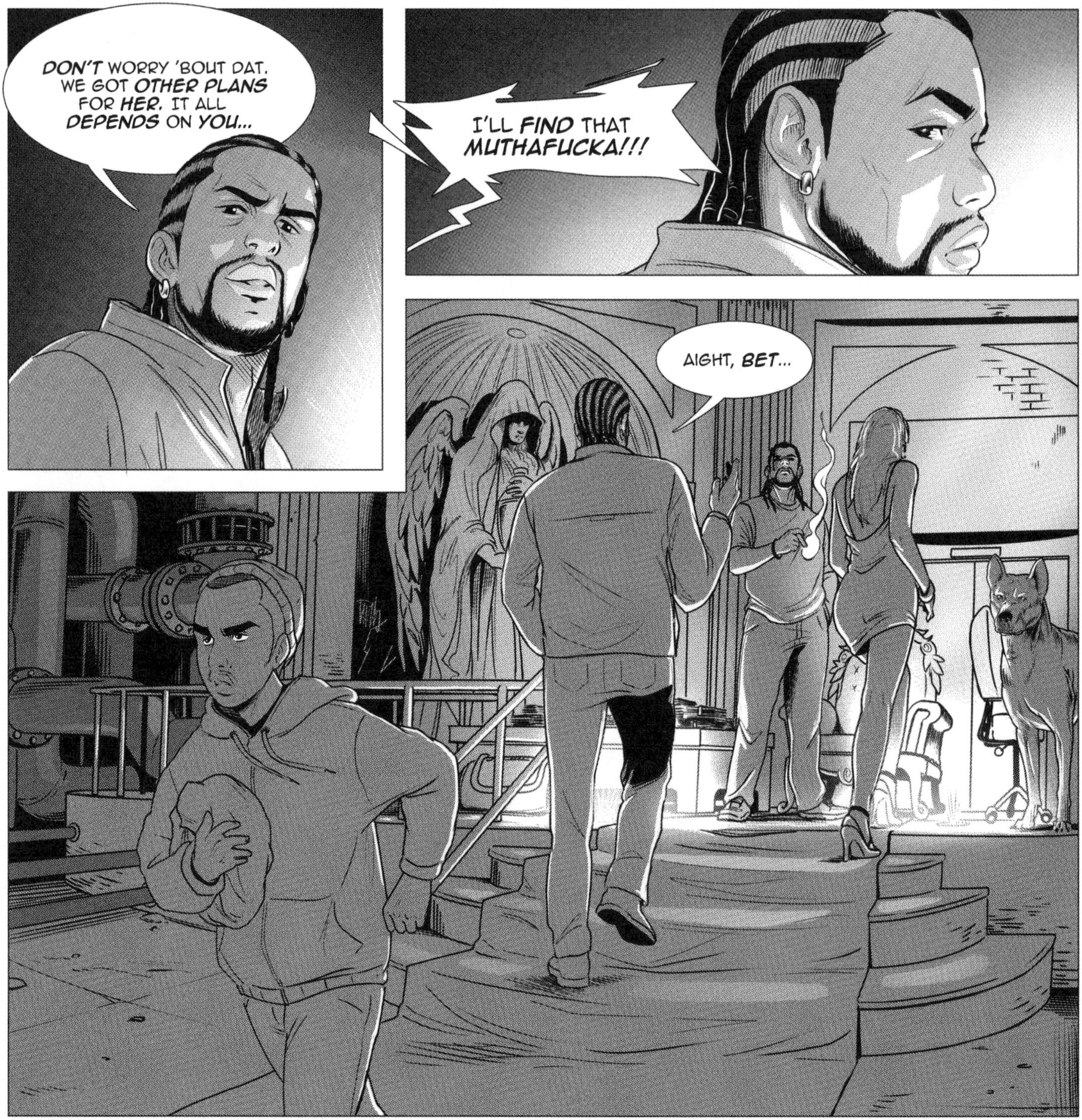
DON'T WORRY 'BOUT DAT. WE GOT OTHER PLANS FOR HER. IT ALL DEPENDS ON YOU...
I'LL FIND THAT MUTHAFUCKA!!!
AIGHT, BET...

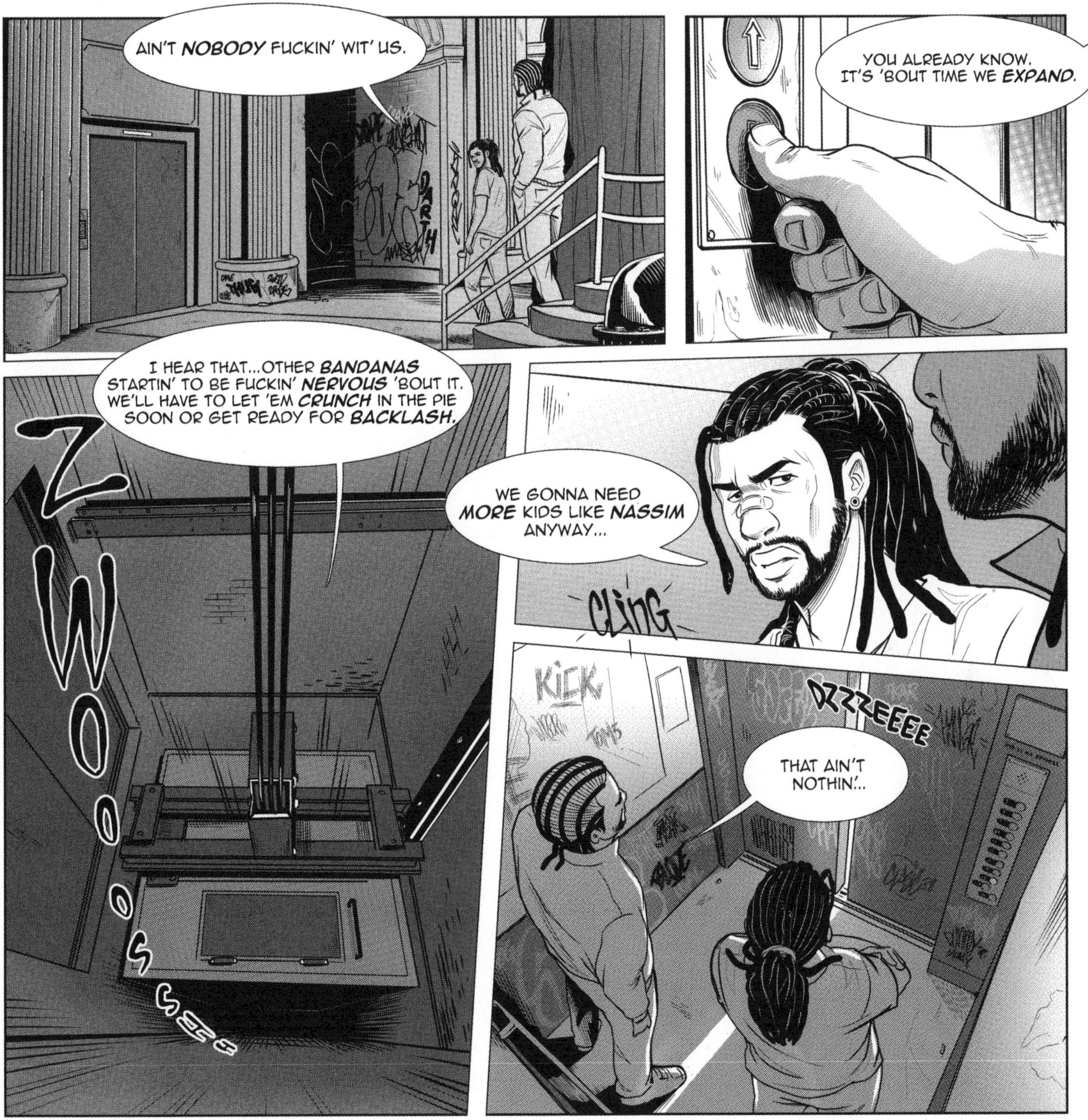
AIN'T NOBODY FUCKIN' WIT' US.
YOU ALREADY KNOW. IT'S 'BOUT TIME WE EXPAND.
I HEAR THAT...OTHER BANDANAS STARTIN' TO BE FUCKIN' NERVOUS 'BOUT IT. WE'LL HAVE TO LET 'EM CRUNCH IN THE PIE SOON OR GET READY FOR BACKLASH.
ZWOOOSSHH
WE GONNA NEED MORE KIDS LIKE NASSIM ANYWAY...
CLING
DZZZEEEEE
THAT AIN'T NOTHIN'...

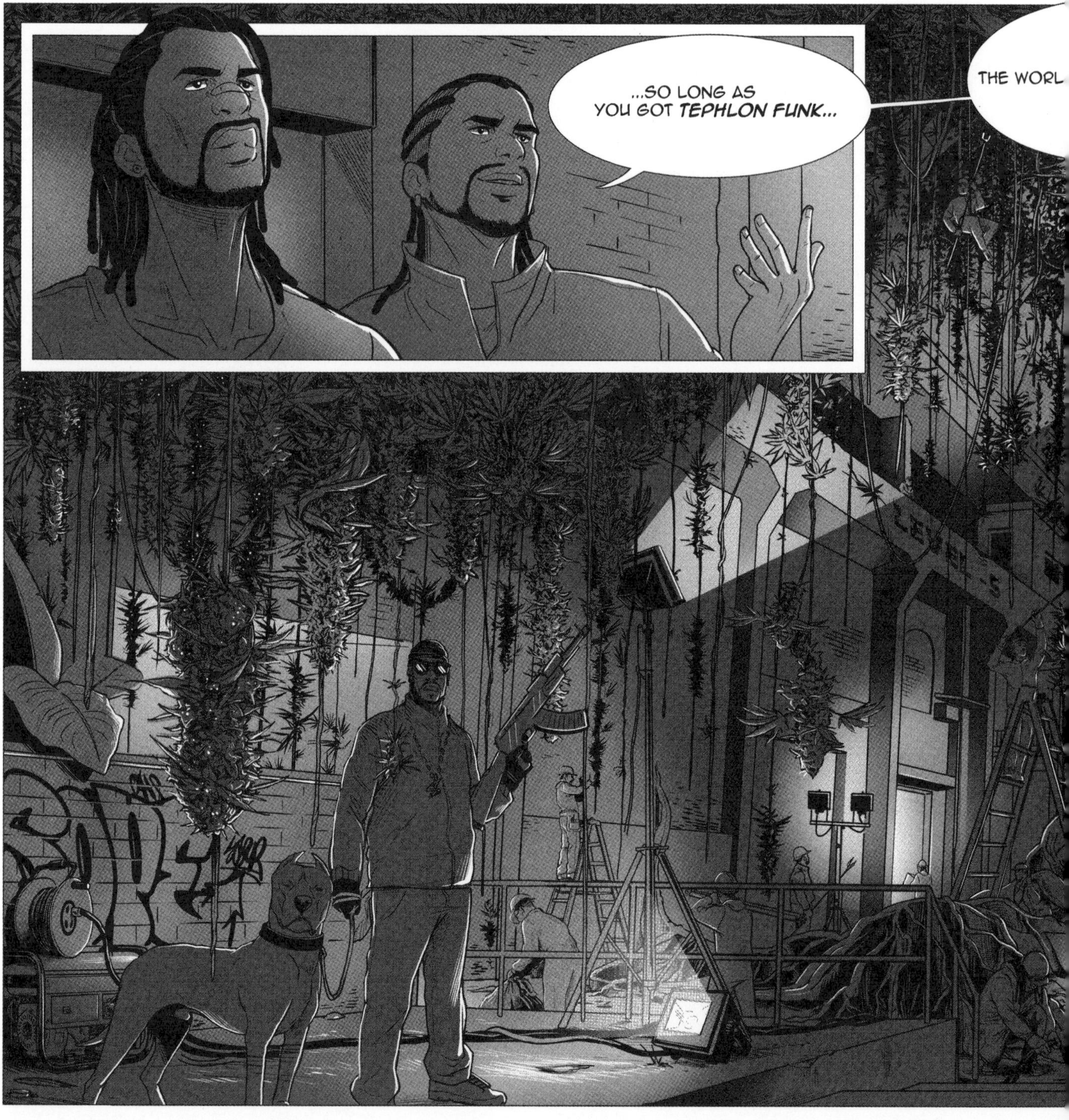
...SO LONG AS YOU GOT TEPHLON FUNK...
THE WORL

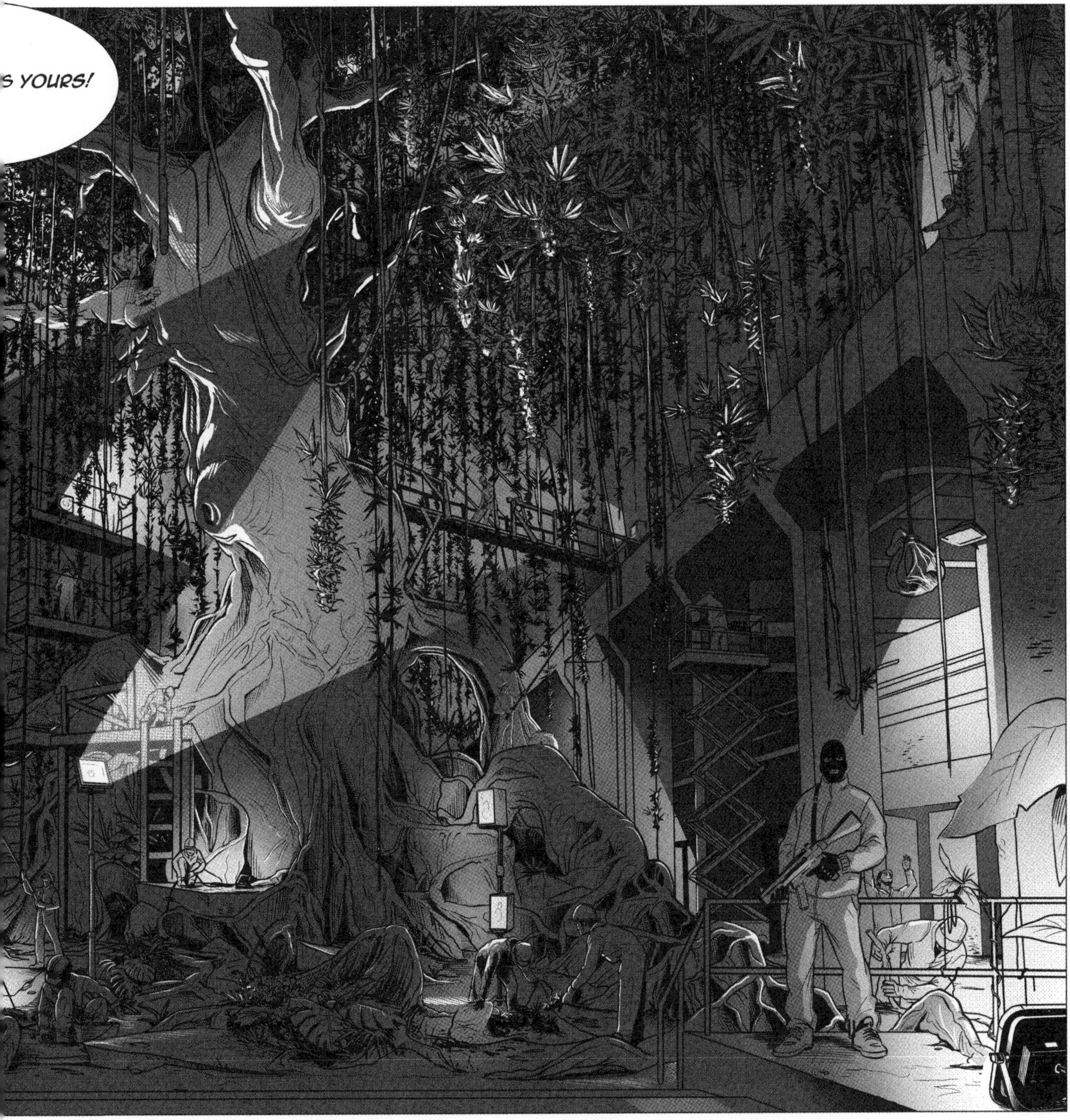
S YOURS!

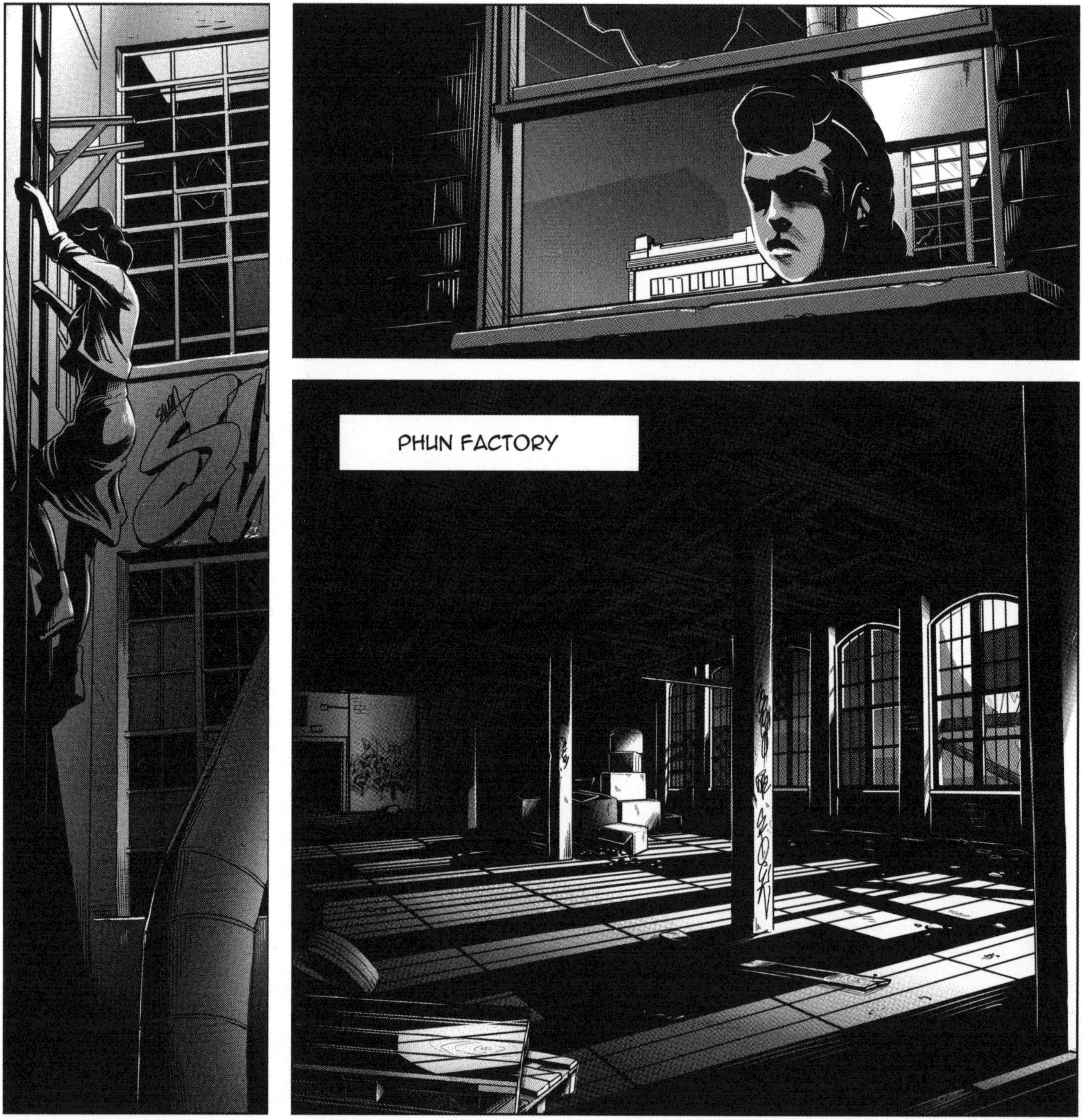
PHUN FACTORY

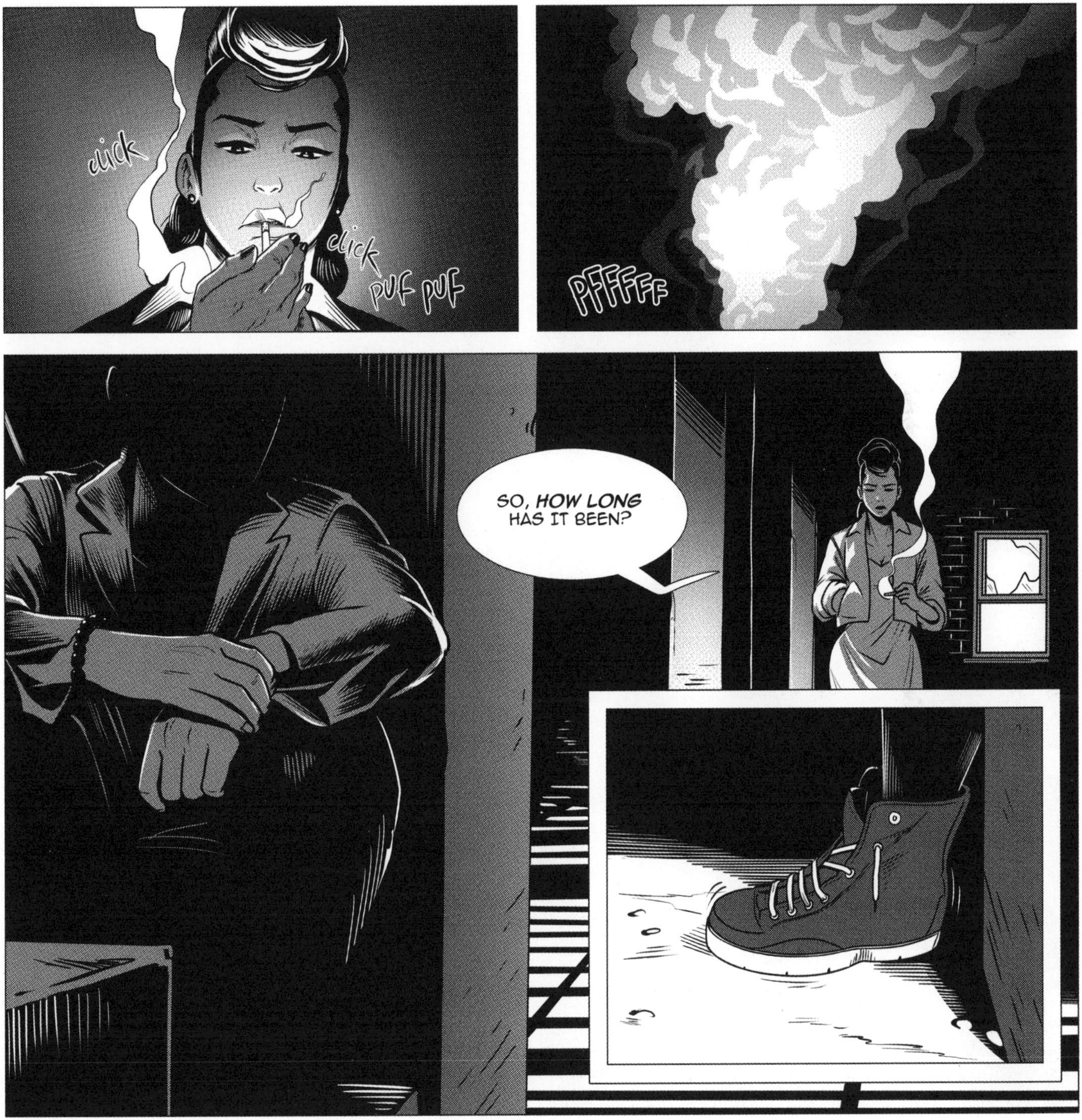
click
click
puf puf
PFFFFFF
SO, HOW LONG HAS IT BEEN?

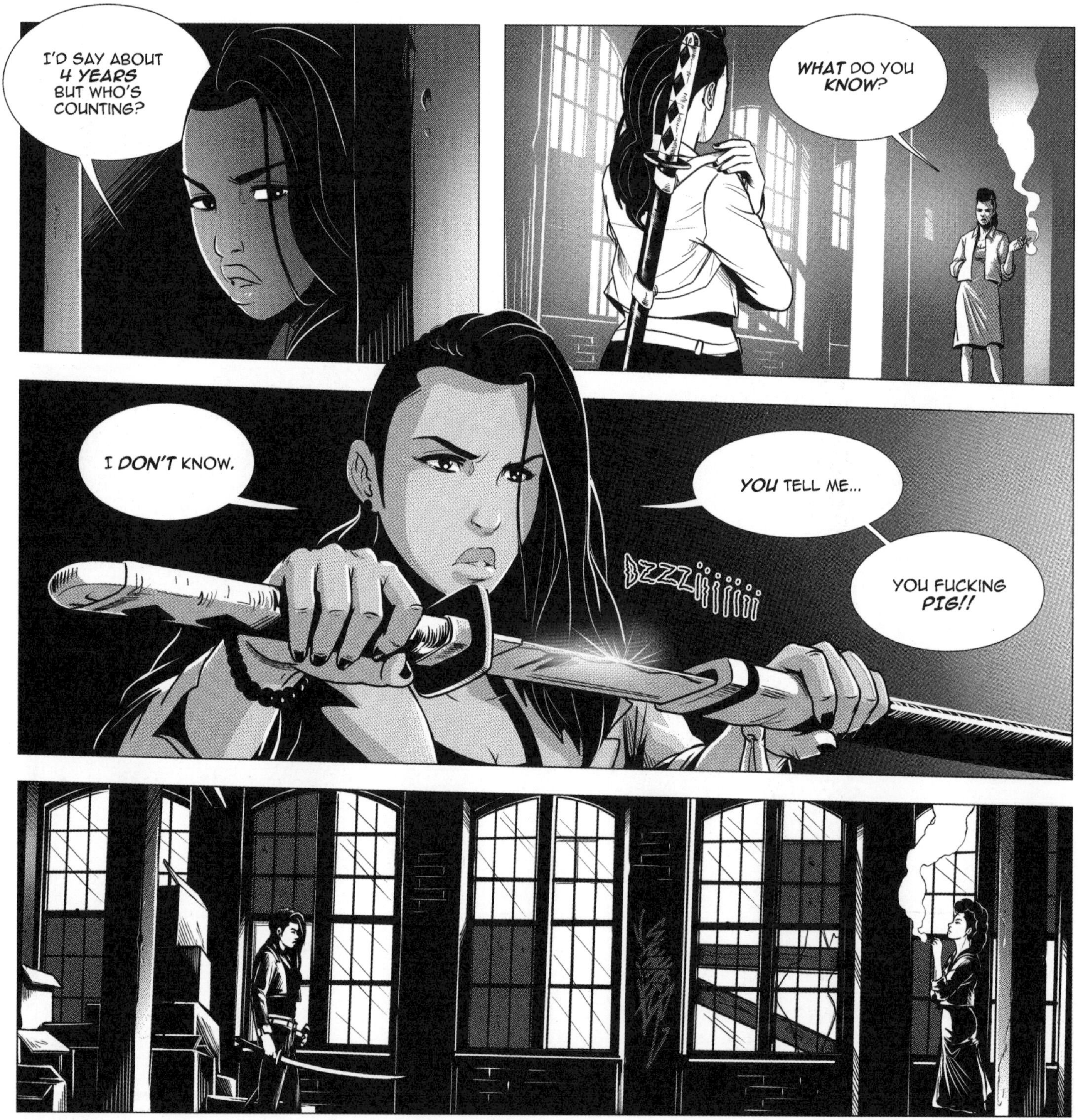

I'D SAY ABOUT 4 YEARS BUT WHO'S COUNTING?
WHAT DO YOU KNOW?
I DON'T KNOW.
YOU TELL ME...
BZZZiiiiiiii
YOU FUCKING PIG!!

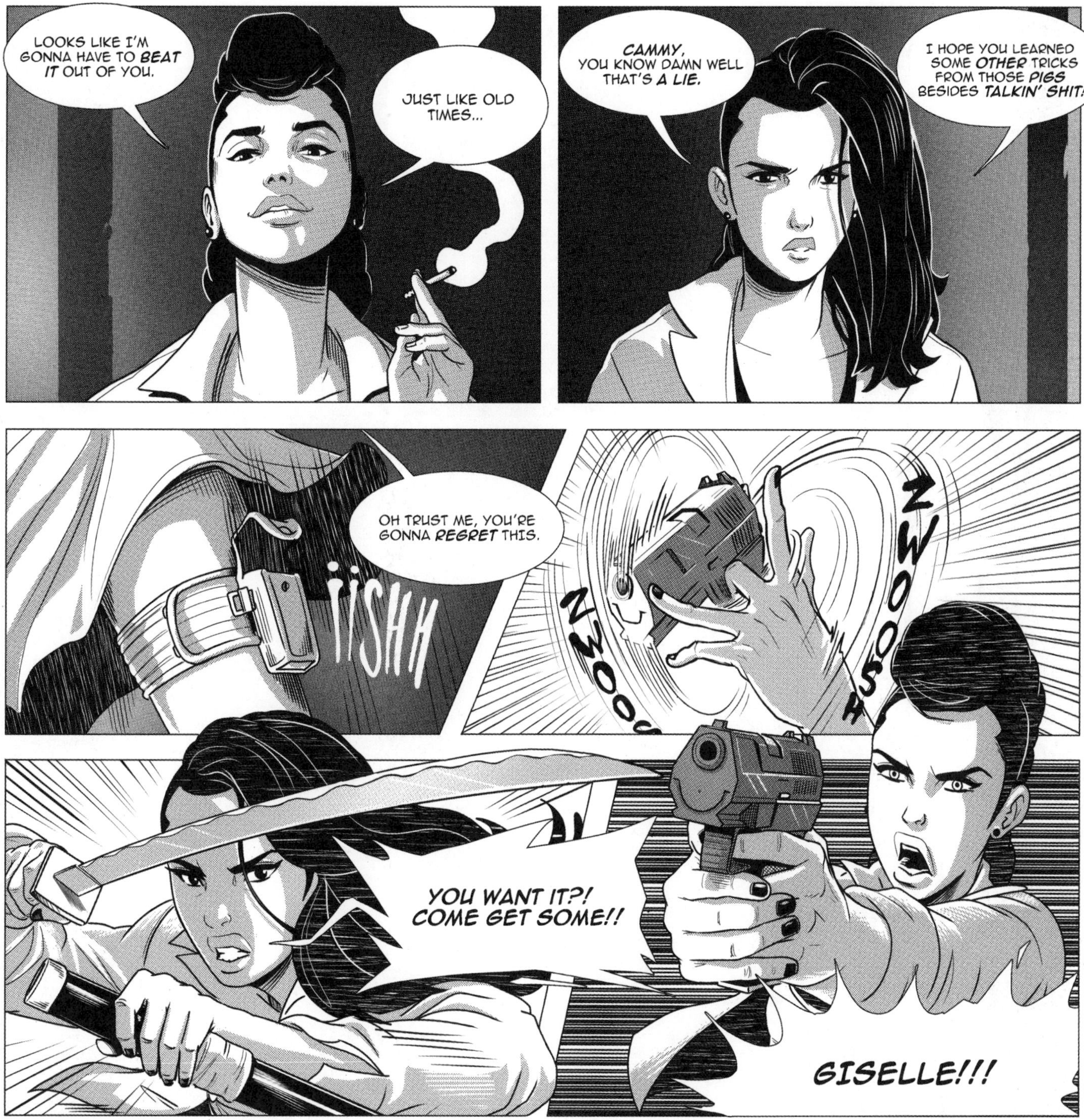
LOOKS LIKE I'M GONNA HAVE TO BEAT IT OUT OF YOU.
JUST LIKE OLD TIMES...
CAMMY, YOU KNOW DAMN WELL THAT'S A LIE.
I HOPE YOU LEARNED SOME OTHER TRICKS FROM THOSE PIGS BESIDES TALKIN' SHIT!
OH TRUST ME, YOU'RE GONNA REGRET THIS.
IISHH
ZWOOOSH
ZWOOOSH
YOU WANT IT?! COME GET SOME!!
GISELLE!!!

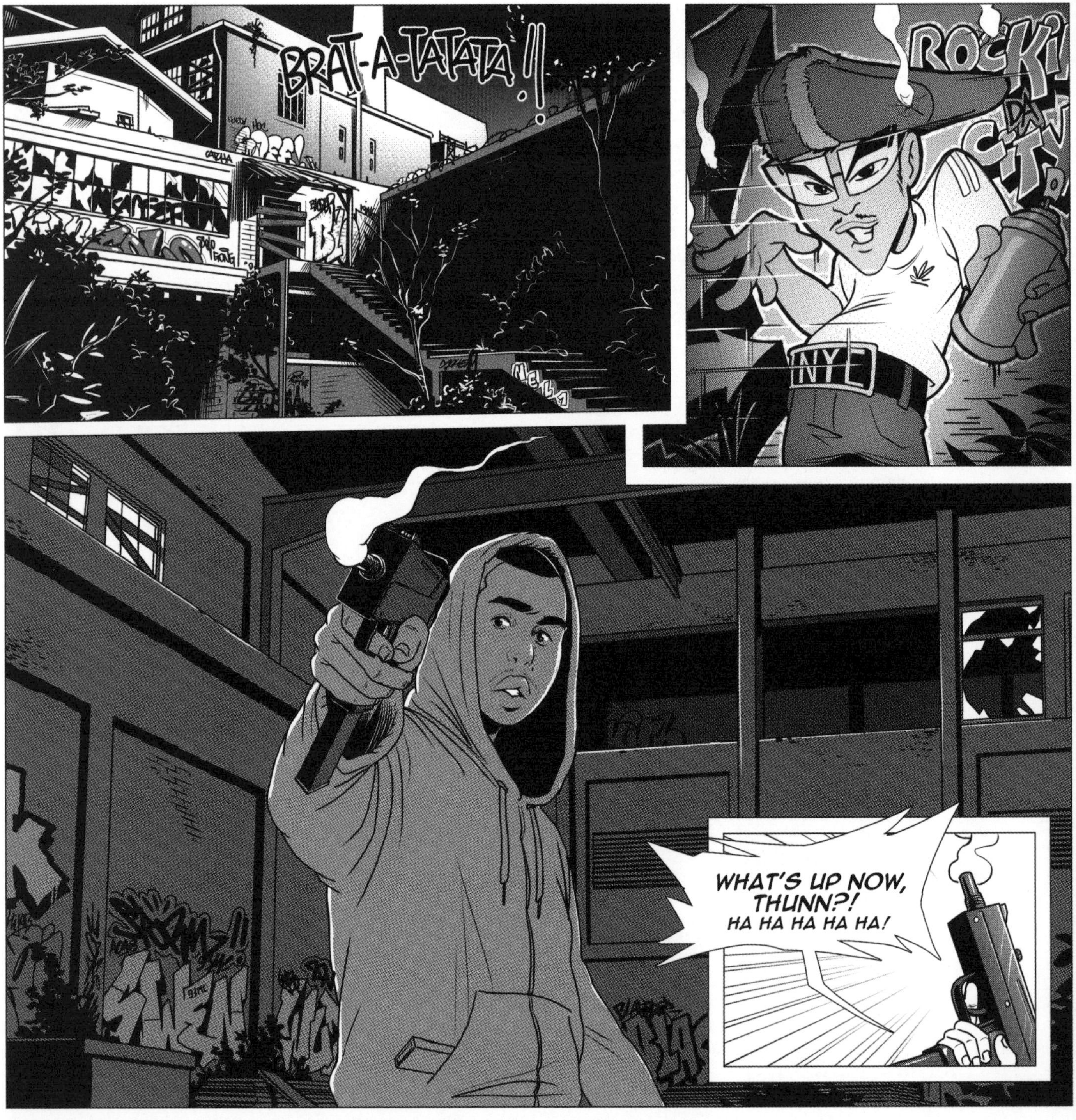
BRAT-A-TATATA!!
WHAT'S UP NOW, THUNN?!
HA HA HA HA HA!

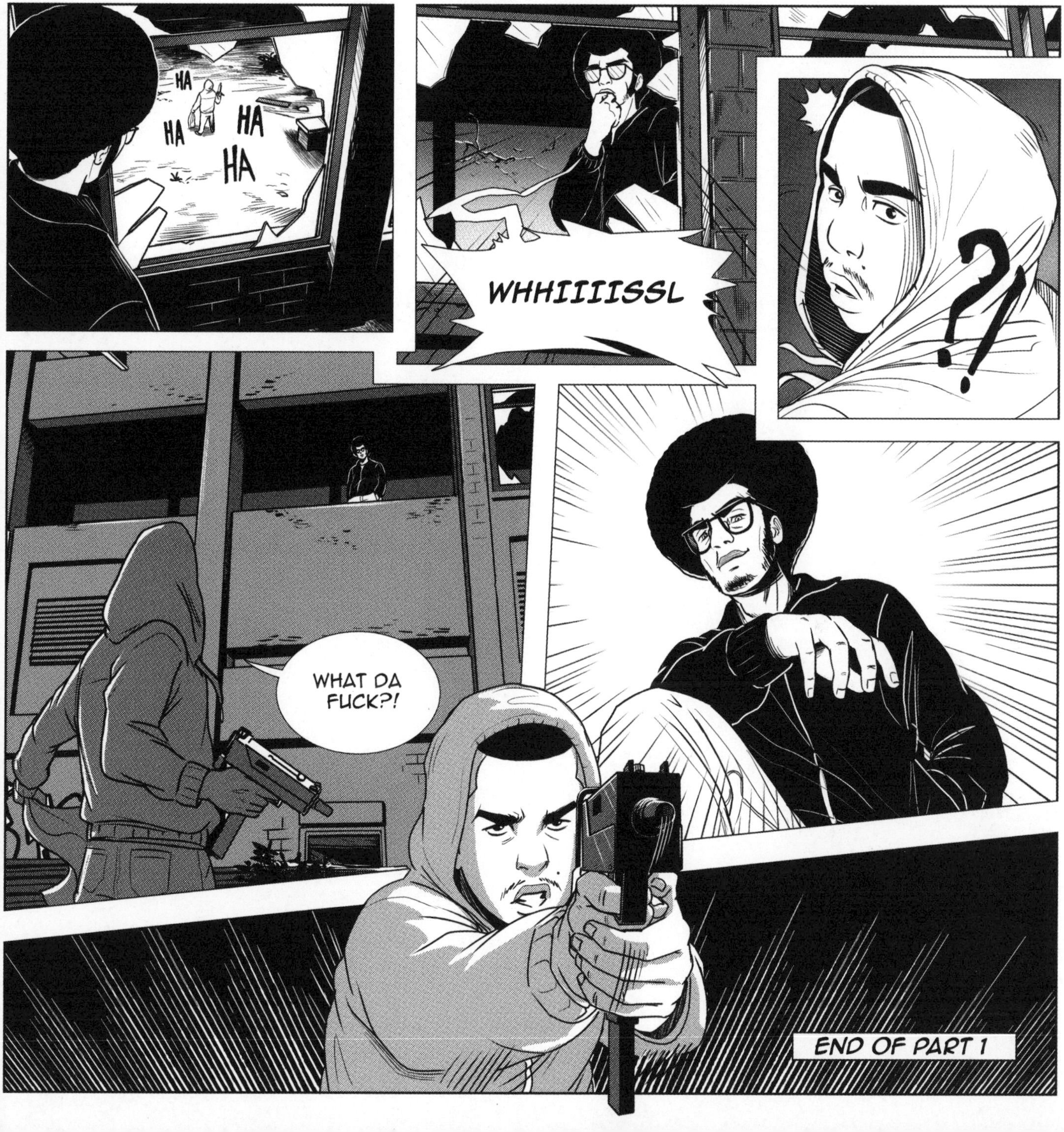
HA
HA
HA
HA
WHHIIIISSL
?!
WHAT DA FUCK?!
END OF PART 1

H·N·Y·C

Tephlon Funk
Art Gallery

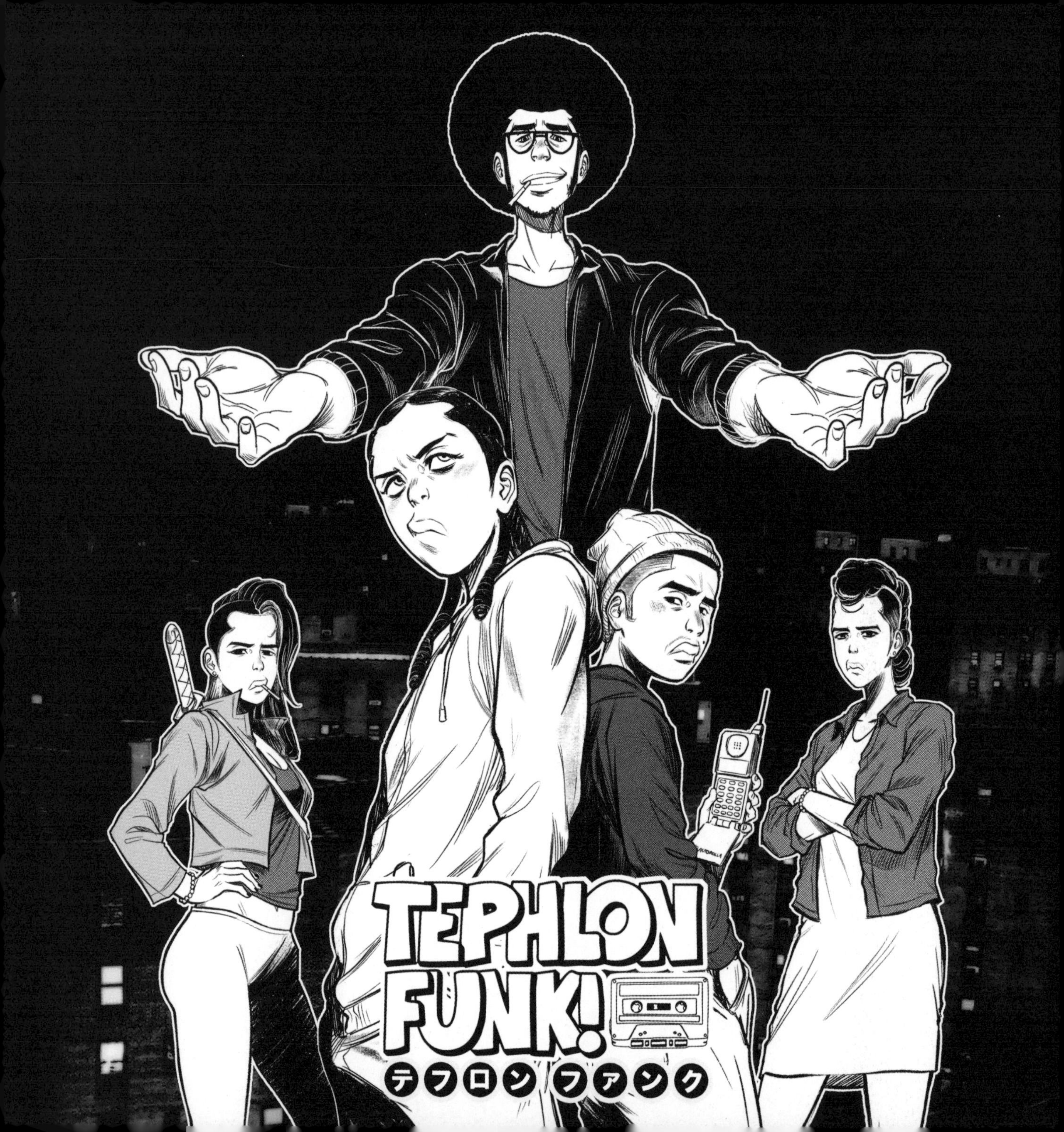
TEPHLON FUNK!
テフロン ファンク

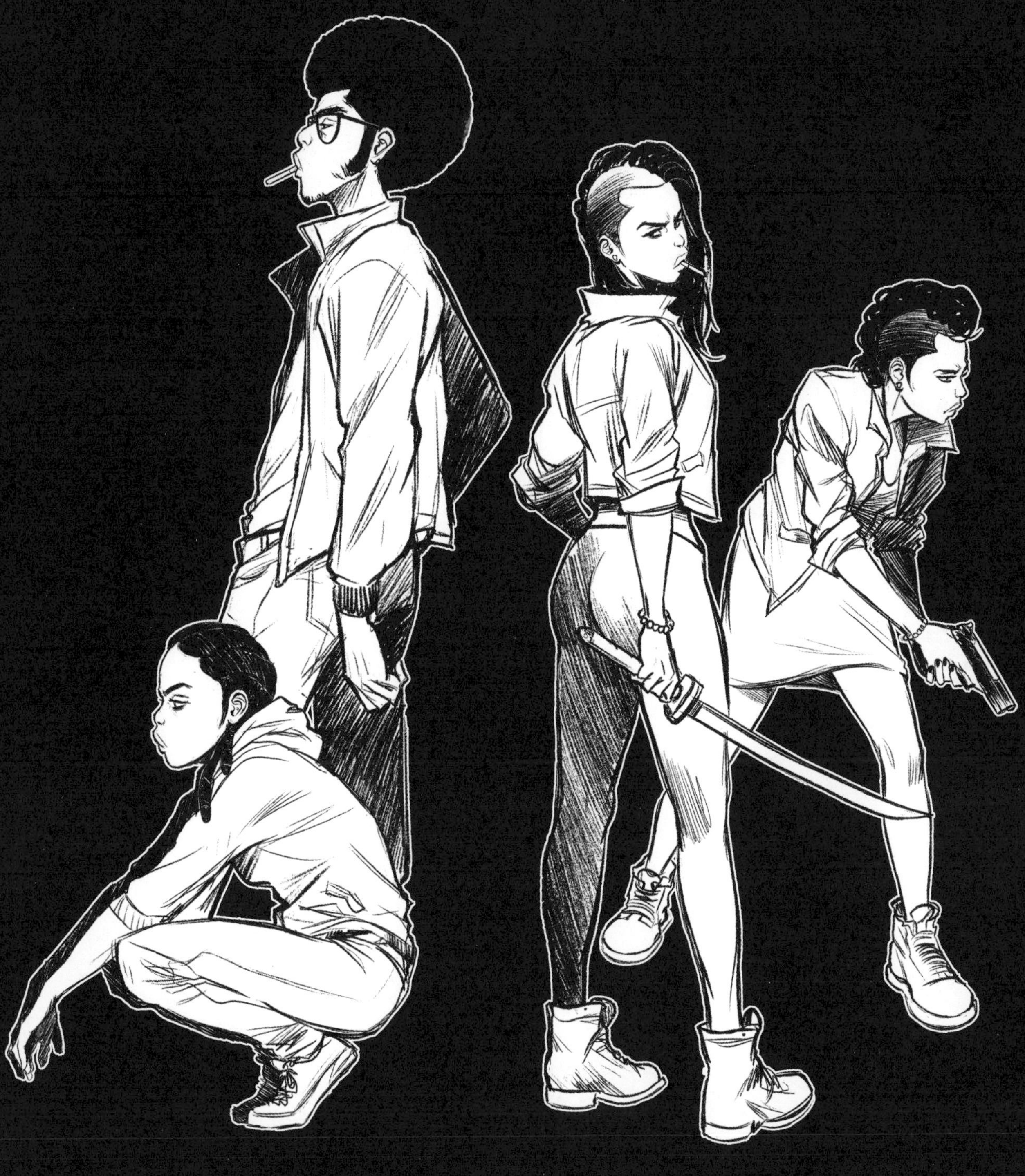

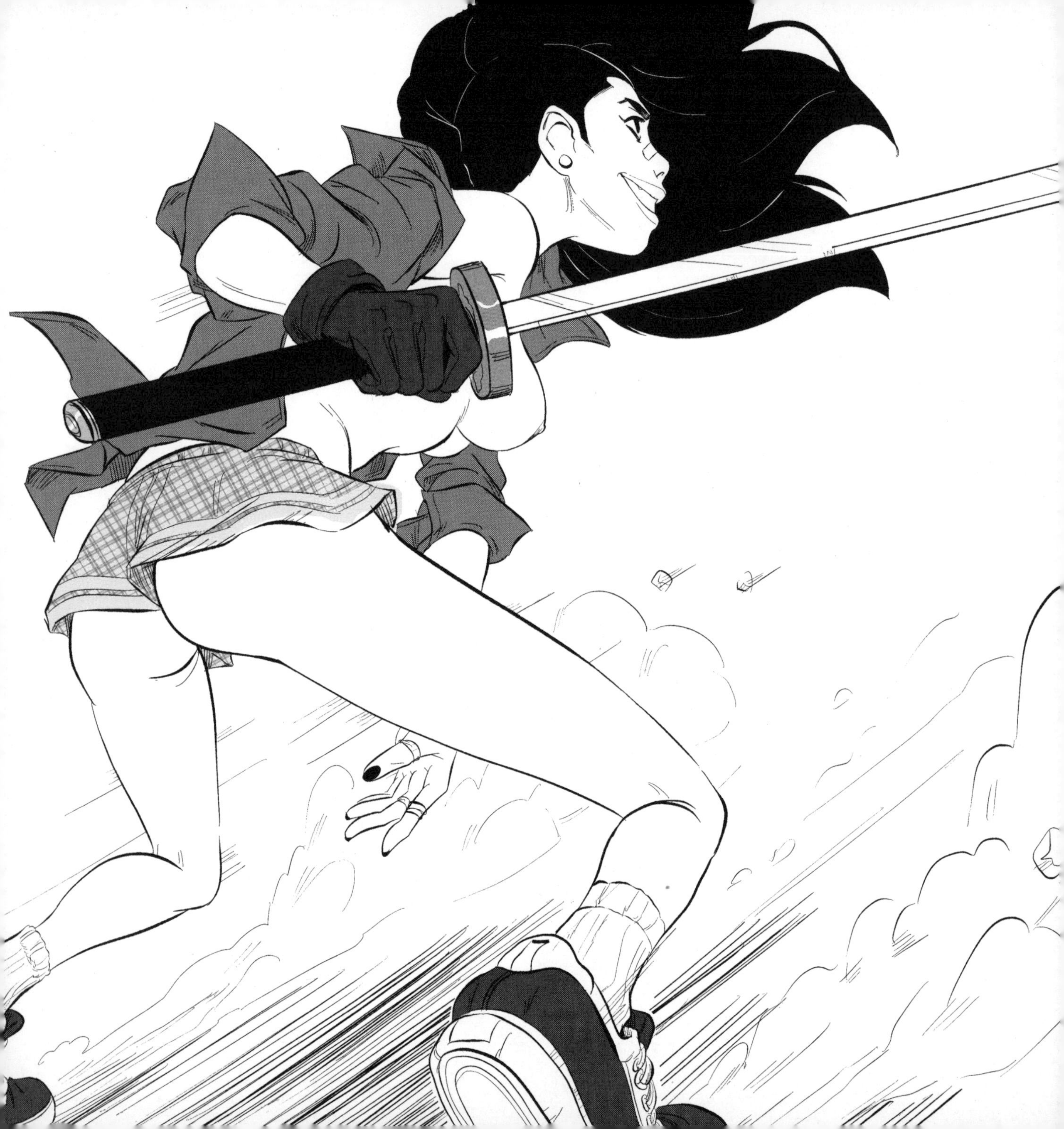

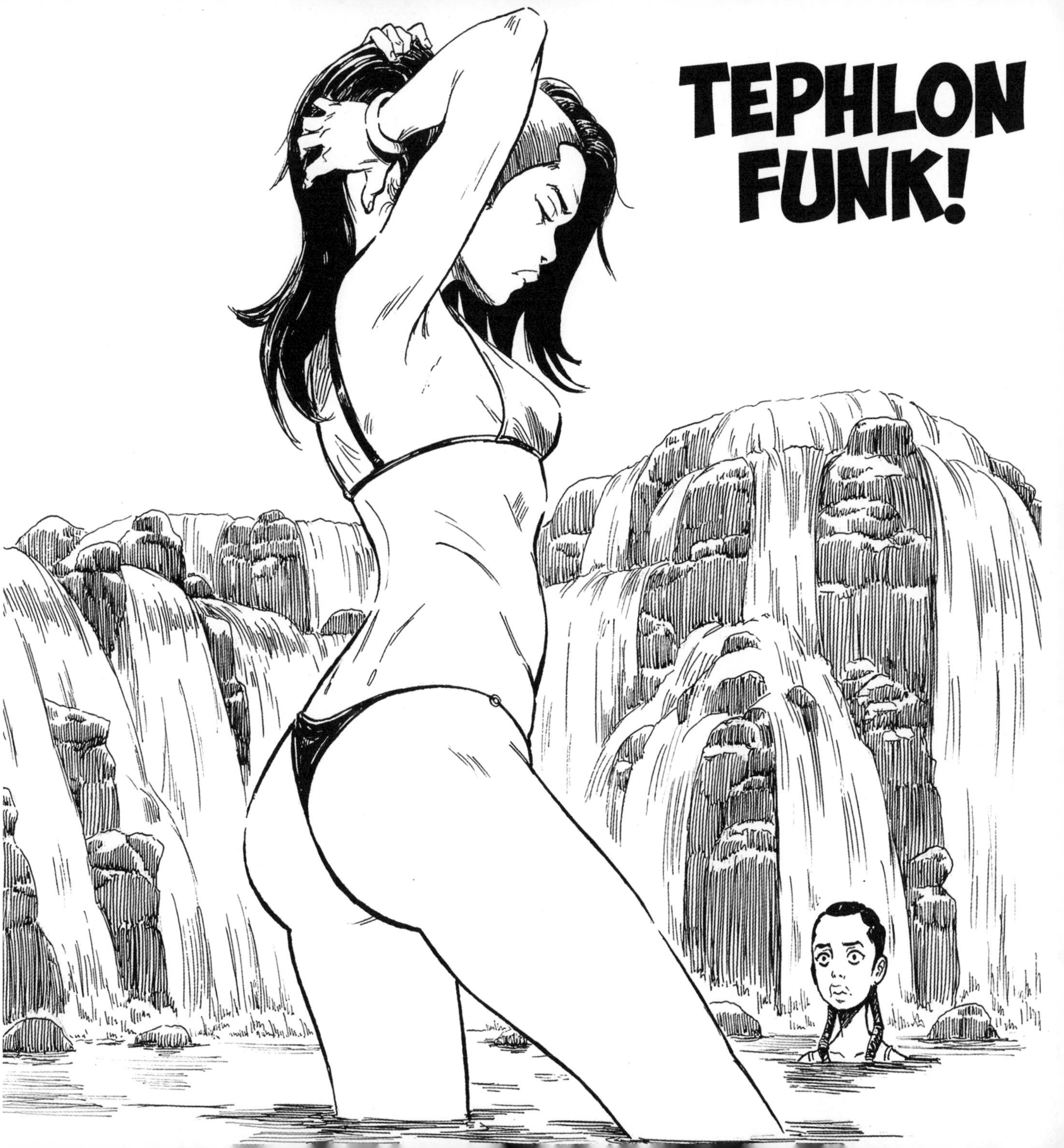
TEPHLON
FUNK!

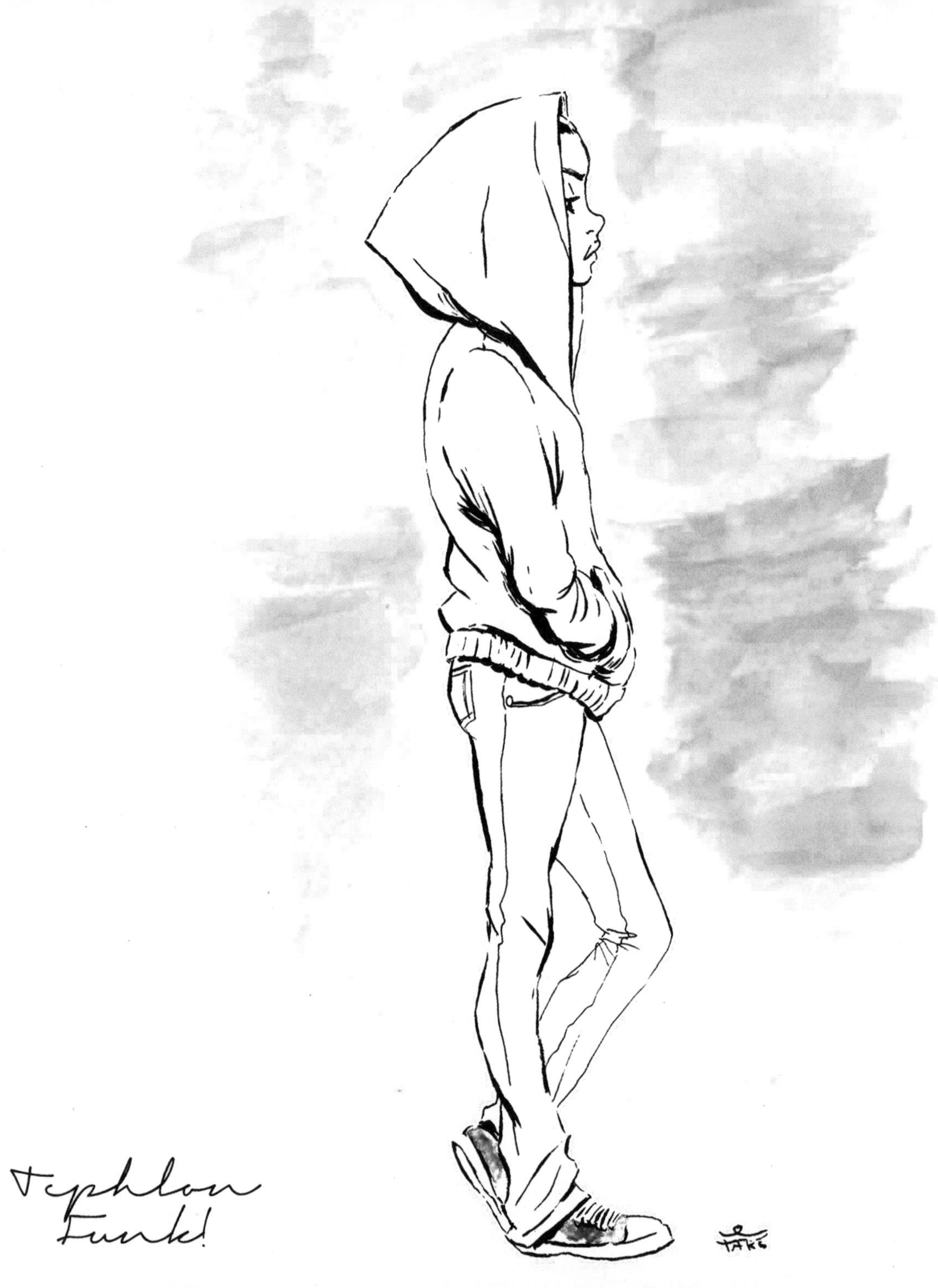
Tephlon
Funk!

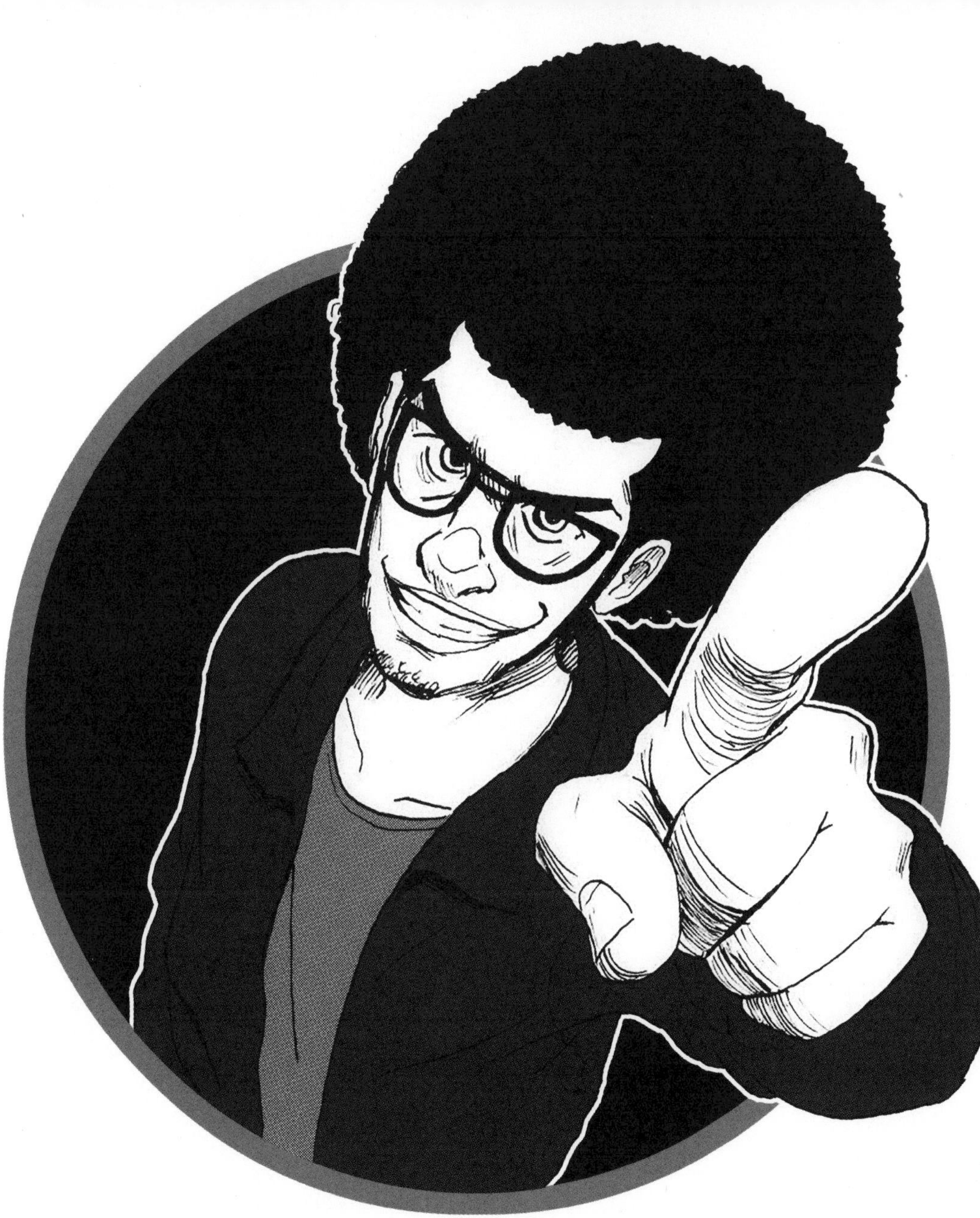

ザーブリーエル

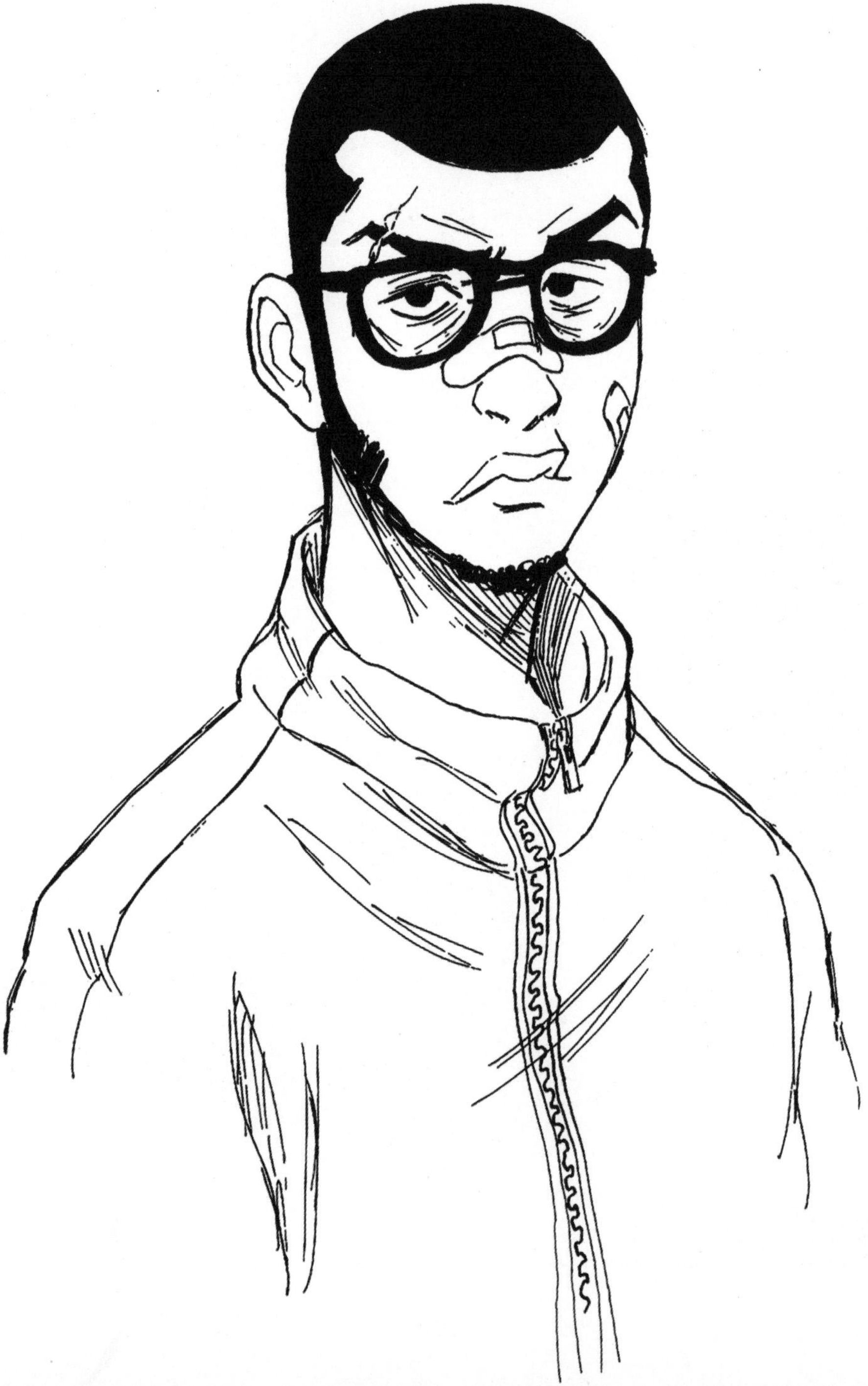

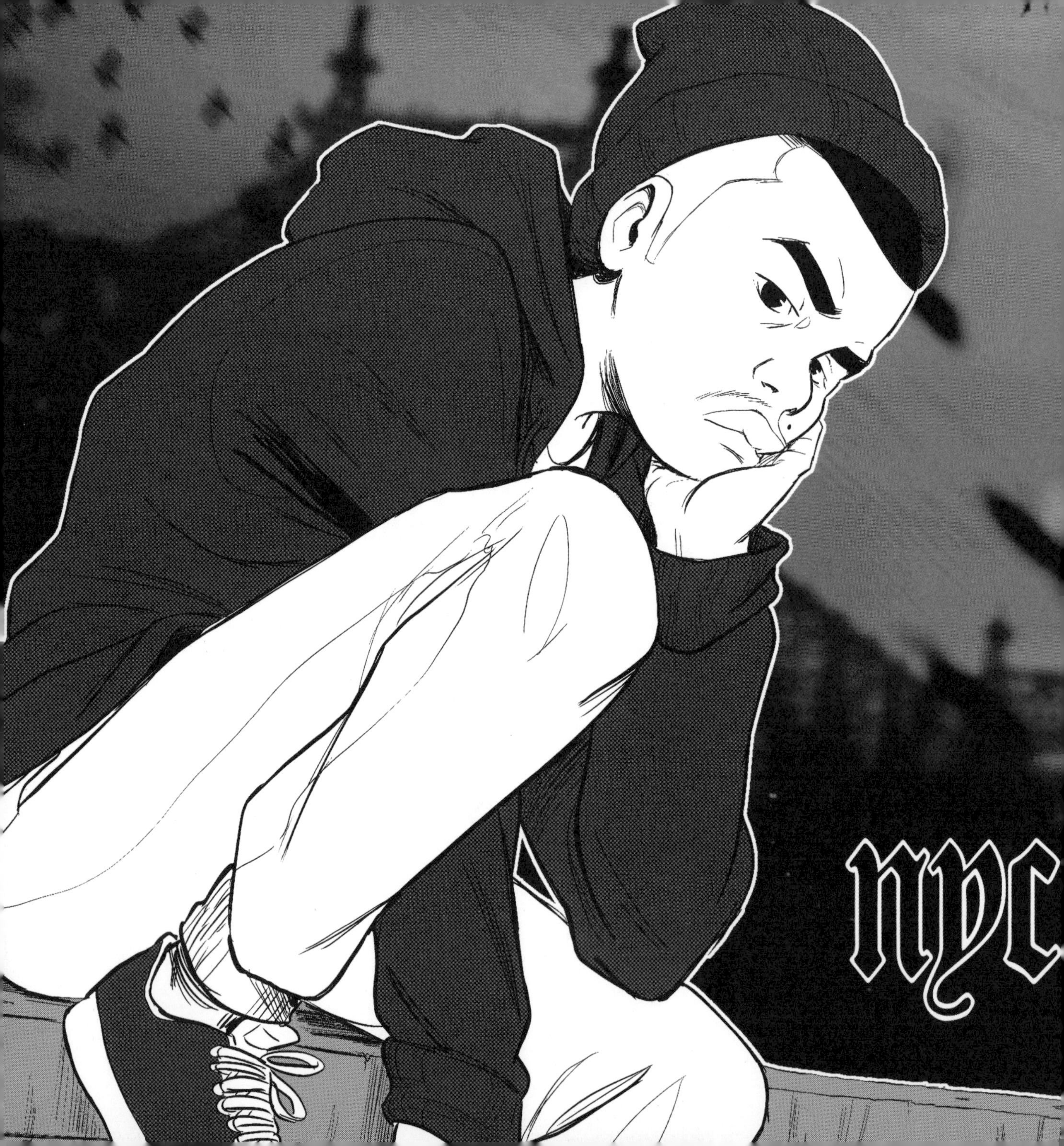
nyc

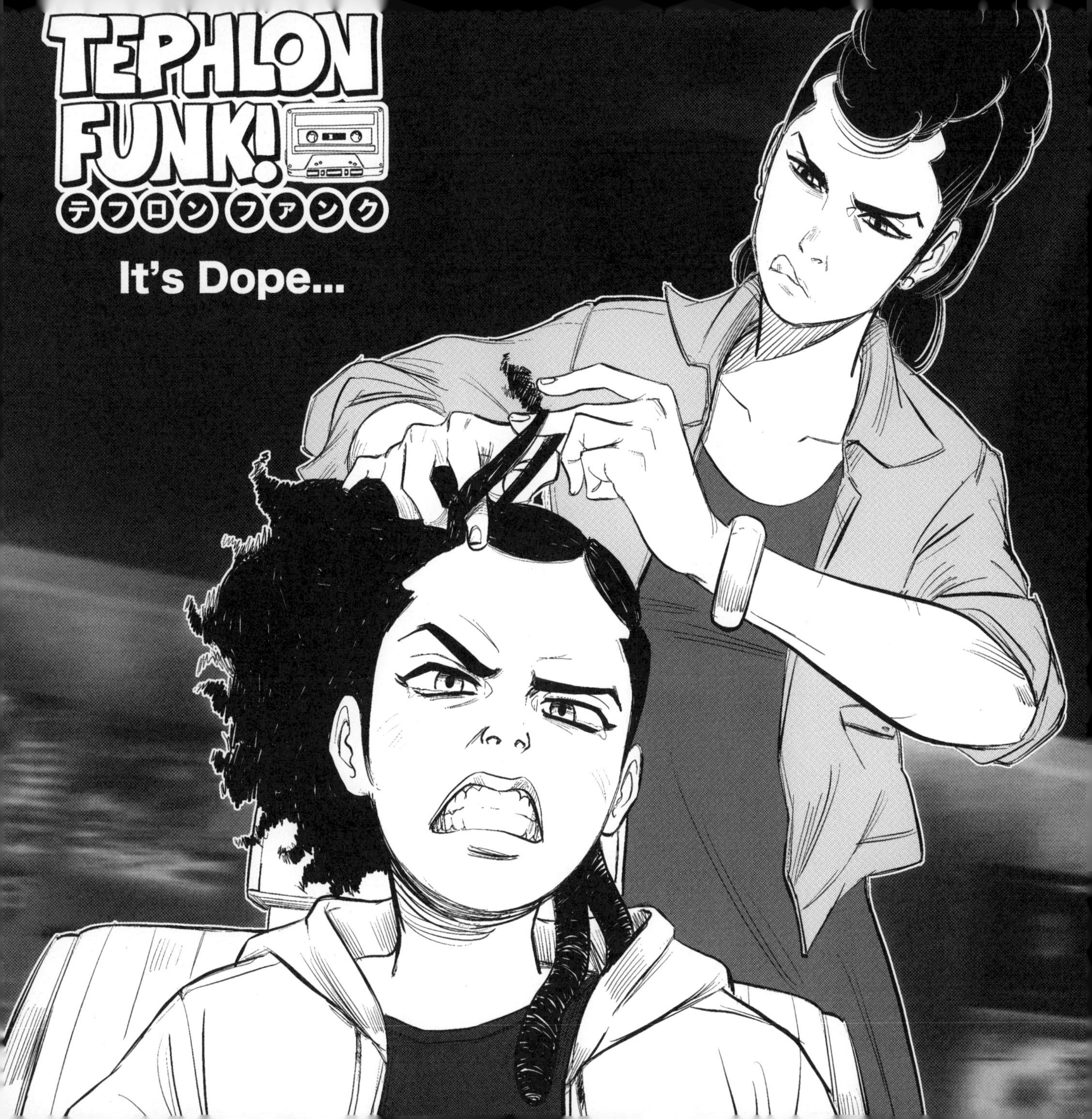
TEPHLON FUNK!
テフロン ファンク
It's Dope...

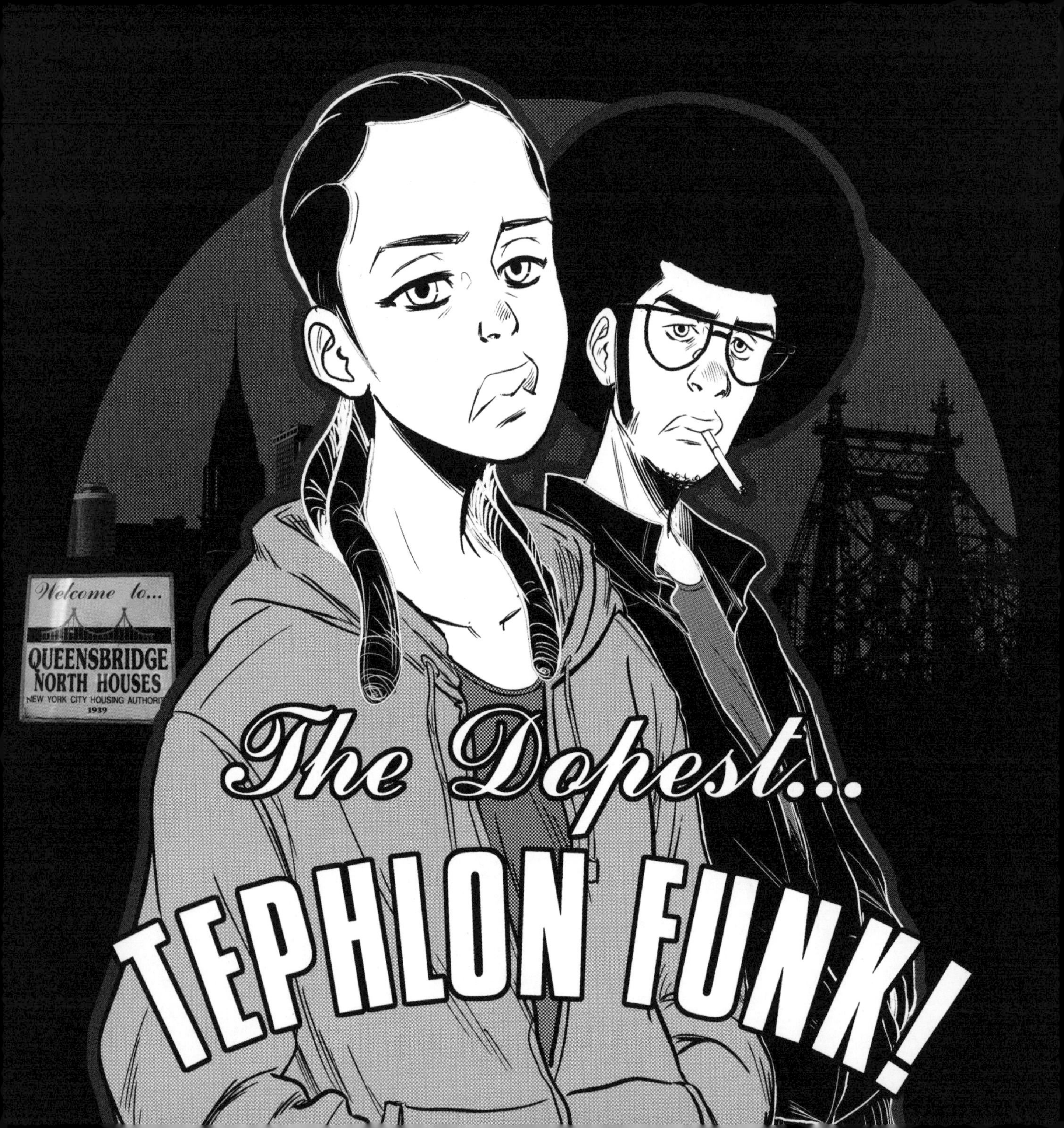
Welcome to...
QUEENSBRIDGE
NORTH HOUSES
NEW YORK CITY HOUSING AUTHORITY
1939
The Dopest...
TEPHLON FUNK!

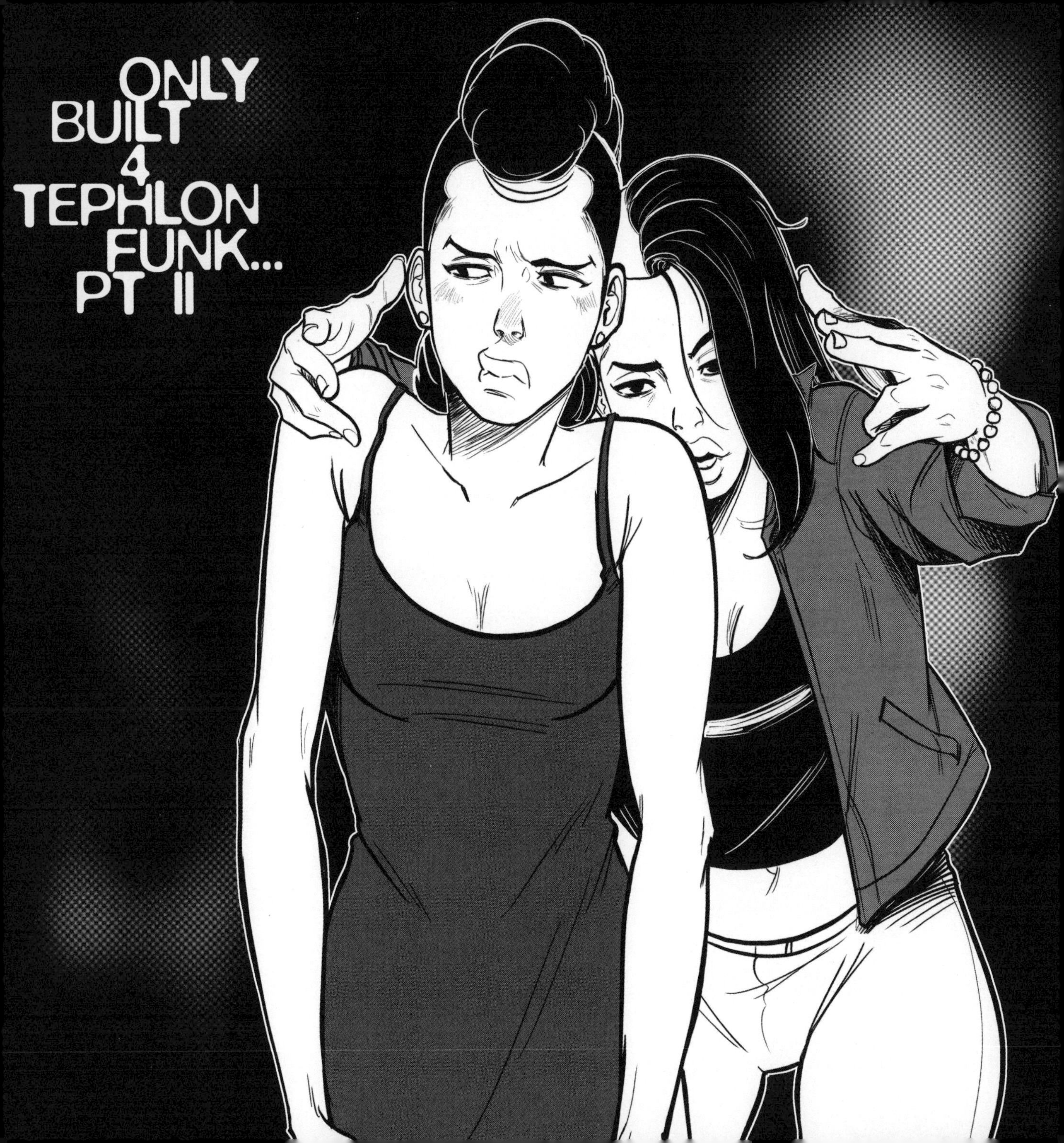
ONLY BUILT 4 TEPHLON FUNK... PT II

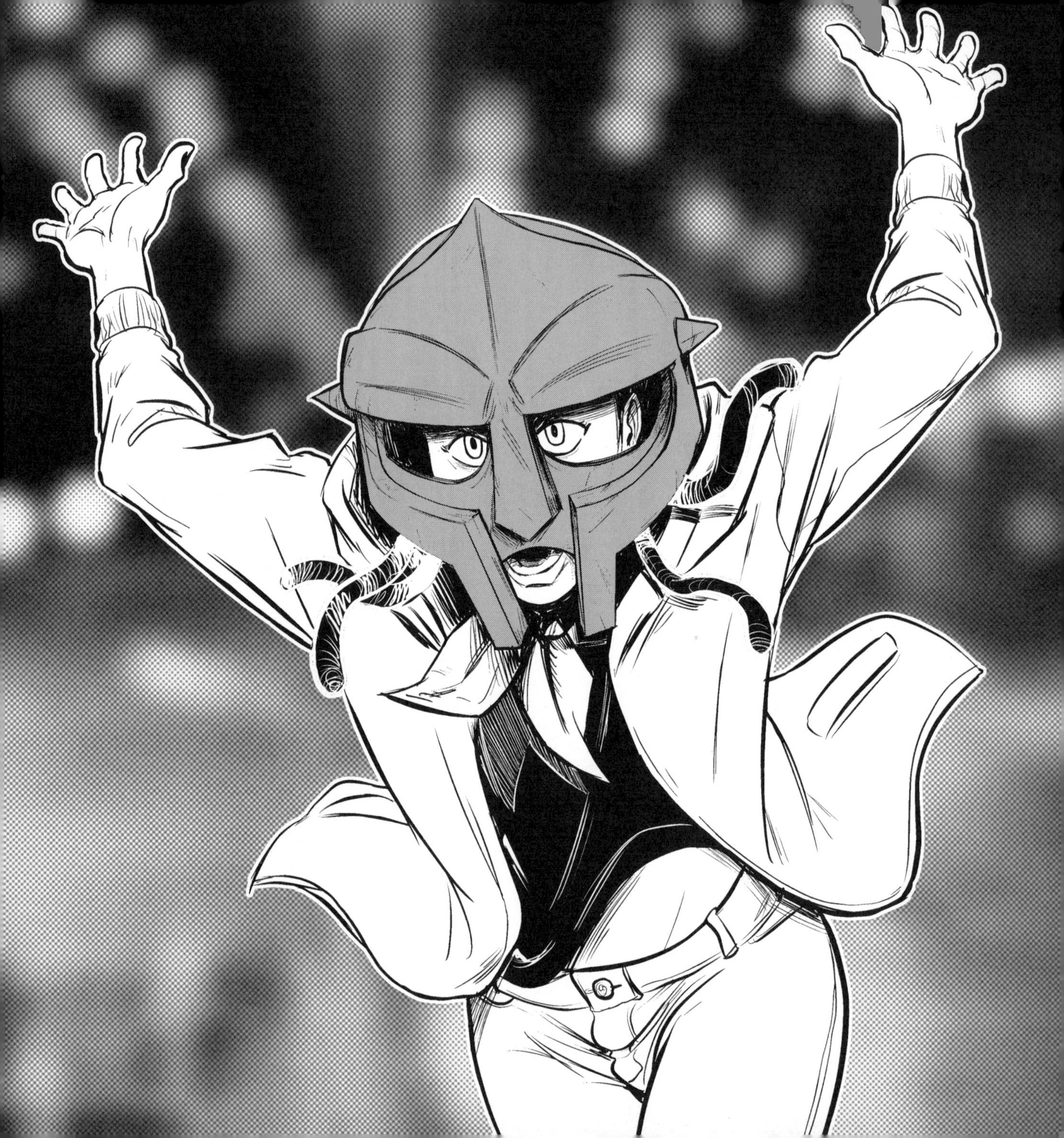

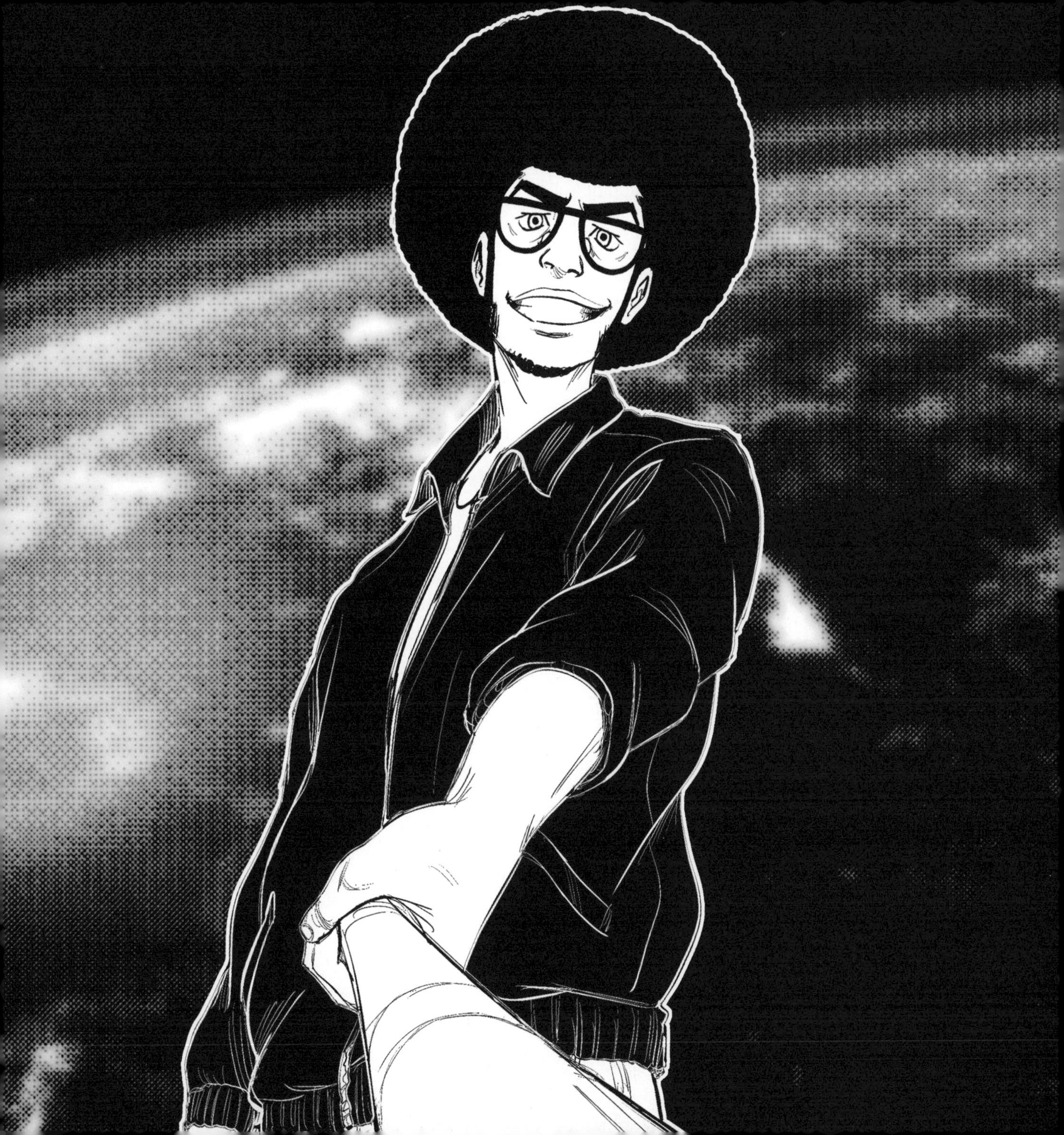

SHOUT-OUTS

A big shout-out to my dad, Gerard Metayer, for putting up with my silly dreams. My big sister, Tessa Metayer, for being my backbone through the very tough times. My cousins, Geoffrey and Dayon Richstone, for giving me the confidence that I needed to never give up. Calvin Reid, for guiding me along the world of book publishing. John Jennings, for giving me the opportunity to vend at our first comic book festival. As well as the team, David Tako, Nicolas Safe, and Fat Jon, for helping me take *Tephlon Funk!* to places I never imagined. Lastly, I'd like to thank our editor, Judy Khuu, for reaching out to us. God bless you all.

—Stephane Metayer

Shout-out to my parents for suffering my bullshits, and to all my 45 Dept people (Coolos first in line). Shout-out to my London crew, my ZDV Boyz, and the elders 93mc and TAP crew. Shout-out to Babs, Sapi, JP74, Oussou, and Jeanne, living in our hearts forever!!! Shout-out to all the people who follow us and helped us with the project at the beginning—thanks a lot for everything! Shout-out to David for involving me in this; I owe you once again, bro! Shout-out to Stephane for his trust, patience, and passion! Shout-out to Dark Horse Comics and Judy; it's just awesome! And final shout-out to all those who love and live that fucking hip-hop! Peace!

—Nicolas Safe

Huge love, respect, and thanks for my bros Nicolas and Stephane for everything they did for me and for *Tephlon Funk!* Can't wait to go further with you guys!

—David Tako

STEPHANE METAYER   CREATOR I WRITER I GRAPHIC DESIGN
An artist from Queens, New York City. His inspirations include Spike Lee, Jean-Michel Basquiat, Shinichirō Watanabe, Bengus, Akiman, Kentaro Miura, and Kazuhiko Katō. Stephane's biggest influence would have to be the rapper Nas, specifically his 1994 classic debut album *Illmatic*.

This finally pushed him to create *Tephlon Funk!* all the way back in 2004. This series is his first project, which he hopes will help inspire and influence others. A true fan of both hip-hop and anime, more than fifteen years later, he's now ready to take the next step.

DAVID TAKO   ILLUSTRATOR I CHARACTER DESIGN
A French artist from Paris, born and raised loving animated films, comics, manga, and video games. He's always had a great passion for Japan and its culture. His inspirations are Satoshi Kon, Naoki Urasawa, Hayao Miyazaki, Yoshiyuki Sadamoto, and Toshihiro Kawamoto.

After animation school, he worked on mobile games and several animated projects. Now he's illustrating and doing character design for *Tephlon Funk!* along with his own personal French comic influenced by manga called *Green Class*.

NICOLAS SAFE   ILLUSTRATOR I BACKGROUNDS
A French graffiti artist from Paris who grew up with Franco-Belgian traditional comics until he discovered manga and American comic strips. His inspirations include '90s hip-hop, Katsuhiro Otomo, Humberto Ramos, William Vance, Masamune Shirow, and Yoshiaki Kawajiri.

Since animation school, he has been working with a collective of artists teaching graffiti and drawing to kids at youth centers, doing canvas walks, and creating frescoes for city halls, associations, or himself, as well as working with David Tako on a few other projects.

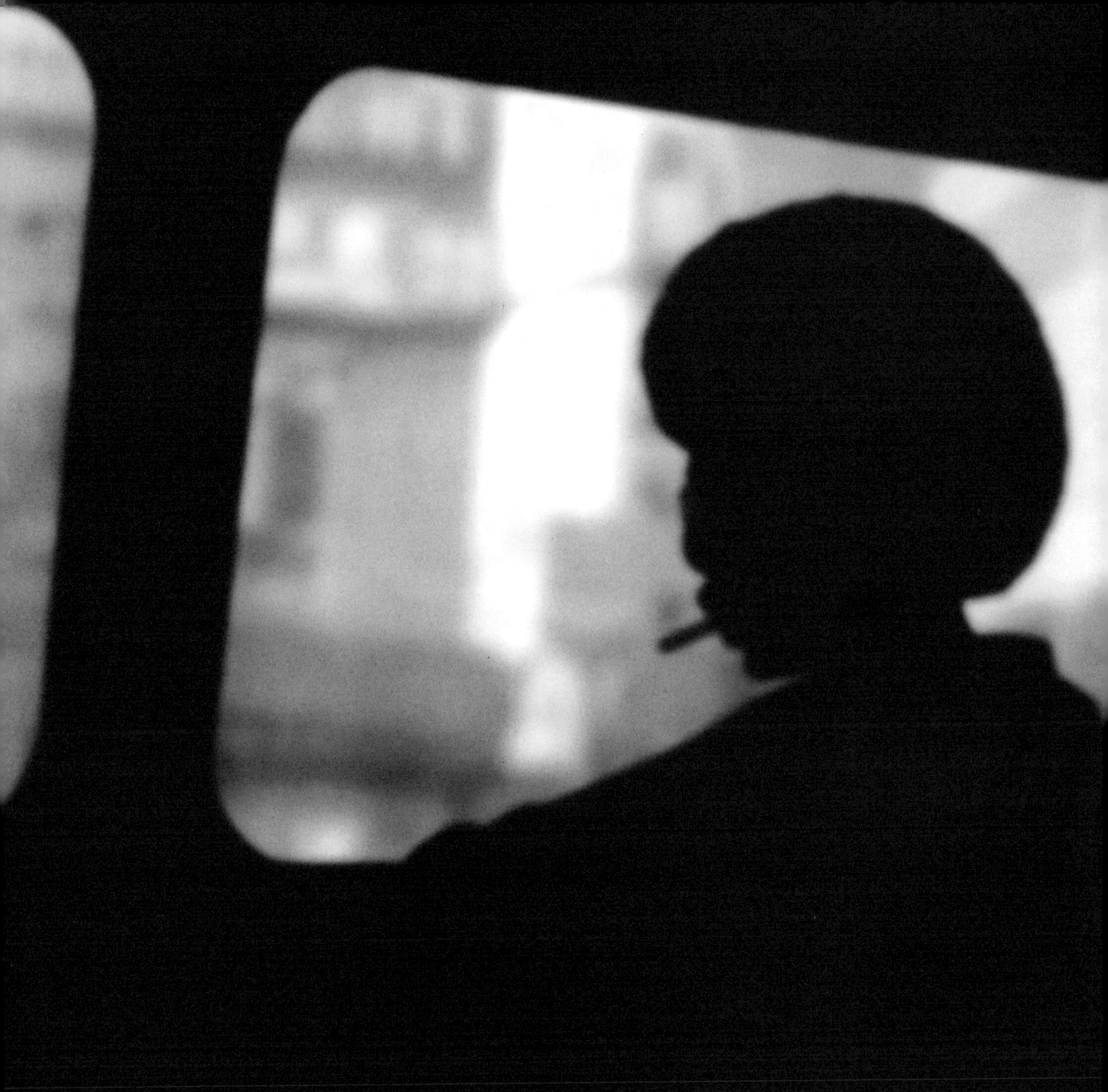

SEE YOU LATER HOMEBOY . . .

President & Publisher
MIKE RICHARDSON

Collection Editor
JUDY KHUU

Collection Assistant Editor
ROSE WEITZ

Collection Designer
JUSTIN COUCH

Digital Art Technician
TYLER LI

Logo and Graphic Design
STEPHANE METAYER

Published by Dark Horse Books
A division of Dark Horse Comics LLC
10956 SE Main Street
Milwaukie, OR 97222

DarkHorse.com

To find a comics shop in your area, visit comicshoplocator.com

First edition: November 2022
Ebook ISBN 978-1-50673-402-6
Trade Paperback ISBN 978-1-50673-401-9

10 9 8 7 6 5 4 3 2 1
Printed in China

MIX
Paper from responsible sources
FSC® C016973
www.fsc.org

Library of Congress Cataloging-in-Publication Data

Names: Metayer, Stephane, writer. | Tako, David, artist. | Safe, Nicolas, artist.
Title: Tephlon funk! / writer, Stephane Metayer ; artists, David Tako, Nicolas Safe.
Description: Milwaukie, OR : Dark Horse Books, 2022.
Identifiers: LCCN 2022022343 (print) | LCCN 2022022344 (ebook) | ISBN 9781506734019 (trade paperback) | ISBN 9781506734026 (ebook)
Subjects: LCSH: Hip-hop--Comic books, strips, etc. | Drug traffic--Comic books, strips, etc. | Queensbridge Houses (New York, N.Y.)--Comic books, strips, etc. | New York (N.Y.)--History--20th century--Comic books, strips, etc. | LCGFT: Graphic novels.
Classification: LCC PN6727.M484 T47 2022 (print) | LCC PN6727.M484 (ebook) | DDC 741.5/973--dc23/eng/20220606
LC record available at https://lccn.loc.gov/2022022343
LC ebook record available at https://lccn.loc.gov/2022022344